Praise for *Blues Highway Blues*

"**Like a Muscle Shoals guitar lick that you can't get out of your head**, Eyre Price has penned a debut novel that you can't put down. You'll want to go down to the crossroads to finish *Blues Highway Blues*."
—Rick Robinson, Grand Prize Winner at London Book Fair for *Writ of Mandamus*

"Eyre Price deftly weaves **page-turning action, suspense, and humor** into **a top-notch primer on the history of modern American music**. As a music lover and reverent fan of great storytelling, I thoroughly enjoyed the *Blues Highway Blues* **thrill-ride, all the way through**."
—Laura Roppe, award-winning singer-songwriter and author of *Rocking the Pink*

"By turns heartbreaking, funny, and terrifying, *Blues Highway Blues* tells the story of a jaded music promoter whose fate is tied to a sadistic Russian mobster, a pair of mismatched hit men, and a mysterious old bluesman who is more than he seems. With pitch-perfect prose, Eyre Price weaves humor, horror, and a touch of magic into **an epic adventure that keeps the reader wondering what lies at the end of the Blues Highway—redemption or damnation**."
—Jaden Terrell, author of the Jared McKean Mysteries

"*Blues Highways Blues* is a musical road trip camouflaged as a great thriller. Anyone even remotely interested in the real history of Rock 'n' Roll has to take this ride. Not since Wyatt and Billy headed out to find the true America have I had half as much fun traveling her highways. Reading Eyre Price is like taking a road trip with a friend who knows music inside out and has an undeniable talent for sharing his knowledge."
—Robert Pobi, author of *Bloodman*

BLUES
HIGHWAY
BLUES

Published by Thomas & Mercer
P.O. Box 400818
Las Vegas, NV 89140

ISBN-13: 9781612183534
ISBN-10: 1612183530

BLUES
HIGHWAY
BLUES

BY EYRE PRICE

THOMAS & MERCER

For Jaime, my everything.
And for our son, Dylan, the love we share.

ACKNOWLEDGMENTS

Writing is not a solitary pursuit. There may be only one name on the cover, but every book is a group project. I'd like to thank and acknowledge all of those who were instrumental in helping me put my name on this cover.

Thanks to my agent, Jill Marr, and everyone at the Sandra Dijkstra Literary Agency, and to Andrew Bartlett and everyone at Thomas & Mercer.

Dr. Mark R. Harris provided expert opinions on just how much mayhem the average man could reasonably endure. Steve E. Lewis offered equally expert advice on just how one might go about delivering said mayhem. Robert Pobi also needs to be thanked for the literary inspiration he's provided me.

To my friend and collaborator, Tim Miller, who has worked to bring to life songs that would otherwise be confined to these pages. His album, *Blues Highway Blues: A Novel Soundtrack,* is the culmination of that shared dream.

On a personal note, I'd like to thank my mother and father. There would be no *Blues Highway Blues* without the love and support of my wife, Jaime. I am also indebted to my son, Dylan, who shared with me the trip of my lifetime: a music-filled road trip down the Blues Highway.

CHAPTER ONE

It takes more than two hundred million lights and over fifteen thousand miles of neon tubing to create the you-can-see-it-from-space light show known as the Las Vegas Strip. Against the ebony abyss of the desert night it twinkles and shines like God's own Lite-Brite set.

And in all of Sin City, from Sunset Road clear up to East Charleston, there is no better venue for viewing this spectacle than from Hotel du Monde's penthouse balcony. From this unique vantage point—the highest in the state—the lights below spread out in all directions and create a celestial tapestry that humbles the stars above.

Unless, of course, the view is all you can see while a muscle-bound wall of meat named Moog dangles you upside-down from said balcony by your ankles. In that case, the lights completely lose their incandescent beauty and all that strobing and flashing just intensifies the throbbing terror felt in each desperate heartbeat. From that perilous point of view, the garish glare only heightens the vertigo as a mad swirl of pulsating colors blurs into a bottomless vortex that seems to suck everything down, down, down.

"What do you want!" Daniel Erickson screamed frantically as he swung back and forth like an inverted human pendulum. "What did I do?" His confusion was genuine, but his headfirst predicament really shouldn't have come as any surprise.

What he'd done was made a deal with a devil.

A year earlier he'd been seeking backing for a reality show project: a can't miss, in-the-bag, "sure thing." His concept—called *Rock and Roll Redemption*—was to follow the members of that once-great glam-metal band, Mission, as they struggled with sobriety during a career-resuscitating tour of state fairs and AA ballparks. Middle-aged sex, no drugs, and rock and roll. What was there not to love?

Opportunity may knock, but genius calls collect—and sometimes the charges to accept that call are more than a man can afford. Daniel had the concept but no coin. A costly divorce had drained him of all but his "rainy day" cash, and his personal implosion in its emotional wake had caused his business as a music promoter to come crashing down around him like a Malibu mud slide. The cumulative effect was a "Road Closed" sign across all of the traditional avenues of financing his project.

In the darkest of days, hope was as thin as a small-town girl trying to break into "the Business" and it seemed Daniel might never get the chance to exploit drug-addled, has-been rockers for a syndicated cable audience. He was "investing" his last hundred dollars of liquidity in a last-ditch "creative financing" venture when he happened to meet a Russian entrepreneur right there at the craps tables.

Daniel had rolled boxcars on the come-out and the bank had taken that last Benjamin, but he and his new friend had a few drinks and shared a few stories. They had some more drinks and discussed investment opportunities in the exciting world of show business. They had even more drinks, smoked some cigars, and before the night was through, Daniel had all the cash needed to shoot and promote a pilot episode, "No prob-leem."

Four hundred and fifty thousand bucks for a six-man film and sound crew for six weeks?

"No prob-leem."

A hundred and thirty thousand for editing and studio work?

"No prob-leem."

Two hundred and fifty thousand for this and that?

"No prob-leem."

Everything was "No prob-leem." Until, of course, there was a prob-leem; and then it was a big fucking prob-leem.

In the end it turned out that even by forgiving post-Soviet standards, the man at the craps table, the one who'd fronted all those expenses, could hardly be considered an "entrepreneur." No, Filat Preezrakevich was a Russian mobster, through and through.

As the USSR collapsed, the former FSB directorate had made a seamless transfer of his brutal skill set from the Lubyanka to the burgeoning Russkaya Mafiya, shooting to the top of the Organizatsiya like a Kalashnikov slug. There was no shortage of men who were willing to do "whatever it takes," but Filat was disturbingly eager to perform the twisted, unspeakable acts all those lesser sociopaths didn't have the stomach for. His uniquely depraved brutality quickly made "the Raging Runt of Rublyovka" one of the most feared (and revered) men in the early days of the Wild, Wild East.

Give a rival's young daughter her mommy's head gift-wrapped in a pretty box with a bow as a Christmas present?

"No prob-leem."

Drop a shipping container crammed with a hundred Chechen women who'd been promised "new lives in America" into the

Golden Horn Bay just "to send a statement" back to their fractured homeland?

"No prob-leem."

Escape his enemies in the Bratva and cover his tracks by setting fire to his own mansion—with his wife and five children murdered inside?

"No prob-leem."

Filat Preezrakevich was notorious throughout all of the former Soviet republics and his murderous deeds were well known to the *Moscow Times'* readers and viewers of RT, but his vast criminal empire never made it to the pages of *Variety* or *Billboard* and he never mingled at a Grammy or AMA after-party, so Daniel was completely ignorant that his funny little friend he'd made at the craps table was living as a self-imposed exile after amassing more enemies than even *he* could kill.

No, when they'd met on the casino floor Filat had been wearing fuchsia silk pajamas and a red silk robe. His salt-and-pepper Phil Spector hair shot straight out of his head like someone had dropped a Russell Hobbs toaster into his Cristal-filled Jacuzzi tub. Oh, the crazy had been on full public display all right, but under the cover of flagrantly displayed wealth, it seemed like harmless eccentricity. And if there was an advantage to be had, Daniel had been confident he could make it his.

Blinded by hubris and greed, Daniel had rushed straight into the fire without heeding the flames. If he hadn't been so desperate to make that deal, if he'd only once looked into Preezrakevich's eyes when their vodka-fueled conversation had turned from "How much you need?" to "When can I get it?" maybe then he would have been warned off, maybe then he would have seen the same soulless pits of black that stared down at him now as he hung helplessly from the balcony with nothing between him and the pavement but the cold night air.

But "ifs" and "maybes" don't matter to the laws of physics. Or Russian mobsters.

The cold, hard facts were simple and few: Gravity is an unforgiving bitch. Daniel had taken Preezrakevich's money—almost a million dollars of it. And now there wasn't a goddamn thing to show the Russian for his investment except, "Points! I gave you points!"

"I don't want points!" The Russian leaned over the railing so Daniel could see the cruel smile such a ridiculous suggestion brought to his face. "How do I spend points of show you cannot sell? How do I pay for all this with your fucking points?" Filat gestured over his shoulder toward the lavish suite. Inside, a party that had been intended to celebrate the deal Daniel had failed to close was raging on without anyone noticing—or at least acknowledging—what was happening to the guest of honor out on the balcony. "There's reason they call it *Cash* Vegas, no?"

As the brisk February wind blew through his crazy hair, the Russian shook his head, amused by his own joke. "*Droog*, this world takes cash, not points." His voice turned colder than the night. "And I want mine. Now!"

"We had a deal," Daniel reminded him.

"And now you are hanging above Strip," Filat countered matter-of-factly. "Things change."

Daniel tried not to struggle, but his body jerked in uncontrollable spasms. He took a deep breath and tried to focus, but cognitive thought was difficult to form and even harder to express. "That's not how business works."

"You explain to *me* how business works?" Filat snapped indignantly. "How about I explain to you how gravity works?"

The Raging Runt snapped his fingers and nodded at his well-dressed gorilla. Understanding his cue, the big man dipped Daniel as if he were letting him go. It was just a foot or so, but more than enough to create the sensation of what the other six hundred forty-nine feet would be like on the way down.

"Moog drop you. You fall. Whomp!" Filat smacked his hands together with delight. "Then you sidewalk borscht. That how gravity work."

"No, God!" Daniel closed his eyes tightly. "Please, don't!"

"I want my money!"

"I can get it!" Daniel screamed in a desperate gasp, terrified every syllable might be his last. "I swear to God."

"God!" Filat sneered as he held his hands up to the pitch-black heavens like some psychotic Pentecostal preacher. "Unless He is paying debt for you, God mean as little to me as you do."

If the life he was terrified of losing had taught Daniel anything in his short forty-seven years, it was that three little words make the world spin on its axis. Just three.

With his hold on life no better than another man's grip around his ankles, he knew his only chance was to scream those three words as loudly as he could: "I. Have. Cash."

"You have cash?" The little man was intrigued.

"I do!" Daniel felt his socks beginning to slip in the big man's hands. "I do! I have it! Just pull me up!"

The Runt was intrigued but not necessarily convinced he wanted to call off the night's *zalupa*-dropping festivities. "How much?"

"I have all of it!" Daniel shouted desperately. "I have the million!"

"A million?" A million dollars. Cash. For that kind of payout perhaps he could wait to see Daniel's midair ballet. For a little while, at least. "Really?"

"I swear!" The big man's arms were beginning to shake with the strain and Daniel knew he was running out of time. "Just pull me up! Please, just—"

"Where you get million dollars?" Rumors of Daniel's financial collapse had circled him like buzzards above a fat man in a broken-down rental car in the desert outside Pahrump. "I hear you lose everything."

"No. I just wanted my wife's lawyers to think—" Daniel was fighting to remain conscious. An upside-down explanation of his personal finances was almost impossible. "I took a little." His breaths were shallow and painful. "Here." He wanted to vomit. "There." His head spun. "For rainy day."

"Rainy day?" the Russian repeated with a Grinchy grin. "Guess what? Dibble, dibble, dopp. It's about to start raining… *you!*"

"No! I swear!" Daniel knew if the interrogation continued much longer, the big man was simply going to lose his grip and drop him. "Just pull me up!"

Preezrakevich considered the possibilities, scratching his butt through fuchsia silk pajama bottoms as he did. "Where is cash?"

"My. House." Full sentences were too hard to form. "Malibu."

"I know Malibu," the Russian snapped. "I don't give you money and not know where you live. Where in house?"

"Safe."

The Russian was becoming increasingly frustrated. "Where?"

"Black. Velvet." Consciousness began to roam around Daniel's head like a bored guest waiting for the earliest opportunity to make a dash from a dead party. "Painting. Elvis."

7

"And combination?"

"Won't." Each breath was harder to take. "Work."

"Even man like Moog," Filat said, patting the three hundred fifty pounds of muscle that was Daniel's only tether to planet Earth, "has only so much stamina. Perhaps he—" He nodded at his henchman, who pretended to drop Daniel again.

"No, goddamn it, no!" The sensation of falling didn't bring Daniel any montage of his life's memories, only a clearer recollection of the combination. "Two...three...nineteen...fifty-nine."

"Good." The Russian smiled, obviously satisfied that the threat of extraordinary violence had once again proved the most reliable path to the truth.

"But. Won't." His words were little more than desperate croaks. "Work!"

Preezrakevich was not amused. "Why?"

With consciousness dimming, Daniel struggled to focus. "Voice activated. Need my voice—my *live* voice."

Filat took a minute to consider his options. And to scratch his crotch. On one hand, he wanted to see the sniveling *zhopa* hit the sidewalk at terminal velocity and make a Jackson Pollock of flesh and broken bone all over the pavement. But on the other hand, a million dollars was...well, a million dollars. He scratched his crotch some more and decided he could wait to drop his human water balloon.

The Russian nodded and then grudgingly gestured toward the balcony deck.

The man mountain named Moog flexed his massive arms and pulled Daniel up over the railing, laying him on the exact spot he'd been shown. He took a step back and rubbed at the cramps burning his bicep. The worries of Daniel's life over the last few years had whittled his six-foot frame down to a mere 175 pounds, but it was still a considerable weight to hold suspended for such a long time.

"Get him on his feet," the Runt ordered.

Moog reached for Daniel and pulled him up, forcing him to stand on trembling legs that weren't ready to bear weight. When he wobbled and collapsed, the big man threw an arm around him like a puppeteer working a middle-aged Muppet.

Filat approached them. "Here's how this will happen." Daniel could smell the fresh caviar and stale smoke on the Russian's breath. "I let you go now."

A way out was more than Daniel could have hoped for a heartbeat earlier. "You will?"

"I'm surprised too," he said with a shrug. "In old days, I cut belly open, tie guts to railing, and throw you over. Make you human yo-yo." The Russian's eyes sparkled at the thought of it. "But for million dollars, I let you go get my money." That didn't mean he'd given up on the idea of trying to "rock the cradle" with Daniel's entrails, but there was no advantage in making that clear now. "Bring it back to me in twenty-four hour."

"I will," Daniel assured him. It was a hard bargain, but a minute earlier he'd been praying just to touch solid ground. Another day, regardless of the price tag attached, was definitely a win. Everything else could be worked out moving forward. "Thank you."

"Don't thank me." Filat flashed the evil smirk that was infamous from Abakan to Zverevo. "You think I let you go alone?" He chuckled at such a ridiculous notion. "No, no. You have traveling companions."

He walked over to the Frigidaire-size henchman decked out in the Jamie Dukes suit and patted the man's unnaturally broad chest with a pet lover's affection. "You already meet Moog." Michael Jackson had a chimpanzee. Mike Tyson had a tiger. Filat Preezrakevich had a pet who could beat Champ's cat to death *with* that fucking monkey.

"'Sup." The big man raised his catcher's mitt of a hand as good-naturedly as if they'd just made acquaintances at a garden party. Moog was, after all, a businessman, a contractor who got things done—*whatever* needed getting done. If that meant breaking bones, he snapped them. If blood needed spilling, it flowed by the bucketful. And if some guy needed to be hung over the balcony like Old Glory on the Fourth, then he was a human flagpole. But it was all business; there was no reason to be personally unpleasant.

Filat circled around behind Daniel and gestured off to the shadows at the far edge of the balcony. "And this one—"

Daniel hadn't noticed another man on the patio, but one stepped out of the darkness as he was introduced. "*Hola, puta.*"

"This is Señor Jesus Arturo Castillo del Savacar," Filat announced proudly, pointing at the *asesino* who was no taller than he was, but whose eyes were considerably crazier. A deep scar ran down his face, from his left temple across his thin, sneering lips, and then over to the right side of his neck. "But his friends and foes call him Rabidoso." The Russian put his hands on the Mexican's shoulders. "He came to me from Cártel del Golfo. Like me, his own men tried to kill him because they feared him."

He looked proudly at his protégé, like a father passing on the family mantle of murder and mayhem. "If you try to fuck me, he will kill you in a way that when you finally die you will be surprised because you will think you already spent two weeks in hell." A broad smile spread over the Mexican's severed lips, pleased that someone appreciated his special skills. "And when he's done with you," Filat continued, "he will kill your family. Your friends. Your family's friends. Your friends' families." He checked himself. "There will be a lot of killing. You understand."

"Mr. P.," Moog interrupted hesitantly, looking first at Daniel and then uncomfortably at the Mexican. "I can do this on my own. I don't need no—"

"What you need, Moog"—the Russian's tone was like a rolled-up newspaper across his dog's nose—"is to do what I say."

The big man's posture was respectful, but it was clear he had something more to say. "It's just that, you know, I roll alone."

"Don't question me, Moog." He glared the big man down. "There are reasons I am where I am and you are where you are. I would think after what happened in Costa Mesa you would understand that."

"Yes, sir." Even the big man knew it was the truth. "I was just sayin'—"

"I have reasons," Filat snarled, daring him to take issue further. "You don't need to *know* the reasons. You just need to *do* the job."

There was more Moog wanted to say, but he held himself to a respectful, resigned nod and a "Yes, sir."

Filat turned his attention back to Daniel. "There one more thing we need discuss before you go." He took an Urso Venice cigar cutter from the left pocket of his robe and a Cohiba Behike from his right. He rolled the cigar between his fingers and listened to the subtle sound of the leaves as he clipped the tip with a surgeon's precision. "Collateral."

Daniel wasn't sure he understood. "Collateral?"

"Before you go," Filat explained as he stalked over to the patio bar to retrieve a glass of Russo-Baltique that was waiting for him there, "you need leave something behind." He savored a sip of the vodka. "A show of good faith until you return."

"Leave something behind?" Daniel wondered if the Russian wanted his watch. Maybe the cash in his pocket. Perhaps the title to his car.

"Hold him," the Russian instructed.

An instant later, Rabidoso was behind Daniel, twisting his left wrist high above his back, using the leverage to force him forward at the waist. Daniel bent in compliance but couldn't escape the sharp pain that ran up his arm. He tried to resist, to raise a pained objection, but all he could articulate was an anguished "Ahhhhh!" through gritted teeth.

The Russian stepped forward, grabbed a handful of Daniel's thinning hair, and lifted his head until he had no choice but to look into his tormentor's eyes. "Maybe you have million dollars. Maybe this saves your life. Who can say?" The predatory glare in the Russian's bulging eyes didn't seem too optimistic about the possibility of salvation. "But anyone who fucks with Filat Preezrakevich pays with flesh and bone and blood!"

The Russian moved behind him and a second later Daniel felt something slip over his left pinkie. It took a second to process what was happening to the hand held painfully behind his back. The realization came as a flash of pain in his left pinkie, sharper and more intense than anything he'd ever felt before. He screamed out in a voice so loud and feral that it scared him, as if the cry were coming not from his own contorted mouth but from the gaping maw of some tortured demon howling at the endless agony of an eternal flame.

It had been a nice dramatic touch, but even with its precision-honed blade, an Urso Venice cigar cutter was simply not the tool of choice for the smooth removal of a human digit. With the thin blade wedged into the bone, the Russian struggled to force it completely through the finger, working the steel back and forth. With each failed attempt, Daniel screamed louder and louder, struggling convulsively against Rabidoso as the pint-size assassin fought to maintain his hold. Filat pushed the blade farther into the bone, trying in vain to claim the resistant trophy, but after a dozen tries, even he had to admit stronger measures were needed.

"Moog." Filat pointed at his dilemma, and then walked away from it. The big man amiably ambled over and took hold of the mangled mess of steel and bone. With one blow, his giant fist drove the stubborn blade clear through the finger. The severed digit dropped to the ground.

Rabidoso let go of Daniel, pushing him away and then stepping back quickly as if he was releasing something wild and dangerous and wasn't sure whether the beast would run off into the underbrush or turn and attack.

Daniel brought his arm around, cradling the maimed hand like it was something delicate in need of nurturing. "What the fuck!" His wide eyes focused accusingly on the Russian who held the severed finger, considering it curiously. The sheer outrageousness of the act far exceeded the excruciating pain it caused or the fear it should have inspired. "What the fuck!" His finger. They had taken his finger. "What the fuck!"

"Don't be so upset," Filat advised, pointedly looking at the front of Daniel's suit pants. "It could be much, much worse."

The big man tossed Daniel a bar towel as casually as if a spilled drink had made a little mess in front of him that he might want to wipe up. Daniel wrapped the cloth around his hand as tightly as he could, frantically trying to stop the bleeding. "What the fuck!" Given what had just happened it seemed worth repeating.

"Now," Preezrakevich said, ignoring Daniel's cries of outrage and holding up his hard-won prize, "I will keep this here until you get back." Then he casually dropped the finger into his drink like it was his garnish of choice and suavely swirled the glass to mix the blood with the vodka like he'd just discovered the hip cocktail *du jour*. "But if you try to fuck me again." He stared into Daniel's eyes, now wide with shock, and then took a deep drink. "You're dead man."

CHAPTER TWO

"We're going to do this nice and simple." Moog's voice carried a soft assurance that all of Daniel's problems could be worked out with just a little cooperation. But his onyx eyes contained the stone-cold promise the problems would just be beginning if there was any confusion.

Daniel understood and nodded. Without a word, he stood between his two mismatched chaperones, concentrating on nothing more than controlling the bleeding from the stump on his left hand. There were two bar towels wrapped tightly around his hand and another wrapped around them to conceal the blood that had leaked through.

The three men rode the elevator down to the lobby, silent and with all eyes forward. The car stopped only once. At the forty-third floor, two potbellied conventioneers and two women who were almost certainly not their wives tried to get on.

As soon as the doors slid open, Rabidoso was there to stop them. "Elevator's full." He leered at the more attractive of the working girls. "But I got something you can ride up and down, *chica*." He dissolved into hysterical laughter.

Whether the two men actually saw the pistol tucked in his low-riding jeans or simply had a self-preservation reaction to the inner maniac twinkling in his eyes, they both avoided getting all chivalrous and challenging the little man. Without a word, they pulled their "dates" back from the open door. "We'll take the next car."

The trio rode the rest of the way without any other interruptions.

Before the doors opened on the lobby, Rabidoso took a knife from his pocket, snapped it open, and pressed it against Daniel's throat. He expertly used just enough pressure to cause discomfort without actually cutting the tender flesh. "Don't think you'll be safe in the crowd," he warned. "If you try anything out there, I will cut your heart right out of your chest like a *tlatoani* and hold it over my head for everyone to see."

"Hey," Moog interrupted angrily. "Put that away. I already talked to him."

The crazy eyes burned with defiance. "Yeah? Well, I'm talking to him now."

"You're talking to the whole damn world." Moog pointed to the security camera mounted in a mirrored ball on the roof of the elevator car. "Put the toys away, fool."

The tone of Moog's voice was disrespectful enough that had it been any other man, Rabidoso would have cut him from ear to ear. He wanted to slice the big man too, but he held his blade. He'd been given his orders. And he could wait.

Before the situation could ferment further, the elevator doors slid open and there were a thousand people milling about the hotel's lobby and main gaming floor. It seemed surreal to Daniel to be back among the living, and he envied every one of them.

Moog put a hand on Daniel's shoulder and steered him forward. "Let's go."

Together the three men headed toward the du Monde's main doors. It was middle-of-the-day bright along the walk-through corridors and Daniel squinted against the glare. It was painfully loud too. Jackpot bells rang here and sirens sounded over there; winners celebrated their moment of good fortune with cheers and losers groaned as money they couldn't afford to lose disappeared into the house's coffers.

Even for a Saturday night the floor was crowded. High rollers and low riders. Those with money to burn and some with nothing left to lose. They all roamed the carpet looking for luck. And the big man cut a path right through them.

They'd almost made it to the doors when a voice called out. "Dan! Dan!"

"Keep walking," Moog insisted.

They did, but the voice grew louder and more insistent. "Dan! Dan!" Finally, it couldn't be ignored any longer without drawing unwanted attention.

The trio stopped in their tracks and Moog whispered, "Turn around slowly. Make it quick and don't get cute."

"Or I will kill you," Rabidoso inserted.

Moog sighed. "I told you I got this."

"You don't tell me noth—"

Their squabbling was interrupted by a man in his late sixties who was stuffed into a tuxedo he must have purchased when lapels were wide, bowties were fat, and Reagan was president. On his arm was a woman of a similar age who was poured into her gown like a glass of wine into a shot glass: a terrible mess, with too much spilling over everywhere.

"We thought you were going to walk out on us," the man said, before exploding into laughter.

Daniel had met the Ledons twenty-five years earlier, when his first song was just climbing the charts and Larry was already an established booking agent for second-tier talent. They'd never been friends exactly, but they weren't bad people and they'd always seemed oddly sincere in the superficial cordialness. "I'm sorry, Larry. I didn't hear you."

"Oh, I understand." Larry gave Daniel's back a hearty slap. "Helen hasn't listened to me in thirty years."

She gave him an "Oh, you!" look and a loving slap on the arm as she joined his laughter—until she noticed the wad of towels wrapped around Daniel's hand. "Are you all right?" There was genuine concern in her voice, like she planned to do something if he said he wasn't.

Daniel squeezed his hand, putting more pressure on the cloth he'd wrapped around it. It hurt. A lot. "I think I will be."

"Somebody's claimed their pound of flesh?" Larry erupted in more laughter, trying in his own way to make the moment less awkward—but failing miserably.

"Nothing like that." Daniel was growing afraid he might pass out.

"I know, I know," Larry sputtered. He had a last laugh anyway and then abruptly changed the topic. "So, what have you been up to lately?"

"About sixty-five stories." Daniel couldn't resist the line, but it only heightened Moog's uneasiness and he instantly regretted it.

The couple stared back blankly, unsure what their response should be. Larry remembered the rumors that had swirled about Daniel's suicide attempt and understandably thought the comment was referencing the night's other disaster. "I heard your pilot didn't sell." It was an overly kind way of acknowledging that no one at the North American Syndicated Television Trade Show (the "Nasties," as they were known for good reason) was interested in a sloppy and depressing pilot that had necessarily been retooled as *Rock and Roll Relapse*. "But there's no sense in taking the bridge just yet, there's still the foreign rights." He offered his best "Keep your chin up, champ!" smile.

Daniel wondered if there was anything—short of a sixty-five-story drop or an impromptu finger amputation—that hurt as much as well-intentioned pity. "Sure."

"We gotta go," Moog whispered into Daniel's ear. "Now."

Daniel was quick to pass it on to the Ledons. "I'm sorry, but I've got to go."

"Aw, just one drink," Larry pleaded. "It's still dark out." Another big laugh.

The guffaws were interrupted by Rabidoso. "Hey, *pendejo*, why don't you and the *puta* stagger back to whatever *burdel* you snatched her ancient ass from. *Esse* here has to take a ride with us right now." When he was finished, his small, gnarled nose was just six inches from Larry's bulbous red one.

The Ledons were, at their core, just a nice couple from Calabasas. They'd never encountered anyone even remotely like Rabidoso before, and so they just stood there, completely unsure of what to do next.

Daniel offered, "I'm sorry."

But before he could say more, the mean little man had given him a sharp push and an even sharper, "Get going or *I'll* make you sorry."

There was no choice but to turn and walk away, but Daniel looked over his shoulder as he left. The Ledons were still standing there, statue still and mouths agape. With every step he took, Daniel realized he was moving further and further away from the life he'd known before. It made him sad. A little.

And scared him. A lot.

"Was that necessary?" Daniel demanded, even though he knew the question would cost him.

"I'll tell you what's necessary," Rabidoso hissed as he moved for his blade.

Moog moved even faster and put his big paw on the little man's shoulder. "I'm not going to tell you again." He looked up at the security cameras providing complete coverage of every activity on the floor.

"You're not going to tell me anything, *esse*."

Without breaking his stride, the man mountain said simply, "Oh, I'm going to tell you this. If Mr. P. doesn't get his money because you stuck the Music Man here, you're the one that's going to get dropped off that balcony." He looked down at his unwanted partner. "And you can call me Air Moog, 'cause I'm the one that's gonna slam-dunk your ass down those sixty stories, got it?"

Rabidoso took his hand from the knife but maintained his defiant posture.

Moog let him have that.

At the valet stand, Moog told Daniel, "Have 'em pull your car up."

Ten minutes later a black BMW 730i came screeching up the drive and an acne-faced kid in a maroon windbreaker jumped out and held the driver's door open. All three men moved toward it, but it was Moog who slid behind the wheel. "Where do you two think you're going?"

Rabidoso conceded the wheel to the big man (he told himself he didn't want to drive anyway) but on his way around to the shotgun seat he opened the trunk and gestured to Daniel. "Get in."

Daniel stopped and looked over to Moog, whom he'd already concluded was his best chance of living through the ordeal.

"Don't look at him," Rabidoso chided him. It was now a point of honor and he wasn't about to be called on it. "I told you—"

Moog looked at his watch impatiently. Twelve minutes into this little adventure and already his patience was strained to a breaking point. "What exactly is it about security cameras you can't get into your little bean head?"

Rabidoso stopped dead. "What did you call me?"

"Don't start that shit with me." The big man was unimpressed with the furious display of righteous indignation. "I meant bean, like tiny and stupid, not beaner." Completely impassive, he focused his attention on pushing buttons and flipping switches he hoped would adjust the seat to accommodate his frame. "When we finish this job, I'll hear any complaints you got about racial insensitivity. But right now we got work to do. And that don't include getting stopped by LVPD two blocks down the Strip because hotel security saw you stuff this guy in the fuckin' trunk." He shook his head with exasperation. "I'm starting to think your crew wanted you dead 'cause you're such a…" His voice softened to an inaudible mumble.

"What did you say?"

"I said get in the goddamn car. Everybody in the goddamn car!"

Still fuming, Rabidoso took the shotgun seat. That left Daniel relegated to the backseat of his own car. It was the first time he'd ever sat there.

Daniel unwrapped the outer layer of towels and found the other two were saturated with blood. "I think I need to go to a hospital."

"Just wrap it back up," Moog instructed. "Keep pressure on it and you'll be fine. I once knew a guy outta Denver got his leg cut off just below the knee—"

"I could bleed to death," Daniel interrupted. "I need to go to a hospital."

"Look it, *esse*," Rabidoso said, peering over the top of the seat. "We're not taking you to any motherfucking hospital. We're taking you to go get your fucking money. If you don't make the trip, we'll just bury your ass in desert. So try not to fucking die."

Daniel tried to convince them by showing him the wrapped wound. "But I—"

"No fucking hospital," Rabidoso repeated.

"But I—"

"Listen," Moog intervened. "We get out of the city, first stop I'll get you some gauze and some Neosporin or something."

"Neosporin?" Daniel asked incredulously. "You cut my fucking finger off!"

"Yeah," Moog said. "Well, you should put Neosporin on it."

With Moog's eye on the speedometer and his foot carefully hovering over the accelerator, they made their way out of Vegas. Careful not to exceed the posted limits, they made their way past the speed traps set up along the I-15 to lighten returning Angelinos of whatever coin they hadn't already dropped on the tables.

As soon as they reached the deserted stretches of highway cutting across the Sandy Valley, Moog made up for lost time, punching the six-figure engine until its low, throaty roar was the only sound in the cabin except the barely audible drone of "Today's Top Hits!" on KLUC.

Somewhere on the high desert, the radio signal finally surrendered to static. Rabidoso switched off the stereo, folded his arms across his chest, and hunkered down in the hand-sewn leather passenger seat with his eyes shut.

By the time they crossed the state line, Moog's eyes were beginning to glaze and once or twice the tires screamed as he veered past the painted white sideline and onto the raised rumble strips.

The job at hand didn't include falling asleep at the wheel, so to keep awake he began humming a tune under his breath. It wasn't recognizable to the others, but every once in a while he punctuated it with the high-pitched refrain, "Cal-eeee-forn-iiii-aaaa."

"Whatchu doin'?" Rabidoso finally complained after a half dozen refrains.

"What?" Moog seemed genuinely surprised the others were still awake. "It's a little 'California Love,'" the big man explained, as if identifying the tune explained everything. "You know, we just made the state line and I—"

"'Chu kiddin' me?" Rabidoso's scarred mouth sneered.

The reaction just confused the big man. "What's wrong with a little love for Tupac?"

"Love? For Tupac?" Rabidoso turned back to the window and whispered mostly to himself, "*Mano, eres tremendamente maricon.*"

Moog brought his size 14 Ferragamos down hard on the chromed brake pedal and the BMW came to a complete stop in just one hundred twenty-five rubber-smoking feet—exactly as the promotional materials had promised. "Don't think 'cause I ain't rockin' no motherfucking sombrero, I don't know you just called me a fucking pussy."

Like a snake about to bite without giving its victim the benefit of rattling first, Rabidoso sat up straight in his seat but said nothing.

"Now," Moog challenged, "You wanna say it again?"

"Hey, hey!" Daniel leaned forward, getting his hands between them. "Let's not do this. Here." He looked out the windows. "In the dark. In the middle of nowhere."

It had briefly occurred to Daniel that his immediate problems might be solved if they simply killed one another, but the thought was short-lived. He knew it was much more likely that one of them would kill the other—leaving him the only witness to murder. And if his fate hadn't already been sealed, *that* would certainly do the trick.

No, Daniel had come up with a plan. And to pull it off, he needed to prevent them from killing one another—for the time being, at least.

"Guys, let's just take a minute here." He looked at each of them and was relieved to see their postures soften just a little with his intervention. "There's nothing wrong with a little love for Tupac. God rest his soul."

"Damn straight," Moog affirmed defiantly. "Pac's the biggest thing ever come out of LA."

It wasn't an important point. And Daniel knew he should just leave it alone, even as he heard himself cautiously correcting the big man, "Well, the Eagles…"

"What?" Moog asked.

"The Eagles," Daniel repeated solemnly, realizing the foolishness of his comment but unable to stop himself from making it. "They were from LA. And their *Greatest Hits* has sold more copies than all of Tupac's discs combined."

The little man laughed under his breath.

The big man made a low, growling sound under his.

"Not that Tupac's not great," Daniel was quick to amend.

"*Mierda*," Rabidoso sneered to himself. "Enrique Iglesias has sold more records than Tupac and the Eagles combined."

"Enrique Iglesias?" Moog repeated incredulously. "Who's the *maricon* now?"

"I will show you *maricon*," Rabidoso shouted, again stiffening his back in preparation for a standoff Daniel couldn't afford to have go down.

"Guys, guys," he pleaded. "There's no need. It's all good. All of it. Tupac. The Eagles." He paused a moment and then forced himself to continue, "Enrique Iglesias. It's all good."

They all sat there silently. Moog snorted to himself and then pressed back down on the accelerator. "I just don't stand for no one calling me no *maricon*," he grumbled as the car built up speed.

"Hey," Daniel hopped in like a UN peacekeeper at a Haitian election. "Let's not revisit all that. Let's just agree it's all good." Neither one up front said anything.

"Music," Daniel continued, fully aware he was ad-libbing for his life. "They played it when they laid us in our cribs and they'll play it when they lay us in our graves. And everything in between, all of it's got its own soundtrack, right? Everything we hang on to, all our memories, they're all bound to us by music." He looked nervously at his still-tense companions who were keeping the animosity level uncomfortably high. "You know what I mean?"

If they did, neither would say so.

"I remember what song was playing when I drove my first car off the lot. And when I crashed it." Daniel could laugh at the memory of it now. "I remember what was playing when I had my first beer. And when I puked it back up." The recollection was so clear he felt nauseated all over again. "Hey, do you remember what was playing when you lost your virginity?"

There was silence and for a moment Daniel feared he'd pushed things too far.

Moog smiled and nodded, volunteering, " 'Uhh Ahh.' "

"What?" Rabidoso looked over from the window.

" 'Uhh Ahh,' " the big man repeated. "You know, Boyz II Men." His mind drifted off into the darkness and a boyish smile crept across his perpetually grim countenance. "LaTanya Harris. Up in her room. While her daddy and brothers were downstairs watching the Chiefs game." He laughed to himself. "Man, they would've whooped my ass if they'd—"

" '*Si Tu Te Vas*,' " Rabidoso interrupted in a soft voice that made him sound almost human. It seemed to surprise him as much as anyone.

"See Too Who What?" Moog couldn't resist instigating just a little.

His mischievous jab went unnoticed by the cold-blooded assassin, who seemed lost in romantic memories of his own. " '*Si Tu Te Vas*.' You never heard it? Enrique Iglesias?"

"Man," Moog protested, good-naturedly this time. "You gotta stop with that whole Enrique Iglesias thing you got goin' on."

Rabidoso was undeterred. "I don't remember her name." His voice trailed off as he fell into an abyss of his own recollections. There was no telling what he found there, but when he returned, he looked out of the window at the passing night. "When it was over," he said with a note of melancholy to his whispering voice, "I had to kill her."

The car's cabin fell silent for an awful moment.

"But we can all agree," Daniel interjected quickly, pretending (and praying) he hadn't heard what he'd just heard. "Music provides the page our life stories are written on." He took a deep, desperate breath. "No matter, you know, how disturbing those stories may be."

Both of them considered his philosophical assertion. And silently reached an understanding.

Miles passed without notice as songs and singers were recounted, revered, and ridiculed. Memories were recollected. Stories were told. And more than once "Bullshit!" was called—but no one was stabbed, shot, or beaten to death because of it.

Before they knew it, the sun was rising behind them and the waters of the Pacific, still shrouded in darkness, were stretched out to the horizon's end.

CHAPTER THREE

Daniel stopped the story he'd been performing long enough to lean forward and point out the long drive leading away from the Pacific Coast Highway and up an impossibly steep canyon side. "It's right here."

Moog made the turn. Daniel leaned back in his seat to relish dropping the moral of his tale on his captive audience. "And that's how I learned the one absolutely irrefutable rule of the music business. Maybe, the one irrefutable rule in all of life." He paused for storytelling effect and lowered his voice for maximum impact. "Never trust a man who wears leather pants."

"Why's that?" Moog wanted to know.

"They're an absolute telltale sign of a jerk-off who doesn't care about anything but creating an image. You get a pair of leather pants on and it's like twisting your junk in a freaking lanyard. And, man, the stink that comes off a pair after an hour or two is like opening a casket in the summertime. They're bullshit with pockets and a fly."

"And you learned all that from that U2 dude?" the big man wondered out loud.

"Well, I've owned a pair or two myself." Daniel confessed with a wry smile. "Should we go inside?"

The house had been designed by a student of John Lautner, with two stories of glass and steel and concrete that looked like a postmodern alien—more Bowie in *The Man Who Fell To Earth* than E.T. in *E.T.*—had crashed his luxury starship into the side of a cliff. Daniel had lived there for almost ten years, though he'd never really owned it per se.

The arrangement was so convoluted, he still wasn't entirely sure how it was supposed to have worked, but somehow the house had been leased to a holding company, then to another, and then rented back to him in a scheme his accountants had promised would be absolutely bulletproof. Tragically, the overly complicated tax dodge proved not to be estranged-wife-proof.

It had been on the market for more than two years. Almost since the day she left.

"This your house?" Moog asked, though it wasn't so much a question as a statement of amazement. "You some kind of rock star?"

"No." Daniel shook off the suggestion like it contained something offensive. "I make them." He reconsidered the answer for a moment. "Or I used to." He looked up at his house, admiring it as if he were seeing it for the first time. "That's where the real money is."

"How do you make a rock star?" Moog wanted to know that too.

When he looked back on it, Daniel couldn't help thinking the process was an easy one. "You put down your own guitar and give up the misguided notion that lightning's ever going to strike for you. Then you get serious about learning how the business works and who makes it work. The club promoters. The A&R guys. The assholes who pretend to be A&R guys. The journalists. The critics. The groupies. The hanger-oners. You get to know people. You learn your way through the labyrinth."

Moog couldn't see how all of that made the down payment on a crib like Daniel's. "Then what?"

"Then every kid with a pawn shop guitar and a rock-and-roll fantasy will sell you their soul if they think there's even the slightest chance you can make their dream come true. And if you're lucky, one of them catches that bit of the lightning you never could. Only this time you've got contractual rights to half of it."

Moog still didn't fully grasp the profit potential. "Half of what?"

"Everything," Daniel answered with a pirate's smile. "For me it was a kid named Scott West. Wrote a song called 'Driving You Out Of My Mind.'"

The big man thought for a moment before coming up blank. "Never heard of it."

Daniel's voice was cracked and strained as he sang the simple chorus that had transformed his entire life.

Another minute and I'll be another mile
Another mile on down the line
I'm not sure where I'm going
I'm just driving you out of my mind

"I know that." Moog's eyes lit up with recognition. "It's that song from that Ford commercial with that guy—"

"Chevy," Daniel corrected.

The connection to the jingle seemed to impress the big man even more than the house. "And you wrote that?"

"Not a single word, not a goddamn note. But I own half of it as part of my deal with the guy who did. And when it hit the top of the charts, I had my name on a number one single. I had money. I had success." He felt momentarily nostalgic.

"And the thing about success is that it makes being successful a hell of a lot easier. People treat you differently. Opportunities open. The more successful I became, the more people wanted to work with me. The more people wanted to work with me, the more they were willing to give away to me." It was simple.

"If you such a playa," Rabidoso interrupted, "how come your ass so deep in the hole?"

That was simple too. "Life changes. On a dime. One minute you got it all and the next it's all got you." All too simple. Daniel seemed to drift for a moment into melancholia, but it didn't last long. "Live long enough and you'll find that out for yourself," he promised the little guy.

"What the hell is that supposed to mean?"

Daniel just smiled knowingly. He took a deep breath of the early-morning ocean air; it seemed sweeter than he'd ever remembered it. "Come on, let's go inside and get your money." With that, he led the other two up the tiered walkway of offset granite trapezoids that climbed to the house. All in all, he seemed a bit more cheery than one might have expected from someone about to turn over a million-dollar nest egg.

If Moog and Rabidoso weren't both so fuzzy-headed from the long, late-night drive from Vegas, they might have picked up on just how inappropriate his demeanor was. They might have read it as a warning sign, a portent that something was "off." Maybe if they'd been on their game, if they hadn't both written Daniel off as a harmless chump, they might have been more prepared when it all went down.

But "ifs" and "buts" don't matter to men who think they're bulletproof. They both blindly followed him inside.

"*Hola*, Maria," Daniel called out brightly to the middle-aged woman who was too engrossed by *Al Diablo con los Guapos* on the living room's oversized flat-screen TV to even pretend to be vacuuming.

She wasn't startled by her boss's sudden appearance and she didn't seem concerned she'd been caught more engaged in her telenovela than her domestic duties. "*Hola*," she responded absentmindedly, never taking her eyes from her stories or paying him any real attention

That is, until she noticed the towel, now spotted with blackened blood, wrapped around his hand. "*Mi dios. Lo que paso en la mano?*" she asked, though all Daniel understood was her concern. And alarm.

"*Lo hice*," Rabidoso answered proudly.

Maria had not noticed the other men at first. When she did, she instinctively drew back in fear. "Mr. Erickson?" she asked, seeking some reassurance that they weren't what she thought they were.

"Don't worry." Daniel smiled warmly and (considering the circumstances) convincingly. "They're with me. We came to pick up something. Everything's all right."

She nodded nervously but didn't believe him. She'd seen too many men like Rabidoso in her lifetime to believe anything would be all right with someone like him in the house. "*Señor?*"

Daniel could sense her concern but ignored it as he led his escorts past her to the stairs. He looked down at his hand, surprised that the massive amount of adrenaline pumping through his system had numbed the throbbing pain. He looked down at his hand. Adrenaline had numbed the throbbing pain. Or maybe it was the "quitcherbitchin" Vicodin that Moog had pressed on him during the trip. Halfway up, he stopped and turned back to her. "Maria, I need you to run out and pick up the dry cleaning."

"Dry cleaning?" she asked, her brow furrowed with confusion. "You no have dry cleaning, Mr. Daniel."

The murderous odd couple on either side of him looked hard at Daniel, letting him know he'd wandered dangerously close to crossing their invisible line. He knew and understood, but he couldn't be frightened out of making this play. Before anyone could say anything to the contrary, he called out again, sharper this time. "I have some things at the dry cleaners. I want you to go pick them up. Now."

She waved him off. "I go after my story. Five minutes."

"Now!" he repeated, his voice as sharp as she'd ever heard it. "You'll go now!"

"All right, all right," she called back, before muttering under her breath a string of Spanish obscenities about him and his cohorts. She waited until he'd resumed his ascent before she turned back to the television to rejoin her stories.

Daniel climbed the rest of the stairs, two flights of steel twisted at odd angles in their ascent like something out of an M.C. Escher etching and then led them down a long corridor to the room he used as his office. It was an impressive space, with a curved wall of glass at the far end through which the Pacific could bee seen in the distance. The other walls were strewn with all sorts of musical memorabilia, concert posters, and framed autographed photos of musicians who had crossed Daniel's professional path at one time or another.

There were also a number of guitars hung up for display. A 1955 Gretsch White Falcon. A Gibson L-5 that had once belonged to Hank Garland. A Rickenbacker 360 12-string. A butterscotch 1953 Telecaster. And a Gibson Kalamazoo, the prize of the lot.

Moog stood admiring the collection. "You play?"

With other things on his mind, it took Daniel a moment before he realized the question was meant for him. He looked up at the instruments, pausing as if he needed some time to remember the answer. "I did. You know, when I was first starting out. Now I just collect them as invest—"

"No one gives a fuck," Rabidoso interrupted. "All we want is the money."

All anybody ever wanted was the money.

Crossing the room to a framed black velvet painting of Elvis—the fat and sweaty period—Daniel pulled it open like a cabinet door and revealed a safe exactly as he'd described.

Daniel took a deep breath.

He wasn't agonizing over losing the money as the other two naturally assumed. No, he was trying to prepare himself mentally for what he had to do once he opened the door.

"Come on, come on," Rabidoso prodded. "Let's go."

Daniel nodded and then took another deep breath. Delay wasn't part of the plan. If it was going to work, he had to act quickly. He knew this, but still couldn't shake his reluctance. It wasn't that he was scared, not really. Not for himself anyway. It was just that he'd never killed anyone before.

He hadn't even really *thought* about killing anyone before. There may have been a time or two during the worst part of the divorce when the liquor and pills had set his mind off wandering into the darkness like a misguided pilgrim, and he'd momentarily flirted with the prospect of killing the punk who'd stolen his wife, but he'd never really seriously or soberly thought about actually taking someone else's life. Not really.

Now he was planning to take two.

All through the long night, he'd spent the endless hours of the drive west making a plan, and then walking through it in his mind. Over and over. And never once had he questioned his resolve.

Now, however, with the time at hand, he began to question whether he could really follow through. He told himself he had to. But telling himself was a long way from getting it done.

His hand reached for the tumbler and he turned it twice to the left.

"Hey, wait a minute!" Rabidoso objected. "I thought you said the safe was voice activated."

Daniel offered a sly smile. "I also told you I'd owned a pair or two of leather pants before, remember?"

"Whoa, slow your roll, fool!" Moog seemed concerned about the turn of events. "You fucking lied to us?"

"I got myself off that balcony," Daniel admitted. "I did what I had to do. If I hadn't tricked you was there any way I was walking out of this?"

Moog thought about it...and then smiled. "Fuck, no. We woulda dumped your ass in the desert." He smiled more broadly. "Good for you, man."

Daniel was relieved to see the big man's grin.

"But if you fucking lie to me again, I'm going to turn you over to this crazy Mexican motherfucker."

"Yeah," Rabidoso concurred, until the words settled in on him. "Hey!"

"Don't worry about it," the big man told his unwanted partner and then turned his attention to Daniel. "However you open the fucking thing, open it and let's get going. It's been a long fucking night."

Daniel set back to work and when the final turn produced an audible *click* in the mechanism he let a skittish little laugh escape past his lips. "Ta-da!"

Neither of the henchmen closely watching him seemed particularly impressed. There was no more stalling. It was now or never.

Daniel tried to act nonchalantly, like there was nothing extraordinary about being kidnapped by hired killers, like it was perfectly natural to be blowing them away. He tried to act like he wasn't afraid of any of it, but his trembling hand made a liar out of him. He slowly pulled the safe door open as he offered his captors a smile, hoping it would distract them from the final part of his plan, the part where he shot them both dead.

Inside the safe was all of the money Daniel had left in the world. Just north of a million, he'd put the cash stash together a dollar or two at a time—sneaking some here, stealing some there—over his twenty-odd years in the music business. A trust fund he'd hoped he'd never have to raid.

Besides the money, the only other item in the safe was a Ruger semiautomatic 9mm. Daniel had locked the pistol away as a suicide precaution; ironically, it was now part of the plan to save his life.

He'd worked the plan out in his head: He would reach into the safe like he was going for the money but pick up the pistol instead. As soon as his fingers touched the steel, there would be a fleeting instant when the advantage of surprise would be his. In that single moment two hardened killers would pay a steep price for underestimating what he was capable of when his back was put to the wall. In that split second, he would turn from the safe and shoot them both dead.

Daniel took one last deep breath and mentally walked through the plan a final time, step by step: Pick up gun. Turn. Slide the safety off (Don't forget!). Find targets. Moog was off to his right, still looking at the guitars. Rabidoso was ten feet behind him, off to his left. Squeeze the trigger. Squeeze! Don't *pull* it! Squeeze!

He took a deep breath. He was ready.

He wondered what it would be like when it happened. Would it be like the movies? Would they die quickly and quietly? Somehow he knew it wouldn't be anything like that at all. It was going to be worse. Much worse.

Stop it!

It was him or them. Survival.

He reached into the safe...and was caught completely off guard.

The scene had played out in his head a thousand times. Probably more. And in all those brief mental rehearsals, he'd never— *not once*—opened the safe and discovered all of his money was gone. All of it. Just. Gone.

It couldn't be, of course. There was no way a million dollars could've just disappeared. It simply couldn't have happened.

And yet the safe was empty. Absolutely empty. Absolutely, completely empty.

Nothing. Not a thing. Except for the Ruger.

And a CD.

A CD?

He picked up the plastic jewel case and turned it over slowly, examining it with all the wonder and disbelief of some isolated aboriginal tribesman who'd just discovered it like a gift from the gods dropped from the sky. It was impossible. And yet there it was in his hand: a silver CD on which someone had written in black Sharpie. "The Blues Highway Blues/Dockery Plantation."

The whole situation was so surreal and Daniel's disbelief was so completely overwhelming that it seemed as if time itself had been stopped. He turned back from the empty safe in what felt like an exaggerated slow motion, like drowning in glycerine. Each scene moved frame by frame, with all of the voices behind him slowed down until the individual words were garbled and lost in thick bottom depths of bass. The words being shouted sounded something like, "Heeeeeeeeeeeee's gooooot aaaaaaa gun!"

It was only that "gun" part Daniel heard with absolute clarity.

And by then it was too late.

Daniel held up his hands. "No!" As he did, he realized he was still holding the CD in his hand. In that one moment, Daniel realized neither man would be able to differentiate between the mysterious jewel case and the pistol, which he'd foolishly left in the otherwise empty safe. "It's not a gun!" And even as he was shouting it, he knew what was coming. There just wasn't time to stop it.

Rabidoso pulled the Colt 9mm from the low-slung waistband of his baggy jeans and drew down on Daniel, who instinctively dove to the ground as five quick shots zinged over his head.

There would've been three more, but the weapon jammed. "*Coño!*" the pint-size assassin screamed as he furiously tried to pull the slide back.

Daniel recognized that brief moment of silence as his cue to get up and get moving. He sprang to his feet and ran toward the double doors that led out onto the deck—not with any plan in mind—but like a wild animal caught in a corner who sees a way out.

Holstered under Moog's massive arm was a pistol as big as he was—a chromed Desert Eagle. While he was no quick draw, when that hammer fell it sounded like a clap of thunder from the gods, and the room's curved glass wall instantly dissolved into a shower of falling NanaWall.

Daniel ran straight through the crystalline downpour and out onto the deck as a second shot from Moog's .50 rang out, but his escape was short-lived. A metal railing ringed the deck and the only way off it was a fifteen-foot drop to the brush-covered slope of the canyon below. He was still trapped, he'd just traded cages.

He turned back over his shoulder, thinking he might be able to get back into the house. Instead, Daniel saw the big man pulling up his oversized pistol and bracing to take a third shot.

There's no bravery in not wanting to die, no cunning in following a simple mammalian survival instinct. Without a thought, Daniel hopped over the deck railing. There might not be anywhere to go, but whatever awaited him on the other side was better than standing on the deck and giving Moog a target he couldn't miss.

It took longer to fall those fifteen feet than Daniel would've thought. There was plenty of time to anticipate the fractures and dislocations he knew he was about to suffer, to chastise himself for having done something so stupid. He tried to brace himself for impact, but hit the ground with an *umph* and then tumbled forward, a floppy pile of flesh and bone, rolling over once or twice before coming to a stop.

A very practical person had gone over the railing, but a true believer had landed in the dirt: he didn't have any of the fractures, dislocations, lacerations, punctures, or serious abrasions he'd been expecting. He was absolutely fine—and aware he probably shouldn't have been.

Beside him on the ground was the mysterious CD case, also unbroken. Daniel wasn't sure where the jewel box had come from, but he knew it was the only link to whoever had taken his money. He picked it up and tucked it into his shirt.

"I got him!" Moog's voice boomed, as powerful and loud as the sidearm dangling at his side. Daniel looked up at where he'd fallen from and there was the big man at the railing pointing down toward him. "I got him."

A second later a shot bit at the ground near Daniel's head. He flinched instinctively then looked back to the deck to find Rabidoso with his un-jammed pistol still smoking in his hand. "Like hell! He's alive!"

Daniel sprang to his feet, but the grading of the slope was too steep for anything that didn't have horns and hooves. With his very first step he pitched forward, hit the ground on his right shoulder, and then began to roll uncontrollably.

Rocks and brush scraped and cut him with every revolution he made. He built up speed quickly, rolling faster and faster until he was spinning through a painful blur: Rocks. Rocks. Sage scrub. Rocks. Dirt. Deerweed. Rock. Deerweed. Sage scrub. Rock. Rocks. Rock.

And then he was falling free. Just for an instant.

When he landed again, it wasn't on desert brush. The ground he hit was hard, cold, and black. He recognized it immediately as the drive lane of the northbound Pacific Coast Highway. Dizzy and disoriented, Daniel looked up and saw nothing but a set of tires and an oversized chromed truck grille coming straight at him.

There was no time to run. His body tensed and he only barely managed to roll away onto the highway's shoulder before the Hummer sped past. The truck's horn blared and whoever was overcompensating behind the wheel screamed out, "Asshole!"

His legs were shaky and unsteady, but Daniel forced himself to his feet. He looked out at cars rolling past, trying to gauge speed and traffic patterns like he was a small amphibian trapped in a life-size Frogger game.

One after another: a Mercedes sedan, then a Prius and a Wrangler. A Lexus and a Mustang convertible. There was no end in sight. And nowhere to go.

Behind him was a hill he couldn't climb and two killers waiting for him at the top even if he could have. To his left was the base of his driveway, from which he expected his BMW to come racing after him soon enough. To his right was just more highway, where the killers driving his car would catch him easily enough.

With nowhere else to go, Daniel looked hopefully to the other side of the highway as the only place of refuge. The distance wasn't that great, no more than a couple hundred feet, but given his current condition it might as well have been a million. His wobbly legs wouldn't let him dodge the oncoming traffic across six lanes, no matter how great his motivation to get over there. He tried to flag down a passing car, but the shocking sight of a disheveled man with his left hand wrapped in blood-stained gauze didn't motivate any of the passing motorists to stop.

And then he turned. It wasn't a specific sound or movement; he simply sensed *something* behind him. He looked up the steep slope, all the way back up to his house, and there was Moog doing his best to make a controlled descent of the ground Daniel had just tumbled down.

The big man had not been designed by his creator for mountaineering. He tried to move nimbly, but his muscular bulk wasn't balanced for that sort of terrain and his fine Italian shoes weren't ideal footwear for making the mountainous descent. Looking like a drunken grizzly on a Slip 'N Slide, he was forced to scoot most of the way on his formidable backside. The whole scene might have been funny in a YouTube-worthy sort of way if that big, bad bear wasn't headed down—with a .50-caliber pistol in his paw.

A Range Rover sped past Daniel. Then a Ford F-150 towing a landscaping trailer. An Audi A4 followed way too closely by a Celica with Oregon plates.

Daniel was desperately aware he had to do something before Moog reached the bottom of the hill. Still, a corpse is a corpse. Ending up as a hood ornament wasn't any better than becoming sidewalk pizza after a sixty-five-story fall or getting perforated with a .50 slug. In the end, it was all just dead.

The cars kept coming. So did Moog. Time was running out. Daniel had to do something. *Just do something*, he told himself.

Daniel looked down the line of traffic and saw the next car to pass him would be a Lotus Elise being driven cautiously by a gray-haired man who'd obviously addressed his impending mortality by signing lease papers. The tiny sports car gave Daniel an absolutely idiotic idea. A plan with almost no chance of working and every probability of getting him killed. Still, with Moog sliding closer, a stupid idea was better than none at all.

With a deep breath but no second thought, Daniel stepped out onto the highway and directly into the path of the oncoming Lotus.

Unsure whether to brake hard or swerve around the mad man in the center of his lane, the startled driver made the mistake of doing both—at the same time. A heartbeat later, the shiny yellow sports car started spinning like a hand-finished fiberglass dreidel, crossing across all three northbound lanes and skidding right past Daniel. After four and a half full revolutions, the Elise came to a suspension-shaking stop and the driver probably breathed a sigh of relief thinking he'd avoided a more serious incident.

The Lotus's driver had, but the motorists behind him weren't so fortunate. A split second later there was a catastrophic chain reaction. A cacophonous symphony of squealing tires built quickly to a crescendo of collisions, punctuated by the high tenor of shattering glass and the percussive pops of metal hitting metal. Within thirty seconds the northbound lanes of the PCH had become completely impassable.

"I'm so sorry," Daniel said to the moaning driver as he ran up to the Lotus. "I know I've just made this a really shitty day. And I hate to make it worse. But I need your car."

"What?" The driver suspected he might be lapsing into shock, but even that didn't explain such a bizarre request. "What the hell are you—"

"I need you to get out of the car." Daniel pulled open the door like a valet waiting on a celebrity outside the Beverly Hills Hotel. "Please."

"Are you carjacking me?" There was genuine disbelief in the man's voice as he tried to determine if this was just a post-concussive hallucination.

Grand Theft Auto hadn't been Daniel's original intention, but the more he thought about it the more obvious it became to him. "Yes. Yes, I am. I'm carjacking you."

"But you don't even have a gun," the driver pointed out.

"No," Daniel admitted, "but he does."

A second later a shot from Moog's hand cannon hit the Lotus's fiberglass frame and tore through it like it was fifty grand worth of cotton candy.

"Holy shit!" The driver looked back through his now-shattered rear window as if there might be something back there to see besides his impending death.

"Get out of the goddamn car!" Daniel tugged at the driver, now trying frantically to free himself from the seat restraint. As the man came loose of the harness, Daniel climbed over him and slid into the cramped cockpit.

A quick glance into the shattered rearview mirror showed Daniel a kaleidoscopic image of the big man purposefully advancing on him, slow and steady. In the spiderweb of broken glass, it looked as if a dozen Moogs were raising their arms, each one aiming his own chromed cannon at him.

Daniel hit the starter and the stalled engine miraculously came to life. He pressed the clutch, threw it into gear, and then let the clutch pop out as he stomped the accelerator. The car jumped like a Jesus bug skimming across the surface of a pond and thick black smoke rose from the squealing, spinning tires.

Moog's second shot hit the pavement right where the car had been stopped a second before.

Daniel stepped hard on the gas and a feeling of exhilaration overcame him as the acceleration shoved him back in the seat and the sports car took off like an AMRAAM missile shooting straight up the now abandoned roadway. "Wooooooooooooo!"

Behind him a crowd of people cursed him. One of them wanted to kill him—two, if he counted the Lotus's owner.

He had nowhere to go, but he was getting there fast. He was free. And alive. Nothing else seemed to matter.

His exuberance, however, didn't last longer than a mile marker or two.

The realization hit him harder than a slug from the .50 would have. Even racing as fast as the Lotus could go, he hadn't gone more than five miles before the most terrible realization hit him. His heart sank and he put the accelerator all the way to the floor.

"Zack!"

There *was* somewhere to go. And he had to get there even faster.

CHAPTER FOUR

"Where do you think you're going?" Rabidoso didn't bother to tuck the pistol back into his pants. It dangled loosely from his hand as he slowly descended the stairs.

Maria had disobeyed Daniel, staying behind to finish her soap opera. When the shooting started she'd sought refuge behind the couch. The sustained silence had tricked her into believing it was safe to finally make her escape. "*Por favor, señor.*" Maria backed away slowly, knowing she had no chance to outrun him.

He shook his head with feigned concern. "You're in a lot of trouble here."

"*Por favor, señor,*" she repeated aloud, though in her head she began reciting the Ave Maria, hoping some celestial force might show her the mercy that a man with such hateful eyes never would.

He pointed to the leather couch she was trying to back around. "Take a seat."

"*Por que?*" The question warbled with her fear.

"Sit!" He screamed the command with more authority than she could defy.

She did as she was told, but begged, "*Señor!*" Tears streamed down her cheeks, salty evidence of her growing desperation. "I have six children, *señor*. Four grandchildren."

"Family's a blessing." He wasn't immune to her tears, only excited by them. "Losing them is the curse."

She gasped audibly, "Oh, *señor*. Please—"

"My partner and me, we're FBI. *Federales*. He smiled proudly at the lie. "And I'm not looking to make any trouble for you."

She couldn't help but be relieved. "*Oh, gracias, señor. Gracias—*"

"Unless I have to." His voice was cold and sharp like the knife he kept in the pocket of his jeans. "But right now you're the only one in a house with fifty kilos of *cocaína* upstairs. Do you understand?" He liked this lie even better.

"*Cocaína?*" The stream of tears became a flood. "*Cocaína?* *Señor* Erickson?" She'd never really liked the man, always thought him weak, but that was why she couldn't believe he'd be involved in such a dangerous enterprise. "Nooooooooooo." She drew out the word like an overexcited *fútbol* announcer to stress the depth of her disbelief.

Rabidoso just stared at her. "Well, if it's not him, it must be you."

She was quick to rethink her position. "*Señor* Erickson, he is in the music business. Always there are musicians coming and going here. You know—"

"I know," he affirmed. "Well, your Mr. Erickson just shot at two *federales*. Now he's running. I need to know where he's running *to*."

"Oh, I don't know, *señor*." She shook her head vigorously. "I know nothing."

Rabidoso knew something. "I was looking around upstairs. There's a room, a boy's bedroom. Does your *Señor* Erickson have a son?"

"*Sí.*" She answered quickly, thinking of her own boys. "A son. *Señor* Zack."

Like a viper pressing the scent of its next meal to its Jacobson's organ, Rabidoso knew he'd found his prey. "Where do I find him?"

"I don't know, *señor.*"

"Maria, you're in deep *mierda*. Not only with the *cocaína* upstairs—"

"I swear—"

He held up a hand to stop her. "The *federales* are going to want to talk to you."

She knew what he was suggesting. "I'm a citizen," she declared as indignantly as she dared.

"They're going to want to talk to *all* your people. I know, because I am the *federal* that's going to do it." He gave her a sinister smile so she'd understand exactly what he meant.

She was a good woman, but she wouldn't sacrifice her family to save Daniel's. "Mr. and Mrs. Erickson. They get a divorce two years ago. The boy, he lives with her."

"Where?"

She considered lying for a minute, but the predatory glint in her inquisitor's eyes made her think better of such a gamble. "Westlake Village. Wynnefield Avenue. One seven one five zero. I clean her house on Thursdays."

He laughed contemptuously. "So, they got joint custody of you in the divorce."

"That's all I know."

"Well, that's too bad, *chica*. 'Cause I got one more question." She looked at him blankly. "Your Mr. Erickson brought us here because he said he had a lot of money in that safe upstairs."

"No." She shook her head. "There no safe up there."

He just laughed. "No, there is, because it's up there open right now. And it's empty. No money." He cleared his throat. "I want to know where the money went."

Her eyes went wide. "I know nothing about any money."

Rabidoso had a long history with people offering him desperate denials. His personal policy was to ignore them until death proved them right. "He called you last night, didn't he?" he pressed. "Told you to move the money? To put the gun in there?" With every question he moved closer, until finally he was just a hot, stale breath away.

She would have backed away farther, but there was nowhere left to retreat. "I swear, I don't know." She was caught between the mad man and the Ibris Blue couch.

"I'm going to ask you again." This time he prefaced the question by dragging back the hammer of the pistol until it cocked. "Where's the money?" He pressed the pistol's barrel against her forehead and she quivered at its icy touch.

"I swear, I don't know anything about any money." Her words dissolved into gasping sobs. But her thoughts turned immediately to what she knew was her only chance for survival and she began to recite the Ave Maria in her head. *Santa Maria, Madre de Dios.*

He reached down and took hold of the neckline of her uniform dress. "Where is the money, *puta*?" He tugged at her top, again and again until neither the fabric nor her desperate efforts to cover herself could resist his savage violence. A shriek escaped her trembling lips as he tore her free and pushed her to the carpet.

He straddled her and she was helpless beneath him, unable to even raise her hands to protect her head and face from the butt of his pistol as he brought it down on her. "Don't lie to me, *mami*," he screamed with each blow. "*No me mienta, mami!*"

"I swear." Her tears ran into the gashes he'd opened and mixed with the blood streaming down her face. "I told you everything." Her voice failed her, but there were no more words to be spoken.

Ruega por nosotros pecadores.

He drew closer still, so she would have to look up at him, so their last moment would be an intimate one, with her looking into his eyes and him looking down into hers. His lips twisted into a wicked sneer as he leaned forward and whispered into her ear, "I believe you. Now." He tucked away his pistol.

And drew out his knife. He placed the blade against her throat, smiled, and then traced a path down to her belly.

Ahora y en la hora de nuestra muerte.

CHAPTER FIVE

Parenthood is a man's greatest vulnerability.

Over the course of his last twelve hours, Daniel Erickson had been held over a sixty-five-story balcony, had a finger chopped off, been shot at a dozen times, fallen forty feet, rolled down a canyon slope, and almost been hit by a car—twice. Still, with the memories of all those events as fresh in his mind as the wounds they'd left on his body, there was only one fate he truly feared. Only one outcome he wouldn't allow himself to consider.

Daniel raced the school-bus-colored sports car harder and harder until the non-intercooled supercharger pinned the RPMs near the red. A hundred and twenty miles per hour. He felt like he was speeding through a series of still photographs and the passing suburban scenes were pages in some pretentious coffee table book.

In that chaotic calmness, he absentmindedly scratched at his midsection and was surprised to discover the cause of the irritation was the mysterious disc he'd slid into his shirt. He pulled it free and considered it for a moment, wondering who'd left it for him. And why.

He opened the case and slipped it into the CD player.

As the first track keyed up, a pair of acoustic guitars began a slow throbbing twelve-bar blues vamp. The recording sounded like it was eighty years old, but Daniel knew it wasn't. The engineer had simply boosted the mids and then added some high compression to keep the track's volume level, maybe blended some gray or white noise low in the mix to enhance the antiquated effect.

The vocalist who began to sing was clearly not the black man he was trying hard to emulate, but there was nothing patronizing in the imitation. It was the sincerest form of adulation, like a young Mick Jagger on the Rolling Stones's version of Willie Dixon's "I Just Want to Make Love to You" or Keith Relf on the Yardbirds's take of "Smokestack Lightning."

Daniel turned up the volume so he could hear the lyrics more clearly.

Little Robert Dusty couldn't play like Son House on guitar
He wandered into the wilderness and came back a shooting star
Some say he made a deal with a demon, tall and black
But I think it was an angel who brought his lost soul back

He rode that stretch of blacktop, it runs to heaven
And straight through hell
One more hard luck story than any man could tell
Of the ones who made that music
Unafraid to pay their dues
And his songs still echo in the night
The Blues Highway Blues

It wasn't anything Daniel had ever heard before. And there was no reason he could think of for why it had been left where his million dollars should have been.

Granddad told lil' Chester there were wolves out in the night
And I'll be damned if that old man didn't have that story right
Their guitars sound like wild beasts, snarling and growlin'
And when that boy heard their blues, Good Lord, it sent him
*   howlin'*

He drove that stretch of blacktop, it runs to heaven
And straight through hell
One more hard luck story than any man could tell
Of the ones who made that music
Unafraid to pay their dues
And their songs still echo in the night
The Blues Highway Blues

At the end of that second chorus, the song shifted into an instrumental with two dueling acoustic guitars taking their turns, swooping in and out from one another like birds of prey sharing the same sky for their hunt. One player worked a slide, while the other finger-picked his part. From a modern standard, neither was technically perfect—maybe not even proficient—but what they lacked in technique they more than made up for with unrestrained passion. There was a rawness to their playing that Daniel hadn't heard in a long time.

Under other circumstances his initial impression of the mysterious band calling itself Dockery Plantation might have been more favorable. If he hadn't been running from killers or racing off in a stolen car to head off the unthinkable, he probably would have been intrigued by the possibilities for a band like this. But given his life-or-death situation, his only conclusion was that there wasn't anything in the track worth a million bucks.

It was the most troubling part of the mystery. If the thief already had his money, why had the culprit left the CD for him? And then he heard the third verse.

Poor mannish boy, Danny, hear me singing straight at you
You know you sold your soul. And now you've lost that money too
If you wanna earn your soul back, find where your money's hid
Better get down to the crossroads like young Robert did

You just follow that blacktop, it runs to heaven
And straight through hell
One more hard luck story than any man could tell
Of the ones who made that music
Unafraid to pay their dues
Their songs still echo in the night
The Blues Highway Blues

You got the Blues Highway Blues
You got the Blues Highway Blues

Dust your broom, Danny, you're a travelin' man now

You got the Blues Highway Blues
You got the Blues Highway Blues

The track built in bluesy fury until it concluded with a single shot of guitars. And then silence.

In the deep background of the track there was some unintelligible conversation between the members of the band, but no matter how loudly Daniel replayed it he couldn't make out the words.

There was nothing else.

Daniel played the track several times, but that was the only thing on the disc. He frantically searched his mind for some glimmer of an idea that might explain who had taken his money. He replayed the lyrics in his head, trying to distill some meaning that might explain what was happening to him. He searched for an answer but could only conclude that whoever had taken his money had left him with nothing but "The Blues Highway Blues."

CHAPTER SIX

Across the cul-de-sac from his ex-wife's McMansion lived a dentist who had called the cops to report noise violations when one of Zack's bands was practicing too loudly. Daniel decided the nosey neighbor could spend his afternoon explaining to those same cops why there was a stolen sports car in his driveway and left the Lotus there. As stealthily as he could, he crossed the circle and walked to her front door.

When his life first began to fall apart, there were plenty of well-wishers who offered Daniel the same worn-out platitudes about fish in the sea and time healing wounds that get offered to the heartbroken. That was two years ago. He was still waiting for just one of them to ring true.

She answered the door and just the sight of her standing there stirred in him a feeling that wasn't unlike the upside-down-and-falling-fast sensation that had gripped him when he was hanging over the du Monde's balcony and thought Moog might drop him to the ground. "Daniel?"

She was still beautiful. No one could dispute that, although he would have understood if some might have insisted on adding "for her age" as a caveat.

It wasn't just the passage of time though. The divorce had been tough on both of them, but somehow all of the anger and bitterness had stayed in her face even after the proceedings had concluded. Somehow the mean little scowl with which she'd purposely regarded him at the time had distorted the fine lines in her face, leaving her eyes permanently pinched in a squint, her mouth in a perpetual sneer.

But while time and temperament had taken a toll on her physical attributes, neither one had lessened his feelings for her. Nothing had. Not the merciless lawyers or the court-ordered bloodlettings. Not the psychologists, the psychiatrists, or the prescriptions. Not even his breakdown. Nothing. Nothing could lessen what he still held in his heart.

He was self-aware enough to recognize his feelings were pathetic. Any number of trained professionals had convinced him of that fact. Family, friends, and business associates too. And yet at the same time he couldn't help thinking there was more than a shred of nobility in his boundless romanticism. If every man had a fatal flaw, he was content to have her be his.

"What do you want?" She made no effort to hide her contempt, maybe even exaggerated it for her own effect.

Daniel didn't care. Not this morning. "I need to come in, Connie."

"What the hell happened to you?" She sounded more curious than concerned. "You look like shit." She noticed the blood-stained bandages wrapped around his hand, which he was trying to conceal behind his back. "What the hell happened to your hand?"

"It's nothing, but I look better than I feel." He checked over his shoulder. "I need to come in."

"I'm a little busy right now," she purred, tucking a strand of auburn hair behind her ear and adjusting but not pulling closed the silk bathrobe and negligee that did little to conceal what he couldn't force himself to forget.

He looked her up and down, from the mussed knot of red hair on the top of her head to the fuzzy, stuffed mallard duck slippers on her feet. Stuffed duck slippers?

"Come on, babe," a man's voice bellowed from somewhere upstairs. "It's wabbit season!"

Daniel offered her a look, somewhere between judgmental and prurient curiosity.

"I'm making up for all the lost time I spent married to *you*." It was the only explanation she was willing to offer.

Her words weren't the most painful part of his morning and without waiting for the invitation he knew she'd never volunteer, he limped past her into the two-story Mediterranean she'd bought with booty plundered from him in their divorce. She could've stopped him easily enough, but she didn't. Instead, she closed the door and followed him into her living room.

There were two suitcases packed and waiting by the stairs.

"Are you going somewhere?" he wondered aloud.

"I'm going up to Portland to see Grace."

He nodded, grateful she was going to be somewhere else.

Concealed in a back room somewhere, a dog—big and loud and thoroughly pissed off—was barking furiously at the intruder. "Hades!" she screamed in a voice he'd only ever heard her use toward him. "Shut up, Hades! Shut up!" All the yelling did nothing to silence the canine's snarled threats.

She turned back to Daniel. "Why do you look like somebody actually *did* to you what I've been dreaming of doing for years?"

She wasn't the only one who wasn't offering explanations. "Where's Zack?"

"Zack?" A tinge of concern seeped into her voice. "What do you mean?"

What did he mean? It was impossible to explain the simplest thing to her, but how could he possibly make her understand why there might be hit men from Vegas hunting him down? Or why those same bad men might now want to find her only child?

There were no words to make her comprehend that Daniel's escape had put these men on the hook. How could he make her understand that if these very bad men wanted to live out the rest of the week themselves, their only hope was to bring back Daniel *and* his money. And because of that, they were likely to come straight for what meant the most to Daniel, whatever—or whomever—he could not bear to lose.

"Zack." He struggled hard to contain his own growing panic. "Where is he?"

"I don't know." She was more than concerned now. Maybe even scared. "What's this all about?" She was certainly angry. "What the hell have you done now?"

"How can you not know where he is?"

"He's nineteen," she reminded him. "It's not like he keeps me up-to-date on his comings and goings."

"I'm not asking you to manage his social calendar, Connie." He ran his good hand through his thinning hair. "I'm asking you to know where our son is. I would've thought if you could cash the child support checks, even you—"

"What the hell does that mean?"

He was more than willing to meet her challenge. "It means—"

"Whoa! Whoa! Whoa!" There was a young man's voice at the top of the stairs, but it wasn't their son's. "I think you better take a second to rethink how you're talking to my lady there, chief."

Daniel rolled his eyes. The last thing he needed this morning was the D-list character actor whose only meaningful role had been as the casually tossed cigarette that started the personal forest fire that burned Daniel's life to the ground. "This doesn't concern you, Randy."

"Oh, I think it does." The beefy young man who descended the carpeted stairs wore nothing but a pair of boxer briefs and a red and black buffalo-plaid Elmer Fudd hat. Still, his chest was puffed out in some misguided mammalian attempt at establishing dominance. "If it's happening in my house—"

"This isn't your house," Daniel was quick to point out. "It's Connie's name on the deed and my money that makes the mortgage. So why don't you just turn right around and go finish whatever you've got started up there all by yourself."

Randy descended the stairs two at a time. "How 'bout I come down there and finish what it looks like somebody else started?"

Daniel didn't have time for another pissing match. He turned back to Connie. "How do I get in touch with Zack? I called his number but it goes straight to voice mail."

"You're scaring me, Daniel." She pulled her robe tight around her and tied the belt. "What's wrong with Zack?"

"He's fine." It was true for the moment, but he recognized the way he'd voiced the words didn't inspire confidence in her.

"Is this about the last time that you two—"

"The last time what?" What had Zack told her?

It hadn't been much. "He said the two of you had a fight. You told him you were cutting off his money."

That wasn't quite right. "I told him I was cutting off his money *if* he doesn't go back to school."

She rolled her emerald eyes. "He doesn't want to go to school."

"Nobody *wants* to go to school, but most people recognize it's a necessity."

"You never went to school." The way she said it suggested she might have retained some small vestige of admiration for him, but she was quick to catch herself on it. "Don't get me wrong. You're still an asshole. But you've done all right for yourself."

"I *am* an asshole," he freely agreed. "But the days of making money simply by being an asshole are coming to an end." The words sounded unexpectedly dire once they'd slipped out of his mouth. Dire, but true just the same.

"Well, he wants music."

"Then he can go back to school for music."

"He wants *his* music." She arched her well-shaped eyebrow and he knew it was the end of any meaningful discussion on the subject.

He knew he didn't have time for *this* conversation and steered the conversation back to finding Zack. "Is he off with Alistair?"

She shook her head. "No, Georgie went back to UC San Jose for spring semester."

"Then who is he off with?"

A shrug. "He started playing with a new band, but I don't know any of the boys. We asked him—" She stopped short, caught on something she didn't want to say aloud.

He'd seen that look in her eyes too often to mistake it: guilt. "What did you do?"

She struggled for a response. And then gave up with a sigh.

"We told him we needed some time and space." It was Randy who offered the answer she couldn't. Or wouldn't. He stood behind Connie and wrapped his artificially bronzed and chemically bloated arms around her. "We're a couple here." He kissed the back of her neck and she did not resist him. He looked at Daniel and smiled like he knew a secret. "We need the space to do all the things that couples are *supposed* to do."

Daniel wasn't deterred by the insinuation. "You threw Zack out?"

"We didn't throw anybody out," Randy countered quickly.

"I'm not talking to you about this." Daniel looked directly at Connie. "You put our son on the street and didn't tell me? What kind of mother are—"

"What kind of father are you?" she snapped defensively. "He didn't turn to you, did he?"

He wanted to slap her with a response every bit as sharp and painful, but he knew she was right. In a morning filled with a whole world of hurts, the most painful thing he had to endure was the simple realization that when his son had been put out into the world he hadn't come to him for money or a place to stay. He hadn't come to him at all.

"He's over eighteen," Randy interrupted in a tone suggesting there was no need for anyone to be concerned. "When I was eighteen I was—"

"Just the same plastic-ass boy toy you are today, Randy." Daniel was uninterested in whatever "school of hard knocks" anecdote the guy wanted to share.

Daniel closed his eyes tightly, trying to contain his building anger and focus on what he needed to do. In his head he drew up a bullet-point mission plan: How to Find Zack. Step One. "I need to borrow a car."

"Call Enterprise," Randy suggested.

"What happened?" Connie was intrigued. Even under the circumstances, she seemed delighted by the humiliating possibilities. "Did they repossess the Bimmer?"

"I just need a car." How much farther could he get in a stolen car?

"I need the Jag," she insisted.

"And I get to keep the Escalade, right?" Randy whined.

She pulled his arms tighter around her. "And Randy needs the Escalade."

Daniel didn't care anymore. Not about any of it. "I just need four wheels. I'll take the Kia."

"Maria needs it to run errands," she protested.

"I'll have it back by Thursday." He knew he wouldn't, but the lie was clearly a condition for getting the car. "I promise."

"All right. If you promise to—"

"Can you just give me the keys?"

She trotted off to fetch them.

"This is it, ace," Randy whispered when they were alone.

"Excuse me?"

"I don't want you coming back here again, dillhole." Even for his size—six foot two, 240 pounds—it was hard for a man wearing undies and a cartoon hunter's cap to look intimidating.

Given what he'd been through so far that day, Daniel tried not to laugh. "What?"

"I got your boy outta here." He made a quick gesture with his thumb. "And if you come back here again," he looked to see if his support system was coming back yet. He then turned back and drew his index finger across his throat. "You're a dead man."

"Here they are," Connie called out as she rejoined them, unaware the tension between them had risen to historic heights. She dropped the keys in Daniel's hand. "Don't forget. Thursday."

"Thanks." It was all Daniel had left to say.

"Thursday," she reminded him. "So have it back here Wednesday night."

"Make sure you top it off," Randy added.

Daniel just nodded. "If Zack calls, tell him to call me. It's important."

"This thing," she couldn't keep herself from asking. "With Zack. Is it something *I* should be worried about?"

Life is just one troubling moral dilemma after another. "I'd take my time at Grace's." Daniel cast a quick glance at the man he hated more than any other in the world—and that included the killers hunting him. "I'd bring Fudd with you too."

"I'm not going anywhere," Randy announced defiantly. "I can handle whatever you couldn't."

Daniel shrugged and turned back to the woman he hated himself for loving. "Then I'd leave soon."

"The only one leaving is you," Randy interrupted. "Now."

Daniel looked to his ex-wife, not asking for compassion or support, just the decency not to let another man—*the* other man—throw him out of a house in which he couldn't help feeling he still held some interest. He looked, but there was nothing there for him. "You need to go, Daniel."

There was so much he wanted to tell her—a lifetime he wanted one last chance to try to explain—but even he knew better than to try to say anything more than, "I'm sure you'll both be fine."

"She's got me." Randy tightened his arms around her, flexing biceps ringed with barbwire tattoos—the mullets of personal ink.

"I've got Randy." She backed into him and pulled his pharmaceutically inflated arms around her, not to twist some emotional blade in Daniel's cuckolded back, but simply because she had found her home there.

And that was all there was to that.

After the grand drama that had played out between them, it seemed oddly anticlimactic to Daniel that such a small gesture could convince him completely of what he'd fought for so many years to deny. For the first time he saw her clearly. Not as his wife. Or his ex-wife. Or even Zack's mother. He saw her simply as the woman she was.

She wasn't his. She never would be. And maybe she never had been.

Daniel felt like a condemned man who'd spent years fearing the gallows door, dreading the moment it would fall beneath his feet with a fatal *BANG!*, only to find there was no deadly drop after all. Only release.

"All right." If he chose to, he could simply walk away. "Good luck with that, then." The first step was surprisingly easy to take. And so were the others that followed. He didn't feel the need for one last look and he had no parting word for this stranger he now realized he had never really known. Daniel had troubles of his own and he was running out of time to set them right.

CHAPTER SEVEN

Legend holds that the engineers who built the Great Pyramids were entombed at the center of their ingenious creations as a practical precaution to prevent their secrets being revealed.

And tales are told that after Peter the Great saw St. Petersburg's storybook skyline, he had all of the architects who contributed to its design executed so they could never duplicate it for another monarch.

Death is, after all, the only completely trustworthy confidant.

Daniel, however, was neither pharaoh nor czar, and death had not been an option on his service contract with Brentwood Safe & Vault Installation. So Terry and—Daniel couldn't remember the name of the guy with the paint-speckled Padres cap who reeked of cheap weed—knew all about the safe they'd installed behind the Elvis painting.

That meant anyone Terry or the whacked-out Padres fan might have shared that information with knew about it too. And whoever *those* people talked to…and on and on, exponentially, until it seemed reasonable to assume half of metropolitan Los Angeles might be aware of Daniel's not-so-secret safe.

It wasn't just Terry and the stoner either.

In that pathetically desperate period when he was trying to get back on his feet after the divorce—and the subsequent temporary commitment—he'd thrown any number of parties at the house to show just how "right" he was. So there were who-knew-how-many guests (most of whom he'd never met) who might have discovered it on their own. Or, more likely, had suffered through his drunken braggadocio and learned about the money he'd cached away in his hidden safe from his own slurring mouth.

He'd held production meetings for the *Rock and Roll Redemption* pilot at the house with God-knew-who in attendance. Film crews. Editing teams. The members of Mission. Their entourages.

And there was the cable guy.

And the painters.

Maria.

Even the EMTs and police who'd responded to the call when he'd made his suicide attempt had been through the house. Maybe alone in his office. Who could say?

The list of suspects who might have known about the safe and the million reasons to crack it was endless. Still, of all the people who might have wanted his money, Daniel couldn't figure a single one with motivation to leave a personalized blues song at the scene of their crime, particularly one with lyrics suggesting he could get his money back.

All he had were questions, but he was confident their answers must be in the song. And so he went back to it again.

"The Blues Highway Blues."

Daniel was familiar with the titular roadway. Long before Bob Dylan revisited it, Route 61 was the major thoroughfare for itinerant bluesmen as they shadowed the Mississippi River down through St. Louis and then over to Memphis, snaking through the fertile crescent of the Mississippi Delta and then finally delivering its disciples in the Big Easy. It was the historical spinal chord of rhythm and blues, the umbilical chord of rock and roll.

And although a twelve-hundred-mile stretch of highway was an inexact destination, the day's events had left him with three certainties: Moog and Rabidoso were looking for him. They would never stop until they found him. The only chance he had to save his life—and his son's—was to find the money and make a deal.

So, if there was even the slightest chance he might be able to recover his money at the end of whatever wild goose chase he was being sent on, he had to take that trip to where the blues had been born.

He was on his way to the Blues Highway.

CHAPTER EIGHT

Every tick of the odometer was another reason to turn back. Every exit he passed was a missed opportunity to come to his senses. Mile after mile passed with the noise on the radio drowned out by the whispering voice at the back of his mind, constantly chiding that he was on a fool's errand with zero chance to accomplish anything except making his situation even worse.

If another man might have heeded this inner call, something else kept Daniel's foot pinned to the accelerator. He drove as the sun climbed high in the sky and never slowed or stopped as it gradually slipped from its perch, falling and fading, finally melting into a fruit-sherbet sunset that spilled across a desert horizon he could only see in his rearview mirror.

The miles ticked away like minutes on the clock until evening had turned to darkness and all of the sensible souls had called it a night and pulled off for a hot meal and badly needed sleep. Daniel left them all to their motel beds and kept going until the highway was eventually abandoned to the legion of long-haul truckers and other assorted hard cases who for reasons all their own couldn't bring themselves to stop either. He was in their number now, counting down exit signs while the rest of the world counted sheep. Just another lost soul, driving hard, with an uncertain destination.

Yet no matter how high the speedometer climbed, he could not outpace the doubt that dogged his steps or the dark thoughts that accompanied him like a shadowy presence seated beside him in the shotgun seat. Was he making a mistake? Should he just turn back? Would he be able to save his son? Or himself?

There are four million miles of highway crisscrossing the United States, an intricate web of blacktop that provides a marathon driver—whether it's wanted or not—with a reasonable alternative to long-term psychotherapy. The lonely night and endless asphalt will not suffer self-delusion. The miles will coax out the truth.

He'd started his journey as a victim, but somewhere in the pitch blackness of a New Mexico night, Daniel collided headfirst with the realization that maybe his current circumstances were not so unjust. It was a wreck no less painful than twisted metal, shattered glass, and spilled blood: perhaps the missing money and the relentless killers were simply karmic payback for the life he'd led for so many years.

A million dollars had been taken from his safe, but the hard truth of it was that he hadn't really earned a cent of it. He'd skimmed and scammed every artist he'd ever worked with, from Scott West to Mission. There were songwriters whose writing credits he'd shanghaied and overgrown adolescents who were too naive or chemically impaired to translate "Trust me" into the modern working English. There were business partners who'd failed to observe the thin line that separates *business* from *partner* and investors whose bespoke-suited lawyers hadn't been nearly as persuasive as Preezrakevich's gun-toting thugs.

No, if Daniel was being cast out on a stony path to penance, he couldn't deny he deserved to travel every painful step. And he could accept such a cosmic punishment as somehow just. What he couldn't accept was the possibility Zack might have to walk it alongside him.

Halfway between Albuquerque and the Texas state line, he took the Santa Rosa exit and slowed up the ramp until he came to a stop beneath the blinking red traffic signal swinging overhead in the howling desert wind. The only other light was a neon sign glowing half a mile down the road: FUEL. FOOD. BEER. Daniel didn't need any of those things as badly as he needed a moment or two to escape the confines of the car—and the realizations that had found him there. He put on his turn signal (though there was no one within miles to see it) and headed toward the iridescent beacon.

The dashboard clock glowed in the dark. 2:40. Sunday morning. His twenty-four-hour deadline with the murderous Russian gangster had come and gone. He tried to imagine Preezrakevich's reaction but all he felt was the throbbing pain in his left hand.

Daniel wondered how the genial giant and his evil, elfin sidekick had broken the news to their boss. Had they told him at all? It wasn't like losing Daniel and his million dollars was something they could toss out as a casual aside. No, Preezrakevich wouldn't accept their failure lightly. They'd both be lucky if he didn't simply recruit a new team of killers to track *them* down.

That thought hadn't crossed Daniel's mind before, but now it struck him like a shank in the back. Could there be a new team of killers out there? It was unnerving enough to know the big man and the *pequeno* psycho were hunting him down, but the possibility there could be new and unknown players in their death match made his troubled stomach even queasier.

71

He pulled into the fuel stop and parked the Kia at the pump closest to the access road. Silence replaced the high hum of the 1.6 liter, four-cylinder DOHC as Daniel pulled the key from the ignition. There was a slight ringing in his ears like auditory floaters and his head spun round whenever he closed his eyes for more than a moment. His sensibilities weren't much improved when he opened his eyes.

His heart raced so wildly that he clutched at it, half to feel its crazy rhythm, and half in hopes the pressure might slow it down, or at least prevent it from bursting out of his chest. Waves of nausea washed over him as his stomach churned in revolt, gurgling and growling like it'd been invaded by intestinal squatters who'd organized Occupy Daniel's Gut.

Inside his head, some small sliver of instinct throbbed with fear, trying to tell him the small gas station/convenience store posted out in the middle of an endless ocean of impenetrable blackness was not a safe spot to stop, but a pit stop for lost souls wandering the highways like godless nomads. A place where anything could happen.

There were four vehicles in the lot, maybe a dozen people on the property. Daniel was afraid of all of them. The innocent don't travel at that godforsaken hour, that wicked time that night hasn't quite given up on, but isn't yet morning. Everyone looked guilty of something.

And maybe, more than anything else, Daniel was afraid of joining them.

At the next pump over, a kid with a keloid-scarred face, a loser's sneer, and a head of greasy hair pulled back tight in a ponytail was fueling a Camaro that had more Bondo than paint. He looked over at Daniel and flashed a smile, a disturbingly knowing grin that seemed to dare him to get on with it already.

Daniel got out of the car, took a deep breath of the night air, and tried to shake off his growing paranoia. For a brief moment, he felt better.

The kid at the pump probably had a connection for some crystal or weed. And it wouldn't have surprised his own mother if he'd slapped around one of his baby-mamas or had snatched a TV or laptop from a trailer he knew was temporarily unattended, but he was no assassin for the Russian mob.

And neither were any of the rest of them. A fat, old man with a Burl Ives beard. A tattooed lady with the shakes impatiently waiting for the cashier to fetch her a carton of smokes. A scarecrow of a man coupled with a woman who could've been dropped on a witch. No, there was no killer elite among them.

And even if there was an assassin hidden in the motley bunch, how could any might-be assassin have found the desolate outpost before he did? Daniel wasn't quite sure where he was; how could anyone else know?

He forced himself to take a deep breath and then swiped his credit card at the pump before plunging the fuel hose into the Kia's tank. As the gas began to flow and the LED numbers started rolling, it occurred to Daniel that even though he had a wallet stuffed fat with cash he'd planned on dropping in Vegas, as a matter of habit, he'd put everything since he'd started his adventure on plastic. Every tank of gas, every Diet Sunkist, every pack of pumpkin seeds had gone right on his Amex. Every single stop he'd made. Every purchase. Everything.

His mind began to spin faster than the numbers on the pump. He knew the government could track credit cards. For half a second he wondered if Filat had those sorts of connections too.

It was a nauseating realization: of course he did. People with Preezrakevich's stash of cash have connections to get *whatever* they want. Daniel doubted obtaining an activity report on his credit cards would be all that troublesome for the former KGB officer. And that meant that every step of the way Daniel had been leaving a neat trail of receipts for Moog and Rabidoso—or whoever else was trying to kill him now—to follow.

What little he'd eaten began to rise in his stomach. It was more than a feeling now; he was certain he was about to vomit. The fuel pump shut itself off and Daniel jumped at the sudden click it made behind him. He didn't bother to replace the fuel hose but ran straight for the bathroom, afraid he wouldn't make it in time.

The graffiti-covered room beyond the swinging door marked MEN reeked of methane and gasoline. It was almost too filthy to retch in. Almost.

When he was certain he had no more road snacks to lose, Daniel turned away from the bowl and staggered over to the sink stained with what he hoped was rust. He ran the tap but the water never got more than lukewarm and smelled suspiciously like what he'd just pumped into his car. He splashed whatever it was that came out of the spigot over his face and then glanced up at his reflection in the mirror. The face staring back didn't look even vaguely familiar. He braced himself against the porcelain basin and tried hard not to cry.

He might have been successful in restraining his tears, if his phone hadn't rung at that exact moment. He pulled the device from his pocket and there on his iPhone screen was a boy's smiling face. *His* boy's. It was Zack.

Unable to control his emotions any longer, he let out a barking sob as a trembling finger pressed Accept Call. He ground his teeth until he thought they might shatter, took a deep breath, and sniffed. "Zack! Where are you? I've been looking all over for you."

The response on the other end was a piercing shriek, so loud and shrill Daniel could almost feel the excruciating pain that had caused it.

"Zack?" Daniel's stomach sank and his heart raced. "ZACK!"

"Oh, he's here, *papi*." The voice on the other end was familiar. Not his son's. "But maybe he can't hear you so well. I just cut off his fucking ear."

Daniel lowered his phone, but he could still hear Rabidoso's psychotic cackle on the other end.

CHAPTER NINE

It had been a good day for Randy Baldwick. He'd awoken for an early session of "Wabbit Season" with his middle-aged Sugar Mama and then dropped her off at LAX to start an entire week of living the life he regretted leaving behind: Running with the old crew. Hitting the clubs. Chasing after—and catching—women who were still young enough to make him feel young too.

The house was completely dark when he got back from his first night out. He thought he'd left the outside lights on, but his recollection of all the night's events was more than hazy. His ears were still ringing from the clubs' deafening *THUMP-THUMP-THUMP*. His head was still swimming in a sickly sweet sea of cranberry and vodka. His body was still tingling from the blonde he'd taken out to the Escalade. And the brunette who'd joined them there.

It had been a good day. A very good day.

His unsteady hand finally found the lock with his key and the tumblers clicked as he turned it. He pushed the door, but something on the other side resisted his efforts to open it. "What the fuck?" He shoved it harder but still couldn't budge it. He lowered his shoulder to the stubborn portal and put all his weight to it. Whatever had been blocking the door finally gave way.

There was a light on at the far end of the house, but the foyer was completely black. He felt the wall for switches and flipped them, but no lights came on. He stepped into the darkness, unable to see there was something wet and slippery spilled on the marble floor. Without warning, his foot slid out from beneath him and sent him falling onto the flat of his back. He landed hard, smacking his head on the foyer tile.

Did he lose consciousness? What little he could make out by the single, distant light was blurry and swirled around his now aching head. He turned over and struggled to get his knees beneath him. On all fours, he lifted his head just slightly and discovered what had been blocking the door.

There on the foyer floor, split open and splayed out like a Staffordshire bull terrier rug, was his beloved Hades. He was surrounded by a pool of thick, slippery blood.

"Oh, Jesus Christ!" Randy tried to get to his feet but the tile was impossibly slick and his "goin' dancing" shoes offered no traction. "Oh, Christ, no!" he screamed as he fell.

Like a mouse caught in a porcelain sink, he frantically tried and tried to get up, his feet scurrying again and again, until he finally managed to get a steady foot beneath him. He started to rise. And that was when the pipe came down on the back of his head.

There was no question he'd been unconscious this time. Given the choice, he would've rather stayed in its dark depths, but a pain—much sharper than the throbbing gash that had been opened across the crown of his head—dragged him out of that black refuge. He tried to fight it, but consciousness fought back, grabbed him, and wouldn't let go. When he finally came to, his hands were bound tightly behind him and there was a man kneeling on his chest.

Rabidoso leaned forward, so close to where the young man's ear had just been that he could almost taste the sweet, salty blood spilling out of it. "Where is the money?" he whispered into the wound he'd opened.

Randy screamed in pain as his oversized arms struggled vainly against the restraints. A small fist, curled up tight like a cue ball, smashed into his left cheek and shut him up. "Where's the money, sonny?"

Confusion hit him as hard as the fist had. "The money? I don't know anything about—" But before Randy could finish, a steel blade carved a crimson path across his not-so-handsome-anymore face. His howl would have split the soul of any man who'd had one, but it only further excited Rabidoso.

The Mexican adjusted his grip on his victim who was slick with blood and sweat. "I know your *papi* gave you the money."

"No." The word was nothing more than a whimper slipping past Randy's severed lips, but it was impossible to tell whether he'd uttered it in response to his interrogator's accusation or as a preemptive plea for mercy.

Rabidoso looked around the well-appointed living room. "This your *mami*'s house?" He didn't wait for an answer. "My *mami* used to tell me I was *el diablo*'s child, not hers." He showed Randy the knife blade covered in his blood. "And do you know what?" He paused for effect, enjoying a long look into Randy's terrified eyes. "She was right." He jammed the point of the blade into Randy's thigh. "I killed the *puta*." He freed the knife, only to plunge it back in again. "I killed them all. Killed them hard."

Randy began to shiver violently, maybe from shock caused by blood loss, or maybe just as a physical expression of his over-whelming emotions as desperation and terror fought for control of what remained of his senses.

Looking into his victim's tearing eyes, Rabidoso tenderly brushed away a strand of sandy, blond hair that had stuck to the young man's sweat-covered brow. "And if I would do that to my own *mami*, just imagine what I will do to you now."

"I swear I don't know anything about any money!"

The Mexican knelt down next to him, so close that his gestures almost seemed like the prelude to a romantic interlude. "You wouldn't lie to me, would you?" His hand slithered into the front pocket of Randy's blood-soaked jeans and pulled out an iPhone. "Why don't we just call Daddy and see?"

A flash of understanding struck Randy when he saw the cell phone he'd taken from Zack the night he'd thrown him out of the house. "No, that's not mine," he cried.

"It's in your pocket, *esse*." Rabidoso put his finger on the screen above the Contacts icon. A list of names and numbers appeared on the screen. He scrolled through them and then pressed the listing marked DAD. Rabidoso grinned triumphantly as a picture of Daniel appeared on the phone. "Let's just call *papi* and see what he knows."

"No," Randy pleaded. "That's not my dad. That's not my phone."

A self-satisfied sneer spread across the Mexican's scarred mouth. "Riiiiiiight."

A second later, Daniel's voice was on the line. "Zack! Where the hell are you? I've been looking all over for you."

Rabidoso leaned forward so that his lips brushed Randy's left ear. "This for lying to me," he whispered to his victim, but his words were drowned out by Randy's piercing shriek as the Mexican's blade sliced off the ear.

"Zack?" Daniel called out from nine hundred and forty miles away. "ZACK!"

"Oh, he's here, *papi*," Rabidoso answered for him. "But maybe he can't hear you so well. I just cut off his ear." The little man cackled.

The line was silent for too long. Rabidoso had no intention of making this easy. "You there, *papi*?"

"I'm here."

"Well, *that's* the problem, *pendejo*. You're *there* when you should be *here*."

"You better not—" Daniel warned, his voice shaking with emotion.

"Better not what?" Rabidoso dared. "Do something like this?"

A second latter there was a bestial scream on the line that made Daniel wince and pull the phone away from his ear again.

"Now your boy's missing an ear—and a nose," Rabidoso relayed. "You better shut your mouth, *esse*, 'cause baby boy's running out of parts here."

"Please! Please!" Rabidoso's victim cried out from beneath him.

The voice was barely intelligible, distorted by gasps and sobs, but Daniel recognized it right away. Relief replaced horror. "What do you want?"

"What do I want?" An exaggerated explosion of laughter. "What the fuck do you think I want? I want you and the money back here in an hour."

"I can't make it there in an hour." Daniel was certain of that.

There was commotion on the line, the phone being passed around. Daniel could hear the exchange. "Come here and tell your daddy what I'm going to do to you if he doesn't get his ass here in an hour."

"Please," the voice begged. "Tell him I don't know anything." As fractured as it was, Daniel knew the desperate plea was

Randy's. In its echoes, everything else fell into place. Randy must have taken Zack's iPhone. And then Rabidoso understandably assumed the young man in his early twenties was the son, not the ex-wife's lover.

"Erickson, you sonofabitch," Randy screamed into the phone. "Tell this fucking psycho I'm not your—"

From the first sleepless night spent walking the floor with a crying infant in their arms, every parent comes to wonder what they'd be capable of doing for their child under the darkest of circumstances. Some have limits, moral or otherwise. Some don't have any bounds at all. "Zack," Daniel called out, though he knew it was a lie.

The best way to help his son at the moment was to convince the sadistic psychopath that he already had him. If protecting Zack's life meant offering Randy's life in its place, then it was a bargain Daniel was willing to strike. And if making that trade was the moral equivalent of wielding the knife himself, Daniel was OK with having that sin on his soul. "Zack, listen to me."

"What are you talking about, Erickson!" It wasn't clear from Randy's voice whether he was more terrified of Rabidoso's knife or Daniel's treachery. "Tell him I'm not your fucking son!"

"I'm sorry, son," Daniel lied softly, though the "sorry" part of it was true enough.

Randy Baldwick had stolen Daniel's wife, sent his life into a near-fatal tailspin, and finally put his son out on the street. There was every reason to hate him—and Daniel did—but there wasn't any vindictive satisfaction in turning him over to such a sadistic monster. It wasn't personal; it was simply what had to be done.

"I'm going to send his soul straight to *Santa Muerte*," Rabidoso hissed into the phone, breathing hard from his exertion. "That what you want for your son?"

"Zack." Daniel gripped the restroom's filthy sink so hard he felt the nine fingers he had left might all snap off. "I'm sorry, Zack. There's nothing I can do for you. You're on your own."

"Please," Randy pleaded desperately. "Why are you doing this to me?"

Daniel knew if his plan was going to work, he had to sell it completely. He had to make certain Randy never had the opportunity to convince Rabidoso there'd been a mistake. If he was going to save Zack, he had to make sure that Randy died. "I'm never coming back, Zack. Never. So tell that psychotic, spic cocksucker there's nothing he can do that will ever make me come back!" He wanted to cry—or vomit, again—but he forced himself to keep his voice steady and strong. "Tell him to go fuck himself. And his *puta mami.*"

A scream went up, so pained and soulless that Daniel wanted to join it with an expression of his own torment, like two wolves howling in shared mourning. He didn't want Randy to die without knowing he was sorry, maybe offer him a word of consolation. Or thanks. But Daniel couldn't afford to say anything that might betray his scheme, so he remained silent and sank to the restroom floor as he wept.

The screaming on the phone intensified, becoming higher and more frenzied until Daniel was certain it couldn't get worse.

He was wrong.

Randy Baldwick was a royal douche bag. There was no doubt about that. And no one could have blamed Daniel if he'd wished for terrible things to happen to him. But not this. Never. Not even in the darkest, most twisted corners of the basement of his soul could he have wished this on anyone.

"Ear." Rabidoso called out the body parts he was systematically removing. "Finger." The screaming became more and more intense with each severed item identified. "Eye." Until finally the shrieking didn't sound like Randy, didn't even sound human anymore.

"You think I can't make you come back?" Rabidoso's voice was crazed with fury. "I hope you didn't want grandchildren!" There was a shriek so agonized that it slashed at Daniel's soul with the same ferocity as the madman worked his blade. "You get your fucking ass back here right now or I swear to *Santa Muerte* I'll skin every inch of your little bastard."

Whether he'd been justified or not, Daniel had done what he'd done. Listening to the tortured aftermath of those actions wouldn't change anything. With a touch of his finger Daniel ended the call and with it, he knew, Randy Baldwick's life.

Still on his knees, Daniel Erickson bowed his head and intertwined his nine fingers. Between his gasping sobs, he prayed to whatever god would hear him—not for forgiveness or compassion, which he knew he didn't deserve—but for the strength to do whatever he had to do to spare his son from Randy's fate. He leaned against the filthy bowl like it was an altar and squeezed his hands together, pleading, "Please, please, please," over and over again.

When he was finished or had simply concluded divine intervention wasn't going to be bestowed on him in the fouled stall of a roadside restroom, he climbed back up to his feet. The only thing his prayers had accomplished was to reopen the wound on his finger, now puss-filled and certainly infected. There was blood all over the floor and toilet bowl where he'd knelt, making the crap booth look like Jackson Pollock had gotten his hands on a can of red paint or some unlucky chicken had found itself on a sacrificial altar.

He washed his face again with the Petro-shit-water from the sink and packed his finger stump as best he could in wads of brown paper towels. Knowing he couldn't stand to see his spec-ter of a reflection, he left the restroom without stopping to check himself in the stained mirror and stepped out into the conve-nience store area.

Above him, the bright fluorescent lights burned his blood-shot eyes. The pop music piped in over speakers in the ceiling made his head hurt even worse. He wanted to leave but felt a nag-ging obligation to at least buy a candy bar or soda pop. The beige metal shelves were lined with every artificially colored/flavored/preserved/enhanced snack food known to man, but Daniel didn't think he could stomach any of them.

He stumbled around the aisles searching but soon realized the only thing he was finding was unwanted attention. The old man eyeing up what hot dog he wanted to choose from the roll-ers pretended not to notice Daniel. The kid checking out with a Mountain Dew and a pack of Lucky Strikes didn't bother to hide his interest in the obviously distressed man pretending to be interested in the display of snacks.

The attention was more than he could stand. Daniel gave up the act and went straight for the door.

"Hey," the young Puebloan woman behind the counter called out to him before he could push it open. Daniel stopped dead. "Can't find what want, huh?" Her voice was playful and light.

He turned and awkwardly shook his head. "No. I can't seem to find what I'm looking for."

"Of course not." The voice that left her scarlet-glossed lips no longer fit her bright eyes, but was deep and raspy and masculine. The change was so sudden and complete that Daniel couldn't help thinking that it wasn't her talking at all. "You need to get back out on the road," something inside her croaked. "That's where you'll find what you lookin' for, *mi key!*" And then, without warning she burst out in raucous laughter, like the voice within her had just told the funniest joke of the night.

Daniel stood there for a moment, stunned and watching her laugh at him. Nobody else in the store seemed to be taking any notice of the odd encounter, and in his fragile emotional condition, the experience left Daniel wondering if he was staring back at a ghost. Or something worse.

He turned and ran out into the night. The door closed behind him with the *ding-dong* of the security sensor, but he could still hear her laughing.

He returned the fuel hose to the pump and climbed in behind the wheel. An unsteady hand fumbled with the shifter as a shaky leg stepped on the accelerator. The Kia lurched and then jumped forward, its tires squealing as Daniel pulled out of the service station parking lot and raced back to the highway.

He drove through the night, through those hard hours when it seems that it's been dark for so long that a soul should give up hope the skies will ever lighten again. He kept the speedometer pinned well past eighty, but the speed would not let him outrun the savage guilt he felt for what he'd done. Mile after mile sped by, but the distance gained did little to clear the lingering stench trapped in his nostrils or soften the night clerk's odd remarks and haunting laughter echoing in his ears.

He slept for an hour or two alongside the highway outside of Conway, Texas, but woke feeling no better. At the Elk City exit, he found a diner and forced himself to eat some of the hot roast beef sandwich he ordered.

Somewhere in the endless abyss of the Sooner State, he finally succumbed to the endless highway's hypnotic spell, and the miles began to pass without much of a thought about anything at all. He was grateful for the undeserved chance to rest his mind, and yet he was aware the road had to end somewhere. He was painfully aware that a man can't outrun his regrets and failures. Not for long, at least.

And so, he drove the rest of the way like a man who can see a funnel cloud in his rearview and needs to keep speeding just to stay one step ahead of the storm.

CHAPTER TEN

The back door opened and closed. Footsteps approached, but Rabidoso didn't hear them. Or, at least, they didn't stop him.

"The only thing I could find open was a Del Taco," Moog called out from the kitchen as he casually tossed the bags of burritos and tortilla chips on the counter. "But then I figured that Mexican had to be a'right with you," he joked as he continued walking through the house toward where he'd last left his partner.

"Hey, where'd you—" He stopped dead as soon as he stepped into the living room. "Jesus Fucking Christ!"

Moog rushed over to where a crazed, dazed, and exhausted Rabidoso was still plunging his knife into the clearly lifeless body beneath him. "What the fuck are you doing, man?" The big man picked the pint-size killer up and tossed him across the room like a bored child discarding a worn-out plaything.

Shaken from his frenzy, Rabidoso was back to his feet almost before he'd hit the ground. He wiped his foaming mouth, too short of breath to answer.

"Oh, Jesus, man!" Moog rubbed a hand over his closely cropped hair as he tried to make some sense of the two-hundred-and-some pounds of ground meat at his feet. "I fuckin' told you I was going to get us something to eat while we waited for someone to show up here. I said, 'Don't do anything till I get back.' Remember that? I told you *not* to fuckin'—"

"No one tells me," the Mexican gasped between panting breaths, "anything."

Moog ignored the adolescent rebelliousness and looked down on what only vaguely resembled a man. "Who the hell's he?"

"He's his—" Rabidoso tried to wipe the blood from the corner of his mouth but only managed to smear more crimson across his badly scarred face. "He's his son."

The big man's eyebrows arched, as if he had reason to doubt it. "Well, whoever he is, he's no goddamn good to us as a motherfucking corpse, is he?"

"He didn't know anything," Rabidoso said in his own defense. "Besides, the fucker told me he wasn't coming back for him." The little psycho shook his head as if that was some coldness even he couldn't comprehend. "His father, man. Wouldn't give the money up for his son's life."

"What?" None of what he'd heard made any sense. "What do you mean *he* told you? *He* who?"

"Erickson, man." Rabidoso didn't understand his partner's confusion and held up the blood-smeared iPhone as if that explained everything. "I had him on the phone. Fucker said he wouldn't come back. Not even to save his son."

The big man hit the living room wall with his right fist, but it was only so he wouldn't make a similar hole in the partner he hadn't wanted in the first place. "You had Erickson on the phone?"

"That's what I just said." Rabidoso didn't see the problem.

"And you didn't think to talk to him *before* you started getting all 'carvey' with this kid?"

"I thought—" Rabidoso started to explain, but the truth of the matter was that once he pulled his blade out he never thought about anything but getting "carvey."

"No. You didn't think." Moog looked down at the body again and then surveyed the mess surrounding it. The high pile carpet was saturated with thick, dark blood. The walls were splattered with an assortment of crimson Rorschach tests. Across the foyer was a pooled lake of death. "You killed the goddamn dog?" He shook his head in disbelief that bordered on genuine remorse. "The dog was in the fucking laundry room. Why would you kill the dog?"

"I don't like dogs." It seemed like a perfectly good explanation to Rabidoso.

But not to Moog. "You better get this shit straightened up. You've put enough evidence down in this goddamn place that the Westlake Village PD is gonna be able to make a case on us." Moog shook his head in disgust. "And they roll all volunteers."

The little man puffed up his chest. "I'm not worried—"

"Not worried?" Moog wasn't sure he'd heard him right, but he was certain this was why he worked alone. "Well, you better get worried. Cause I ain't pullin' no forty years in Chico 'cause you too fuckin' stupid to be scared." He fought hard to regain his composure as he looked around at the blood-splattered walls and gore-drenched carpet. "And you got a lot of shit to clean up here."

"Clean it up?" Rabidoso looked around at the carnage. "What's the point?"

"The point is that the more evidence you leave here, the more evidence they have to lock up your ass." He was losing patience. "But the real fucking point is that I told you to do it."

Rabidoso didn't answer, but his burning eyes silently warned there was a price to pay for talking to him like that. No one talked that shit to him and lived. Not for long, anyway. Without a word, he turned and walked away like he had business to attend to.

The big man didn't give a goddamn for what he saw in any man's eyes. "Now get moving! We can't be waiting around all damn day." He straightened his tie and walked away.

No, Rabidoso didn't like the big man's tone at all. It was the same one his *mami* had used with him—and look where that had gotten her. He was a good soldier, but it was getting harder and harder for him to follow his orders.

CHAPTER ELEVEN

Vernon "Moog" Turner was ducking under doorways by the time he turned twelve. He could press five hundred reps before he could drive, and when he dropped out of the tenth grade, he tipped the scales upward of three fifty. Even on the hard streets of Kansas City, east of Holmes Road, everyone feared the man-size boy who was filled with all the rage of a campsite-raiding bear.

Elma Mae Nutdon needed the stepstool from her pantry to kiss her grandson's cheek and she never saw a day when she weighed more than a hundred and five pounds. Still, what she lacked in size, she overcompensated for with spirit. She was not slow with a belt or a broom or the back of her hand and she raised her baby boy's baby boy with all of the love and discipline she had left in her.

"Vernon Turner!" she'd holler, and her Frigidaire-size grandson would come running like a puppy, obediently accepting whatever punishment she'd decided to mete out for his latest offense.

One Sunday afternoon Vernon showed up at the supper table with a Chiefs hat on, cocked to one side with the price tag still dangling from the brim. The old lady took one look at it and then removed it from his head—with a back swing that sent the offending cap sailing across the room. "Don't come to my table looking like one of them clowns. Hats on sideways. Pants falling down. Fools and clowns!

"Pride!" She wagged her arthritic finger right in his face. "A man without pride don' have nothin'! Ain't no man at all."

Elma knew her grandbaby wasn't going to grow to be an angel, but she wouldn't stand for him being less than his best. "Lord knows I tried. But whatever you're gonna do, Vernon, you do it with pride. You don' go around like one of them street clowns. You take pride in how you look. In what you do. In who you are."

His reply wasn't anything more than a meek "Yes, ma'am," but from that day on he was a changed man. He dressed for business. Carried himself like he was someone to be respected—or reckoned with. And no matter what his job required, he always went about it like a professional. From top to bottom. Through and through. He was a professional.

That was why the partner he'd been unwillingly burdened with bothered him so much. Rabidoso was undisciplined. So goddamn sloppy. So bat-shit crazy. He left messes everywhere he went, and that kind of shit was how your ass ended up in prison. Or a grave.

The cell phone in Moog's pocket vibrated and he put it to his ear. "Good evening, Mr. Preezrakevich."

It was the wrong way to begin their conversation.

"No, sir. I know it's not a *good* evening, I just meant—" He held the phone away so the yelling would just be an annoying buzzing in the near distance.

"Yes, sir." Moog's eyes never came up off the ground as he paced back and forth listening to what his employer had to say.

"No, sir. I understand." He paused to listen to the runty Russian's tirade but kept pacing the carpet Rabidoso had scrubbed as best he could.

"Yes, sir." Pause. "No, sir." He curled a fist but had nowhere to throw it. "No, sir. There's no need to involve any outside talent in this. You have my word." He held the phone away from his ear again as his boss made it deafeningly clear just how little his pledge of honor meant.

"Yes, sir. I understand." Moog ended the call and put the phone back in his pocket.

"What did he say?" Rabidoso asked, as he twisted the last of the trash bags and tied it shut.

The big man hadn't slept in two days. His Alexander Amosu suit was ruined. His Hermès tie and his Ferragamos too. And he was in no mood to recap the verbal whipping he'd just gotten for the Mexican madman he'd been chained to. "He asked if we needed help. I told him I didn't. And he told me to go get it done."

Rabidoso considered the news and then translated it in his head. "You think he's going to kill us?"

"Don't know." Moog shrugged off the suggestion. "But you can be goddamn certain dropping a million dollars in Mr. P.'s lap is going to improve his mood some. So let's just focus on doing what we need to do to get that money."

Rabidoso nodded like he understood.

The not-so-gentle giant wanted to make absolutely sure that he did. "That means, you need to stop fucking killing everything." He shook his head in frustration, knowing he was close to losing his temper and making a bad situation worse. He took a deep breath and counted to ten. "From now on you don't kill anything you don't have to. Nothing. Got it? You don't swat a fucking fly—"

"You work your way," Rabidoso smirked as he turned his knife over and over, checking it for some stubborn, telltale trace of Randy Baldwick's blood on its shiny steel surface. "And I'll work my—"

"You'll work *my* way!" Moog's voice boomed like the .50 holstered beneath his arm. "You don't kill anyone else unless you absolutely have to."

Rabidoso concluded the blade was clean enough, casually folded it, and returned it to his front pants pocket. "And how do I know if I absolutely have to?"

"You'll know when it's time for killing because I'll be the motherfucker doing it." The big man locked eyes with his unprofessional colleague like a laser-assisted sight. "And if you try and cross me up on this, I'm going to start all that killing with you."

"You threatening me?" Rabidoso's dark, empty eyes seemed to brighten at the prospect of a challenge.

"Consider it a professional courtesy," Moog shot straight back. "I'm telling you straight off so you won't die wondering what you done to get yourself killed." Then he shrugged the rest of it off. There was work that needed doing. "Come on, I don't have time for this. We got some driving to do."

"Where to?"

Moog turned and walked to the front door of Connie Erickson's freshly scrubbed Mediterranean McMansion. "Mr. P. got word Erickson used his credit card at a service station in New Mexico."

"New Mexico?"

"Well, there ain't much room to run west, is there?"

Rabidoso followed, struggling with a black plastic bag that was stuffed with soiled rags, used cleanings supplies, and parts of what had once been Randy Baldwick. "When all of this is over, *esse*, you and me—"

The big man turned and stopped him there. "If we're both alive when this wraps up, you can have your shot at the champ. For now, you just concentrate on cleaning up your shit. I ain't going down 'cause you do a sloppy job. I work clean. I'm a professional. I take pride in my work."

Wherever she was, Moog knew his Gramma Mae was looking down on him. And even if she wasn't proud of what he was doing, he knew she was proud of how he was getting it done.

CHAPTER TWELVE

The blinding sun that had forced Daniel's eyes into a pained, Eastwoodesque squint as he drove across the long stretches of Oklahoma prairie had dimmed and all but abandoned him as he rolled into Arkansas. By the time he'd crossed the Mississippi River, the night had grown darker than Delta soil.

Without a moon above to light the way, he raced over the twisting and turning back roads like a moonshine-running native as the odd barn or boarded-up storefront indicated he was getting closer and closer to what passed for a town. When he hit his first stoplight in Mississippi, he looked over toward the side of the road where a sign illuminated by his high beams proclaimed "The Birthplace of the Blues." He had arrived.

Highways 49 and 61 intersect at what passes for the town center of Clarksdale, Mississippi. Without much else going on, Clarksdale has made a nice little cottage industry of its place in blues history with a dozen boutiques and souvenir shops, a classic guitar shop, and even a celebrity restaurant club— (Morgan Freeman's Ground Zero blues club is just two or three blocks over). And the good folks down at the Chamber of Commerce will tell whoever's passing through that their town square is the exact spot where a young Robert Johnson traded his mortal soul for immortal guitar prowess. And to lay claim to that legend, the town has erected a twenty-foot signpost that boasts a trio of oversized cutouts of baby blue electric guitars. (It's an odd tribute to a man who was never known to play anything but a battered Kalamazoo acoustic.)

Daniel had no desire to stick around until morning just to pick up a Muddy Waters T-shirt or a Little Walter blues harp refrigerator magnet, but still he couldn't shake the song that kept playing on an endless loop in the back of his head. The lyrics of "Blues Highway Blues," the mysterious words he'd tried to decipher a thousand times over the course of his pilgrimage, had told him:

> *If you wanna earn your soul back, find where your money's hid*
> *Better get down to the crossroads like young Robert did*

Daniel had long ago given up on the idea of ever recovering his soul, but he was in desperate need of the cash. So he parked his Kia at those crossroads—in the gravel parking lot that served double duty for Delta Donut and Atlas Bar-B-Q—and waited patiently, too tired to explain to himself just what he was waiting for.

He focused his frayed attention on the glowing lights of the Kia's dashboard clock. A minute before midnight. If something was going to happen at these fabled crossroads, the witching hour seemed like the perfect time for it.

And then, at the exact moment the 11:59 changed to 12:00, at the very stroke of midnight…the witching hour…absolutely nothing happened.

Outside in the cold distance…a dog barked.

A truck drove past.

And then another.

But nothing extraordinary happened. Not in this world. Not in some underworld of Southern legend and lore. Not in any world, as far as Daniel knew.

There was nothing extraordinary about it. Not the place. Or time. None of it.

Daniel wasn't sure why he felt so disappointed. Had he really expected the song would be anything other than a diversion? Could he have possibly believed there was a hope in hell of getting his money back?

Of course he could have.

If he looked back at his life, the entire path was clearly marked with a string of similarly stupid acts and piss-poor personal judgments as trailblazers: Following the thief's riddles to this godforsaken crossroads. Thinking he could recreate his career with a reality show. Financing the doomed project with a Russian mobster's money. Self-destructing in the wake of his divorce. Falling for Connie in the first place; believing the lie of her love. Making music his business. Picking up the guitar in the first place.

Forty-seven years of unbelievable blunders. One leading to the next and then the next, like notes in a song—the worst song ever.

He hit the steering wheel as hard as he could. "Goddamn it!" There was nothing else he could do, nowhere else to go. No more cards to play. No hope. Nothing.

He closed his eyes and folded his arms across his chest, not to sleep but just to take a moment to gather up all the disjointed thoughts scattered across the floor of his consciousness like a dropped deck of cards. If there had been a prayer left in his soul, it would have only been the same tired one he'd screamed to the unhearing heavens a thousand times before: "Please, just let it stop. Let everything just fade to black. Forever."

Tap. Tap.

The sound was so faint at first he wasn't sure it was a sound at all. *Tap. Tap.*

Daniel sat up in his seat, looking for the source of the slight sound slowly building in volume and insistence. *Tap. Tap.* But he couldn't see a thing. *Tap. Tap.* The windows had fogged in what seemed like an instant and turned an eerie opaque. *Tap. Tap.* He couldn't see a thing out in the night. Including whatever was making the sound. *Tap. Tap.*

Daniel rubbed at the glass, trying to wipe away what he assumed was frost, but found the window was dry and clear. *Tap, tap, tap.* No, whatever was coating the windows had come from the outside. *TAP. TAP. TAP.*

The rapping was focused on the driver's window. Tentatively, Daniel put his palm to the window, like he was reaching out to whatever was now banging at the glass. *TAP! TAP!* Like he was reaching out to touch what he knew he shouldn't.

And then suddenly—silence.

From out in the darkness, from the other side of the window, another hand appeared against his, pressing its palm against the glass. Daniel pulled his hand back, recoiling in shock. And then he watched in horror as the hand began to wipe away whatever gelatinous film was covering the window.

At first it had seemed simply opaque, and then as black as the night itself. But as the phantom hand wiped the window clean, Daniel could tell the substance wasn't black, but red. A dark, dark red. "Oh, Jesus," he whimpered. The windows were covered in blood. Gallons and gallons of blood. A second hand appeared on the window, trying to assist the other in clearing the blood away.

And then a face pressed against the glass, twisting and contorting in an effort to get a look into the car's cabin. A face, but not quite a human face. At least, not human any longer. The nose had been cut off. The ears too. An eye had been removed. And yet the remaining parts were all too familiar. The bloody mess of a face was Randy Baldwick's.

Daniel jumped back in his seat as if there were somewhere to escape in the compact's cramped cabin.

The face pressed closer to the glass, the remaining eye filled with a hateful fury focused on Daniel. The slashed remnants of a mouth curled in a cruel sneer as it growled hoarsely. "You. Are. A. Dead. Man."

Bang. Bang. Bang. "Sir, roll down your window."

Daniel sat up in his seat with a start, shielding his eyes from the painfully bright beam of a Clarksdale patrolman's Maglite. Lingering disorientation left him unsure which was the dream, and Daniel let out a low groan.

"Sir, roll down your window," the officer repeated, his free hand resting nervously on the Sig Sauer holstered at his more-than-ample waist.

The sight shocked the dream out of Daniel's foggy head. "That's what I get for praying," he moaned to himself as he slowly cranked the window down. "Yes, officer? Is there a problem?"

"Been drinking tonight?" The accusation slipped from his jowly mouth just as easy as the first piece of sweet potato pie out of the tin.

"I don't drink." It was the truth—for the last eight months or so, anyway. "I'm just tired. I must have dozed off."

The officer's beam started to explore the cabin of the car, seeking to illuminate something he could call *probable cause*. "Sometimes that can be even worse."

"That's why I pulled over."

"Well, this here's a private parking lot, it ain't no Motel Six." The patrolman matter-of-factly requested, "License. Registration. Proof of 'surance."

As he reached for the documentation, Daniel began to wonder: Had they traced the stolen Lotus and that whole PCH mess back to him? Had they found what Rabidoso might have left of Randy and figured *him* for the murder? The night air was cold, but Daniel began to sweat.

The cop noticed the beads forming on Daniel's forehead. "Is there a problem there, mister?" he asked suspiciously.

There were lots of them, but none that Daniel wanted to explain to a Mississippi cop. "No problem." He fished his license out of his wallet, opened the glove box and pulled out the car's paperwork, then handed it all over.

"Wait here and don't start your ve-hic-le." Without another word, the chubby cop returned to his patrol car.

As unpredictable as his life had been, Daniel had never—not even once—foreseen a scenario in which he was taken into custody by a night-shift patrolman in Clarksdale, Mississippi. If he wasn't struggling to contain a fear-induced impulse to vomit, he might have laughed out loud.

After what seemed like a long while, the cop returned, his slightly crossed eyes squinty with grim suspicion. "Sir, can you explain why the address on your license don't match the registration of the ve-hic-le?"

That was an easy one. "Connie."

"'Scuse me?"

It was karmically perfect that she'd ultimately be responsible for his tragic end, sending him off to a life in the Mississippi State penal system. "My ex-wife. She's got the Jaguar and the Escalade and I had to come begging to use the goddamn Kia."

The cop's jaw clenched as a jolt of anger sparked in his off-set eyes. For a second Daniel was convinced he was completely fucked. And then, an instant later, the policeman's countenance softened. "Goddamn, don't I know that one." His jowls wagged as he nodded his understanding. "Had me a 2010 Superduty F-250 King Ranch. Beaut-i-ful. V-8 Turbo Diesel. Eight-foot box. Had her jacked up on a Skyjacker lift kit."

Daniel had no idea what the patrolman was talking about, but he was grateful for a diversion from his situation and faked an enthusiastic "Wow!"

"Yeah, 'Wow!'" The portly cop stopped to take a deep, cleansing breath, a process Daniel thought the guy must have learned in some court-ordered anger management class. "Turned out my bitch of an ex-wife was fuckin' my best friend." Another deep breath, although this time it was more of a snort. "She ended up takin' damn near everything I had. Now I'll be damned if that sonofabitch ain't drivin' my truck!" It was clear the cuckolding hadn't been the worst of it as he shook his head sadly over the loss of his truck. "If I hadn't sworn an oath under God as a law officer—" He didn't finish his declaration, but Daniel guessed the unspoken threat was where the court-ordered anger management had come into play.

Daniel felt sorry for the guy, even if he was about to slap the iron bracelets on him. "It's not right."

"No. It ain't." There was a moment when the patrolman seemed like he might say something else, but instead he drifted off into his own dark thoughts. (It must have been a hell of a truck.)

When he finally surfaced again, the cop simply handed Daniel his license and paperwork. "Sorry 'bout this, but we keep a sharp watch on this corner. Get all sort of freaks come down here." He snorted contemptuously. "Think they're gonna see some goddamn ghost story or somethin'."

"Really?" Daniel did his best to sound surprised.

"On account o' all that crossroads bullshit," the officer explained halfheartedly as he pointed up at the guitars overhead. "Dumb shitheads," he laughed to himself. "It ain't even the right crossroads."

"It isn't the right what?" Daniel tried to contain his surprise—and interest.

"Shit, no." The cop laughed a little, amused by all those misguided musical pilgrims. "I don't listen to *that* kinda music, mind ya."

"No. Me neither," Daniel lied, trying to build some common ground with his new redneck friend—besides the cuckoldings and financially disastrous divorces.

"Give me Skynyrd any damn day."

Daniel weakly tried a few bars of "Freebird."

The patrolman grinned a good ol' grin. "Or Stevie Ray."

Daniel obliged with the chorus of "Pride and Joy," croaking it like an out-of-tune human jukebox.

"That's why I won't ever get on no air-o-plane," the officer observed solemnly.

Daniel nodded as if his precaution made perfect sense, and then quickly redirected the conversation. "But this isn't the crossroads?"

"Hell, no. You ask any of the old-timers 'round here. More than a few of 'em knew that ol' boy, most all of 'em knew someone who did. They'll all tell you Robert Johnson played 'round here

EYRE PRICE

but never lived here. So if'in he went to some damn crossroads or whatnot, he'd done it down there on Dockery Plantation."

If the night hadn't already put a chill into Daniel, hearing the name of the band that had recorded the mystery song would have done the job. "Dockery Plantation, huh?"

"Yeah. Down 'tween Ruleville and Cleveland. Bunch a' them blues guys came outta there. But you ask anyone and they'll tell you the *real* crossroad's down there. Corner of Dockery Road and Highway Eight."

"Dockery Road and Highway Eight," Daniel repeated, trying hard not to sound like his very life depended on it.

"Now, you best get yourself off the road as tired as you are." There was more than a little paternal tone to his voice. "I don't wanna come haveta' pull you outta some ditch in an hour or two."

"No. You wouldn't—"

"Too much damn paperwork," the cop laughed a little more. "Seriously, you get yourself just down the road there and check into the Sleepin' Inn. You tell 'em ol' Ronnie Granger sent ya and they'll treat ya right."

"I'll do that," Daniel lied again.

"The hell you will," the cop said with a knowing chuckle, his voice suddenly alarmingly deep and raspy. "You a goddamn liar." It was the same voice he'd heard escaping from the convenience store clerk back in New Mexico. "You got miles to go and you better get going, *mi key*."

The sound of it was no less horrifying than the apparition at his window. "Excuse me?"

"I said, 'Have a good night now,'" the policeman clarified in his thick, gentle Southern drawl. He cocked his head, clearly wondering whether he'd made a mistake in not having written a ticket.

Unnerved, Daniel forced himself to say, "I'll try."

The patrol car pulled past him and headed on down the highway, but Daniel couldn't shake the feeling he was still being watched. Carefully, he turned the Kia around and headed south down 61. When the lights of the northbound patrol car finally faded into the black, Daniel picked up speed. He saw the Sleepin' Inn off to the right…and drove right on past it.

He was headed south, down to the Dockery Plantation.

CHAPTER THIRTEEN

For all the dark legend it holds, there is nothing to distinguish the intersection of Mississippi Route 8 and the old Dockery Road from any of the other countless dirt paths that cut away from the macadam highway and snake off through the tall grasses only to disappear beyond some creek bed or on the far end of a stand of cypress. There's not a plaque or historical marker for Robert Johnson. No monument to the man who reinvented the blues (and everything else that sprang forth from those magical musical seeds). There's not so much as a handmade cross to mark the spot where he supposedly struck his sinister deal for the powers to do it.

The only notice to alert a traveler (or pilgrim) of that particular crossroad is a green road sign reading Dockery Road, so small that it's easy to drive right by without noticing. Daniel was almost a quarter mile down the road before his road-weary brain realized what he'd just glimpsed in his peripheral vision.

It was another eighth of a mile before he could find a spot to turn around. Off to the left was a small service station with a two-pump island out front. Its windows were darkened, making it impossible to tell whether it was simply closed for the late hour or had been abandoned altogether.

Daniel pulled into the station's gravel-covered lot and palmed the steering wheel hard to the right. As the Kia came round its turn, its headlights lit up an old barn a hundred yards beyond the gas station. Its roof was faded from a hundred summers and its side planks were weathered gray. Across those ancient timbers, someone had painted in whitewash letters three feet high: DOCKERY FARMS.

Daniel stopped the car and sat for a minute, staring at the words. Although they'd clearly been painted decades ago as part of a historical preservation effort, they seemed to him to be a mean-spirited personal taunt. Maybe his senses had been compromised by fatigue or stress or shock; but it seemed like someone had put them there all those years ago, knowing even then on some dark night in the future he'd stand before them and see them there. It was as if whatever force was responsible for dragging him out to such a desolate spot was bragging about its omniscience, its total control of time and circumstances—warning him, perhaps, that he'd come too far to ever turn back.

Turning back, however, was exactly what he decided to do. When the Kia started moving again, it was shooting gravel from its rear tires like the Union artillery at Vicksburg. He peeled out of the lot, and spinning rubber hit pavement with a banshee's squeal as he went shooting off down the road, headed back the way he'd come.

By the time he approached the fabled crossroads for a second time, he'd managed to catch his breath and his heart had slowed to a more comfortable 4/4 backbeat, although he was far from calm. His grip on the wheel made his knuckles ache.

In the pit of his sour stomach there was a gnawing feeling—a certainty, really—that he should keep driving, just get as far away from that cursed spot as a Korean subcompact could take him. Deep inside that little voice was screaming, "For the love of God, just keep driving!" And for once in his life he was determined to listen.

It wasn't until the very last minute, until he'd almost driven past it for a second time, that Daniel pulled the wheel hard to the right. The Kia left the highway too abruptly, hitting the dirt road far faster than the little car ever should have. The tires slid and the car began to drift to the right as he instinctively stomped on the brakes and tried to regain control. The mini-hatchback fishtailed and skidded and then came to a sudden stop.

Daniel sat panting behind the steering wheel as the dust he'd churned up settled back down to earth, illuminated in the headlights like drifting brown snowflakes. "Goddamn it!"

Through the dirt blizzard, Daniel's eyes traced the road ahead as it crossed over a small one-lane bridge and then disappeared behind a number of blight-stricken pines. Not wanting to do the same, he decided the best thing to do was to turn around. He tried to convince himself retreating was simply the most reasonable reaction to his predicament, but the truth was that a growing uneasiness gnawing at his gut had become a panicked *need* to get out of there before it was too late. And a whispering voice inside his head teased that he'd already missed that train.

The road was too narrow to make a U-turn. (Daniel cursed himself for not having paid closer attention in his high school driver's ed class thirty years earlier.) In his first pass of his "K" turn, the Kia's grip on the dirt road gave just a little. With the second maneuver, the car swung around to point out toward the highway, but then slid a bit on the loose surface as it began to move forward. Already jittery and jumpy, Daniel panicked and tried to accelerate his way back into control.

The tires spun wildly on the loose surface and then, as they dug down to find some purchase, began flinging mud and gravel everywhere, spewing like an LSU coed at the end of a long game night. The Kia lurched forward once, but soon that throaty growl of tires clawing through dirt turned to the high-pitched whine of wheels spinning through mud but going nowhere: the unmistakable sound of *stuck*.

"Goddamn it!"

Out of pure frustration, Daniel stepped harder on the accelerator, no longer believing—or even caring—that it would set him free. The tachometer jumped up dangerously close to the red line as the car rocked and trembled but refused to move an inch.

"Goddamn it!"

He threw off his seat belt, exploded out of the car, and stomped around behind to see just exactly what the problem was. He was no automotive expert, but the difficulty was obvious enough: the right rear tire was buried clear up to the frame in deep, dark Delta mud. He wasn't going anywhere.

"Goddamn it!"

The blasphemy was so loud it should have produced a clear echo, but the only return was the faintest of whispers, barely audible above the whistle of the winter wind in the tall grasses of the fallow fields. And while the word that came back was the same one he'd uttered, Daniel had an unsettling feeling the voice repeating it wasn't his.

As far as he could tell, there was nothing around him in any direction except pitch black. He was absolutely alone. Not a soul. And yet he'd heard a voice. Or thought he had.

The possibility that the darkness in which he was entombed hid something with a voice left Daniel momentarily paralyzed. He just stood there behind his car, frozen in fear like an armadillo caught on a highway, unsure whether to go left or right, to stay or to run.

There was another sound. *Grrrrrrrrrrrrrr*. Not loud, but distinct enough to break him from his trance. It resolved all indecision and he moved toward the Kia as quickly as he could.

Just as he reached it, something moved through the grass off to his right. The sound stopped him again, left him as motionless as one of the stone statutes of long-forgotten Confederate generals dotting the landscape of their defeat.

With the terrified concentration of a fawn in the brush, he listened as whatever it was bounded back and forth through the tall grasses, moving closer and then farther away. He wanted to believe it was just a dog from a nearby farm making a night for itself chasing raccoons or rats, but he knew it was moving too quickly for that—and then too slowly. It was so loud he could hear it clearly and then so soft he began to doubt whether there was anything to hear at all.

Alone. In the middle of nowhere. Drowning in darkness. Surrounded, but unsure by whom. Or by what. Daniel suddenly found that the antiquity of the earth beneath his feet was impossible to escape and his mind began to open to the possibilities it might contain: fantastical, nightmarish possibilities.

Perhaps there was truth in every legend, even if that kernel lay only at the point of its origin. Maybe there was a very good reason for the primal terror that lies in every human heart, a forgotten understanding that there are some things that cannot be explained or understood, and yet still deserve to be feared.

Science would scoff at the notion, but science needs a light in the darkness. It's dependent upon some reasonable shelter and the safety found within four walls and a roof. Science needs the time and opportunity to think it all out. It's easy to be brave in a classroom, and skepticism can flourish freely in a laboratory's controlled environment. Alone in the darkness, however, every soul is reminded with certainty that "there is more of heaven and earth..."

And then it was quiet again. Quiet and still. Daniel took as deep a breath as he dared. He waited. Still nothing. Another deep breath and his senses slowly returned. Rationality began to lap over him like the tide at the foreshore. He chastised himself for panicking, for having surrendered so freely to a momentary free-fall into superstition's fetid pool.

The night was just an effect of the regular rotation of the earth.

The lonely stretch of roadway where he was stranded was just another old farm road. If he could have seen it through the impenetrable dark, the landscape was probably quaint and picturesque in a G. Ruger Donoho kind of way.

The stories of young Robert Johnson trading his soul for complete command of the guitar were just stories. A way to entertain folks in the dark ages before radio or television. Or the Internet. There was only one path to mastery of the guitar: practice.

And even if Robert himself claimed he'd made such a deal— and he did—it was just a bluesman's bravado, another way of promoting the act. Something Daniel knew only too well. Just a clever marketing angle. Nothing more.

Daniel told himself all of this, and yet he couldn't help but imagine a young Robert Johnson standing just across the road from him now. He could almost make out the shadowy silhouette of the young man waiting there in the darkness, defeated and disgraced, driven to the most desperate of measures—exactly like Daniel was now.

He wondered if Robert Johnson had been frightened too. Had the young man's imagination played tricks on *him* in the night? Had he wanted to go back to wherever he'd called home or had he simply been too determined to turn and run? Had he come to that crossroads doubting the legends, or had he believed in its powers and been willing to give up anything in order to get what he wanted most? Just like Daniel.

There was another sound. He wasn't sure where it came from or what it was, but he was certain it was something. Out in the fields, there was quick movement through the tall grasses. Could he hear paws on the ground? Or were they feet?

Something rustled in the bushes not twenty feet away. Was that a growl?

Yes. Yes, it was a growl. A large growl. *Grrrrrrrrrrrrrrrrrrrrrrrrrr.*

Robert Johnson died as a young man, just a few years after his meteoric rise to prominence. Musical historians have concluded he was poisoned by a vengeful man whom Robert had made a cuckold, but there were others—folks who knew the man personally—who insisted his death could not be so easily explained. And the dark legend that begins with a boy at the crossroads ends with a man dying on his hands and knees, barking like the hellhound he'd claimed had been chasing him since the night he'd made his pact.

Supposed pact, Daniel corrected himself.

It was just a legend. Just a legend. Daniel repeated it to himself over and over.

Legend or not, as Daniel reached for the Kia's door handle his heart was beating faster than a Gabber bass line. He took one last look off into the darkness, trying to convince himself there wasn't anything stalking him in it. Just a legend.

There was, however, something wet and sticky all over the door handle. Instinctively, Daniel recoiled at the feel of it. In the faint light of a thin sliver of moon, he could see the door was streaked with three lines of blood. He felt a sharp pain in his hand and realized it was his own. The festering wound consuming the stump of his severed digit had opened up yet again. "Goddamn it."

He considered his maimed hand for a moment with a detached curiosity, as if the bloody mess were someone else's. He watched with wide-eyed wonderment as a thick drop of his blood dripped from the wound and fell to the dark Delta mud at his feet.

"*Well, I'm goin' where the Southern cross the Dog,*" a voice, rough and raspy, sang out in the darkness.

Daniel whirled around to face whoever had snuck up on him, but as soon as he'd turned, the voice's point of origin seemed to change again.

"*Goin' where the Southern cross the Dog.*"

Was it coming from behind him? From the road? From the fields?

Daniel could hear feet on the road now, each step keeping time in the cinder-sprinkled dirt with a steady *tramp-tramp-tramp* as the singer moved closer. "*Goin' where the Southern cross the Dog.*"

Daniel couldn't place the singer's position in the night; the vocal was almost quadraphonic, as if it weren't coming from any one place, but from everywhere all at once. The footsteps continued to fall in a steady rhythm. *Tramp-tramp-tramp. Tramp-tramp-tramp.*

Daniel turned back toward the Kia…and the man was just standing there.

"You lookin' for me?" The voice was deeper than the darkness and rougher than the road he'd walked.

The shock of the man's sudden appearance hit Daniel like the blast from a 32-20. "Oh my God!" He stumbled back, slipped on the mud, and fell to the ground.

"Not even close." The man's voice rolled into a deep belly laugh.

The passing clouds parted for a moment, letting just the slightest bit of moonlight through as if some celestial stage director had cued a baby spot to illuminate the man. He was taller than Daniel. Thinner too. The silver hair beneath his straw porkpie hat and the gray mustache and beard circling his smile were evidence he was older. The glint in his eyes suggested he knew something Daniel didn't—and perhaps that he was crueler.

He looked down on Daniel. "How long you gonna lie there in the mud, son?"

Daniel tried to get to his feet, but they slipped out from beneath him.

"Maybe you just need a hand up." The old man offered his. It was thin and bony, but thickly calloused and surprisingly strong. With little effort, he pulled Daniel to his feet.

Daniel wasn't sure whether he should be grateful. Or frightened. "Who are you?"

"Who am *I?*" the man said with a laugh. "You gonna call me Atibon. *Mister* Atibon."

The introduction did little to lessen Daniel's confusion. "But, *who* are you?"

"I done told you, son. I'm Mr. Atibon. You gotta learn to listen, son." The old man made it clear his patience was already exhausted. "You ain't a dummy, is you? Can't make a bargain with no dummy."

Daniel answered, "No." But he wasn't so sure anymore.

The reply was enough to satisfy the old man, who seemed uninterested in anything but business. "So now the question is: Is you the one I's lookin' for or ain't ya?"

"I don't know—" Daniel fumbled.

"He say if I come all the ways out here, there'd be some fool come lookin' for this." The old man pulled a small manila envelope from inside his coat pocket. "You dat fool?"

Daniel reached for the envelope, but it disappeared right back into the old man's coat. "He said you'd come *lookin'* for it, but I didn' say nuthin' 'bout you gettin' it."

Even without the envelope, Daniel thought the mystery might still be solved with a single question. "Who told you I'd come?"

"That youngest Handy boy." The old man stopped to consider just which one that was. "Willie, I think they call him."

The name meant nothing to Daniel. "And he gave you that envelope? This Willie Handy?"

"Wellllll," Mr. Atibon stretched out the word to buy him time and he stroked his beard as he thought up a response that wouldn't answer the question. "Let's jes' say he's the one I got it from."

Daniel was undeterred. "And where did *he* get it from?"

"Didn' say," the old man confessed. "He was over the Po' Monkey braggin' how he gonna get paid big money for what he got here." He pulled out the envelope again and then returned it just as quickly. "Well, I figure it's better me gets that money than him. So I helped myself to this here," he tapped his coat pocket, "while he was sleepin' off his Saturday night."

Nothing the old man said made any sense, but Daniel figured that only meant it dovetailed nicely with everything else that had happened to him. "All right. Well, here I am. I'm your fool."

"Willie was sayin' you was gonna pay him five hun—" The old man stopped mid-demand and took a long, hard look at Daniel, reappraising just what kind of sucker he'd snagged on his line. "A thousand dollars for what's inside."

"A thousand dollars?" It seemed a bit steep to Daniel. "What exactly is inside?"

"Somethin' worth a thousand dollars," Mr. Atibon snapped. "Didn' I just say that?" He took a harder look at Daniel. "Just what's wrong with you, son?"

"I'm trying to figure that out," Daniel admitted as he pulled out his wallet. "It's the middle of the night and I'm in East God-damn-nowhere, counting out cash to buy something I don't know from a man I've never met. Maybe I'm a dummy, after all."

When he was done counting out the cash he'd planned on dropping in Vegas two nights ago, he offered the bills—and an admission. "All I have is eight hundred and—"

In the blink of an eye, the bills disappeared from Daniel's hand and reappeared in the old man's. "I'm gonna take this as a down payment."

"It's all I got," Daniel tried to make clear. "And it's all you're getting."

"I'm gonna take *this*," Mr. Atibon held up the money, but not nearly close enough for Daniel to snatch it back. "And your good word on the balance."

"No, you don't understand." After twenty-odd years in the music business, Daniel had become a sophisticated negotiator, and the time had come to deliver a graduate course in how a deal gets done. "I'm not going to pay you a thousand dollars."

"Then I'm keepin' this here for expenses." The old man tucked the bills in the front pocket of his work pants.

"Wait a minute!" This was not on Daniel's syllabus. "Eight hundred dollars for expenses?"

"And a penalty on bad faith," the old man added indignantly before turning to go.

Daniel knew it was ridiculous to pay a thousand dollars for the envelope. Just as ridiculous as it was to think a man could become a guitar virtuoso through anything but natural talent and hard work. And yet sometimes the ridiculous is exactly what happens. "All right, all right. Keep the money."

It was no concession to the old man. "I already told ya I was gonna."

"I'll give you the rest as soon as the banks open."

"Gas station out on sixty-one got one of them money machines." Mr. Atibon pointed the way with a walking stick that was darker than the night and more gnarled than he was. "Open all night. No need to wait for nothin'."

"All right. I'll go get you your cash." A couple hundred dollars was money well spent if it led him to his million. "But I want the envelope. Now."

Mr. Atibon thought it over. "If'in I give it, you ain't got no reason ta' give me what's I got comin'."

That wasn't entirely true. "Except I said I would."

"And you think that's enough, do ya'?" The old man cocked his head, like he was searching Daniel for the unspoken answer to his question.

Two years ago...two months...even two days ago, it wouldn't have been. But things were different now. "Please, Mr. Atibon."

"A man's word ain't no substitute for cash money, but I'll take yours." With a shaky hand, he offered Daniel the envelope—and a warning. "But I got a razor in my back pocket and I'll slice your ass like a Sunday smoked ham if you tryin' to trick me."

Daniel took the eight-by-ten-inch envelope and looked it over, but in the intermittent moonlight, he couldn't see it with any detail. He opened the car door and both men shielded their eyes from the awful glare of the dome light. Daniel slid into the driver's seat.

"Where you think you're going?" Mr. Atibon wanted to know.

"I thought I was going to that gas sta—"

"And so we are, but—"

"Do you want to follow me?" Daniel had asked the question before he'd recalled that he hadn't heard a car approach, just feet.

"I'm like Big Mama Thornton, son."

Daniel didn't get the reference.

"I gots the walking blues." Daniel only looked back blankly. "My dogs are barking," Mr. Atibon tried again and this time he tapped his work boots with the tip of the black walking stick. Still nothing. "I could use a damn ride."

"Right."

"Now, what the hell is this?" the old man asked, looking suspiciously at the little Korean coupe.

"It's my car." He thought that over for a minute. "Well, it's *a* car."

"Son, this ain't no car." The dark stranger shook his head with a mixture of contempt and dismay. "Now, there was a day I had me a car. A Rocket 88. V-8 motor. Black convertible."

"Well, then maybe *you'd* rather drive," Daniel quipped from behind the wheel.

"No need to be like that," the man grumbled as he moved around to the Kia's passenger side. "I made a deal wit' you, didn't I?"

Daniel flipped the lock and Mr. Atibon slid into the passenger seat, which was not intended to accommodate a man of his height. He closed the door and awkwardly tried to adjust himself to the confines while finding a suitable resting place for his walking stick. "All right, let's go get me my money," he said after he finally settled on the fact there was no way to get comfortable in a subcompact.

Daniel, however, was focused on the envelope. By the light of the car's dash, he could see there was nothing written on either side. No clues at all. He opened it carefully, but it only contained the jewel box he'd been expecting—and half fearing.

"What that?" Mr. Atibon asked.

"A CD."

"I ain't Amish, boy," the old man snapped. "An I already take a peek when I snatched it from the Handy kid, so I know it's a goddamn CD. What I's askin' is what make it worth a thousand dollars?"

It was Daniel's turn to smile. "Let's find out." He slid it into the car's stereo.

Where the original mystery track had been all acoustic guitars, the second one featured a boogie-woogie piano line that laid down a melody but kept its own rhythm with an incorporated rumba beat. After a twelve-bar vamp, the same vocalist who'd sung "The Blues Highway Blues" broke in:

> Everyone of us has lost face, and we've all lost our faith too
> Measure of a soul is "Whatcha gonna do?"
> Ain't no sin in sinning in a moment of doubt
> No shame in an eight count if you don't go count you out
> You may suck the sour sponge or drink that loving cup
> But when you get beat-down-stomped-on, just you get back on up

"What this?" the old man asked.

Daniel waved him off, anticipating the next verse, and turned up the volume.

*Now they say that they warned them, "Get on out 'fore it's too
    late!"*
But if you ain't got the "whatfor" then you can't evacuate
Georgie said, "I got this!" But his Brownie dropped the ball
*And as soon as them skies cleared up, ah, there came a water
    wall*
Well, you can't hold back the river with just a paper cup
But when you get beat-down-stomped-on, just you get back on up

There was a little piano boogie-woogie interlude. Not the
smoothest of solos, but a passionate pounding of the ivories.

*Well he played on sixty-eight, what most folks can't play on
    twenty more*
He was the King of Mardi Gras but he wound up scrubbing floor
Still you could not stop the Bald Man or his Shuffling Hungarians
And the Fess ruled the Fest as a sexagenarian
And at the entry to his altar is where you'll find your next cut
You been beat-down-stomped-on, Danny, just you get back on up

The piano led a raucous parade for a joyous minute or two
before coming to a rumbling stop and a quick run up and down
the keys.

When it was over, silence resumed its hold on the night.

The old man turned, not understanding how what he'd just
heard could possibly be worth a thousand bucks. "What the hell
was that?"

"I'm not sure." Daniel was focused on running through the
lyrics in his head. "Something about New Orleans, I think."

"Of course, it's 'bout Nawlins, you damned fool, but—"

"I didn't get that last part though." Daniel reached for the rewind.

"It's the Professor," Mr. Atibon said gruffly.

Daniel was lost in thought. "What?"

"I didn' make a deal with a dummy," Atibon mumbled to himself. "I made a deal with the king o' the dummies. Gonna call you King Dummy from now on."

The new title didn't matter to Daniel. "What professor?"

"Fess? The Bald Man?" The old man offered clues, but they meant nothing to Daniel. "They talkin' 'bout Professor Longhair," he finally exploded, exasperated that he needed to explain it all.

Still distracted with his own analysis, Daniel only repeated the key points he'd heard. "Professor Longhair. New Orleans. Right."

"That's who they trying to play like on that song of yours," the old man scoffed with more than a note of contempt in his voice. "Only no one play like the Professor." He smiled like he had a secret—and it was one he was willing to spill. "Nobody ever play like the Professor on account he learnt on a broken piano. Had to play 'round all them broken keys. That's how he learnt to play like that."

"He could play on sixty-eight—" Daniel eagerly inserted.

"What the hell you talkin' 'bout, son?"

"All right." There was a note of hope in his voice. "I think I got this."

"You got what?"

"It's a long story," Daniel said as a polite way of dismissing an explanation.

"You gots the time," Mr. Atibon assured him.

Daniel hesitated, trying to decide just what and how much to share with the stranger. "I had some money," he began.

"I gots me some money right now," the old man boasted as he patted his pocket. "How much money *you* talking about?" His question reflected more than a glimmer of self-interest in his eyes.

"A little," Daniel answered self-consciously.

"You lyin' like hell." The old man laughed, amused by Daniel's sorry effort. "If you give a man a thousand dollars 'cause he ask for it, then we talkin' more than a lil'." He considered the possibilities. "Or maybe my lil' is a lil' different from your lil'." He laughed again.

"It doesn't really matter." Daniel tried to shake off the subject.

"To you," the old man objected.

"It's just someone took some money from me and they left a song in its place."

Confusion lifted the old man's growl an octave higher. "A song? Stole money and left a song?"

Daniel nodded instead of answering. "And the lyrics of that first song led me out here. To you." He pointed at the dashboard where he'd inserted the disc. "And the lyrics of this second song seem to be leading to—"

The old man understood. "Nawlins."

"Right."

"So, it's like a treasure map." The thought of it made the old man smile.

"What?"

"Your songs," he said plainly. "They like singin' treasure maps."

"I guess so." Daniel hadn't thought about it quite like that. "But, yeah, I guess so. They're supposed to lead me to get my money back."

Mr. Atibon shook his head, a gesture of equal parts amusement and exasperation. Then he pointed at the road ahead. "Well, let's get goin', then."

It was only then that Daniel remembered his predicament. "Goddamn it!"

"What?"

Daniel slapped the steering wheel. "I've got myself stuck in the mud there. I'm not going anywhere until I get a tow truck down here."

"Tow truck?" The old man's frustration continued to grow. "You ain't stuck. The only man who's stuck is the one won't see the truth. You see the truth?"

"What truth?"

"The truth, son. There ain't but one."

"I'm not—"

"Start the car." The old man seemed confident, like he was aware of something that had long evaded Daniel.

"I told you, I'm stuck."

"Start the car." Mr. Atibon's voice was low and firm, like the command a well-trained owner might give to a dog.

Daniel did what he was told and the engine came to life.

"Now let's go." The old man nodded forward.

"I told you," Daniel protested. "I'm stuck."

"You got some place to go?" Mr. Atibon demanded. "A treasure to find?"

"Yes. But I'm—"

"You ain't never gonna gets nowhere bitchin' 'bout all the reasons why you *can't*. You need to stop that shit and just drive." The old man's gnarled finger pointed the way.

Daniel pressed down hard on the accelerator, for no other reason than to convince his unwanted passenger there was no point in it. The tires spun, whined...and then somehow found traction. They rocketed forward so fast that Daniel had to stomp on the brakes to keep from shooting past the stop sign at the highway's edge.

Flustered and flummoxed, Daniel looked over to his companion for an explanation he knew couldn't exist. "How—"

"That's the truth." The old man grinned. "And the truth will set you free."

CHAPTER FOURTEEN

The service station was there, just off the highway, exactly as the old man had said. Daniel pulled into a spot outside the station's convenience store and turned the engine off. "You gonna come in?"

Mr. Atibon shook his head. "Don' need no one knowin' I come into money." His voice was uncharacteristically quiet, like he was worried someone in the store might overhear. "Jes' go in and get me mine," he instructed, then added, "We got a deal."

Daniel was good to his word and five minutes later, he counted the rest of the money out into Mr. Atibon's hand. "And that makes a thousand. So we're good?"

"We're jake," the old man said with a satisfied smile.

There was an awkward silence, during which Mr. Atibon didn't do anything except put the folded bills into the front pocket of his pants and then settle on back into the passenger seat.

Daniel was eager to get on with his trip, but he didn't want to leave the old man stranded. He felt obliged to offer, "Can I take you somewhere? Give you a ride home?"

"Home?" Mr. Atibon laughed out loud. "Son, I got a thousand dollars cash money in my pants. How the hell I'm gonna spend all that in Ruleville, Mississippi?" He shook his head in a way that Daniel had already become familiar with—and oddly fond of. "You need to learn to use your head, son."

Daniel hadn't quite put all the pieces together. "But if you're not going home—"

"I got a thousand dollars and a good friend goin' to Nawlins with a goddamn singing treasure map." Mr. Atibon grinned. "Now start using your head and tell me where I'm goin' to."

Daniel got it. "New Orleans?"

"Goddamn! Now you usin' your head," the old man declared proudly, like he'd just taught Daniel an important life lesson. "If you don' set here gabbin' all night, we can make the Crescent by daybreak and you can buy me pecan waffles at the Camellia Grill."

Route 61, as it runs through the Mississippi Delta, is one of the longest straightaway of any highway in the world. It would be logical to assume this makes it the easiest highway to drive, but it's actually a deceptively dangerous stretch of roadway. Over the years more than a few drivers—drunk, tired, or distracted—have been hypnotized by the seemingly endless asphalt.

A pickup truck passed the Kia more closely than it should have and then shot on ahead. Its red taillights burned in the night like the devil's own eyes staring back at them mile after mile. They unnerved Daniel at first, and then hypnotized him. A tossed cigarette sparked as it hit the road and sprayed the night like Satan's sneeze.

"Whoa!" the old man yelped.

The strange sound he made was more startling than the foot or two Daniel had begun to drift toward the embankment. "What?"

"Your mind and the goddamn car," Mr. Atibon scolded. "Ya gotta keep 'em both on the road."

"I am," Daniel answered defensively, although he realized he had absolutely no memory of the miles he'd just driven.

"Bessie Smith died right along this stretch of road." The old man looked off into the impenetrable darkness like he was searching for the exact spot. "Car wreck."

Daniel scanned the passing darkness like there might still be wreckage to rubberneck. "She did?"

"Isn't that what I jes' said?" Mr. Atibon shook his head. "You gonna have to listen up if you're gonna make it through this world. Sometimes it's the chords ain't played that ring truest."

Although he wasn't sure exactly what the old man had meant, Daniel nodded eagerly, like a mop-headed pop star who'd been given an audience with a yogi.

The old man didn't seem to notice. Or care. "Voice of an angel." The depth of the heartbreak in the old man's growl suggested he was something more than a fan. "They let her die at the side of the road like a dog in a ditch." If he had more to say on the subject, he didn't share it with Daniel. He fell silent and turned back to the window like he was searching for something he knew should be there but wasn't.

"I'm sorry." It was all Daniel could think of to say.

"Why?" The old man turned. "You didn't drive past her, did ya?"

They drove on in silence, with one mile bleeding into another, until after a while Mr. Atibon began to absentmindedly drum on the dashboard with his long, gnarled fingers. *Tap-tap-tap. Tap. Tap.* The same steady, driving beat over and over. *Tap-tap-tap. Tap. Tap.*

Daniel thought he recognized the rhythm and began to sing along as a well-intended gesture to generate some common ground, "*Bo Diddley. Bo Diddley.*"

The old man stopped tapping and gave Daniel a disapproving look that didn't need to be translated.

"That's the Bo Diddley beat, right?" Daniel asked innocently, as he drummed it out on the dashboard himself. *Tap-tap-tap. Tap. Tap.*

"That ain't no Bo Diddley beat," the old man declared, and then paused almost immediately to reconsider. "Well, Bo mighta claimed it, but he didn' come up with it."

"No?" Daniel had always thought that rock's seminal rhythm—*Boom-boom-boom. Boom. Boom.*—was created by the great Bo Diddley. "Well, who—"

"You know what that beat is?" Mr. Atibon interrupted impatiently as he began to tap it out again. *Tap-tap-tap. Tap. Tap.* "That's the heartbeat of a woman just got herself some good lovin'." *Tap-tap-tap. Tap. Tap.* "That's how you can tell you put some sugar in her bowl. Her heart be beatin' just like that." *Tap-tap-tap. Tap. Tap.*

There was a note of boyish wonderment in Daniel's voice. "Really?"

"Listen to you, '*Really?*'" The old man laughed to himself. "I'm talking 'bout the blues, son. Truth don't never stand in the way a' good story." Then he turned back to the window and laughed to himself as if he was hearing his own joke for the first time. "Used to give ol' Bo fits when I tol' that story on him. I just laugh an' laugh."

Daniel had another "Really?" ready to drop, but he was too sheepish to step into another of the old man's traps so soon.

Instead, he drove on through the last vestiges of night with nothing but the car radio to keep him from falling asleep.

Somewhere between Blind Willie Johnson's "Motherless Children" and Big Joe Williams's "Shake 'Em On Down," Daniel's traveling companion sat up and announced, "Now that's the real stuff. Blues needs to be played by a man don't got nuthin'. Nuthin' but six strings." He considered that and laughed. "Most times those six strings don' belong to him neither."

Daniel only nodded.

"Now that other stuff you had there." Mr. Atibon pointed toward the stereo's disc port. "That's just playin' *at* the blues."

Daniel didn't necessarily disagree, but he didn't say anything at all.

It was clear Mr. Atibon was disturbed by the silence that followed, though Daniel had no idea why. The old man fidgeted in his seat, moved his walking stick, adjusted his hat, and then finally, after a dozen more miles, just asked what was on his mind, "How that work?"

"The CD player?" Daniel asked innocently enough.

"I know how the goddamn CD player works," he snapped, although he really didn't. "That song there. The treasure an' all. How it all work?"

Daniel thought about it. "I don't know." He was surprised to hear the admission aloud, but it was the truth. "Someone stole some money from me and left a CD. That's all I know for sure. The lyrics of the song, they seemed to point me to that crossroads where I met you."

"Crossroads," the old man repeated with a scoff. "You know, mos' folk end up in Clarksdale. They got a whole big thing up there."

"Yeah. I know." Daniel had learned enough not to let on *how* he knew.

"Maybe you ain't such a dummy after all." Mr. Atibon didn't allow Daniel an opportunity to respond and prove him wrong. "And that song there?"

"Don't know," Daniel admitted. "Guess I'll find out when I get to New Orleans."

"Don' seem like much of a plan."

"It's not."

"And you think these people jus' gonna give your money back?"

"It doesn't make any sense, I know," Daniel conceded, but then shrugged. "I just have to take the chance."

"Have to?" The note of desperation piqued the old man's curiosity. "Why's that?"

"Because there's some guys after me and—"

"Whoa! Just pull the handbrake, son." Mr. Atibon sat up straighter than he had during the whole trip. "You said you was after a treasure, you never said nuthin' 'bout nobody being after *you*."

"There's bad guys," Daniel said plainly.

The old man finally felt free to comment on what he'd observed when they first met. "Bad enough to take a man's finger from his fretting hand?"

Daniel hadn't thought of it in those terms before, but not having a pinkie was going to take a little something off his guitar playing. "Yes." He looked down at the missing digit and the infection that had replaced it. "That and worse. Much worse."

The revelation made Mr. Atibon grumble, "Well, it's late for that now. We lil' more an hour outside of Nawlins and you jus' tellin' me there's folks huntin' your ass like some rabid ol' opossum."

Daniel understood the old man's concerns, but he had learned not to take them too seriously. "I can let you out if you want."

"Out!" The offer alarmed Mr. Atibon more than the news they were being pursued by finger-taking bad guys. "There ain't nuthin' out here but gators, snakes, and rednecks—and I'll be goddamned if 'in I can say which is worse."

"Well, you can make your own way when we hit the city."

"Don' think I won't," he vowed defiantly.

"That's probably best."

"Damn right that's best." Mr. Atibon was quiet for a moment, but just a moment. "You gonna buy me pecan waffles for my troubles first," he added. "Then I'm gone."

Daniel turned his head so the old man wouldn't see him smile. "Fine."

"Damn right, that's fine."

Another mile passed in silence before Mr. Atibon again found he couldn't contain his curiosity. "Sho' must be whole lotta money."

Daniel was lost somewhere between deep thought and drowsiness. "How's that?"

"Lot of money," the old man repeated. "Goin' to this trouble, with folks after you cuttin' your finger off an' whatnot."

"It's not the money."

Mr. Atibon scoffed, "It's always the money."

"Well, it's the money," Daniel conceded. "But just because I need it to save my son from—"

"Son?" Something in his question suggested the old man knew about having a boy.

Daniel nodded. "What I'm really afraid of is what they'll do—"

"The finger-cutters?"

Daniel nodded again but couldn't help thinking back to Randy's last phone call. "They're worse than that. And I know what they'll do if they find my son before they find me."

Mr. Atibon thought on this for a minute. "Where your boy at?"

Daniel shook his head sadly. "I don't know."

"How's that happen?"

Daniel thought about the possibilities, even the unthinkable ones. "I'm not quite sure."

Mr. Atibon didn't say anything for a while. When he broke his silence, his voice was soft and shaky. "Terrible thing, havin' a child."

Daniel was a little taken aback, not by the statement, but by the emotions that cracked the old man's voice. He disagreed, but did it as gently as he could. "It was the best thing ever happened to me."

The old man nodded, but it didn't change his mind. "That's 'cause you ain't lost yours yet." He looked off into the just-brightening sky, searching for the fading moon's remains. "Havin' a child jus' gives Fate a hostage. This is a mean ol' world, old friend. You're better to live alone."

"You had a child?" The question was out of his mouth before Daniel could consider its propriety or sensitivity.

Mr. Atibon's face was turned to the window so all Daniel could see was the silent nod of his head.

"What happened?"

The old man was slow to answer and Daniel knew better than to press the matter. After a few silent miles the old man announced, "I had me a son too. Beautiful boy. Eyes as dark as the night sky, sparkled just like they was filled with stars." He stopped for a moment, as if he didn't want to talk over the memories he'd just conjured. "And they was." He shifted in his seat. "Filled with stars."

He cleared his throat to continue. "But things was never right with his mama. She moved him all over the goddamn place. Here and there. Married herself a *proper* man an' they gave *my* boy *his* name." No matter how much time might have passed, it was clear the old man was still furious about it. "Ain't that the goddamnedest?"

Daniel nodded that he thought it was.

"Never got to spend much time with him—not one-on-one—but I watched over him every day o' his life, you can be sure." He took off his straw porkpie hat and rubbed the grayed tufts of hair still on the top of his head. "Every goddamn day."

He replaced the hat when he was ready. "Tried to do right by him. Gave him everything I could—an' then some. But he was wild." Mr. Atibon laughed to himself. "Just like me."

"Where is he now?"

"Well, I tell ya," he started to explain. "Every man got a kind a woman he fancies. Fat woman. Skinny woman. Mean woman. Sweet woman. We alls gots our desires."

Daniel didn't say anything, but his thoughts drifted off to Connie as if to prove the old man's point.

"Every man like what he likes, and my boy, he liked *other men's* women." The old man looked hard out of his window and his voice grew as cold as a tomb. "Some cowardly sonofabitch poisoned him."

Daniel had only meant to make enough conversation to pass the remaining miles. He instantly regretted having trespassed into something so private. And painful.

"Strychnine in an open bottle of whisky he handed my boy as a friend. Took him three days to die." The old man wiped away what he would've denied was a tear. "He was just twenty-seven." Then he wiped away another.

"Don't you worry though," he cleared his throat and his voice regained all its rough edges. "Death don't have no mercy in *this* land. I set out on that sonbitch like a hellhound unbound. My boy, he died easy compared to what I put him through." The old man pounded his walking stick once against the Kia's floorboards as his thoughts faded into memories that were darker than the south Mississippi night.

The old man sniffled. "They let these fields get overrun with that giant ragweed—like regular ol' ragweed weren't bad 'nough. Make my eyes water like I been cuttin' onion all damn day." Alibi laid, he wiped his eyes. "And nothin' grows like it grows in the Delta."

Daniel looked out past the endless expanse just beginning to become discernible in the gathering dawn. "I remember seeing all the news coverage last year when it all flooded." He wondered if he'd lost track of time. "Was that two years ago?"

Grateful for the opportunity to change the topic of conversation, the old man pronounced with certainty, "Last year. This year. The ol' Delta, she'll flood again this spring. But you can cleanse your soul in that muddy water. And it's the floods bring the dark soil make this place so damn fertile. That's why the blues grow here too. People think they all sad songs, but that ain't right. Don' get me wrong, every blues song 'bout one kind a flood or another, but they got the hope for rebirth in 'em too. That's what we all lookin' for, jus' another chance."

Daniel thought the old man was right, but neither one of them said another word until New Orleans.

CHAPTER FIFTEEN

Nancy Ravensong knew she'd seen the man in the photograph just the night before. He'd come into the station in the middle of the night and right away he'd struck her as odd. Troubled. Seriously troubled. Even among the road-weary, hard-traveling flotsam and jetsam that drifted through the double glass doors every night, he stuck out as someone in some very deep shit.

And yet at the same time, she had only the haziest memory of him. His hand, wrapped in filthy bandages. Fresh blood. Lots of it. And then nothing. Absolutely nothing. Just blackness. An awful blackness that frightened her.

Why couldn't she remember more?

"I don't know." She handed the photo back to the well-dressed black man. "I can't remember any more. I just don't know."

"What the fuck do you mean, you don't know, bitch?" The mean little one had a voice as sharp as the serrated edge of a hunting knife.

"She means she don't know." The big man's voice was low and soft but filled with force as he calmly slipped the photo back into his suit coat. She was grateful for his intercession and relieved he was calling an end to their questioning.

"He was here," she repeated, trying to demonstrate her willingness to cooperate. "I just can't remember anything else." Why couldn't she remember?

"We appreciate you trying," the black man assured her.

"Thanks." His big brown eyes had no kindness in them, but she thought they smiled at her just the same. Self-consciously, she brushed a loose strand of her long, black hair behind her right ear.

"That's it?" the Mexican demanded of his traveling companion.

"No," the big man replied, apathetic to the other's obvious agitation. "We also need fifty dollars on pump six. And—" He paused to consider his options. "A pack of the Phillies." He fished his wallet out of his pants pocket and put two Grants on the counter.

Nancy took the bills and credited the pump. She rang up the register and then handed him his change and the smokes. "Is there anything else?"

"Yeah, there's something else," the little one insisted. "Why don't you fucking tell us whatever you're holding back before I jump this fucking counter and—"

"Hey, hey, hey!" The big man put an oversized palm on his partner's chest. "There's no reason for this."

"No reason? She fucking knows something. I can see it in her eyes."

"She already told us. He came in here last night, gassed up, and got out. Just like a couple hundred other folks. You think he told her where he was going?" The big man didn't make any effort to conceal how ridiculous he thought his partner was being. "We knew it was a long shot. We took it and got what we got. Now, let's gas up and go."

"She knows more," the little man insisted. "I can see it in her eyes.

The only thing Nancy knew for certain was that her memory of the past night had a deep, dark hole in the middle of it. "I'm not keeping anything." It was the truth, but it sounded like a lie to her too. "I swear."

The big man left a twenty on the counter. "It's cool."

"It's not cool!" his partner insisted.

"If I say it's cool, then you can motherfucking *skate* on it." Nancy had been right: they weren't kind eyes. And they focused on the little man with a threat of imminent violence that needed no words to be heard. "Got it?"

The little man tried not to look kowtowed. "Whatever." But it didn't work.

The big man turned back to Nancy. "You have a nice night now."

She smiled. "You too."

He turned to his partner. "Let's go."

The two walked toward the door, but before they got there the little one stopped. "You go gas up. I'm going to take a piss and grab a Red Bull."

"Take a piss, then drink some piss," the big man joked. A thought crossed his mind and he looked back at Nancy behind the counter, then at the little man. "We got no time for any more of your psycho shit," he warned.

The little man brushed off the unspoken suggestion. "I'm going to take a piss. You can shake off my dick if you don't trust me."

"I mean that shit!"

"Go gas up. I'll be right out."

The big man took a last look at the girl behind the counter and decided that not even his partner could be that off-the-rails twisted. "All right."

The glass door hadn't closed shut behind him before the little man went to the door and threw the deadbolt. The click it made locking in place caught Nancy's attention and she looked up, alarmed to find him advancing toward her.

"Now, let's try this again," he snarled. "My way, *puta*."

She didn't see the blade in his hand until he was already over the counter.

Ten minutes later the little man slid into the BMW's passenger seat and tried not to let on he was out of breath.

"What took you so fucking long?"

"Nothing. Let's go."

The big man put the car in gear. "The boss called while you were in there playin' with yourself."

"Fuck you."

"They got another hit on Erickson's credit card. Used it for a cash advance."

"Where?"

"Cleveland."

"Ohio?"

"Mississippi."

"Fuck."

"We goin' down to the Delta, boy."

"Don't call me 'boy.'"

Moog hit the gas and the BMW pulled off into the night.

Billy Gibbons had a place about ten miles down the way and was a regular at the station. He was still grumbling to himself about the BMW that'd cut him off by the highway entrance ramp when he pushed open the doors to the convenience store and found her there in a pool of her own blood.

Nancy Ravensong had slipped off into an awful darkness.

CHAPTER SIXTEEN

Compared to some New Orleans institutions, the Camellia Grill may not be as universally associated with the Crescent City as others, but it's an honest-to-God institution just the same. For more than seventy-five years, the city's socialites and sinners have crowded into the small dining room—its walls painted a dreary shade of pink like some unmarried great aunt's bathroom—and bluesmen and businessmen have sat shoulder-to-shoulder around her counters.

It was just after five in the morning when Daniel and Mr. Atibon stepped in from beneath the flickering torch above the door, and the grill room was uncharacteristically empty. It was too late for the last of Bourbon Street's revelers, who had already choked down their Chef Special omelets and stumbled off toward wherever or whatever they called home. And it was still just a bit early for the ambitious business folks and meaningfully employed types who'd yet to arrive for the most important meal of the day.

When he heard the bell on the door tinkle, the dreadlocked counterman called out, "Take a seat anywhere, mon," but he never took his eyes off the grill he was scraping. Even with his scraggily beard, the kid couldn't have passed for more than twenty. He was tall and lean, with a voice as smooth as Caribbean rum and a relaxed manner that made it clear he was still running on "island time"—which is even slower than "NOLA time."

When he was finished with his greasy task he turned toward the morning's newest customers, now seated on stools at his counter. "Now, what can I do for you?" His tone was playful and his movements as fluid as Montego Bay. Until he saw Mr. Atibon sitting in front of him. That sight stopped him dead.

"Whatchu doin' here, ol' mon?" The kid's eyes grew as big as the plates stacked neatly under the counter. He took a step back and desperately searched the room for available exits, genuinely alarmed by the unexpected visitation.

Daniel first looked up at the counterman and then over at his traveling companion. "You know this guy?" he asked, although it wasn't clear who he was asking.

"I know lotsa people." The old man smiled. "In lotsa places."

"Whatchu want, mon?" The kid's island accent was tinged with suspicion and as much defiance as he dared to manifest. "I already pay you what I owes you."

"Oh, quiet yourself, boy." Mr. Atibon gave him a dismissive wave of his hand. "You know some debts you don't ever pay in full." He spoke matter-of-factly, but there was an undeniable element of menace crouched and hiding behind his words. "But donchu worry 'bout none of that today. Right now all I want from you is waffles." He grinned. "For now."

"Ain't got none, mon." There was more than a measure of relief in the counter guy's response, like the absence of waffles meant there was no more reason for the old man to stick around. "Dat waffle iron busted." He pointed at the broken appliance in case anyone had any doubts. "Dey got a guy comin' over later today, but it won't heat up right now."

Mr. Atibon looked up at the counterman like he was a willful child trying to keep a secret from a parent—and failing miserably. "Go check it."

"I'm tellin' you, mon. It no work for two, tree days," the young man protested as he walked over to the waffle iron beside his grill. He reached out to touch the appliance to prove his point—and then jerked his hand back with a yelp as his flesh hissed against the hot surface.

He sucked on the burnt tips of his fingers, then looked over at Mr. Atibon with a troubling blend of reverence and terror. "Whatchu want with the waffles, mon?"

"Bacon." Mr. Atibon grinned triumphantly. "And leave some 'oink' in it, don't go cookin' it all to leather on me." He stopped to scan the laminated menu. "And some fries. Fresh basket. Nothin' been sittin' longer than I have. An coffee." He looked to Daniel, who was still amazed by what he'd just witnessed. "Same thing for this one."

Daniel didn't object to the order, but he had to know, "How did you—with the—" He couldn't find the words and so he simply pointed over at the supposedly broken waffle iron the counterman was now filling with batter.

"Who knows?" the old man said with a shrug. "World's filled with book-learnt folk who'll tell ya they understand how everything works, but they don't know a goddamn thing—not a thing matters, anyway. Hell, every one of those know-it-alls will fall in love. Love," he scoffed. "How do you explain that? Ain't nobody knows, but crazy shit beyond our control or understanding happens every damn day."

"It's not the same," Daniel insisted.

"Now you take a guitar," the old man continued. "Seventeen frets. Six strings, 'lessen ya use five an' tune it down like some of 'em do. A man got five fingers each hand." Mr. Atibon looked at Daniel, and then at his conspicuously missing pinkie. "'Lessen he's you. But even still, a country's boy math-a-matics will tell ya there gotta be a limit to what a man can play before it's all been played before. But, I'll be goddamned if those six strings ain't an infinite universe if a man's gots soul enough to find it."

"But there has to be an explanation," Daniel interrupted, but there was no stopping the old man.

"Explanation?" The old man took a sip from the coffee cup the jittery counterman had half-spilled in front of him. "Bah! Folks is only concerned with explanations for their questions so long as there's no hellhound nippin' at their heels. Once they hear that ol' dark dog barking down their trail, all they want is answers. Not explanations. Answers. Answers to prayers."

Daniel took a sip from his coffee too. "Not me."

"That right?" The old man grinned like he knew better. "Ain't got no prayers?"

"I have prayers," Daniel admitted. "They just don't ever have answers."

"There's all kinds of answers, son," Mr. Atibon said, slurping at his coffee. "A man just can't always see 'em. Don't always come from where you expect. Sometimes it seems like nothing at all, other times it's—"

"Waffles," the counterman said as he set two plates in front of them.

Mr. Atibon set to buttering his waffles and then drenching them in syrup, adding salt and a blizzard of black pepper to his potatoes. Without lifting his attention from his preparations, he asked casually, "So if it weren't a prayer sent you down to the crossroads, just what was it?" He took a large mouthful of breakfast. "The truth."

The insinuation that he'd been less than honest caught Daniel off guard. "I told you. I followed the clues in that song. I came down there for that CD I bought—"

"And I give it to you for your cash money," Mr. Atibon acknowledged. "But we both know it ain't what you come there for." Another mouthful, even bigger this time. "Not really."

There was a puzzling certainty in the old man's words. "What do you mean?"

"I mean just what I say, son." He said it plainly and washed it down with another swallow of hot, black coffee. "I always do."

Daniel didn't like the old man's words. "And so do I. I came to the crossroads for—" He faltered for a moment but didn't know why. "I went there for the next clue in—" He thought for a moment. "This game. Or whatever it is."

The old man refused the words like Satchel Paige shaking off a pitch call from Josh Gibson. "You can lie to yourself, son. Most souls do. But you can't lie to Mr. Atibon. No one can. Some try. But Mr. Atibon knows better. 'Cause I see the truth."

"I got what I came there for." Daniel meant the words as he said them, but they sounded tinny and empty. Even to him.

"Sooner or later everyone finds their way to the crossroads." The old man slurped at his coffee. "It's where you go *from* there that matters." He popped the last bite of waffle into his mouth. "You got a long, hard road ahead of you and if you gonna walk it all the way to its end, you're gonna need what you came down there for. What you *really* come there for." He left the cryptic warning hang for a second. "And, son?"

Daniel hadn't touched his breakfast yet. "What?"

"It's gonna cost you." Mr. Atibon pushed his empty plate across the counter and wiped the telltale traces of syrup from his grin. "Not no cash money. It's gonna *really* cost you."

Without another word, the old man got to his feet. "Well, I do believe I'll dust my broom. It's time for me to be moving on."

"Yeah, all right." Daniel wasn't sure why he felt so disappointed. Or scared. "I need to get some sleep anyway," he said, exaggerating his fatigue to ease the awkwardness of their parting.

"Sleep?" Mr. Atibon shook his head reproachfully one last time. "I need somethin', but it sure ain't sleep." He laughed contentedly, his belly full of pecan waffles, his pocket flush with cash, and his heart burning with prurient intent.

"I keep wanting to thank you for something," Daniel offered as he pushed his untouched plate away. "But I'll be damned if I know what for."

"Oh, you're damned all right." Mr. Atibon laughed. "But you know just what for." He took Daniel's hand and shook it. "I'll see you on down the road apiece. You keep goin', I'm right behind you, *mi key.*"

"Excuse me?" The phrase sent a jolt of electricity through Daniel. "*Mi key?*" It wasn't the first time he'd heard the odd phrase in the last few days. Its repetition had punctuated the most alarming events of his odd odyssey. "What does that mean?"

The old man smiled and shook his head dismissively. "Just a little something they say where I come from."

"And just where is that?" Daniel couldn't help wondering aloud.

"Aww now," Mr. Atibon dodged. "Ain't about where a man from, it's 'bout where he's goin'. " He flashed a big grin and put his hand on top of Daniel's. "And it looks like you're on the road to healin'. "

Daniel peeled down the bandages and looked down to what he thought would be a festering wound. It was now impossibly clear of infection. The remaining stub had completely scarred over as if he'd lost the digit two years ago, not two days. He stared in amazement, panicked and unnerved by what he knew was impossible. "How did you—" Shock slowed his words and before he could finish the question, the old man was gone. Just gone. A shiver ran down his spine.

Daniel called over the counterman. "The man?" he asked, pointing at the empty stool Mr. Atibon had just occupied. "You know him?"

"Don't know nothin', mon." The kid cleared the plates like they were something he shouldn't be touching.

"Just one thing, then." He raised a hand to stop the kid before he ran off. "He called me *mi key*. Do you know what that means?"

"He call you that?"

Daniel couldn't tell from the kid's reaction whether it was an honor or an indictment, but he nodded just the same.

"It patois," the kid replied, as if that should be answer enough.

Daniel titled his head like a dog that's not sure whether its master has really thrown the tennis ball or just hidden it behind his back.

"Island language, mon," the kid continued when he realized he had to. "It means something like *my old friend*." He shuffled the dirty dishes in his hands. "Dat old man been callin' you dat?" He pointed with a nod at the now vacant stool.

Daniel recalled the woman at the gas station in New Mexico. The cop in Clarksdale. "A couple people have called me that."

"No, no." The young man shook his head. "It's all him, mon."

"No," Daniel tried to explain, "I mean a couple people said that to me."

"I'm tellin' you." The young man shook his head more vigorously. "It's all him, mon." He looked around the empty room like he was nervous someone unseen might be listening. "It's all him. Every-ting. All him."

"I don't understand."

"Some t'ings got no explanation, mon."

"Like love and music?"

The kid nodded. "And dat old mon."

CHAPTER SEVENTEEN

Hotel rooms in New Orleans can be expensive and hard to come by any time of year. In the first weeks of February, they're damn near impossible to find and cost more than a FEMA director's *per diem*.

Sixteen desk clerks had already laughed him out of their lobbies by the time Daniel Erickson finally found an available cancellation at the Hotel d'Lafayette later that morning. And when they advised him it was hotel policy to insist on securing a credit card imprint in order to rent a room, he was too tired to be concerned about anyone tracing the transaction.

His iPhone woke him sometime later, ringing and vibrating on the nightstand beside the bed. He opened his eyes, disoriented to time and place, unsure whether he had just slept for twenty minutes or twelve hours. He was still as tired as when he'd first laid down, and with blackout blinds on the windows it was impossible to judge the time of day.

He rubbed his eyes and the clock on the nightstand came into focus. 8:36. The realization he'd slept through the entire day wasn't as disconcerting as the realization he'd slept through the entire day and was still exhausted.

Still groggy, he peeked at the screen identifying the caller. It wasn't Rabidoso, but he wasn't any more eager to answer the call. It was someone much worse. Against every impulse, he picked up the phone and touched Accept Call. "Connie?"

"Daniel?"

He sat on the edge of the bed for a moment, silent and running a hand through his thinning hair as he tried to gather his thoughts. Words failed him, so he tried for something simple. The emotions he was wrestling choked him off before he could utter anything more than, "Hey."

"Are you there?" The question didn't express concern as much as it demanded a response.

"Yes. I'm here." But he wished he wasn't.

Her voice was more agitated than he'd heard it in a long, long time. "I've been trying to call you since—"

"I've been away from my phone." It was the best explanation he had—and not exactly a lie.

"What the hell is going on, Daniel?"

"Nothing." It was as big a lie as a soul could tell, except maybe, "Everything's fine." And then his heart sank. He was suddenly panicked his lie might not be as bad as whatever truth she'd called to share. "Have you heard from Zack?"

"No."

Relief replaced panic, but they both stayed on.

"I haven't heard from Randy either," she announced. It was a simple statement, but she phrased it like an accusation.

"What does that have to do with me?"

"You tell me."

Daniel was prepared to deny the charge vigorously. "A middle-aged woman goes away for a weekend and now she can't get in touch with her twenty-something boy toy? The only mystery you've got there is how you think your sordid mess involves me."

She wasn't deterred in the slightest. "Whatever's happened, you brought this shit to our door."

And he was prepared to keep denying. "I didn't bring anything to your door."

"Oh, come on, Daniel. You show up unannounced—and there's a court order saying you can't do that—you look like someone threw you down an elevator shaft, and you're desperate to find Zack." She took a breath, but he could tell she was just bracing herself before asking, "Just how bad is it?"

"It's nothing." Another grievous lie.

"I'm not playing games, Daniel." She wanted that understood. "I'm serious. I'm not being a drama queen like you with your make-believe suicide attempt."

The snide comment cut as deeply as she'd intended. "I wasn't playing," he snapped before he could stop himself from taking her bait. A familiar anger began to rise within him and he felt his ears grow warm.

"Is Randy in danger? You owe me that much." She spoke with such conviction that no one would've doubted she truly believed what she was saying.

But Daniel knew he wasn't the only one telling lies now. "I don't owe you anything anymore. You can ask the California Family Courts."

"I'm not talking about the goddamn money, Daniel." Her words were sharp and edged with contempt. "That's what you never got."

"Really?" He wasn't the only one telling *biiiiig* lies either. "Then why'd you take so much of mine?"

She sighed. "Money was never my reason for doing anything."

"There were reasons for what you did?"

"Yes, Daniel," her voice was frosty with condescension. "Maybe not reasons that make sense in your narrow little world, but ones that work just fine in mine." She paused, clearly debating which specific examples she was willing to share. "I just didn't want to feel like *that* anymore."

"Feel like what?" he pressed.

"Like my life was ending with Zack leaving for college. I didn't want to be your well-tended little ghost, haunting my own house. I wanted to *live*. I wanted to do all the things people *need* to do for no other reason than they're still living."

"I'm sorry you didn't think you could do that with me."

"Me too." She was silent for a moment. "And now if you've taken all of that away from me somehow—"

"Just because your boy toy takes off the minute you go to visit your sister, don't think you're going to put the noose around my neck. Not again." His anger was like an old friend he hadn't seen in a while, but with whom he could take up like they'd never parted. "Maybe he's sick of haunting *your* house. Maybe *he* just wants to feel alive again. Did you ever think maybe he's just a twenty-three-year-old guy who wants a piece of ass that's not twice his age?" Wait for it… "Oh, of course, you did."

If their conversation had been one of those martial arts video games Zack had played in his anger-filled adolescence, Daniel's venomous comments would have been followed by a slow-motion image of Connie being lifted up off her feet and landing on the flat of her back while an announcer screamed, "KO!"

Instead, there was just silence on the other end of the phone.

There was no honor in what he'd done. Not even satisfaction in having wounded someone who'd casually and carelessly hurt him irreparably. If his words could have been addressed like a factual mistake printed in the *New York Times*, he happily would have made the Page Two retraction. But they both recognized the sad truth in what he'd said and nothing could take that away.

It was a moment before she could reply, and even then, it was only a soft, "You're right."

If he'd hurt her worse than he'd meant to, he still had no apologies to offer. All he could say was, "I'm sure everything's fine."

And *that* was the exact moment she became absolutely certain everything was not fine. Something in the way he tried to reassure her only served to convince her that everything was all kinds of fucked up. She paused for a moment as the realization overtook her like an emotional tsunami: fifty feet high, five miles deep. There was no point in trying to survive it. Something had changed and it would never be all right. Not ever again. "Whatever's happened to Randy…" Her voice was suddenly calm, zombified in her resignation.

"I'm sure Randy's fine." He had no desire to extend her suffering, but couldn't tell her anything that might draw the police and, in so doing, reveal his lie to Rabidoso.

It wouldn't have mattered anyway. She'd given up listening. "Whatever it is, I want you to know that I blame you. And I'll never forgive you." She took a hard breath. "But if any of this comes back at Zack, if he gets hurt in any way, I swear to God I will do what you didn't have the guts to do yourself. Do you understand?"

He did, but he didn't care. If he failed his son, he'd beat her to it.

He was done with her now. With a touch, the line went dead.

CHAPTER EIGHTEEN

In New Orleans it's only reasonable to expect the impossible and improbable. And, sure enough—without even having to circle the block—Daniel found a parking spot right on Tchoupitoulas Street.

It was a tight fit, even for a subcompact, but in only a half-dozen moves he'd squeezed the Kia between a black Mercedes with a Tulane School of Law license plate frame and an El Camino that had been painted like a runaway Mardi Gras float.

The lyrics of "Just You Get Back On Up" on the second CD had led Daniel straight to the Crescent City. And they'd been equally clear in pointing him toward one of its greatest musical icons: Professor Longhair.

The man who'd been born Henry Roeland Byrd did not invent the piano. Music historians might dispel the notion he was the originator of jazz or the blues, but no one can dispute that the man took the popular music of his times to heights no other pianist could reach. What he did on the keyboard created a unique sound that joined rhythm to blues, and it gave rock its roll. From Little Richard to Jerry Lee Lewis, from Fats Domino to Stevie Wonder, from Ian Stewart to Roy Bittan, it all started with the Professor.

The man is long dead. But if one happens to be searching out the spirit of Professor Longhair—for musical inspiration or, perhaps, in an attempt to regain a stolen sum of cash—there would seem to be no better place to start looking than the corner of Tchoupitoulas and Napoleon. That particular intersection is home to Tipitina's, a decent restaurant, respectable bar, and world-renowned music venue. It is also a living shrine to the illustrious Professor.

As he walked to the front door, Daniel heard a familiar voice call out behind him. "You think this it, *mi key*?"

He turned and wasn't at all surprised to see Mr. Atibon step out of the shadows cast by the ancient oak ripping up the sidewalk. Perhaps he should have been alarmed, but all he felt was grateful. "What are you doing here?"

"You gots a singin' treasure map," snapped the old man, as if there was no need to ask that question. "Where the hell else would I be?"

"I thought you were going—"

"Done it, son," Mr. Atibon announced proudly, flashing a bright smile. "But I'm an old man and it don' take all day *an'* all night no more." He shook his head with more than a little regret. "Had me a second go at those waffles and then came over here where I knew your fool ass would show up sooner or later."

"Tipitina's, right?" Daniel announced proudly, like he'd finally gotten one right.

"I can read my damn letters," Mr. Atibon growled defensively. "I ain' ignant."

In their short time together, Daniel had gotten used to the old man's gruffness, maybe even developing a fondness for it. He'd certainly learned to ignore it. "You know, like Professor Longhair's trademark song."

"I know the damn song." Mr. Atibon recoiled at the suggestion Daniel could explain something like that to him. "Who you think introduced Ol' Fess to Tina in the first place?"

"You knew Professor Longhair?" Daniel wasn't surprised by anything anymore, but the question slipped out anyway.

"You tellin' me all 'bout the song like I ain't never heard it a thousand goddamn times. What you think that song 'bout anyways?"

"Tipitina" was the Professor's signature number, but when faced with a question about what the often-garbled lyrics were actually about, Daniel had to shake his head and admit, "I have no idea."

"Tina." The old man closed his eyes. The name obviously brought back a memory or two he wanted to savor for a second. "Man, that ol' girl could fix whatever ailed ya."

"And the 'tipi' part?"

"Ol' Tina sold the meanest reefer in the whole damn city." Mr. Atibon laughed to himself, like he knew that to be the God's honest truth. "One day she's done gone into town just as high as she could get, bumbling and stumbling along. And goddamn if a streetcar don't run over both her feet. Slices 'em both clean off like they was a roasted beef on the cutting board at Mother's." He shook his head with disbelief.

If there was a connection between story and song, it had eluded Daniel. "And…"

"You *really* gotta learn to listen, son." Mr. Atibon adjusted his porkpie hat and rolled his eyes to the starry sky above. "Girl had no damn feet. Weren't ya' payin' attention to that part? No feet. From then on in, she had to go tippy-toeing all over town." He paused for effect. "Tippy-Tina."

Daniel had grown jaded. "Is that true?"

"If it ain't, it oughta be." The old man snorted, too pleased with himself.

Before Daniel could ask him any more about it, Mr. Atibon turned his attention to the sign on the side of the building's façade. "Why the hell there a banana up there? You ain't dragged me to one of those—"

"No, no," Daniel laughed dismissively. "When the place opened they used to have a juice bar." It wasn't the long-lost origin of one of New Orleans's most treasured musical classics, but Daniel was proud of his own bit of trivia he'd just found in a Wikipedia search.

Mr. Atibon looked up, entirely unimpressed. "Well, the last time I was here this place weren't no juice bar." He shook his head disapprovingly. "No, sir."

"You've been here before?"

"Son, I've been everywhere before." He nodded up at the building with his whisker-covered chin. "This here was a juke house in the day."

"A jukebox?" Daniel tried to clarify.

"Juke house," the old man corrected. "A place to get a little jelly roll."

"Like Jelly Roll Morton?" Daniel wondered.

"That's what he woulda had you believe." Mr. Atibon laughed to himself, without any intent to share the joke. "Now, we goin' into your lil' fruity factory here or not?"

As they approached the bar's front door, they noticed there was a young man on a folding chair with a guitar in his lap and an open case at his feet off to the side.

"See that," Mr. Atibon said, pointing to the busker. "That's how it oughta be. That's Today music."

Daniel didn't recognize the tune as anything currently making its way up the charts. "I never heard of—"

"Tooooo-daaaay music," the old man repeated more emphatically. "Music just being played for the here and now. That's how it used to be. You think any those ol' boys left a life of sharecroppin' and their momma's supper table to head out on the open road with a guitar slung 'cross their back thinkin' 'bout anything more than today?" Mr. Atibon flashed a fiery look that dared Daniel to answer.

He didn't.

"Hell, no!" the old man continued. "Ain't no future in bein' a bluesman. *Today* is all a real bluesman ever has. It's all he'll ever have. They didn't pick up a guitar thinkin' they'd get rich. And none of 'em did. Po-lice'd bust 'em 'cause they was easy to pin with what blame needed takin'. Juke joint owners'd cheat 'em. Women'd roll 'em. Shit, none of 'em had nuthin'. No expectations. So every time they set down to play, they went at it like there weren't no tomorrow—because there weren't. Just today."

The old man folded his arms against his chest. "These folks nowadays ain't playin' for Today. They all playin' for Someday: 'Someday I'm gonna get me a big car.' 'Someday I'm gonna get me a big house.' They thinkin' 'bout Someday when they playin' and that's what strips the soul right out of it."

Daniel had never thought that way, but he couldn't disagree. And he felt a little twinge of guilt about all the Someday music he'd created over the years, like so much litter he scattered along life's highway.

"But you listen to this boy." Mr. Atibon held out his hand like he was offering the young man as a gift.

The player was in his early twenties, half as old as the road-worn Epiphone acoustic on his lap. He closed his eyes as he sang in a voice that still held the purity of youth but had gained a smoky edge that more than hinted at heartache and lost innocence.

No woman leaves you all at once
No, they leave you by degrees
And if you want to keep yours, son
You better listen up to me

"See, what I tell you?" Mr. Atibon boasted, as if he'd had anything to do with the performance.

The busker accompanied himself in seventh chords, slowly dragging his right thumb across the guitar strings. It was all much smoother than the combustible good-time tunes Daniel thought of as typifying the New Orleans style.

Now the first time that she leaves you
It might seem like nothing at all
Just a harsh word that you gave her
Or a late night, you didn't call
Second time that she leaves you
Is the first time that she cries
Third time's when she looks at you
Without that love light in her eyes

You know she's going
Gonna set herself free
She's leaving
By degrees

Mr. Atibon elbowed Daniel. "Ain't that the truth."
Daniel nodded, but he felt like he'd been gut-punched.

Next time that she leaves you
She cries herself to sleep

She pretends she still loves you
But she knows it ain't as deep
Then comes the end
One fateful day
Some stranger looks in her eyes
And she don't look away

You know she's going
Gonna set herself free
She's leaving
By degrees

Daniel stood, his arms folded across his chest, and let the music wash over him like a baptismal font. There were no A&R guys. No corporate types who read balance sheets, not sheet music. No one at all like the man he used to be, no scammers or hustlers. No overdubs or Auto-Tune. There was just a man and his guitar, making music together for no other reason than there was a song stuck inside and it wanted out. It was Today music.

And then comes the times
She goes out for the night
She's just about gone
When she won't even fight
The last time she leaves you
She's immune to your charms
She won't heed your begging
She runs straight into his arms

And she won't come back
To see me no more

She won't ever come back
926 East McLemore

You know she's gone
Gone and set herself free
She's left you
Left you by degrees

Daniel reached into his pants pocket and pulled out a wad of bills he'd accumulated over the course of his trip. He'd been too frazzled or distracted to take the time to smooth and sort them out. Without knowing its worth—and without hesitation—he tossed it all into the open case. The best money he'd spent in a long, long time.

"Come on," he told his friend. "We gotta go."

"Doncha' wanna hear him play?"

"I do. But I have to get that money." Daniel thought he detected a glint of mercenary expectation in the old man's ebony eyes and he felt the need to extinguish it quickly. "For my son," he said with emphasis.

"'Course," the old man agreed. "For your boy."

They turned away, but behind them the busker kept up his show—with no other audience but the sky above.

Leaving by degrees
Leaving by degrees

And she won't come back
To see me no more
She won't ever come back

Daniel opened the club's door and they both stepped inside.

Though it wasn't yet midnight—still early by New Orleans's standard time—the main room was already packed with the usual assortment of tourists on Mission: Inebriated, and a healthy cross section of locals, from NOLA's stylized nonconformists to those still-clinging-to-the-whole-preppy-thing LSU alums out for a night.

Up on the main stage, a four-piece band was being led through its paces by a hobbit of a guy with a mop of shaggy gray hair and an even shaggier beard. His mumbled vocals and lazy manner made him sound like he wished he was home watching TV. The guitars were a muddied mess of reverb and the drummer was hitting the skins like they were misbehaving kids, but the crowd that enthusiastically bobbed up and down (mostly) in time to the beat seemed to think it was a sufficient soundtrack for a night of mindless drinking.

Mr. Atibon was unimpressed. "Now what?"

Daniel didn't have a clue. "I guess we'll just know."

"This a goddamn waste of time," the old man groused over the sound the band was trying its best to conjure. It was a soulless cacophony, cynically contrived for a roomful of misguided, middle-aged posers—something like a Jimmy Buffett tribute band trying its hand at Elmore James. Atibon pointed up at the stage toward the leader of the band. "And that damn fool up there looks like a goddamn mud-puppet."

Daniel wasn't sure what he'd heard. "A what?"

"Mud-puppet," he repeated. "You know, like the frog and pig on the TV."

Daniel shook his head, confused by the reference. "You mean a Muppet?"

"That's right. Whenever a fool like this one here tries a hand at the blues, it always ends up soundin' like what they *think* the blues should sound like. But you can't no way *think* the blues. Hell, you can't play the blues, 'less you fucked the blues, fought the blues, and lost to the blues. You can't play the blues till you get so that when you pick up a guitar that's the only goddamn thing that'll come out." He looked back at the band and shook his head with disgust.

"Ignore the Muppet," Daniel said, trying to redirect the old man's attention to the matter at hand. "The clue was about Professor Longhair. This is a club devoted to him. There's got to be something here. This has to be the 'altar' the lyric was talking about."

"Well, son, this ain't no altar. Not to Fess, it ain't. And even if it was, that song of yours said it was at the entrance."

"The entrance!" The tumblers in Daniel's mind all clicked. "The busker we passed coming in!"

"He's a hell of a lot better than this damn Mud-puppet," Mr. Atibon agreed.

"No," Daniel shouted frantically. "He must have been the clue."

"Isn't that what I said?" the old man revised. "You really got to listen, son."

Daniel ignored what the old man was saying and began to clear a path through the crowd. "Come on." He gingerly pressed past frat boys and slid between groups of Bohemian girls. Mr. Atibon followed and together they pushed their way through the swelling crowd and back out of the club.

The busker was gone.

"Goddamn it!" Daniel threw his hands up in the air in frustration and let them fall to his hips. "Goddamn it!"

"I told ya' we shoulda listened to him," Mr. Atibon reminded him.

"You know, this is really not helping right now," Daniel snapped, so sharply that the seemingly indefatigable Mr. Atibon was momentarily stunned.

Unsure how to make an apology, Daniel turned from the old man and saw a group of four soon-to-be-partiers approaching down Napoleon. An attractive couple, arm in arm, and two women. One pretty, brunette, and petite. The other beautiful, blonde, and impossibly tall.

"Excuse me," Daniel prefaced as he approached. "There was a guy with a guitar playing here." He gestured toward the spot in the empty shadows beside the door. "Did you pass a guy with a guitar coming down the street?"

"Dude," the guy with the shaved head smiled. "This is Nawlins. There's a guy with a guitar on *every* street."

It was hopeless. Daniel nodded and rubbed his temples, hoping it might stave off the aneurysm he was certain he felt coming. "It's just that we were supposed to meet this guitar player right here." He pointed back to the spot. "Right outside the door at Tipitina's."

"Maybe it's the other Tipitina's," the brunette offered.

A sinking feeling washed over Daniel. "The other—"

"There's a Tip's down in the Quarter," the beautiful blonde told him, her honey voice spiced with contempt. "Everyone knows that."

Daniel didn't. "There is?"

Mr. Atibon shook his head mournfully. "King o' the dummies."

A minute later Daniel had directions. He turned to his friend, "You coming?"

"You the man with the singing treasure map." Mr. Atibon adjusted his porkpie hat. "Lead on, *mi key.*"

CHAPTER NINETEEN

For more than three hundred years, New Orleans's French Quarter has enjoyed a hard-won reputation as the ultimate destination for those wishing to demonstrate a complete lack of self-control. Over any given weekend, the tight colonial streets originally laid out as a military encampment come alive as a single throbbing mass of humanity: one drunken, screaming, flashing, fighting, groping, puking entity that stretches shoulder-to-shoulder-to-shoulder from daiquiri bar to oyster bar, from leather bar to biker bar and back again.

On Lundi Gras—the last full party night of the annual bacchanal that is Mardi Gras—the Quarter is transformed into something much more depraved. On that particular night, those seventy-eight square blocks become an inter-dimensional portal through space and time to some alternate, thoroughly debauched reality—Disneyland reimagined by Charlie Sheen.

Although they'd been at it for the better part of an hour, Daniel and Mr. Atibon had managed to move only a block and a half through the sweaty mess. There were more people than there was space for people and so simply walking from one point to another was almost impossible.

"You can tell everythin' 'bout a soul by what they think of the Quarter at Mardi Gras," Mr. Atibon shouted into Daniel's ear loudly enough to be heard above the deafening rumble of revelry. "It's either your heaven or your hell. But it ain't nobody's purgatory."

Buried alive in a living, breathing grave of partiers, Daniel felt too dizzy and nauseated to try to respond. If he could have taken a free breath, he would have answered, "What's worse than hell?"

"Y'all right?" the old man yelled, with something approaching genuine concern.

"I'm fine," Daniel assured him, though the heat, smell, and impossibly close quarters of the crowd had completely overwhelmed his senses. He couldn't breathe or hear much more than a high-pitched whine in his ears. All he could do was concentrate on not passing out and falling into the crowd. He kept pushing on like a modern-day Mr. Stanley, cutting a path through a jungle of drunkards, hoping it would lead to his Dr. Livingstone—a kid with a guitar and a very important song.

And then suddenly, no more than ten yards ahead of them, the solid wall of humanity divided like Moses separating an inebriated Red Sea. At the very point where the crowd broke, an oversized man moved through the masses like an Arctic icebreaker in an Alexander Amosu suit. Behind him, a diminutive demon strutted as proudly as if he were the unstoppable force shoving drunken tourists out of the way.

Without thought or hesitation, Daniel turned as instinctively as a rabbit with the smell of wet dog suddenly in the air. "Come on."

"What's wrong now?" Mr. Atibon asked, struggling to follow Daniel's abrupt change in direction.

"Let's just go this way," Daniel shouted.

Mr. Atibon turned to follow but looked back over his shoulder. It didn't take him long to find the reason for their detour. He saw the big man pushing his way through the crowd and realized immediately what was happening: the finger-takers were closing in.

Between Daniel's detour and the streets clogged with inebriated revelers, by the time they reached the front door of Tipitina's French Quarter branch it was well past two in the morning. If there had ever been a busker outside the door—and it seemed doubtful a man could've ever played a guitar in the midst of such madness—he was gone now.

"Goddamn it!" Daniel yelled, though nobody but his friend heard. "We're too late."

Mr. Atibon put an uncharacteristically reassuring hand on Daniel's shoulder. "Maybe he's inside."

Daniel nodded brightly. "Right." He moved toward the front door with his hopes momentarily restored. He managed only a step or two before he ran straight into a wall of muscle, four sides of beef in tight, black T-shirts.

The meanest looking one put his hand on Daniel's chest and stopped him dead. "We're closed, Chief."

Daniel didn't resist the manhandling man. He raised his hands as a plea for just a moment in which to plead his case. "I've got to get inside—"

"Not gonna happen," Meanie assured him. The three other bouncers crossed their bulging arms and glared in solidarity. "Why don't you take yourself home, Ace."

"No, you don't understand. I'm supposed to meet someone in there," Daniel continued to protest. What he'd failed to factor into the equation was that guys like that don't do anything they're not paid to do and Meanie wasn't paid to understand. Or care.

"Well, then you fucking missed him," Meanie informed him. "You can wait for him over there." The hand that wasn't implanted in Daniel's chest pointed in the general direction of the corner of Iberville and North Peters. "But you ain't gettin' in and you ain't waitin' here."

He couldn't have come all this way just to be turned away at the door. "I have to get in there!" He couldn't let the clue slip through his hands. He had to save his son.

In a moment of paternal desperation, Daniel tried to make an end-run around Meanie. He got about a step, but no farther. He was intercepted almost immediately by Almost As Meanie, who grabbed Daniel and then pushed him back as hard as he could.

If the streets had been empty, Daniel might have sailed clear across North Peters and several rows into the parking lot across the way. The crowds, however, were so heavy that he was driven back only a foot or two before he smashed into a wall of people. Staggering partiers were jostled. Some of them spilled their "go" cups. And others fell back into others who fell back into others—like a set of drunken dominoes.

Someone, annoyed by the collision or having spilled his "walking around" Hurricane, took hold of Daniel from behind and pushed him back toward the bouncers.

Daniel collected himself and regrouped for another go at breaking through the muscle-bound Maginot Line. He took a step, but this time Mr. Atibon put an arm out to stop him. "It's no use."

Daniel could see from the determined sneers spread across the four faces opposing him that it was true. His quest had run straight into a black-T-shirt-wearing wall. He'd come too far to turn back, but there was simply no way to move forward. There was no way to move at all. "Goddamn it!"

"Hey, hey!" Although he'd been the one to stop Daniel, Mr. Atibon reached out and took a grip of his arms. "Can't give up hope." His gravel road of a voice was now earnestly paternal. "That what the blues is all about."

"The blues?" Daniel couldn't help but scoff at what seemed to be a fundamental contradiction. "Hope?"

"That's right," Mr. Atibon answered, not in the defensive snap Daniel had come to expect, but with simple reassurance. "Folks think the blues is sad music 'cause it come from hard-pressed people doin' one another wrong jus' 'cause they don't know no diff'rent, cause they feel they ain't got no choice."

The old man offered a consoling smile. "That's where the blues comes from, but it ain't what they're 'bout. Blues all 'bout that blessed belief if'in you put everything you got—your heart, your soul, your flesh, your bone—if you give everything, you can rise up above all that other shit. It's deliverance in twelve bars."

Daniel's faith was lost in the crowd. "I need more than music to deliver me now."

"All ya need is hope in your heart—even when it seem the whole damn world fixin' to stomp it outta ya. They say the blues come straight from hell, but nothin' that beautiful could from somethin' less it had a pure soul. And that means you too." The old man stopped to clear his throat. "And if you wanna know, *that's* what I told my boy." He put his hand on Daniel's shoulder. "And that's what you're gonna get the chance to tell your own."

Another sniff. "Now we gonna go find whatever the hell you need to find to get dat done. But it ain't here."

Daniel stopped and looked into the old man's eyes. "Thanks."

Reinvigorated, they turned together and found even their exit strategy was blocked. They were surrounded by seven guys in matching motorcycle club leathers. It was like if Snow White had come upon unwashed, meth-fueled, hog-riding petty criminals instead of dwarves. Daniel was sure they already came with cool biker names, but he would have called them Potbelly, Ponytail, Shorty, Zit-Face, Toothless, and Ape-Face.

Daniel would have named the one who grabbed him by the shirt and held him up in the air asking, "Is this the guy?" Sven because he had a braided moustache like a Nordic raider.

"Sure looks like him to me," Potbelly grunted.

Daniel's arms and legs flailed vainly in the air like a turtle being examined by an overcurious eight-year-old. "We don't want any trouble," he assured them, which was an unintentionally funny thing to say considering his feet weren't touching the ground. "Whatever happened, we can work it out."

Mr. Atibon marched right up to Sven as if he mistakenly thought the two were roughly the same size. "Put him down, ya damn fool. He ain't got no money." The Viking regarded the old man like he was a potential food source. "I ain't got no money neither."

"This don't concern you, old man," Sven growled.

Daniel wasn't sure what was happening or why, but he knew getting beaten by a biker gang was a distraction he couldn't afford. "Listen, guys, I'm sorry about whatever happened here, but I don't have anything you'd want."

Potbelly just sneered. "You *are* what we want."

"Me?" Daniel asked innocently. "What did I do to you?"

Potbelly began, "It ain't what you did to us—" but he never finished.

Potbelly's jaw dropped and as his eyes grew wide. The other bikers looked suddenly awestruck. Sven swallowed hard and slowly lowered Daniel to the ground.

Daniel didn't need to turn around to know what had happened. "I was wondering when you were going to show up, Moog."

"Hey, *papi*!" Rabidoso chimed in. "Remember us?"

"You shouldn't oughta run, Daniel." The big man didn't have to raise his voice to be heard above the crowd. "Running always makes everything worse."

"For me or for you?" Daniel wondered aloud.

"Same thing," Moog tossed off casually, though he was clearly eyeing up the bikers gathered behind Daniel. "What makes it worse for me, makes it worse on you."

"I'll keep that in mind."

Moog shook his head. "Won't matter for you no more." He reached out to take Daniel by the arm. "Come on, we got miles to go."

No one wanted to challenge the mountain, but all the bikers looked to Sven. If he didn't feel the call to action in his heart, he clearly felt a need to represent his brothers and their club. "Wait a minute," he called out as he caught Moog's wrist and wrapped his heavily tattooed hand around it. "This guy ain't going anywhere with you."

"Fuck off, *puta*," Rabidoso spat, before Moog had a chance to speak for himself.

Both Potbelly and Ponytail thought they could take the undersized Mexican without any problem and they were quick to step up. "I'm gonna kick your fuckin' spic ass," Potbelly promised.

"I'm goin' count to three," Moog told Sven calmly as he adjusted his tie. "If your hand's still on me when I get there, I'm gonna put it so far up your ass you're gonna have to snap your fingers to shit."

And then the third front of that perfect storm blew in. Meanie, Almost As Meanie, and the others behind him approached the group. "Listen, fellas, y'all need to take this fuckin' daisy chain down the street. You're blockin' our door and you gotta go!"

Somewhere there was a thunderclap, but it was impossible to tell who threw the first punch.

Mardi Gras is intended to be a joyous celebration—and it almost always is. But a crowd that's been drinking for days and then crammed into close confines, pushing and shoving, is like a gas-soaked Christmas tree thrown on the Fourth of July bonfire: it really doesn't matter where the spark comes from. When a spark hits it, it all goes up in a big, fucking *WHOOOOOOSH!*

Complete chaos descended on the Quarter in all the time it takes to throw a punch. Bouncers hit bikers. Bikers smacked bouncers. Bikers and bouncers missed one another and struck bystanders. And then the bystanders struck back. Punches were thrown wildly. People kicked at whatever was near them. Whatever they happened to have in their hands became missiles, the sky raining down beer bottles and rocks and street signs.

In an instant, what had been merely a melee degenerated into a full-fledged riot. Revelers ran in all directions, pushing the weaker or drunker partiers out of their way, even if that meant down to the street. More side fights broke out. The truly crazy stopped in the midst of the raging storm to shoot the human hurricane on phone cameras.

In all the chaos, Daniel and Mr. Atibon were perhaps the only ones who demonstrated any sense. Daniel grabbed the old man's coat collar and pulled him close. With his arm around him offering protection, they ran through the frantic crowd looking for a way out. Any way out.

Rabidoso saw the pair running away, serpentining through the crowd. He pulled the pistol from his waistband and took aim on the center of Daniel's back. His index finger began to tighten on the trigger—and an oversized hand swatted the Colt 9mm. "What the fuck, man?"

"Are you kidding me?" Moog shouted, as he watched Daniel and Atibon disappear into the eye of the storm. "This is New Orleans," the big man reminded his partner. "Half these motherfuckers are carrying. The other half are still *crazy* motherfuckers. You fire off into this crowd and you'll turn this whole damn city into Afghanistan." He pointed Rabidoso in the direction they'd seen Daniel running and gave him a push. "Come on. They can't be far."

Daniel and Mr. Atibon moved as quickly as they could, dodging the frightened partiers who ran in any direction they thought would lead them out of danger and avoiding the brain-addled testosterone freaks who howled as they did their best to fan the fires of violence. They worked their way through the crowd until they reached its edge at the Riverwalk, the Quarter's eastern border, an asphalt walkway that runs parallel to the Mississippi. There was nowhere for the pair to run without getting wet.

Daniel stood for a moment, a riot behind him and a river ahead. He was afraid to run back into the mayhem, but more frightened still of the part of him that wanted simply to jump into the river and be done with it. Unsure what to do, he was relieved when he felt Mr. Atibon's hand grab him around the arm. "Come on. Best thing now is just lay low."

The old man led him north, up the Riverwalk about two hundred yards and then off into the shadows behind a row of restaurants and shops that fronted onto North Peters. Mr. Atibon checked the loading bays and back doors, but all hiding spots were predictably locked up tight.

The only available hiding spot was behind a Dumpster, which, from the smell of it, was overflowing with bad fish and vomit. As nauseating as that sanctuary was, Daniel figured they could stay there until Moog and Rabidoso realized the folly of searching a raging sea of humanity for a single face.

The plan worked perfectly. For about a minute. And then the dim light of a nearby streetlight was eclipsed by a less-than-celestial body. Warily, Daniel stuck his head out from behind the Dumpster like a middle-aged raccoon.

His heart raced as he hid in the shadows and watched Moog and Rabidoso tracing the steps he'd just taken. They walked down the Riverfront path, scanning the crowds at the far edge of the mayhem for the faces they were after.

Daniel couldn't hear any of the words they were sharing, but it was clear from their actions they were both more concerned with moving quickly than with searching carefully. They hurried along until they finally reached the general vicinity of Daniel's hiding spot. The stench coming off the Dumpster, however, was so overpowering that they turned quickly and kept moving right past where Daniel and Mr. Atibon were crouched and hiding.

Daniel let loose a sigh of relief—a nauseating mistake so close to the Dumpster. And unfortunately premature.

Thirty seconds after he offered whispered words of thanks to the heavens above, he peered around the filthy edge of the Dumpster to make certain the coast was clear, and there was the mismatched pair walking back as if they'd realized simultaneously they'd overlooked something meaningful.

Daniel could tell from their aggressive postures and their sharp, violent gestures that they were fighting about something. Rabidoso shouted something, emphasizing his point with an extended index finger. Moog threw his hands up in obvious frustration.

At that moment, a spotted mutt—post-Katrina New Orleans still has a tragic number of strays—broke out of the darkness and scampered past the two men. Perhaps the pup had been frightened by the rioting crowds or it was simply in search of a much-needed meal, but it was clear that it meant no harm as it skittered along the edge of the walkway just behind the two killers.

Moog didn't pay any attention to the dog, but Rabidoso jumped at the sight of it. Moog burst into laughter at "the fearless assassin" recoiling with fear at the sight of the stray.

Maybe it was being laughed at by Moog. It could have been just that he didn't like living things. Whatever his motivation Rabidoso picked up a broken brick lying at the side of the pavement and heaved it as hard as he could at the mongrel's head. The missile hit its target dead on, striking the pup and knocking it to the ground with a whine that faded to a soft groan and then to silence.

Daniel was so fixed on hiding from the killers that he'd all but forgotten about his gray-haired friend until he felt Mr. Atibon push past him as he rose from his crouched position like a soldier suddenly called to duty. "*Me a guh bax yuh!*" the old man threatened under his breath.

The outburst startled Daniel, not just because he didn't understand (or recognize) the language, but because it was spoken with a seething, visceral fury. It was like Death as a whisper.

"I got some business to settle up here now," Mr. Atibon announced, looking over at the dog splayed across the pavement and then down at Daniel. "And you need to get runnin', son."

"But they'll see us," Daniel said worriedly, trying to pull the old man back into the shadow.

"Goddamn right, they'll see me," Mr. Atibon declared, choking up on his walking stick as if he were getting ready to do some heavy swinging. "But you best get a move on. It's time."

There was an alarming finality in the old man's voice and it left Daniel uneasy, like a kid dropped off at school for the very first time. "What do you mean?"

"Everything has its season, son. We've had ours for the time bein'." The old man looked off toward where Moog stood yelling at Rabidoso, who was poking that dog with a stick. "Now's the time for me to settle this score and then get back to my Marie."

Even given their circumstances, the revelation was startling. "You're married?"

"Hell, son, you may be a dummy, but that don't mean I is." Mr. Atibon shook his head, though it was more to brush off the question than deny it. "You let me worry 'bout my sweet boo. You need to keep your mind straight on savin' your boy. And that means, you gotta get gallopin'."

"What?" Moving on alone wasn't anything Daniel wanted to consider. "I can't just leave you here."

"I couldn' save my son," the old man's eyes glistened, "but you can still save yours. Now go!"

"I'm not leaving you." Daniel reached for the old man, but there was no turning him around.

"Ain't you figured it out yet? I'll be there when you need me." Mr. Atibon smiled like he'd just spilled a secret. "Now get goin'. Go, save your boy."

Daniel looked up into his friend's eyes, frantically trying to think of some protest to file or argument to make. There was nothing.

"Go!"

"But go where? I don't even know—"

"Memphis," the old man told him. "That boy you been wastin' your time lookin' for was playin' Memphis soul if I've ever heard it—and I heard it all. I think you best get yourself up there. But you best get goin' right now!"

"But—" Daniel racked his brain for something he could say to change the old man's mind. And came up empty.

"I bid you farewell." The old man tipped his porkpie hat. "And when we meet again, you'll have a helluva story to tell." Without another word, Atibon stepped out into the light.

Knowing what he had to do didn't make getting it done any easier. Daniel couldn't bring himself to break away. "How can I thank you?"

"Ya don't have another grand, do ya?" Mr. Atibon asked slyly.

Daniel smiled. "Not on me."

"Well, until you do…" The old man patted him on the shoulder, turned him around, and pointed the way. "Then get goin'. Now! Go, *mi key!*"

Without turning back again, Daniel got to his feet and ran down the Riverwalk as fast as he could. He didn't look back for his old friend. He didn't check to see if anyone was following him. Or gaining on him. He ran without stopping, block after block until his lungs burned like they'd been used for ashtrays and he'd made it all the way back to the Kia.

He started it up, slid it into gear, and didn't stop again until he'd put the Louisiana border in his rearview. As he drove back through Mississippi on now-familiar roads, his thoughts were twisted with guilt for having left his friend behind and consumed by questions about why he'd done so.

His concerns might have disappeared, his guilt lessened, if he'd stayed to see Mr. Atibon walk down the Riverwalk just as calmly as if he was taking a Sunday stroll through the Garden District, his black walking stick tapping out a rhythm to his cadence.

Moog was the first to notice the old man approaching them slowly but purposefully. Something about the sight stunned him and left him standing statue still like a carved slab of obsidian. Rabidoso drew his pistol at the sight of the stranger, but seemed to lose the nerve to raise it up.

Mr. Atibon approached the pair and looked first at Moog. His eyes scanned the big man, not like he was searching them for something they might contain, but like he was planting some thought with him. "You know enough not to trouble me, boy."

Moog mumbled a confused, "Who are you?" like he was stirring from a restless sleep.

"You know me, Vernon Turner." Mr. Atibon tilted his head and let slip a cautionary smile, like he'd caught the big man trying to play a cheat. "I'm the prayer that ain't been answered. I'm the dream that hasn't come. And I tell you this: that's a good man you're chasing. You'd do well to leave him alone." The old man's voice was like the rumble of thunder in the stillness of a sultry summer night.

"I can't." Moog's voice sounded childish in comparison.

"You a slave?" Mr. Atibon looked harder into the big man's eyes. "You only think you can't. You got yourself all turned 'round. If there's killin' to be done, you should start with what you're runnin' from, not what you're runnin' after."

This time Moog made no response at all.

"As for you." Mr. Atibon turned to Rabidoso, placing his walking stick against the assassin's throat with the swiftness of a snake's strike. The miniature madman seemed unable to do anything to protect himself, and the pistol dangling limply from his hand fell to the pavement.

"So you serve that bitch, *Muerte*, do you?" His words were seething and he punctuated them by spitting in Rabidoso's face. The proud assassin—who'd killed more than once for a glance he'd thought was vaguely insulting—stood motionless as the spittle ran down his cheek, tracing a path against his raised scar. "Well, I'm telling you just the same as I'd tell her if she was here." He spit again, this time on the ground where *she* wasn't. "The pups are mine. Every single one of 'em. If I ever see you hurt one again, I'll bring you to an ending that'll make your fuckin' head go *boom!*"

Without another word, the old man gently touched the handle of his cane to Rabidoso's head. Suddenly, the little man cried out in pain and fell to his knees; a trickle of blood ran from his nose and ears. He pressed his hands to the sides of his head like they were the only things keeping his cranium from exploding then and there. Moaning and whimpering, he rocked back and forth like he was praying as hard as he could—but his prayers were being ignored.

Mr. Atibon smiled with satisfaction and then calmly walked over to where the stray dog had fallen. He stooped down and picked its limp body up into his arms. He brushed his hand over the furry contours of its head, wiping away the blood that had gathered there, and then began to walk purposefully down the Riverwalk and off into the darkness that lay beyond.

As he walked off, he sung at the top of his voice.

And she won't come back
To see me no more
She won't ever come back
926 East McLemore

Leaving by degrees
Leaving by degrees

Moog still stood like a statute. Rabidoso kept rocking back and forth on his knees, his pained howl fading to a soft mumbling.

Neither of them raised their eyes to watch the old man as he walked away and so neither noticed the dog lift its head and adjust itself in the old man's arms. "Good boy," Mr. Atibon told the pup as the two of them slipped off into the darkness. "Let's go check in on Miss Laveau, *mi key*."

CHAPTER TWENTY

Daniel woke with a start. And the unsettling feeling he hadn't actually been asleep. Not for long, at least. He reached for the bedside clock. It read 11:44, confirming his uneasy suspicions and explaining the crushing sensation he felt in his temples and across his forehead.

He tried to get comfortable between the clammy sheets he desperately hoped had been washed since the last time there'd been an occupant in Room 213 of the River Belle Hotel, the cheapest sleep in Memphis. He tried, but his fevered brain refused to let him slip off to the sweet refuge of sleep.

Instead, he tortured himself with an endless parade of nightmare scenarios: The bloody fate that might have befallen Mr. Atibon. The sadistic price Preezrakevich would exact if the money couldn't be recovered. The horrific end he would face if the musical scavenger hunt was nothing more than an elaborate and sadistic trap. And worst of all, what all of it might mean for his son.

When he couldn't bear his thoughts any longer, Daniel got out of bed and made his escape to the bathroom, gingerly crossing the disturbingly moist carpet. The room was exactly what he feared (and expected). None of the features had been updated since the Nixon administration and using them required concentrating on not thinking about who might have used them previously—or for what purpose.

It was Tuesday morning. Just four days earlier he'd stood in the (much nicer) bathroom at the Hotel du Monde and looked into the mirror, praying the man he saw there might still have enough magic left over to sell his *Rock and Roll Redemption* pilot for a *suh-weeeet* syndication deal.

Now he looked into a chipped, permanently smoky mirror and could barely recognize the hollow eyes, circled with dark rings of exhaustion, staring back at him. The *magic* to sell a television pilot? He didn't even have the magic for a fucking toothbrush...or a razor...deodorant...not even a fresh set of clothes. He didn't have magic for anything anymore.

If he'd eaten anything in past twenty-four hours he might have sunk to his knees and vomited. Instead, he knelt in front of the rust-stained toilet praying that he could. When he finally realized not even *that* prayer would be answered, he got to his feet and stepped into the shower. It left him little more than wet.

He dried himself with a towel that was no cleaner than he was and put his filthy clothes back on. He took a last look at the forlorn character in the mirror and tried to pretend he was ready for a new day. "Magic!"

Daniel sat in the Kia's driver's seat for a long time. He was ready to roll, but there was no particular place to go.

The old man had told him to go to Memphis and, though he still wasn't entirely sure why, Daniel had gone straight there. But the River City comprises more than three hundred square miles and he didn't have a clue as to where he should start looking in first. Even if Mr. Atibon had been right about where the song was sending him, that didn't mean the fractured clue still didn't lead straight into a stone wall.

"Goddamn it!" Daniel hit the steering wheel in frustration. He hit it again because it felt good. Again. And again. Each blow he delivered was stronger and more furious than the last, until finally he set off the car alarm.

Aaaaaawww-aaaaawwww-aaaaaawwww-aaaaawwww!

Car alarms haven't been an effective theft deterrent since the days when cars had their own phones. Nobody stopped to help someone who might be in distress or to stop a could-be thief. Pedestrians passed by, scornfully looking at him from the corners of their angry eyes with a mix of annoyance and amusement as Daniel desperately pressed buttons trying (and failing) to silence the siren. He pushed the button on the key fob and punched the steering wheel some more. Nothing worked. Everybody else went about their business, shaking their heads at *that* asshole.

And how could he help but join them all in laughing at him? As soon as the alarm cried itself out and finally fell silent, Daniel recalled teaching Zack to drive. His son had lost his nerve when he'd stalled and had become enraged whenever speeding Angelinos cut in front of him. It was all understandable, but it was also the worst mistake a driver could make. Over and over again, Daniel had told his son that "behind the wheel" was no place to get emotional. Ever.

The same was true now too. The only way to approach his problem was to think it through. Calmly. Rationally. He took a deep breath, cleared his head, and tried to take the problem step by step.

If the next location was Memphis then the logical place to start looking was…he didn't have a clue.

He sighed. And then started over. The clues never sent him just *any* place. The underlying theme of the twisted lil' game show was: music.

So then the most logical place to look...in Memphis...that had something to do with music...was...

He thought about it for a second or two, but not any longer than that. He shook his head, refusing to believe he could've been so stupid as to overlook such an obvious destination. Memphis, after all, was music's Mecca.

Daniel started the Kia. This time he knew exactly where he was going.

CHAPTER TWENTY-ONE

In 1939, Dr. Thomas Moore built a colonial-style mansion on a parcel of property his wife had received as a gift from her aunt, Grace, in Memphis's Whitehaven community. And for more than twenty years they lived there quite comfortably and without any notoriety at all.

Then one day—completely out of the blue—there was a knock on the Moores' door. It was a middle-aged couple asking if the house was for sale. The inquiring pair was clearly from poor and rural origins—hillbillies would have been an impolite, but not inaccurate, description—and their offer was initially taken as some kind of practical joke. Until they informed the Moores they had $100,000. With them. In cash.

The satchel of money had been given to them by their only son, who'd sent them out on that lazy Sunday afternoon to buy him a house. Any house they liked. And that's just what they did.

In a nation with hundreds of tourist attractions, Graceland is a *shrine*. People take family vacations to the Grand Canyon and visit the Statue of Liberty, but they make pilgrimages to Graceland.

It's Graceland, after all.

And Daniel saw every bit of it. At least those parts left open to the tour.

He took the bus through the iconic "Music Gates" and craned his neck with the rest of his group to see into the living room and the music room. He meandered through the dining room and the kitchen and listened while a guide read a list of all of the food items the King demanded be kept on hand at all times. He pretended to marvel at the television room with the three TVs that could be watched simultaneously. And kept his opinion of the Jungle Room to himself.

Still, after an hour of looking at collections of gold records and gold lamé jumpsuits, gawking at pink Cadillacs and Convair jets, Daniel still hadn't found anything to lead him on to the next step of his musical quest. He was confident he hadn't overlooked anything and so he examined every new display and exhibition with desperate interest as it was presented.

Despite the thoroughness with which he reviewed the mansion museum, by the time the tour guide was directing all the guests to the conveniently located gift shop, Daniel still hadn't found the next clue. But he wasn't at all surprised there'd been nothing to find there.

The game Daniel was being forced to play was all about music. The mansion he'd just passed through, however, had damn little to do with music.

It *was* a shrine, but only to outlandish displays of wealth and the dead-end street of unchecked hedonism. Product had been developed on the site, but music hadn't been made there. As far as Daniel could tell, the only thing actually *created* on the grounds was the grilled peanut butter and banana sandwich.

No one could deny the power in the man's performances. Daniel had been a lifelong fan and nothing he'd seen on the tour had lessened his admiration for that showman. But standing there on the garish grounds led him to the inescapable conclusion that no matter how dynamic the performance, there was something disturbing behind the idol and the cult that had grown up around him.

There wasn't much more than a hundred miles between Graceland's garish gates and the Delta shotgun shacks and juke joints where the music that paid for all of that excess had been birthed and nurtured, but it was just about as far as a soul could get. One was a place that brought a young, awkward boy to life and the other was the crypt where he'd come to die.

"It's amazing, isn't it?" The middle-aged woman with the question had taken note that Daniel didn't seem to be experiencing the same sort of rapture as the corn-fed faithful who were enthusiastically pawing through souvenirs, everything from aprons to Zippos. It bothered her.

"What?" Daniel looked around, wondering what he'd missed.

"All of this," she answered with good-natured determination, her overly made-up eyes bulging with enthusiasm. "It's just a life-changing experience, isn't it?"

"I suppose it has been." It was the truth, but Daniel knew it hadn't changed his life the same way it'd changed hers.

"To think he was just a truck driver from Tupelo who went into this nothing, little recording studio to record some songs for his momma and POOF!" She said the word like she could actually see it—and it was covered in glitter. "He creates rock and roll."

Daniel knew he should just wish the woman well and walk away, but he couldn't stop himself from saying, "First off, that's not what happened." The jowls wagged when her face fell. "And even as a creation myth, that's not very rock and roll, is it?"

"What do you mean?" she asked, although it was clear she'd already dismissed him as a heretic.

"I mean, rock and roll is meant to be the soundtrack to rebellion. It kind of loses something if it all started with a love-song-singing-momma's-boy, doesn't it?"

If he'd sprouted cloven hooves and a pitchfork right there, the woman in her XXL "ELVIS LIVES" T-shirt wouldn't have regarded Daniel any differently.

"And it wasn't a nothing, little studio. Sam Phillips had already tapped into the Delta's musical mother lode. He'd recorded artists like Howlin' Wolf, Junior Parker, B.B. King, Little Milton."

Her doughy countenance morphed from distress to contempt as her eyes registered an unspoken, "Oh, so *that's* what this is all about."

"When your truck driver walked into Sun, rock and roll had already been born. It was alive and kicking ass mightily. But Sam Phillips was pragmatic and knew if he wanted to sell that new music to people with the money to buy records he'd have to put it in a different package. And that's what your truck driver was: a good-looking cardboard box."

It was clear from the fire in her eyes she wanted to make an impassioned retort to put the blasphemer in his place, but all that came out was, "You're an asshole!"

Finally, something they could agree on. Daniel turned and started off toward what he hoped was the exit.

"If you love all *that* so much," she called after him angrily. "You shoulda gone there instead."

And then it hit him. Maybe Graceland had given him a clue after all.

CHAPTER TWENTY-TWO

There was a group of tourists standing in the driveway connecting Union Avenue to the cramped parking lot behind the red brick building. Some of them were busily snapping pictures of the oversized portrait of "The Million Dollar Quartet" plastered across the side of the building. Others were animatedly recounting the "energies" they'd felt throughout their tour of the building. None of them, however, paid any attention to the little gray Kia until it was almost right on top of them.

Daniel stomped on the brake and then endured the wrathful stares of the picture-takers and storytellers. When they finally cleared the way, he pulled through to the parking lot and found a spot.

If the near collision had been his fault, Daniel didn't pause to apologize as he rushed past the group and hurried toward the modest storefront that had once been a "nothing, little recording studio." The winter sun was sinking in the late-afternoon sky and with little time left in the day, he threw open the door beneath the giant guitar sign and walked in. A bell rang to announce his entrance.

What had once been the front office for Sun Records, Sam Phillips's musical empire, had been converted into a gift shop, with rows of T-shirts and stacks of CDs and books for sale. A few tables and booths had been set up to take full advantage of the tourist trade with a Sun Studio Café.

The walls were covered in photos of Elvis, undeniably its most famous artist. He was joined by Jerry Lee Lewis. Randy Perkins. Johnny Cash. Roy Orbison.

But Daniel was struck that the only reminder of the blues artists on which Sun had been founded, who'd sustained and nourished the studio and arguably given Phillips the millions of dollars to give to that quartet was an eight-by-ten of a smiling Howlin' Wolf. A framed photo of the man about whom Sam Phillips had said, "This for me is where the soul of man never dies," was mounted just over the entrance to the restrooms.

Along the north wall, near the front door, was a long glass counter and behind it, a woman who looked old enough to remember the place before it was nostalgic. "I'm sorry." End-of-the-day fatigue made her voice sound like a telephone recording. "The last tour's already started. We close in ten minutes."

Daniel hoped it would be enough time. "I'm looking for—" He stopped, suddenly aware he had no idea: What *was* he looking for?

She smiled officiously, but the hour was too close to five for her to care what he wanted. "We open again tomorrow at ten."

There was no more time for tomorrows. "No!"

The clock-watching clerk was understandably taken aback by Daniel's unintentionally forceful response, so Daniel repeated it—softer this time—hoping a gentler phrasing would reassure her. "No."

In her head, she wondered why the nutcases always seemed to wait for the end of the day to make their appearances; outwardly, she forced another smile. "I'm sorry, sir." She kept her voice as calm as she could, cautious not to let on just how much his erratic behavior disturbed her. "We're just closing up now. If you could come back tomorrow."

"No, I can't come back tomorrow." How could he hope to make her understand? There was no way to make it sound reasonable so he just asked, "Were there some men in here recently? Or a man? Someone who might have left something behind? An envelope with a CD in it maybe?" They all seemed like pertinent questions as he asked them, but as soon as he'd heard them aloud, the crazy they contained came through loud and strong. He sympathized with her completely and understood the reason for the worried look in her weary eyes.

"I'm afraid I'm going to have to ask you to leave." It was almost dark out and she was alone in the store. Without taking her eyes off Daniel, her wrinkled hand inched slowly beneath the counter for whatever it was that was kept under there to deal with the "problem" customers.

"No, wait!" A thought came to Daniel and he held up his hands, asking for just one more chance. "Maybe someone came in here to record recently. Maybe a song that mentioned me by name? Danny?" Even to his ear, it sounded like an odd question, but it didn't stop him from continuing. "I go by Daniel, actually. But all these songs keep referring to me as Danny for some reason I don't understand."

"Sir—" She was terrified now.

And he understood he was the reason for her anxiety. "I'm just leaving," he assured her before she could say anything else. "I'm just leaving."

She didn't respond, but her eyes were grateful to see him slowly edge to the door and then close it behind him.

Daniel had been certain that Sun Studio was his Memphis destination. But as he walked back to the Kia, he couldn't help but wonder whether Mr. Atibon hadn't made a mistake in sending him there. Perhaps the old man had told a lie or had made up a destination intending only to get Daniel as far away from the dangers of New Orleans as he could. Maybe there wasn't even another clue to be found at all.

The Kia pulled out of the lot, and by the time he'd turned on to Mississippi Boulevard, Daniel's mood had begun to match the gathering gloom of the coming evening. If he couldn't find the money—and he was beginning to doubt whether he'd ever had any real possibility of recouping the cash—then there was only one way left to save his son.

With or without the money, his own fate was almost certainly sealed. But maybe if he returned to Las Vegas on his own—and groveled sufficiently—maybe Filat might be satisfied with just one body cracking the sidewalk outside the Hotel du Monde. Maybe Daniel's body contained all of the blood the Russian would need to consider the debt satisfied.

It wasn't a perfect plan, but it was the only way Daniel could think of to protect Zack now. In his mind, at least, it was settled: the quest was over. He'd just go back to Vegas.

Not tonight, though. He was too tired to spend another night on the highway. He could spend one last night on the River Belle Hotel's soiled sheets and then start for Vegas in the morning. His only goal now was simply to find the dive he'd call home for one last night.

The traffic in downtown Memphis had thickened with rush hour, and the early descent of evening made navigating his way more difficult than he would have thought. Daniel carefully watched the cross-streets go by. Walker. Saxon. Edith. McLemore.

An old man stepped off the curb and straight into the street without looking toward oncoming traffic. Daniel stomped on the brake. The Kia's nose dipped and tires squealed as the subcompact came to a sudden stop. With 500cc of adrenaline coursing through his system, Daniel drew a pained breath of relief and looked for the pedestrian he'd almost made into a hood ornament. The old man was nowhere to be seen, but above him hung a street sign. McLemore.

McLemore.

McLemore.

And suddenly he heard music. With his memory unexpectedly prompted, he heard a tune he couldn't place at first. He hummed the melody and that brought back the image of a kid. With a guitar. The busker outside Tipitina's. It was in the chorus of the song the kid had been singing.

He struggled to pull the words back to his consciousness, but nothing came.

Nothing, at first, and then suddenly he could hear—not the busker—but Mr. Atibon's raspy voice:

And she won't come back
To see me no more
She won't ever come back
926 East McLemore

Leaving by degrees
Leaving by degrees

Daniel stepped on the gas and made a quick, unannounced left turn from the right-hand lane. Horns blared and well-deserved obscenities were shouted in his direction, but he didn't care. He turned onto McLemore and in two short blocks everything made all the sense in the world.

And she won't come back
To see me no more
She won't ever come back
926 East McLemore

CHAPTER TWENTY-THREE

When he recalled his friend's rushed last words, Daniel remembered that Mr. Atibon had sent him to Memphis not because the song rocked or carried on the blues, but based on the soulfulness of the song they'd heard.

The marquee over 926 East McLemore proudly proclaimed: STAX STUDIOS—SOULSVILLE, USA. Somehow Daniel instantly knew he'd finally arrived at his destination. And if that was the case, then maybe there was still some small sliver of hope left.

In its glory, Stax Studios was home to a roster of incredible talent. Otis Redding, Rufus Thomas, Wilson Pickett, Sam & Dave, and Isaac Hayes. And in its time, it produced a sound that was every bit as unique and musically important as anything Sam Phillips created across town at Sun. Yet despite its musical and social significance, when changes in the industry ultimately led to Stax's demise, the original building at 926 East McLemore Avenue was allowed to fall into disrepair and it was eventually demolished.

After the original Stax Studios met the wrecking ball, a replica was constructed on the site and converted to a museum.

Perhaps it was a testament to what Mr. Atibon had described as the quality of hope at the foundation of music.

Daniel parked in the lot behind the building and excitedly walked around to the front doors. He took a deep breath—said a quick, silent prayer—and pulled on the doors.

They didn't budge.

The place was closed.

He cupped his hands over his eyes to steal a look through the small diamond-shaped window in the locked door, but couldn't see anything except a completely deserted lobby. Renewed resignation descended on him and he was just about to turn and go when he thought he noticed something move back in the far shadows of the lobby. He banged on the doors, enthusiastically but respectfully.

Nothing.

He saw something again. He was certain this time. There was someone just at the far edge of what he could see of the museum's interior. He banged again. More enthusiastically, perhaps less respectfully.

Still nothing.

He banged on the door like his life depended on it—because it kinda did.

A young man appeared at the window in the door, his chubby face framed in ringlets of long red curls. "We're closed," he shouted as he brushed errant curls out of his eyes and then returned to whatever he'd been doing.

Daniel banged again, desperate to get the kid back to the door. "Please."

The round face appeared at the glass again. "I said we're closed." He looked hard at Daniel, like he didn't want any trouble but if that was what Daniel was bringing, he was more than able to finish whatever was started—or call someone for help.

"Please," Daniel pleaded again.

"No." The kid turned.

"Please." This time Daniel banged like *his son's* life depended on it. The doors rattled like they might come off their hinges. "Just listen to me."

The kid appeared again, this time clearly angered. "Look, man, I said—"

Daniel held up his hands as a thought struck him. He reached into his pocket and pulled out his wallet. He fished out one of the two twenty-dollar bills he still had left and slid it through the slight space between the twin doors.

The kid just looked insulted.

Daniel dug out the other and pushed the pair through.

The kid looked suspiciously from side to side, like he was concerned the transaction might be a trap set by his employer. He thought about it for a moment or two and then with a single motion snatched the bills. He checked them over and then—satisfied they were legit—slid them into the front pocket of his baggy jeans.

Daniel smiled broadly and looked expectantly at him.

"Thanks, man," the kid grinned triumphantly. "I'm up forty and you're still locked out."

"Please." It was all he could say, all he could do.

"We're closed, man!" There was a plaintive note in the young man's voice, like Daniel was just killing him with all the banging and the begging. "Whatchu want?"

This again. He wasn't sure exactly how to explain what he didn't understand. "I'm looking for something," he began. "Something very important."

"You lost something?" The young man seemed more responsive.

It wasn't exactly what Daniel had intended, but it suddenly seemed like the best chance for getting inside. And it was, in a way, the truth. "More than you could ever imagine."

"Don't bet on it." Whatever the kid was referring to, he took a deep breath and let it go. Then he pulled a ring of keys from his pocket, selected one, and opened the door. "You can have a quick look at the lost and found, but then you're gone. Start any trouble with me and you'll be gone even sooner. Understand?"

Daniel nodded enthusiastically. "Thank you."

"It's over here." The kid led Daniel over to a circular reception desk. On the wall behind it was a large silver plaque bearing the name Led Zeppelin along with artwork from several of the band's album covers.

It struck Daniel as curiously out of place in SOULSVILLE, USA. He was facing more important dilemmas, but Daniel couldn't help asking, "What's with the Led Zeppelin?"

The kid looked over his shoulder and then answered proudly, "Robert Plant's, you know, a big fan. When he was recording up in Nashville he came down here to check us out and gave us that."

Daniel just shook his head. "Nothing like paying homage to the music you sampled for your entire career by presenting a nice big plaque—of yourself."

His sarcastic observation completely obliterated whatever goodwill his forty bucks had bought him. "You want to check the lost and found or not?" the kid asked, clearly personally offended by the observation.

"Please." Daniel smiled as innocently as he could, thinking to himself he should introduce the kid to the fat lady at the Graceland gift shop.

The kid handed Daniel a cardboard box filled to overflowing with an astonishing variety of items anyway. "If you lost it here and someone turned it in, it's in there. Find it and get out."

The box was heavier than Daniel thought it would be. "There hasn't been anyone here, has there?" he asked, as casually as he could while sorting through dropped mittens and abandoned binkies. "Some guys dropping off a package maybe for a Daniel Erickson?"

"Look it," the kid snapped, regretting he'd ever taken the strange man's money. "If what you're looking for isn't in there, you need to go."

"No," Daniel covered. "I'm still looking."

He went through the box item by item. The expected hats and sweaters. Some notebooks forgotten by kids on field trips. A hairdryer? A set of keys. A surprising number of single shoes.

At the very bottom of the box was a manila envelope so tattered and worn it looked like it might have been a remnant from the original structure. It was postmarked from Nashville and addressed to Mr. Danny Erickson.

"This is it," Daniel announced as he held his prize up triumphantly.

"Good." The kid was obviously still fuming over the whole Plant thing. "Now take it and get gone."

"Sure." Daniel followed him to the door and offered his hand. "Thanks."

The kid just looked at the hand and then pointed the way through the door he was holding open. Daniel nodded and stepped back out into the night without another word.

The door locked behind him.

With his package in hand, Daniel started walking back to the lot behind the museum. His attention was so focused on this newest clue that he'd turned the corner around the building and taken a dozen steps into the parking lot before he noticed the Kia was completely surrounded by Memphis Police Department squad cars, their sirens silenced but their redtops flashing.

CHAPTER TWENTY-FOUR

Gerald Feller had turned down his father-in-law's offer to join him in his personal injury practice in Peoria. He'd suffered instead through the rigors of Quantico and then a revolving door of seven different field offices over the course of his career. Thirteen years of paperwork and bureaucracy. Thirteen years of watching less-qualified candidates skip past him on their ascent up the bureau's ladder of command. Thirteen years and all he had to show for it was a failed marriage, a set of swollen ankles that warned him when it was going to storm, and a personnel jacket stuffed full of mediocre agent evaluations.

But *this*. This one was a redeemer. This was a game breaker. A career maker. It was *six o'clock news*–worthy. Front-page photo fodder. It was the case he'd been waiting thirteen years for. And he was determined that the locals weren't going to fuck it up on him.

Clyde Mosby had been born and raised in Memphis. Ward 232. The fact that he'd lived to adulthood put him ahead of too many of the kids with whom he'd run those mean streets. That he'd become a Memphis homicide detective made him notorious in the old neighborhood. That he'd been tapped as a featured detective in the cable reality show *Murder Squad* had made him into a celebrity. Memphis was his city and he was the Man. It was not a title he was willing to relinquish to some tight-ass fed.

The two men met in the center of the parking lot, coming together like Frazier and Cooney out of their corners.

"Look sharp, boys," Mosby called out to the uniformed officers who were stringing tape around their crime scene. "J. Edgar's on the case."

"Special Agent Gerald Feller." He flipped his credentials too quickly to be read, a gesture he meant to convey his lack of interest in anything the cop with the camera crew had to say. "What've we got here?"

"We've got what we got." Detective Mosby looked at the crime scene and then smiled smugly at Agent Feller like he was standing pat with three kings and a pair of aces. "What you got?"

"Jurisdiction."

"Well, you better get DC to recalibrate your GPS for you, J. Edgar, 'cause this vehicle is parked right here in Memphis." He pointed over to the gray compact as proof.

Special Agent Feller wasn't impressed. Or entertained. "Well, it was taken from the scene of a murder in California. And the suspected driver is connected to a second murder out there. He's also a suspect in the murder of a gas station attendant in New Mexico. And we believe he ignited a riot in New Orleans. So what we have here is a one-man crime spree. A crime spree across state lines. And that gives me jurisdiction."

"Gives you? Or the bureau?"

"As far as you're concerned, they're one and the same."

"Oh, is that right?"

The special agent and the detective continued the heated discussion without ever noticing the man who walked around the corner from the Stax Museum and blended into the crowd that had gathered along the sidewalk. Neither one paid attention to the man as he nervously watched what was unfolding in the lot.

Daniel suppressed his first impulse, which was to turn and walk (very quickly) away. As casually as he could, he sidled up to the gathering of gawkers and tried to mix right in. "What's goin' on?"

"Car must be stolen," a pear-shaped man in a University of Memphis hoodie guessed, never taking his eyes off the action in front of him.

"Shit, man, that ain't it," a young man in a fur-trimmed parka disagreed. "They got two suits over there," he said, pointing to a pudgy white guy in a trench coat and a tall black guy in a leather car coat. "They ain't rollin' out on a night like this for no stolen fuckin' Kia. If they here, you best better believe someone call in a one-eighty-seven."

"A what?" Daniel wondered aloud.

The kid in the parka turned to take a look, curious about someone in his neighborhood who didn't know the police code for: "Murder, man."

The explanation sounded more like an accusation to Daniel. "Murder?" he repeated nervously. "That's crazy."

With that, one of the other onlookers, a heavyset woman whose nurse's whites were showing from beneath her black London Fog overcoat, looked over at Daniel, focusing on him until she was confident enough to call out. "Ain't that *your* car?"

As if on cue, everyone turned, clearly considering this stranger's probable guilt.

"Me? That's not my car." For someone who'd spent his adult life in the music industry, his lie was surprisingly unconvincing.

"Yeah, it was you," the heavy nurse said with conviction. "I was just comin' home and saw you parking. Thought to myself, 'He shouldn't be parkin' there. Museum's closed.'"

Daniel tried to laugh the accusation off, but the little noise came out as more of a weak, pained shriek. "Heh."

It was as good as a confession.

"That's him," the nurse repeated, this time pointing a thick finger at him like it was a pistol. She turned and called out to the cops, "Hey! That's him! That's the guy!"

The detective and the FBI agent ignored her completely. But the volume of her voice was enough to make of some of the uniformed officers look up from the dull routine of securing and processing a crime-scene vehicle.

At first, all any of them noticed was the woman pointing excitedly. None of them was sure what she was doing and it took a moment before they realized she was trying to call their attention to a man at the edge of the crowd. By that time, however, all any of them could see was the back of the man as he ran from the scene as fast as he could.

There was confusion at first as the detective and the fed finally broke from their conference. One of the patrolmen filled them both in on what had just happened and they walked over to question the woman who claimed to have seen the driver of the impounded car. She pointed off in the direction he'd run down McLemore, but no one was quite sure where he'd gone.

"How far can he get on foot?" Agent Feller asked as Detective Mosby arranged for all responding units to perform a street-by-street sweep for their fugitive suspect. Suddenly, sirens screamed from all directions, howling in the night like hound dogs converging on a kill.

"Catching a fugitive is just a mathematical operation," Detective Mosby confidently told the patrolmen (and the cameramen). "We'll get a perimeter set up. Then we just tighten the noose. Block by block. Street by street. It's only a matter of time."

Agent Feller looked off into the distance like his ankles hurt and he was unconvinced by the detective. "You better hope so."

CHAPTER TWENTY-FIVE

Mile after mile went speeding past, but every one of them looked just like the last.

"My head is killing me," Rabidoso complained, rubbing his temple. "I woke up this morning feeling like I freebased a rock the size of your head."

Moog's recollections of the night just past were hazy too, but he didn't let on. Or acknowledge his partner's latest attempt to start a conversation.

"How long we gonna keep driving?" Rabidoso asked when he realized there would just be more silence if he didn't. "It's like being on a redneck safari."

The big man shot his unwanted partner a stern look. "We're gonna keep going from one jerkwater town to the next till we get a line on our man, 'cause without him—and without his money— he ain't the only sonbitch running for his goddamn life. Got it?"

Rabidoso's only response was to lean back in his seat and prop his Tony Lamas up on the dashboard.

"Get your goddamn feet down," Moog scolded.

The boots stayed defiantly where they were. "You my *mami*?"

"Get your goddamn feet down off my dash. I'm not going to tell you again."

"This ain't your car," Rabidoso protested.

"You see me over here behind the wheel of this vehicle?"

Rabidoso licked his right thumb, reached forward, and made a deliberately exaggerated motion to wipe away some small spot or smear from his prized boots. "Dude, just 'cause you drivin' don't make it yours." When he was done, he leaned back again and flashed Moog a satisfied grin.

The big man was no longer in a mood to debate what he regarded as the commonly accepted principles of ownership: "If you got it, it's yours."

Nor was he willing to back down from the demand he'd made. In a single motion, Moog's hand backslapped the *asesino a sueldo*'s offending footwear from the leather-covered dashboard of Daniel's BMW.

Before his boots hit the floor mats, the hot-tempered killer started reaching for the pistol tucked in his waistband. He was quick, but not quick enough. He hadn't even touched the Colt's grip before a tree trunk of an arm fell across his body and pinned him to the seat.

The BMW swerved right toward the shoulder and then left across the oncoming lane as Moog struggled to control it *and* his partner. Breaks squealed and tires smoked as the vehicle came to a sudden stop in the westbound lane of a Mississippi back road.

With his right arm burying Rabidoso in the hand-upholstered passenger seat, Moog curled his left hand into a shot put–sized fist and drew back the blow both men knew could settle their differences once and for all. With all of his fury focused like a laser on his target, the big man took a very deep breath and released it in slow, deliberate puffs while he considered his options. None of them were good.

"I could end this now, but I ain't gonna," he said after a while. "'Cause it ain't going to get me nothing but a dead Mexican and a blood-splattered ride. And I don't much feel like cleaning up either one of 'em today."

A series of musical tones sounded off in the big man's coat pocket and he flashed a quick, nervous look down at it before he returned his focus back to a man who, in his own way, was just as lethal as he was. "That's my phone."

Demonstrating he wasn't afraid was more important to Rabidoso than living. "Well, I'm not going to get it for you," he quipped.

The series of tones rang again.

Moog's voice was low and calm. "I need to answer. It could be Mr. P. and we don't need to piss him off more than he is." Slowly he released a little of the pressure his right arm was putting on Rabidoso's chest. "I'm going to let you up so I can get this."

The tones rang a third time.

The big man cautioned, "But I swear to God if you do anything—"

"Just answer your damn phone." Rabidoso pushed the oversized arm completely off him.

Moog nodded to confirm their understanding and then turned his full attention to the still-ringing phone. He answered with a "Yeah."

Rabidoso could hear the muffled murmur of a voice on the other end, but didn't recognize it. He was sure it wasn't Preezrakevich.

Moog listened for a while. "You sure?" He shook his head. "Shit."

More silence.

"All right, thanks a lot, Ruffy." Moog ended the call and gently tossed the cell phone up on the BMW's dash.

Without a word, the big man put the sedan into gear and pulled a tight U-turn. Rabidoso was too proud to give the big man the satisfaction of asking, so he rode quietly in feigned disinterest.

He made it only a mile or two before he had to ask, "What the hell was that?"

"Call from a friend of mine. Friend with connections." Moog didn't offer more.

Another mile passed.

"About what?"

"Erickson."

"And?"

"California has an APB out on him."

That didn't sound right. "An APB?"

Moog nodded. "Murder. Two counts."

"Who he kill?" Rabidoso's question almost sounded jealous.

"He didn't kill anyone," Moog snapped. "They think he killed that maid. And they think he killed his own damn son. Memphis PD found a car they say he stole from his wife's house."

Rabidoso considered these developments. And smiled. "That's good, right?"

"No, it's not good." Moog snorted his disgust. "It draws all sorts of attention to a situation Mr. P. wanted handled discreetly. It also means we're not the only ones looking for this cat now."

"Well, *that's* good, right?" Rabidoso thought the extra eyes should be a positive.

The big man shook his head. "No, that's not good either. Means we got competition now. Means we got to get him before the cops do. 'Cause if Erickson gets popped, he's gonna tell 'em everything. And if he does that, the next thing you know cops are gonna come looking for us."

"I ain't worried," Rabidoso assured him.

"Well, you should be," Moog countered. " 'Cause we get picked up, Mr. P. is sure as shit gonna start worryin'. He's gonna need to cut this shit off and he's gonna start with you and me."

"Still not worried," the little man bragged.

Moog was unconvinced. "What you're not is *smart*. What you're not is *professional*. And what you're *not* is helping me get our asses up out of this shit. So, would you just stop this crazy-ass, psycho shit you got going on."

"That's right, I'm crazy." Rabidoso announced it proudly like it was an achievement. And, for him, it was. He'd been born as a runt in a savage land. His mental state—or lack of one—was all that had allowed him to survive. And prosper.

Moog wasn't impressed. "And if Mr. P. says so, you can get as sick as you want on this dude once we get him. But we gotta get him first. Squeeze *that* into your deranged little mind." Moog tapped his own head for emphasis. "We gotta get this guy. Soon. Before anyone else does."

"I know." Rabidoso nodded like a schoolboy who's been reprimanded but still didn't understand the lesson. And resented the teacher for trying to teach it.

"You know *what*?" Moog asked incredulously. "We had him in New Orleans."

"I almost got him."

"What you got was a motherfucking riot started." Moog shook his head. "And just so you know, 'almost' doesn't put a gag in this guy's mouth and shove him in our motherfuckin' trunk. We can't go back to Mr. P. with 'almost' in the motherfucking trunk."

Rabidoso had nothing to say to that one.

"And the worst of it is that if the cops are looking for Erickson, they'll be looking for his car too. This car." Moog had come to enjoy the smooth-driving sedan. "We're going to have to find a place to clean and drop this."

He shook his head in frustration, unable to believe how such a simple assignment could have turned out so many layers of fucked up. His eyes burning with resentment, he straightened his tie and looked over at his partner. "If I knew I was going to have to clean the goddamn car anyway..."

CHAPTER TWENTY-SIX

Daniel tucked the envelope in his jacket and ran down McLemore Avenue as fast as he could. He wasn't sure where he was going, but he ran blindly until his legs felt like they were about to give out beneath him and his lungs burned like he'd breathed in fire— about two and a half blocks.

There was no use in running. He wasn't twenty any longer, and even for a man in his forties he wasn't exactly a picture of aerobic conditioning. But it was more than just that. Even an Olympic marathoner wouldn't be able to elude the dragnet that was being thrown up around him.

If he was going to make it through the night, he had to get off the streets. And soon. He crossed over McLemore, half limping and half loping, and moved toward whatever temporary sanctuary he could find in the surrounding residential neighborhood. He followed a tree-lined meridian running down the middle of Fountain Court, moving quickly and quietly under the cover of its barren canopy until he came to the end of the street.

Sirens sounded in the near distance. He looked over his shoulder and saw a squad car shoot down McLemore, its red lights flashing and its sirens wailing. He watched it race past and realized it was only a matter of time before he'd be riding in the back.

In front of him was a large white house—much larger than the others in the neighborhood—with a detached garage behind it. Daniel didn't want to take a chance with any of the residents and so it was the garage that interested him most. If he could sneak inside, he could weather the night in relative safety and then head out in the morning once the dragnet had been quit.

The blinds were drawn on all of the windows in the big house, but the light that escaped at their edges suggested someone was at home. Daniel crept through the yard as quietly as he could. It would be darkly ironic to have survived the pair of professional killers and then be shot dead as a burglar by some disgruntled Memphis homeowner.

He tiptoed past the house, satisfied no one inside had seen him or detected his presence on the property. It was an old garage with a wooden door that rolled up on two tracks. Using a discarded fence post he found in the yard, Daniel was able to lift the door just enough for him to squeeze under. Almost.

As he wiggled through the opening, the fence post slipped free and the weight of the door came down on his chest. Daniel wanted to cry out in pain, but his breath had left him. When the air finally returned to his lungs, he allowed himself just one low moan, afraid anything more would alert the homeowner. He tried to move the door off him, but couldn't get a grip—and probably couldn't have moved something so heavy anyway. He was trapped like a turtle on its back.

The February night was cold, but the ground was colder. It was like being pinned to a glacier. He tried his best to stay warm, but his efforts were futile and after a while, he began to shiver. He knew he'd never survive the night on the ground. If it hadn't already begun to set in, hypothermia was certain to take him in a matter of hours.

He wondered how long that might be. Time passed, but he was too disoriented to estimate the rate of its flow. He wondered how long he'd been trapped. And how long he had left to live.

With the weight of the garage door full on his chest, each breath became more difficult than the last. He fought against the pain, struggling not to slip under the surface of its dark contours, but eventually it all became too much for him. The cold and the pain, the labored breaths, and the four days on the road. It all lead to exhaustion. Exhaustion gave way to sleepiness, which faded to black.

He couldn't be sure if he was asleep and dreaming or awake and suffering from shock, but he knew the darkness he was drowning in was deeper than any he'd ever known before. It was all around him, and still he felt like he was falling, deeper and deeper. Plummeting into nothingness.

And then there was light. A puncture in the blackness. A single beam that pierced the darkness right above him. A light. *The* light?

"Hey!" A voice called out in the darkness. A woman's voice. An angel's voice? "What the hell you doin' in my goddamn garage?" Probably not an angel.

If Daniel squinted against the glare, he could make out a figure, but nothing more than shadows. "I could shoot your goddamned ass right here and now," she informed him. "And there's not a motherfuckin' soul who'd say I done wrong."

Daniel couldn't see a gun, but the mention of one made him try again to lift the door that pinned him to the ground.

"I admire your effort, sugar, but I think if you coulda moved that door, you wouldn't be stuck there now." She seemed only amused by his efforts.

He stopped struggling.

"Now the question is," she continued, "What do I do witchu now I gotcha?"

"Please." It was hard to talk with the door on his chest. "Just let me go and I'll get out of here and—"

"Break into one of my neighbors' places?" she scoffed.

"No. I swear to God—"

"Sugar, you trapped on your ass breakin' into my garage. That ain't no position to be callin' on the Almighty for anythin'."

Another squad car raced up McLemore and Daniel jerked with the instinctive reflexes of a fox at the sound of a hound.

For a split second, the flashlight beam was diverted down Fountain Court and then returned to Daniel. "Oh, *that's* what it is," the woman said knowingly. "All that noise and commotion for you?"

There was no sense in lying anymore. "Please."

A motor inside the garage groaned as the door came up off Daniel's chest. Releasing the pressure made him cough violently. He rolled onto his side and the first deep breath he took made him cough until his ribs hurt.

"Come on," the woman said hurriedly. "We best get you inside before they take a turn down this way and see you there."

The offer took Daniel by surprise. "What?"

"Inside. We best get you inside."

Daniel tried to get to his feet, grateful but still unsure what was happening. "I don't understand."

"Whatever you got to say to me you can say inside." A hand gripped him under his arm and helped him up. "But if the po-po catch you, it won't matter what you say to no one." She held him by the arm and led him inside the big house. "Folks call me Ma Horton."

The woman let him in through the back door and then closed it behind them. A ceiling light in her kitchen gave Daniel a first look at his hostess and savior. She was tall and round and something about her size suggested a boundless love of life. Her chestnut eyes twinkled with mischief but unmistakably had seen their share of sorrows and shed an ocean of tears.

"Daniel Erickson." It had been so long since he'd heard his name aloud that he wondered for a second if he hadn't gotten it wrong. He wasn't sure it suited him any longer.

"Well, welcome, Daniel Erickson." She offered him a seat at her kitchen table and, without asking, began making him a plate from the pots and pans on her stove. Ham with a sour cherry glaze. Fried green beans with bacon and onions. Mac and cheese with a crunchy crust of browned bread crumbs on the top.

"Now what the Memphis Police want with someone like you?" she asked, sliding the plate in front of him and pairing it with a can of Coca-Cola she'd retrieved from the fridge.

"It's a long story," he dodged and then filled his mouth with ham.

"Ain't they all." She laughed as she took a seat across from him. She didn't press him further for answers she knew weren't coming, but seemed content to look him up and down like she was making up her own mind about what sort of trouble he'd gotten himself into.

He hadn't felt hungry. If she'd offered the food instead of putting it there in front of him, he certainly would have declined. But Daniel hadn't eaten since breakfast at the Camellia Grill and it took only a mouthful of the heavenly concoctions to convince him he was ravenous. He wolfed down mouthful after mouthful, pausing only to ask her, "Why'd you save me?" Another mouthful and then, "Aren't you worried I may be guilty of something that deserves all that attention out there?"

"Let's just say I'm a good judge of character." She chuckled at what she clearly thought was a major understatement. "And, sugar, I can tell you ain't guilty of nothin' but bein' a fool."

He couldn't disagree, so he didn't. "So why help me?"

"'Cause that's what I do." Her smile grew. "I help the foolish."

When his plate was cleaner than when she'd first dished it up, she took it from him and put it in the sink. "Come on, let me introduce you to my little pride and joys."

She led him through a swinging door into a living room that was completely overwhelmed by a jumbo flat-screen TV. There were six young women—the youngest maybe sixteen, the oldest no more than twenty—circled around it; some lay on the floor, some were draped over couches or slouched in chairs. They were all fixated on their program, but when Ma called out, "Girls!" they all obediently turned their heads.

"This is Mr. Erickson." The girls all waved halfheartedly, completely uninterested in the middle-aged guy who nodded awkwardly at his introduction.

Ma lit up like a marquee up on Beale Street as she singled out each girl, starting with the oldest, a pretty redhead: "This is Rose." The Latina she called "Elsa." She pointed toward the twins with hair as wild as the night wind without making clear which one was "Keisha" and which was "Raven." The blonde whose attention almost immediately returned to the television was "Morgan." And the petite Asian curled in a chair was "Amy."

Ma turned back to Daniel with her hands up in one final display, as if she'd just announced the greatest show on earth. "These are my girls."

Daniel nodded as warmly as he could. "Nice to meet you."

None of them seemed to feel the same way. Or care. Without another word, their attention returned to their program, ignoring him like he was just a ghost that had drifted in with the night.

"Ain't they all beautiful," Ma beamed, shaking her head like even she couldn't quite believe it.

And it was true. Every one of them was attractive in her distinct way.

"An' every one of them is just as talented as she can be."

And then the pieces all came together: Big Ma. Big white house. Six beautiful teenaged girls. Talented. The realization was like a softball hitting the bull's-eye on a dunk tank that dropped Daniel into five hundred gallons of ickiness. "Ooooooooooooh," Daniel said in a long, pained attempt to gain some time to formulate a response.

" 'Ooooooh,' what?" Ma asked, her question edged with a suspicion that she already knew.

"Nothing," Daniel tried to cover quickly.

"No, what?" she dared him.

"Nothing. It's just that..." He didn't want to seem ungrateful for the hospitality. "You've really done enough for me already."

"And I ain't gonna do no more," she assured him, shaking her head with disappointment.

"I appreciate everything," Daniel hemmed and hawed. "But the supper was enough," he caught himself. "Just getting out of your garage was enough." He laughed weakly. "I just don't need any...*talents*...right now." He wanted to make clear, "It's not that they're not all beautiful. They are. It's just that's not really my *thing*. And, besides, I don't have any money."

Ma Horton looked like she was considering sending him straight back to New Orleans—with the flat of her hand. "When I said I could see you was guilty of stupid, I didn't realize your own case o' stupid was a goddamn capital crime."

The look in her eyes made him wish he was back under the garage door.

"Get your skinny, cracker ass back in there," she ordered, pointing the way back to the kitchen. He stepped through the swinging door and once he was there, she told him, "Sit your motherfuckin' ass down."

"I didn't mean anything," he started, but it was weak even for him.

"You men never mean nuthin'," she shot right back. "I know what you was thinkin' 'bout my girls. My *girrrrrrrrls!*" She drew the word out to stress her point.

"No, really," he protested, but it was like trying to calm a momma grizzly while holding her cub.

"Oh, I know what was goin' on in your evil mind." She was all kinds of crazy angry. "Man sees a woman taking care of some young girls and the first thing he thinks is she runnin' a goddamn whorehouse. That's what you was thinkin'!" She dared him to deny it.

"I didn' mean—"

"Let me tell you somethin', Mr. Daniel-I-got-myself-stuck-under-a-goddamn-garage-door-with-the-police-huntin'-my-dumb-ass-Erickson." Her right index finger was just an inch away from his nose. "I pulled every one of those girls out of a home you wouldn't raise a dog in. A home someone like you wouldn't last a goddamn day in. And every one of those girls is just as good as gold. And they don't need the likes of you makin' assumptions 'bout them 'cause of your own lack of character and twisted pre-versions."

"I'm sorry." She was right. There was no excuse, but he wanted to offer her one anyway. "It's just, I'm in kind of a situation."

"What kind of situation?"

"Someone took some money from me." That was the easy part to explain. "And to get it back, they've forced me to follow this trail of musical clues from the blues—"

"The blues?" she snorted. "I shoulda known." She folded her arms across her chest and sat down, her head turned to the side like she was refusing to go where he was leading her.

Her display of contempt surprised him. "You don't like the blues?"

"The blues? The blues ain't nuthin' but a bunch of men sittin' round feelin' sorry for themselves 'cause they think they been put down," she scoffed bitterly. "But then how they go about treatin' us ladies at the end of the day, huh? Their lives are hard, but we only good for two things. And neither one of 'em making music."

She was at the throttle of an angry train and even Daniel knew better than to step in front of it. "Bessie Smith was the best-selling recording artist of her time, but you ever hear name as the greatest blues singer?" She didn't give him time to answer, but he shook his head anyway. "Shit, it's all Robert Johnson this and Muddy Waters that, but they ever give credit to Ma Rainey for what she done? Big Mama Thornton?"

He shook his head again but was smart enough to stay silent.

"You think it was a hard life bein' a bluesman? And just how goddamn hard you think it was doin' it as a woman?" She'd made her point and she knew it.

She sighed heavily and it was like all her fury had suddenly left her with nothing but weariness. "So you do yourself a favor, Mr. Erickson. Next time a woman treats you decent, why don't you consider maybe she's got more to offer you than what she can put on a plate in front of you at the table or what she give up to you in her bed."

"I'm sorry." He was, but she wasn't having any of it.

"Sorry? Well, you can take your sorry and your nasty-thought-thinking ass outta my house and sleep in the goddamn garage till morning." Her voice was even colder than he knew his makeshift bunk would be. " 'Cause there's no way in hell I'd let you under the same roof as my angel-girls."

He understood. And was ashamed. "Thank you."

She shook her head one last time. "*Now* who gots the motherfuckin' blues?"

CHAPTER
TWENTY-SEVEN

Memphis had warmed with the morning sun, but Ma Horton's disposition hadn't thawed at all. She came to the garage with cold biscuits and burnt bacon wrapped in brown paper and asked Daniel where he was headed. When he answered, "Nashville," she offered him a ride to the Greyhound but nothing else.

Though she was clearly hoping he'd refuse her kind offer, he wasn't in any position to let go of a helping hand. He took the silent ride downtown and left her with a "Thank you." And another apology.

She left him on the curb and drove away without accepting either one.

Down the street from the bus station was a pawn shop. He couldn't bear the idea of parting with his Panerai watch and so he tried to convince the clerk with the toupee that the silver ring he was offering had been given to him by Stevie Nicks and was worth at least ten grand in sentimental value alone. He got a lecture on the nature of commerce and two hundred bucks in cash.

Daniel walked back down the block, bought his ticket, and climbed on board a Motor Coach D40 bound for Nashville.

Halfway down the aisle, a young woman was sitting alone. She was attractive in a Southern beauty pageant contestant sort of way: pretty enough to have contended for Miss Jackson County or Miss Kudzu, although she probably couldn't have walked away with the crown.

"Excuse me." Daniel gestured at the empty seat beside her.

Her low-cut sweater was a size too small and showed off her ample bosom and sizable muffin-top. Daniel made a point of averting his eyes from both as she looked up and asked innocently, "Uh-huh?"

"Do you mind if I sit here?"

She looked down at the items she'd set on the empty seat: her purse, the latest issue of *US*, and the letterman's jacket of some hometown boy whose heart she'd just broken—or was about to.

She didn't say anything at all for a moment, hoping her silence would communicate the "You ain't sittin' here, asshole!" she was thinking, but which her mama had raised her to not say out loud. When her prolonged silence didn't work, she moved her stuff and gave him a halfhearted "Sure," every bit as forced as the smile that accompanied it.

He took the seat. "Thanks."

"No problem."

She'd assumed the creep had been looking for a two-hundred-mile opportunity to hit on her, but Daniel had absolutely no interest in joining the "welcoming committee" he was sure would find her once she got to Nashville. He hadn't chosen her as a seatmate based on her appearance, but because she had the one thing he needed: a portable CD player, something of a rarity in the digital age.

"I haven't seen one of those in a while," he commented casually, pointing to the school-bus-yellow Sony Discman, so retro it looked almost futuristic.

She offered an embarrassed smile. "I'm saving up for an iPod," she assured him.

"No. I think those are great."

"I use it for my music," she volunteered enthusiastically. The Southern twang in her voice was as deep as tire tracks in a dirt road after a rainstorm. "My backing tracks and all."

"You're a vocalist?" he asked.

The folks back home—none of whom had ever understood her talent, especially Tommy Ray—always called her a singer, but she liked what the stranger said better. "Mm-hmm." It wasn't the sort of thing she would've expected to hear from a rumpled bus-rider, but his easy use of the term intrigued her.

"I heard you singing along there." Daniel pointed back to the device he needed. "You've got a very strong vocal instrument," he told her—not exactly a lie—but a compliment motivated solely by need.

Vocal instrument? She blushed and revealed a smile that could've won her Miss Jackson County. First Runner-Up, at least. "Ya think so?"

"Yeah, I do." Necessity made him more emphatic. "Really strong."

"Gosh." A deeper blush, a wider smile. "Y'all in the Business?"

Under different circumstances he might have had pity for a girl who said things like "gosh" and "the Business," but he needed her Walkman. "Yes. Yes, I am."

"Oh, wow!"

"Daniel—" he announced, before realizing he was a wanted man. "Danielson. Eric Danielson."

If she found something amiss with his fumbled introduction, it didn't stop her from taking his offered hand. "Honey Amber Wills."

"It's a pleasure."

She was excited by the opportunity that had taken a seat beside her, but she'd heard stories. "Y'all *reeeeeally* in the business?"

"Really. In fact, I tell you what." She was ready and waiting. "I just got this new CD." He took the envelope out of his jacket and showed her the Nashville postmark. She was suitably impressed. "It's a demo from a band I've been working with."

"Really?"

"Really." It was close enough to the truth.

"What band?"

"Dockery Plantation," he said without a quarter note of hesitation.

"Never heard of 'em."

"You will," he assured her. "And if I could just borrow your disc player—"

Her face fell just a bit.

"Just for a moment," he assured her. "I think this track might be stronger as a duet." She was interested again. "And I think, maybe, just maybe, your voice might work perfectly."

She was very interested. "Really?"

"Really." He flashed a deal-sealing smile.

"Well, sure." She handed him the unit. "Here."

It took him a moment to remember how a Discman worked, but when he pressed play and slid on the headphones, he heard a drummer counting time. It was a familiar beat, but it wasn't the blues. A steel guitar whined out a classic (or clichéd) country intro as the drummer kept time with brushes on some toms and a snare. Someone started plucking an upright bass and an acoustic guitar began to strum a countrified version of a classic twelve-bar blues.

And then the now-familiar voice sang out.

Well, they break my heart
You steal my soul
They take what they can
You've taken control
They want what I got
You won't give me release
But in between
The two of you
I've found six feet of peace

Six feet of peace
Is all that I know
Where the summer rain falls
And the winter winds blow
Where the only stars shine
High up in the sky
Six feet of peace
Is all I'll know
Till I die

The young woman looked expectantly at Daniel, eager for his opinion of what she couldn't help thinking might be her big break. He gave her a thumbs-up but didn't say anything for fear of missing something in the track.

Trying to pay off
All the debts that I owed
Hiram and Luke, they
Went out on the road
In a Cadillac rag-top

With a pain that wouldn't cease
Drifting like cowboys
They found
Six feet of peace

He'd always thought of blues and country as musical antitheses. Listening to the haunting track made him realize for the first time that they were more like kissing cousins from different sides of the same holler. It was the same basic E-A-B chord change and lyric progressions. Certainly they both conveyed a similar sentiment. They were just a different way of voicing the same song.

Six feet of peace is all that I know
Where the summer rain falls
And the winter winds blow
Where the only stars shine
High up in the sky
Six feet of peace
Is all I'll know
Till I die

Danny, you lost your love

He hated how the songs each called him out by name. Particularly how they all called him "Danny." No one had called him that since his dad, wanting to make him feel small, and as soon as he left home, he'd always been Daniel.

Now your money's gone too
But they saved your life from
What you wanted to do

You get a new start
You get a new lease
If from your head to your toes
You find six feet of peace

Six feet of peace
What you need to find
Lose the pain in your heart
Quiet the war
In your mind
Six feet of peace
It's yours to give
Six feet of peace
Every day that you live

The band played the tune as the singer hummed his way through another chorus. And then with the strum of an acoustic guitar the song came to an end.

Like the other two, there was nothing on the disc besides that one song. He listened to it again. And then a third time.

His seatmate stared at him intensely, trying to read his every reaction to a song she couldn't hear. When he finally slipped the yellow headphones off, she asked, "So whacha y'all think?"

It took him a minute to place her question in the context of his half lie. "Oh, right." The ongoing mystery left him tired, too tired to continue the game he'd begun with her. "Here. Take a listen," he handed her back her Discman. What could it hurt?

With a youthful exuberance usually reserved for Christmas mornings and trips to Disneyland, she put on the headphones. "This is sooooo great," she told him as she adjusted the ear buds. "Last week I lost my job at Shear Insanity. It's a beauty salon in

Beaumont," she filled in for him. "I left the foil on Miss Beulah a little too long—like anyone would really believe that cranky old bitch wasn't as gray as a porch cat on a foggy morning—so I just took it as a sign from Jesus I should take up my music." She looked at him expectantly.

He did not disappoint. "I think that's probably right."

She pressed play and the song came up. And then the music he'd just heard clearly came back as sonic fuzz, overflowing from her cheap headphones. She smiled at him, a broad, way-too-big-for-her-face smile.

"I liked it," she said when the song was done. "But I don't understand what it's about," she confessed.

He just let out a little puff of a laugh. "Join the club."

"Is it about an alien or something?"

"An alien?"

"Yeah," she responded defensively. "What else has six feet apiece?"

He laughed to himself but patted her hand so she wouldn't think it was mean-spirited. "You're going to do fine in Nashville."

She flashed him her pageant smile. "I know so too."

CHAPTER TWENTY-EIGHT

Nashville is a capital city.

Just *what* it's the capital of depends entirely on your interests.

If you have a legal focus, Nashville is the capital of the state of Tennessee. Its capitol—a striking example of Greek Revival architecture—is just off Charlotte Avenue, majestically perched at the top of a hill overlooking the city.

If your interests are more pious than a politician's or a lawyer's—and how could they not be?—Nashville is also known as the Protestant Vatican City. Its St. Peter's Basilica is the Southern Baptist Convention, a squat, modern structure of red brick and tinted glass located—perhaps ironically—on Commerce Street.

If your interests are neither legal nor religious, then the Nashville you are looking for is the capital of country music. And in that case, her capitol is a lilac-painted saloon on Broadway, just down from Fifth. Tootsie's Orchid Lounge is where country music happened, happens, and will continue to happen until folks get tired of songs about falling in love, broken hearts, and raising hell.

Daniel walked through Tootsie's purple door late on a Wednesday afternoon, but there was already—or still—a healthy crowd at the bar. On a small stage set up by the front window, a young woman who looked like she might have aced poor Honey Amber Wills out of that Miss Jackson County crown was trying her best with "Don't Ever Leave Me Again." It wasn't close to the original, but if Patsy's spirit was present, she was pleased.

Not wanting to interrupt her show, Daniel walked quickly past and headed straight for the bar. Before he could make it to a stool, however, the man tending the bar held up a calloused, been-broken-but-not-set-right ham of a hand to stop him. "Whoa! Hold it up there, Chief!"

The bartender wasn't muscular in an over-developed, Ah-nold sort of way. He seemed more suited for lifting hay bales than iron, but he was solid from head to toe with roughly hewn features like he'd been carved from wood by some hill-country craftsman.

Daniel stopped in his tracks.

"This here is a cash-fueled establishment." The bartender put a country-sausage-size finger on the bar to emphasize his point. "The shelter is up on Eighth." The finger pointed the way.

Daniel was taken aback by such a hostile reception, but only until he caught a glimpse of the tattered, soiled, disheveled char-acter reflected in the back bar mirror. He hardly recognized him-self. But he understood the reaction he'd received.

"Oh, no. I have money." He dug into his pockets and pulled out a crumpled twenty. "Will this do?" he asked, placing the bill on the bar and smoothing it out.

"If the ink on that bill don't smear, it'll do just fine." A smile replaced the bartender's stern scowl. "I'm sorry, mister. It's just that we get more than our share of bums drifting in here thinking they're going to drink for a song."

"Don't worry about it." Daniel wiped away the concern with a sweeping gesture of his hand. He looked himself over and admitted, "It's been a rough couple of days, but I can pay for my drinks."

"Well, then, you've come to the right place," the bartender smiled confidently. "I specialize in treating 'a rough couple of days.' What can I get you?"

What Daniel needed didn't come in a bottle, but he had to start somewhere. His eyes drifted across the bottles lined up with military precision across the back bar, the decades of memorabilia that had gathered on the walls and the glaring neon illuminating the windows. A distant memory of his father came close to him and touched him on the shoulder. "Bottle of Pabst."

"Old school." The bartender put an amber bottle down and took the twenty.

"That's all for you," Daniel offered. "If you can help me answer a few questions."

The bartender looked down at the familiar portrait of Tennessee's favorite son and then back up at Daniel. "Ol' Hickory won't buy you much more than my favorite color or the name of the girl who popped my cherry, but you can go on and ask."

"The name Hiram mean anything to you? Or Luke? Luke the Drifter?" Out of his filthy shirt pocket, Daniel pulled a piece of paper on which he'd written the lyrics to "Six Feet of Peace." He smoothed it out just like he'd done to the twenty and pushed it across to the bartender. "Any of that make sense to you?"

The barkeep picked up the paper, gave it a glance, and then handed it right back. "I told you. I'm in the business of selling drinks, not buying songs."

"I'm not selling anything," Daniel assured him.

The bartender rubbed the bald dome of his head. "And I don't need no lawyer coming in here six months from now dropping paper on me because you claim you wrote whatever's at the top of the charts and I'm the guy who you say must've passed it along to Tim or Keith or whoever."

"It's not like that. It's not even a real song. It's just a clue." Daniel struggled to explain. "It's like a scavenger hunt—"

"Oooooh!" the bartender exclaimed, pointing at Daniel's filthy clothes as if they were the explanation to everything. "I couldn't figure out why a guy in a suit like that looks like he's spent a week digging crooked furrows behind a one-mule turn plow."

"Sure." Daniel didn't understand or care what that meant, he just wanted to know: "Does this makes any sense to you?" He pushed the lyrics back across the bar.

The bartender picked them up, mumbling to himself and brushing his bushy, brown mustache as he read them over.

"I don't understand the first verse," he admitted. "Could be about anything, really. I'd say the songwriter should work on narrowing the scope—"

"It's not a real song," Daniel reminded him.

"Right, right." He turned his attention back to the paper. "And I don't understand this last verse neither."

"That's OK," Daniel said. "I got that one. I'm Danny. So I get—"

"You're Danny?"

"Yes."

"Mmm-hum," the bartender mumbled some more, as if that admission cleared up additional questions he'd had. "But this second verse I understand. I'm pretty sure." And then with an outstretched index finger, he pointed past Daniel and announced. "The man you're looking for is right there."

Daniel wheeled around on his stool, momentarily off guard, but ready to confront his tormentor.

There was no one there.

"Who?" Daniel asked, visibly disappointed and confused.

"Him," the bartender repeated, leaving the "Right there, ya goddamn fool!" unspoken but easily inferred from his tone.

Looking past where he'd expected to find a flesh-and-blood culprit standing, Daniel followed the bartender's pointing finger to a framed photograph on the bar's Wall of Fame.

"Kid Rock?" Daniel asked incredulously.

"Not him. *Him.*" And this time the bartender pointed emphatically at one particular portrait. "Hank. Your song's about Hank Williams." There was more than a note of triumph in his voice.

It was not enough to convince Daniel. "You sure?"

"Lookee here." The bartender's crooked finger traced along the lines.

Trying to pay off
All the debts that I owed
Hiram and Luke, they
Went out on the road

"The world may know him and love him as Hank Williams, but his God-given name was Hiram."

"Really?" Daniel chuckled out loud. "Can you imagine if country music's greatest artist was named Hiram?"

The barkeep failed to find the humor. His dead-eyed glare wordlessly communicated that in Nashville there are figures who are too revered to be the subjects of jokes: Jesus. A man's mother. Whoever is coaching the Vols (as long as they're winning). And Hank Williams.

And on that note, the bartender returned to his lyrical analysis, not out of some notion of Southern hospitality or because he felt a moral duty to earn the twenty he'd already pocketed, but simply because he'd become engaged in the exercise.

"Luke." He pointed to the name on the paper. "Is Luke the Drifter."

"Who's he?"

"He's Hank," the barkeeper answered like he shouldn't have had to. "History has him painted as a drunkard and hophead and carouser, but that wasn't Hank. At least it wasn't all of him. Everybody thinks he was one thing, but he was something completely different."

"Aren't we all?" If it came off as flippant, Daniel hadn't meant it that way. He shook his head with a certain resignation. "They tell you not to judge a book by its cover, but that's exactly how they sell them."

An awkward moment of silence passed and then the bartender gratefully returned to the lyrics. "He was a very spiritual person, but they wouldn't let him record gospel music under his name because they thought it would take away from the Hank Williams image. So he recorded it anyway, but under the name Luke the Drifter." He shook his head with regret.

"And this," the bartender traced the line with his finger.

In a Cadillac rag-top
With a pain that wouldn't cease
Drifting like cowboys
They found
Six feet of peace

"The Cadillac convertible was the car Hank passed away in." Ol' Hank had passed long before the bartender had been born, but there was still a note of personal loss in his voice. "They're not

234

even sure where it happened, just somewhere in the darkness, on his way to the next show. Now, *that's* a musician's death." His voice was a fitting mixture of solemnity and admiration.

"This last bit," he continued. "When Hank could keep a backup band together, he called them the Drifting Cowboys."

Daniel nodded appreciatively. He still didn't, however, have a location for the next clue. "And the 'Six Feet of Peace'?"

The bartender shook his head, the blank look on his face a silent admission he was stumped on that one too. "The closest I can come up with is maybe his grave."

Daniel suddenly regretted spending the twenty on something that now seemed so obvious. "Of course, that has to be it," he concurred, relieved to have finally cracked the riddle. "The next one has to be at his grave."

"The next what?"

Daniel didn't want to get into it. "You don't happen to know where Hank's buried, do you?"

" 'Course I do," the bartender snapped, offended by the suggestion he might not know the location of Hank's final resting place.

Daniel slid off his stool, ready to get started. "How do I get there?"

"You want to take Sixty-Five all the way down cross the 'Bama border," the bartender started.

A confused and panicked look passed over Daniel's face. "He's not in Nashville?"

"No, sir. They put him in the ground down in Montgomery, Alabama."

"Montgomery?" Daniel had to hold on to the bar to keep from falling over. "Alabama?" His head spun like he'd just spent the last twenty minutes drinking malt liquor on a carnival Tilt-A-Whirl. "Montgomery?"

It had been an understandable mistake to assume the Nashville postmark meant he was to go there himself—understandable, but still a mistake. He hoped not a fatal one.

If he'd only stayed in Memphis and taken the time to decode the song instead of jumping to conclusions, he might have realized the lyrics' clues were pointing him in an entirely different direction. Now he was three hundred miles north of where he needed to be. And time was running out.

"You know, a lot of people are quick to write off ol' Hank as just another musician who killed himself with the booze and drugs," the bartender offered. "But it wasn't like that at all. He had a spinal condition; the bones in his back didn't form right. Man, the pain he musta suffered his whole life—" He stopped and looked back down at the lyric sheet. "I guess that's the 'pain that wouldn't cease' part right there."

Daniel was in an agony of his own and couldn't muster more than a weak nod of acknowledgment for the little bit of medical trivia.

"They say back before this place was Tootsie's, Hank used to step out between shows at the Grand Ol' Opry. He'd duck out the back door of the Ryman and cut across the alley out there, come right in the back door for a couple drinks here. Most people write it off as he just had the thirst, but the poor sonofabitch was just trying to get a little relief from the goddamn pain." He shook his head. "Why you think people always gotta make other folks look their worst?"

Daniel wondered that himself. "Human nature, I guess."

The bartender shook his head. "It ain't right. Ol' Hank was just a man in pain looking for a little relief, you know? Just looking for a little—"

"Peace?" Daniel wondered aloud.

"I suppose."

"That alley you said Hank used to cross to get here." Daniel tried to contain his excitement. "How wide is it?"

"I don't know." The bartender's face screwed with confusion. "Twenty feet. Maybe a little less."

"Or if you were taking a little artistic license," Daniel hedged, "about six feet?"

"I think it's wider than that—"

"Maybe." Daniel didn't feel constrained by strict linear measurements. "But if you were writing a song, you might compare the distance he had to travel to the depth of a grave." He pointed to the first verse.

Well, they break my heart
You steal my soul
They take what they can,
You've taken control
They want what I got
You won't give me release
But in between
The two of you
I've found six feet of peace

"Don't you get it?" Daniel's voice lifted. "It's about Hank being torn between his audiences over at the Ryman and his problem with the bottle right here." He pointed at the stool next to him. "And the six feet of peace—"

"I don't get it," the bartender confessed.

"It's the alleyway. When he steps away from the Grand Ol' Opry or pulls himself away from the bar. The only place he finds any peace is the place in between the two."

The bartender brightened a little. "I get what you're gettin' at. You think—"

Daniel did. "Where is it?"

"What?"

"The back door." Daniel shot to his feet, reenergized by his revelation.

"It's right there," the bartender pointed to the magical portal. "But you can't—"

"Sure I can," Daniel told him confidently. "And I'm not even going to offer you another twenty, because I know you want to see what's out there even more than I do."

"Do not," the bartender told him plainly, crossing his arms across his broad chest to demonstrate his resolve.

Daniel just smiled. And waited.

The bartender stood his ground.

Until he couldn't stand it any longer. "Oh, goddamn it, come on," he grumbled as he made his way around the bar and led Daniel back to country music's most famous door.

CHAPTER TWENTY-NINE

The problem with legends—whether they're people, places, or things—is that they're almost always disappointing when encountered in real life.

Despite its place in country-western mythology as a sort of Valhalla's Gate, Tootsie's back door was just a door—and not much of one at that. It was old and creaky and when the bartender opened it, it didn't lead anywhere except out to a narrow alleyway that ran between Tootsie's back wall and the west side of the Ryman Auditorium.

Of course, every once in a while there's a chance encounter with the stuff of legends—and the result is pure magic.

Daniel stepped out into the completely unremarkable alley. The bartender followed. Though neither man would ever have admitted it aloud—at least not sober—both felt Hank's presence between them. Without a word exchanged, they both closed their eyes and instantly felt the unrelenting agony of Hank's twisted spine as if it was their own. Each man took a labored breath as he pondered the staggering career pressures that must have overwhelmed a country boy from Mount Olive, Alabama, who'd only ever wanted to play guitar and sing.

Silently, they each imagined what the night air must have felt like to a man who found himself trapped between the suffocating crowds that filled the Ryman every Saturday and the smoke-choked barroom where he could feel himself slipping away one drink at a time. Moving between the two must have felt like freedom. That small, precious space must have been six feet of peace.

When he finally opened his eyes, Daniel found he was looking at the back wall of Tootsie's. Almost the entire surface was covered with fliers announcing all sorts of concerts and shows and CD-release parties. They were all sizes and colors, but the one that caught his eye most was a bright green one that read:

DOCKERY PLANTATION
TAKE THE MONEY AND RUN TOUR
A Million Reasons to Follow This Band

Daniel approached the poster cautiously, certain it was his clue, but afraid of what he might find. He peeled it from the brick wall and discovered a CD affixed to its underside.

"This," Daniel announced victoriously, "is what we were after."

Still drifting through the mists of time with Hank, the barkeep grumbled at the intrusion. "What?"

"This," Daniel repeated, holding the CD. "This is what I was supposed to find."

It's hard to be disappointed without having had expectations, but the bartender was dissatisfied just the same. "That? What the hell is that?"

Daniel smiled slyly. "Let's go inside and find out."

"It's going to cost you."

"No, it's not." Daniel's smile widened.

The bartender was adamant this time. It was a matter of principle. "If you want to hear that…" He considered his price. "Fifty."

"Not a cent."

The bartender growled. "All right, twenty."

Daniel didn't make any response except that same goddamn smile.

The bartender kept telling himself it didn't matter what was on the CD. It was nothing to him one way or another. Not really. And yet no matter how hard he tried to convince himself otherwise, he couldn't deny that he really wanted to know whatever secret was on the mysterious CD. "All right," he conceded at last. "But you're buying me a goddamn drink."

Daniel's shit-eating grin broadened even wider. "You can have my Pabst."

There were any number of things the bartender wanted to say, but what he settled on was, "Come on."

Back inside Tootsie's barroom, last year's Miss Jackson County had finished her set and the place had settled into silence. A rarity for the place.

"Give it here." The bartender took the disc from Daniel and slipped it into the stereo system behind the bar.

A second later, all the speakers in the joint popped. An electric guitar—six strings of raw, unfiltered nastiness—kicked open the door and a heavy, rolling bass with a siren-wailing harmonica rushed into the room right behind it. The drummer beat his kit like he was mugging it. The tune was classic blues at its heart, but electrified and amplified to give it a bolder, more defiant edge that no mortal hands could have ever wrung from an acoustic guitar.

Immediately, Daniel knew where he was headed next.

"Aw yeaaah," the vocalist screamed and the whole musical concoction started to brew just a little bit hotter.

"We're calling you out!" the lead singer screamed again before the whole band launched into a full-frontal assault.

You got your fancy mansion, maybe three or four
Got a limo and a jet and a bleach blonde Hollywood whore
You got stock and bonds and treasuries
And all that kind of shit
From where I stand
You and your band
Don't deserve none of it
'Cause what you do
Has all been done before and put to bed
And you wouldn't stand a ghost of a chance
Cuttin' heads
With the living dead

"Who is this?" the bartender asked above a raucous blues free-for-all between a mic'ed-up harmonica and two electric guitars.

Daniel just shook his head. "I wish I knew."

Now Charlie Patton played tuned down
But he made that guitar scream
He could play on just five strings
What Page can't on eighteen
Cutting heads
With the living dead

And Elmore James, he was tweaking his amps
When the Edge was still in shortie pants

Jimmie Rodgers rocked the house
John Lee Hooker was the man
And there ain't no one can play today
Like that Magic Sam
Cuttin' heads
With the living dead

Freddy King, everybody knows,
Didn't need no Lego videos
So run along in your suit of red
Cause you'd be in way over your head
Cuttin' heads
With the living dead

B.B. may play sittin' down
But Slow Hand can't ever take that crown
Cuttin' heads
Cuttin' heads

The two guitars then swirled in a duel of their own. Whether either one of them could have stood toe-to-toe with any of the guitarists they'd called out was unlikely, yet there was still something admirable in the intensity of their attempt.

Now, Danny, you played your part too
You whored your soul
You know it's true
And when your world came crashing down
You'd given up your solid ground
So now you're going to have to run, my friend
If you ever want to see your cash again

I'm certain you know where to go
Sweet home, Chicago

The guitars took their last swings at one another and then the whole number came to a four-count, sudden stop.

"They're not bad," the bartender commented, handing the disc back to Daniel.

"No. Trust me," Daniel said, slipping the disc back into his coat with the others. "Whoever they are, they're all kinds of bad."

CHAPTER THIRTY

In the post-9/11 world, the NTSB has managed to make everyone who flies commercial airlines feel like a criminal. It's an annoyance for the innocent but makes air travel an absolute impossibility for subjects of federal manhunts.

Rental cars require a check of driver's licenses and credit cards, a problematic procedure when the hired killers hot on your trail can trace those kinds of things. A bus ticket can be bought with cash and without clearing a security screening. But the trip from Nashville to Chicago—with about a hundred stops in between—takes fourteen hours. Daniel wasn't sure he had that kind of time to waste.

The idea of a train briefly seemed like a possibility, but there hasn't been passenger service to or from the Music City since the Floridian was cancelled in the 1970s.

There was one last option. But at 472 miles, it's a long walk from Nashville to Chicago.

Afternoon slipped into evening. One by one, the honky-tonks and bars lining Broadway lit up their neon signs and readied themselves for another night. Daniel stood beneath their glow, cursing his predicament. He knew he had to head to Chicago and he was fairly sure where he'd find the next clue once he got there, but he had absolutely no way of getting to the Home of the Electric Blues.

The sidewalk traffic along Broadway had increased significantly, swelled by a hardworking legion just looking to take the edge off another day in the trenches, and by some others who were looking to get an early jump on the reason they'd be calling in "sick" in the morning. Stunned by his predicament, Daniel stood statue still, ignoring the jostling crowd as it bumped and bustled by him. He was so oblivious to the constant stream of commotion behind him that he was never sure whether it was an accident or the unseen hand on his back purposely intended to shove him out into the street.

Caught off guard and off balance, he stumbled a step or two and then looked up at the chrome grill bearing down on him. A horn like a thousand vuvuzelas sounded. Tires screeched. Breaks hissed. The truck and trailer came to a frame-rattling stop as Daniel stood looking up at the Peterbilt badge not more than a foot from his face. It gave him an ingenious idea.

What started as an angry exchange between driver and almost-victim quickly turned to a discrete negotiation. It turned out the driver was headed in a most convenient direction. For one hundred and five dollars—all the money he had left—Daniel got a cozy bunk in the sleeper cab and a handshake promise they'd be in Chi-town before midnight.

"Doncha worry," the heavyset man with the full red beard assured him, "I'll get ya dere befores youse knows it. Trust me!" And with that sterling guarantee, Daniel closed the curtain on the sleeper cab, stretched out on the bunk and drifted off to sleep.

The images were so oddly striking that Daniel was aware he was dreaming even while he was shrouded in its veil. He was in a mid-century bungalow in Echo Park, the one he'd bought with

Connie as newlyweds. He wandered from room to room, unsure what he was looking for but desperately searching. Through the windows he could see a lion on the front lawn, agitated and impatiently pacing back and forth. It stopped when it saw him and called out in a voice, deeper and louder than any roar, "You're gonna haveta come out sooner or later. Get out before it's too late." He turned and there was Connie holding a gun in one hand and Randy's hand in the other—the rest of Randy was not attached. She stood there, pointing them both at Daniel. He turned and ran toward the door, less afraid of the lion than he was of staying in the house.

The truck's cab door slamming shut sounded like a shotgun blast in the otherwise silent night. Daniel awoke with a start, not sure if he'd been shot. It took a moment before he realized where he was. And why.

"Are we here?" he asked groggily.

Silence was the only response.

And then from just outside the cab, he could hear muffled voices. He assumed one of them must be the driver's. He couldn't make out every word, but every now and again he could catch bits and pieces of the conversation. The trucker said something about not being a public servant and wanting his goddamn money.

Whoever he was speaking with said something about getting "back behind the perimeter."

The driver answered with something garbled, though Daniel thought he heard "be careful of my goddamn truck."

It struck Daniel as strange, but none of it made any sense.

Confused and still half-asleep, Daniel pulled back the curtain between the sleeper berth and the truck's main cabin. He yawned, unable to shake the grogginess from his aching head. He looked around the cab. He was alone.

He glanced casually through the truck's windshield, hoping he might spot some landmark that would offer a clue as to where they'd stopped. And why.

The skyline in the near distance confirmed they were in Chitown, all right, and apparently parked in the middle of a seemingly abandoned freight yard. Daniel guessed the "why" had something to do with the two dozen CPD squad cars strategically positioned as cover for the officers who had taken aim on the truck cab.

Somewhere just beyond this wall of black-and-whites, a bullhorn squawked and an authoritative voice called out, "You in the truck. This is Agent Gerald Feller of the Federal Bureau of Investigation. Place your hands out of the window and prepare to exit the vehicle."

There was nothing Daniel wanted to do more. He was tired and hungry and sore and scared. He'd grown weary of the malicious game he'd been dragged into and tired of running for his life. If it had been up to him, he would have happily put up his hands and given up then and there. Maybe—with a good lawyer—he might even be able to explain the reasons for why he'd done it all.

There was, however, more than just his life at stake. If he surrendered now, there was nothing ahead of him except a brief stay in the infamous Cook County Jail. And then it would just be a matter of waiting for one of Filat's messengers with a sharpened spoon or the pointy part of a broken toothbrush to finish his ordeal. And while Daniel was lying on a slab in the morgue, Filat Preezrakevich would have his men out looking for Zack.

Daniel didn't give a shit about himself anymore, but if he was caught now, his son was a dead man too.

And so, he simply had to find a way out.

In all the times he'd lovingly told his son, "There's nothing in the world I wouldn't do for you," Daniel had never once anticipated that life might actually call him on his paternal promise or that fulfilling his vow might include driving a stolen tractor-trailer through a hail of bullets and a wall of cop cars.

Still, he'd meant what he'd said; besides, he couldn't think of another way out. He climbed awkwardly into the driver's seat. There were no keys hanging from the ignition, but he found the spare behind the oversized sun visor. He slipped it in and turned…but nothing happened.

"Daniel Erickson," Agent Feller called again, making his order more personal and direct. "Place your hands in plain sight and prepare to exit the vehicle."

Maybe it was the clutch. Daniel pressed it in and tried the key again. Still nothing.

"This is your last warning!"

Daniel noticed a button marked START. This time he turned the key, depressed the clutch, and pressed the button. The third time was a charm. The engine coughed, sputtered, and then roared to life.

"Turn off the engine!" Agent Feller ordered. "Turn off the engine and exit the vehicle. Now! You are surrounded and we are prepared to use deadly force!"

Daniel knew he should be feeling something—there were dozens of appropriate emotions, a full gamut from terror to regret—but all he felt was determined. He focused on the street at the far end of the freight yard. If he could make it that far, he might have a chance of getting free of the trap that was closing on him.

"This is your last chance!" Agent Feller screamed, clearly agitated that his directive was being ignored. "Exit the vehicle! Now!"

Daniel took a deep breath and closed his eyes. He pictured his son, and then the little boy his son had been. The most subtle of smiles turned the far corners of his lips as he forced the stick up into first gear. The grinding gears made a high-pitched sound like a mechanized banshee as the truck jumped, jerking against the weight of the trailer still hitched behind it.

Most of the CPD officers had expected the fugitive to surrender. They all had their weapons drawn and aimed at the truck, but none of them was truly prepared for the truck to start moving forward. When it suddenly lurched toward them, it startled all them—but one of them more than the rest.

A single shot rang out. And *that* startled the other officers too. A second panic shot went off. Then a third. The night sounded like popcorn beginning to pop. An instant later, there was a sustained volley of shots as Agent Feller scrambled to figure out who'd started shooting—and why. And to stop the others.

Shots went high. Shots went low. Some struck the tractor's engine block and others shattered the windshield. But none hit Daniel, who crouched behind the steering wheel and reached for second gear. There was another pained wail of grinding metal as he made the shift, and then the truck began to pick up speed as it rolled closer and closer to the wall of squad cars.

Fifteen miles per hour may not be very fast, but it's plenty fast enough if the moving force happens to be a Peterbilt tractor. The truck barreled through the blockade like it had been hastily constructed of cardboard boxes as the police officers hiding behind them jumped clear of the collision. The truck pushed squad cars out of its way like a bully at the beach, driving them into one another like it was knocking over a set of automotive dominoes.

The officers who'd dived for cover righted themselves and resumed fire on the truck as it rolled past their positions. Their shots buried themselves in the trailer, but it was too late to stop it. Daniel kept his foot pressed to the accelerator and tried to shift up to third. The transmission protested, but he made it. He kept his eye on the chain-link fence at the far edge of the freight yard.

Thirty yards.

Twenty yards.

Ten.

The truck rolled over the fence and Daniel couldn't resist reaching for the air horn to sound a celebratory "Honk! Honk!" The tractor's suspension bobbed slightly as it climbed over the curb and headed out toward Grand Avenue. He'd made it. He was free.

There was another "Honk! Honk!" This one wasn't celebratory.

Fifteen miles per hour may not be very fast, but the Freightliner headed west on Grand was doing almost fifty. It collided with Daniel's hijacked Peterbilt with a force of impact that wrapped the tractor trailers around one another like two Transformers in love.

Glass shattered and steel groaned. Tires smoked and squealed as the now-fused trucks spun wildly in a death spiral down Grand Avenue. The spinning wreckage came to a rest with a final collision that sent Daniel sailing across the cab. He landed with a groan in the truck's passenger footwell.

There were sirens in the near distance and the sharp hissing of steam escaping from the trucks' engines, but everything else was perfectly silent and still. For an instant.

And in that perfectly preserved moment, Daniel realized, "I'm all right." He pulled himself up off the cab floor and tried to clear his spinning head. "I need to go. Now."

Without another competing thought, Daniel forced open the passenger door and climbed down out of the truck. He looked over his shoulder and was relieved to find that the wreckage obscured him from the contingency of cops who'd gathered to arrest him.

He started running toward Westheimer Road as fast as his shaky legs would go. Unfortunately, it wasn't nearly fast enough.

"There he is!" a cop screamed.

Daniel looked over his shoulder again and this time saw two overachieving officers sprinting toward him, closing the gap fast. He tried to run faster, but it was all he could do to simply stay on his feet. His lungs burned until he feared he might not be able to draw another breath. Ever.

His frantically falling footsteps and heavy breathing were all he could hear, until he realized the footsteps and breathing weren't just him. He looked back again and saw the faces of the two cops who were now just a step or two behind him.

It was no use. He was as good as caught. There was no escape from this. He'd failed his son. And the heaviness of that thought slowed him to a stop.

The cops slowed too. One of them reached out for Daniel.

And that was when the black Cadillac came out of nowhere. It drove straight toward Daniel and then screeched like a demon as it turned tightly and stopped just a foot or two from him.

The two policemen dove to the pavement for cover.

The door of the Cadillac flew open and a voice inside called, "Gef en da ca'!"

CHAPTER THIRTY-ONE

Moog Turner prided himself on his self-discipline, both on the job and off. Still, even a man of tungsten-steel resolve has a temptation or two he can't resist. One of Moog's just so happened to be located in Chicago's South Side.

He sat behind the wheel and devoured a third Big Dat, the signature pastry of Dat Old Fashioned Donut. The big man was stressed and cold and tired, but temporarily none of that mattered. He'd been transported to heaven on angels' wings and they were made of yeasty, fried goodness and glazed in sugar.

"You really gonna eat all of them?" Rabidoso asked, more annoyed by the display than amazed by the feat.

"Mmm-hum." Moog's mouth was too filled with bliss to say anything else.

"Come on," the little man whined. "You got a dozen of those big-ass doughnuts. Let me have one."

"Weren't you there? Didn't you walk into the Dat with me?"

"Yeah?"

It was simple. "Well, then you coulda bought your own."

"You were buying a dozen," Rabidoso squealed. "I didn't you think you were gonna eat them all, you know?"

"That's 'cause you never had one. If you'd had one, you woulda known I was going to eat the whole dozen and you woulda got a dozen of your own." Moog licked his fingers clean. "I don't know what to tell you except, 'Now you know.'"

"That's cold, man."

Moog looked lustfully at number four and held it out for the runt to see. "Nooo, baby, that's still warm."

"I don't even understand what we're doin' out here in the first place."

"We're trying to save our asses," the big man told him, finishing off number four and reaching for number five.

"How you figure?"

"I figure Ruffy, my man in Memphis, told me he'd gotten word someone called in to dime out Erickson and collect on the reward. He let me know Mr. FBI had set up this little get-together with the help of Chicago's beasts in blue."

"So what are we supposed to do?"

"I don't know yet." Moog was confident he'd have a plan when it was time to get it done, but for the moment all he could do was take on Big Dat number five.

"It doesn't make any sense just sitting here freezing our asses off," Rabidoso complained.

"Then open the door and go. But quit bitch—" The big man's mouth dropped.

Rabidoso didn't ask why. His own eyes widened with shock. "Holy shit!"

Moog couldn't help but echo the sentiment. "Holy shit!"

"Is that tractor moving?"

Moog nodded in disbelief. "That crazy sonofabitch gonna roll them right over."

"Whoooo!" Rabidoso cackled as the night lit up with a furious volley of gunfire. "Man, that little *pendejo* gone *loco*! Look at those cops scatter!"

With half of number five in his mouth, Moog started the engine and shifted the Cadillac CTS they'd stolen to replace the BMW into drive.

"What are you doing?"

"Ge'ing 'eady?"

"Ready for what?"

"Wha'ver com' next."

The two men stared in stunned silence as the truck Daniel was driving gained speed, rolled through the chain-link fence that surrounded the freight yard, and pulled out onto Grand Avenue.

Rabidoso excitedly pointed at the tractor trailer as it turned onto Grand. "He's making a run for—"

"Honk! Honk!" the tractor boasted.

There was a response, "Honk! Honk!" but neither Moog nor Rabidoso saw the collision coming. The unexpected impact was so viciously violent that they both instinctively flinched, ducking down behind the dash for cover, even though they were fifty yards away.

The remnants of number five fell from Moog's mouth as it contorted in shock. "Holy shit!"

"He's dead," Rabidoso announced with premature finality. "He's gotta be—"

"No, he ain't! Look at that!" Moog screamed, pointing out the figure lurching down the street through the darkness.

"That little fucker's tougher to kill than he looks," Rabidoso admitted.

"Yeah, he is," the big man agreed.

"Let's go get him!" Rabidoso shouted excitedly. "Get him!"

"I know what to do," Moog declared defiantly. He grabbed number six and put his big foot down on the accelerator. The engine whined as the Caddie sped off.

"Hurry, man, those cops are going to grab him before we get there!"

"Watch this." The big man stored number six in his mouth and gripped the wheel with both hands.

Daniel, exhausted and defeated, slowed to a stop. One of the pursuing police officers reached out to take hold of his arm. He was just inches away.

The whole scene was suddenly lit up in the Caddie's headlights. When it seemed certain that Moog would run down all three men, he stomped on the brake and turned the wheel as far right as it would go without snapping off in his oversized hands. The tires squealed and the sedan spun around.

With number six still securely in his mouth, Moog leaned over the seat and threw open the car's back door. Daniel was standing there, out of breath and wide-eyed. Moog yelled to him, "Gef en da ca'!"

CHAPTER THIRTY-TWO

To anyone whose lungs are already bursting and about to go down for the third time, it doesn't matter who's rowing the lifeboat. When plummeting to earth at terminal velocity, it's impossible to care who's wearing the tandem harness. And Daniel never gave a good goddamn who was offering him a way out of his inescapable situation. The door opened and he jumped in.

By the time Daniel realized who was behind the wheel and who was sitting in the shotgun, the Cadillac was already speeding off into the night. As soon as he made the connection, he reached for the door handle—jump, tuck, and roll!—but that gesture was met with the distinct sound of a semiautomatic's slide being worked to chamber a round. Daniel looked up and straight into the single, unflinching eye of Rabidoso's 9mm.

"I'm going to kill you," the little guy snarled. "Then I'm gonna make an offering to *Santa Muerte* that she raises you from the dead just so I can kill you all over again." He pointed his pistol at Daniel's forehead.

For maybe the first time in his life, Daniel didn't flinch. Not an inch.

Gently, but firmly, Moog reached over and pushed Rabidoso back into his seat. "How many times do I have to tell you? We need the guy alive."

"You need me more than alive," Daniel asserted boldly.

"Man," Moog shook his head at Daniel's bold assertion. "Don't stir his shit up like that."

But Daniel couldn't be quieted. "You need my money too." He looked right down the barrel Rabidoso was still aiming at him from over the seat. "So, go ahead. Do what you're going to do. You'd have to tell Filat that *he* wasn't going to get to kill me—and that you lost his money. So I'd die happy, knowing he'd make you pay for every dollar he'd assume you'd stolen. And all three of us know that'd be a hell of a lot worse for you two than a bullet in the head right here and now."

"You want me shoot you?" The Mexican's voice quivered with emotion. "You think I won't fucking—"

"Enough," Moog shouted. "Put the piece away or I will."

Rabidoso looked at the big man as if he'd betrayed him in some way, his brown eyes burning with an unspoken promise that someday soon he'd answer and repay the treachery. Sullenly and reluctantly, he put the pistol away.

"So then," Moog adjusted the rearview mirror to get a better look at his passenger. "Tell me about the money."

Daniel stared right back. "I was trying to tell you when you started shooting back in Malibu."

"You pulled a piece," Rabidoso shot back defensively.

"I had a jewel box," Daniel corrected.

"A jeweled what-now?" Moog wondered.

"You just turned around," Rabidoso corrected, "with a piece in your hand."

258

"It was a fucking CD," Daniel objected. "How can you not know the difference between a gun and—"

"It doesn't matter what happened in Malibu." Moog cut them both off. "Right now the only thing that matters to any of us is where the money's at."

"And that's what I'm telling you," Daniel repeated. "I don't know where it is."

"Wait a minute," Moog said, unconvinced. "You're telling me a million dollars in cash just disappeared out your secret safe?"

"It was all gone when we got there. Someone—I don't know who—took it, and the only thing they left behind was this," Daniel reached for the collection of discs he had in his coat pocket.

Without stopping the car, the big man stretched back over the seat to stop him. "Don't go in pockets like that. Makes me nervous." He let go of Daniel. "Now get what you got there. Take it out real slow."

Daniel pulled out the discs, found the one marked "Blues Highway Blues," and held it up. "This was the only thing in the safe."

Moog snatched it from him and looked at it curiously. "What is it?"

Daniel shook his head. "It's a CD."

"I know it's a motherfuckin' CD!" Moog snapped angrily. "What's on it?"

"A song."

"A song?" Moog slid the shiny disc into the Cadillac's dash player and three seconds later the car was filled with the bluesy intro to the track Daniel knew by heart.

The big man let "The Blues Highway Blues" play all the way through, but when it was finished he was only more confused. "What was that about?"

"It was a clue," Daniel answered. "A musical clue."

"A clue to what?"

"A location. The crossroads where Robert Johnson sold his soul in order to become the greatest guitar player."

"You're shittin' me." The big man was still unconvinced.

"About Robert Johnson selling his soul or the clue on the disc?"

And losing patience. "If I don't give a damn about my own soul, I sure as hell don't care about no one else's."

"Well, I went there and sure enough there was another disc waiting for me." Daniel handed the second disc over. "This one had a clue to go to New Orleans." He thought about his time there. About the friend he'd left behind. "You didn't let him hurt the old man, did you?" Daniel asked as he disdainfully pointed at Rabidoso.

If it was possible, Moog seemed even more confused. "What old man?"

"The old man—" Daniel started, and then thought better of it. He wasn't sure what Moog's lack of memory meant, but he felt relieved and figured the best thing to do was let the subject die.

"In New Orleans," Daniel continued. "I heard a song that led me to Memphis, where I got a disc that led me to Nashville." He gave up that one. "And Nashville led me to Chicago." Daniel completed the collection.

Moog looked at the discs in his hand. "So they just keep sending you—"

"To someplace else." Daniel nodded. "Mostly they just focus on a musician and give a clue telling me where I can find the next clue to a final place where supposedly I can find my money."

"Who does this?" Moog wondered aloud. "Who makes off with a cool million and then plays a game like this?"

"I don't know." Daniel shook his head. "I've spent the last twenty-five hundred miles trying to figure it out and I've come up with nothing. Maybe one of the bands I used to work with. Maybe an old business partner." He was beyond guessing anymore. "I don't know. I just keep following the clues, figuring that sooner or later—"

"Something will turn up." Moog knew the mind-set only too well.

"Yeah."

Moog looked at the discs. "So now where? You got the Chicago clue?"

"Not yet."

The big man had a hunch. "But you know where it is."

"I think I do."

"And where's that?"

"Twenty-one twenty South Michigan Avenue."

The address didn't ring any bells for Moog. "What's there?"

"Twenty-one twenty South Michigan Avenue," Daniel repeated. "You know, like the Rolling Stones song?" It was clear the reference did nothing to help, so Daniel just gave him the answer. "It's the address of Chess Records." He thought better of the description. "Or, at least, it's where Chess used to be before… everything changed."

Moog nodded his understanding. And offered a word of caution. "You better be telling the truth about all this shit. 'Cause it turn out to be just one of your motherfucking leather-pants-lies, you don't have nuthin' to ever put in any kinda pants."

"Understood."

Moog gave Daniel one last look to underscore his murderous intent. "Better be understood." And then he went back to finishing off the box of Big Dats.

CHAPTER
THIRTY-THREE

Other than the children's garden next door, there is nothing in its plain edifice to distinguish the modest storefront at 2120 from any of the other small businesses and "Available for Development" properties that line South Michigan Avenue. There is little to alert the casual passerby that this address was once the epicenter of a distinctly American musical and cultural revolution.

Like its Southern sister, Stax, the former offices and recording studios of Chess Records were left to fall victim to the harsh economic realities of urban America in the early 1970s. After the music business moved west, the building that once played home to musical giants like Chuck Berry and Bo Diddley, Howlin' Wolf and Muddy Waters, gradually deteriorated like so much real estate of unappreciated historical significance.

Ultimately the property was purchased, preserved, and restored as a private museum by the Blues Heaven Foundation, a charity founded by Willie Dixon. Willie's importance in the annals of American music has been lost somewhat in the shifting sands of time, but his contribution is undeniable and he belongs on the short list in any discussion of America's most important songwriters.

Being a musicians' museum, however, the renovated Chess Records keeps musicians' hours. So by the time the simple glass door was unlocked for another day of visiting tourists at eleven o'clock, the trio had already put the morning to good use.

Moog had taken Daniel to a men's store and bought him a black wool overcoat. "You attract attention we don't need with you looking like a goddamn hobo," he said, offering him the garment as a present. "I put a pack of cigs in the pocket. Just in case."

Daniel didn't mean to sound ungrateful, but said, "I don't smoke."

"I don't smoke either," the big man answered. "But there's things a pack of cigarettes can get you in this world that not even cash will buy. Trust me."

While they were waiting for Chess to open, Rabidoso had been tasked with "cleaning" the stolen Caddie. He'd driven off with the promise of wiping it down thoroughly but without the intention of making good on his word. Instead, he left it parked on the street with the keys dangling from the ignition, confident it would be gone before the morning frost had cleared.

Rabidoso's other assignment had been stealing the Caddie's replacement. Once that was accomplished, he returned to their designated meeting spot, particularly proud of his selection.

"Are you shittin' me?" Moog exclaimed when it pulled up to the curb.

"What?" The little man sat proudly behind the wheel, determined not to relinquish what he thought of as a position of authority. "She's a beauty."

Moog was speechless.

Daniel wasn't. "You stole a purple pickup truck? We're on the run from the cops and you stole a purple pickup pimpmobile?"

"It's a Sierra Crew Cab, *pendejo*," Rabidoso spat defensively, leaning out of the driver's window to admire the truck's seventeen-inch, chromed spinner rims.

"It's purple!" Daniel circled around the truck. "It's got a mural of two skeletons in a gun fight and the name Ramirez stenciled on the back window."

"Cool, huh?"

Moog sighed and watched his frustration float skyward as crystalline smoke. "Get in."

It was Daniel who was speechless now. Almost. "Get in? In that thing?"

"We don't have time to argue about it now. Let's just go."

Twenty minutes later, Rabidoso parked the stolen truck on South Michigan Avenue. He volunteered to stay with his ride as Moog and Daniel went into what had once been home of Chicago's electrified blues and the maternity ward for rock and roll.

There was a modest gift shop in the studio's old offices, though truthfully it appeared as if the proprietors had merely scattered some T-shirts and souvenirs around and left the old office otherwise unchanged. At the far end of the room, a middle-aged woman sat behind a desk, working over a pile of papers. She raised her head when the two men entered and offered them a "Good morning."

Neither made any intelligible response.

"May I help you?"

Moog looked at Daniel as if he should know what to do, but Daniel wasn't so confident. "I'm not sure."

The woman began to look vaguely concerned, worried the morning's only visitors—a giant and a nine-fingered man—didn't look much like music lovers.

"I'm looking for something," Daniel began, before hesitating again. "I'm just not sure what it is." He began having a Sun Records flashback.

The woman behind the desk began to look *very* worried.

Sensing where things were headed, Moog flashed a bright smile he hoped might disarm her. "What my friend here is trying to say—" He turned to Daniel and whispered as discretely as the situation would allow, "What the hell are you trying to say?"

"I don't know," he confessed in a whisper.

"Well, how'd you get the other discs?"

Daniel shrugged his shoulders. "Something just always turned up."

"Well, then turn something up!"

Daniel slowly approached the woman's desk as she let her hand drop discretely beneath it. He took a deep breath. "You see, I think someone might have left something for me here, but I'm not sure what it is."

She looked hard at him and in that lingering moment, Daniel wondered whether her hand was on an alarm or a gun. He wasn't quite sure which one he hoped it was.

She cocked her head a bit and then asked directly, "Are you Danny Erickson?"

Her question was simple enough, but he wasn't sure how to answer. He was, of course. But that man was also wanted by police. On the other hand, if he didn't admit who he was, he'd miss out on the next clue. He weighed his options. "Yes. Yes, I am."

The woman burst out of her seat and ran to him, shrieking and throwing her arms around him. "Oh, Mr. Erickson, when we got your gift—" She stopped and placed her hand on her chest to calm herself and take a badly needed breath. "I just can't tell you how much we appreciate your contribution."

"You found it generous?" Daniel asked, uncomfortably looking around the museum he apparently had a hand in funding.

"Oh, yes, sir. Very generous."

"The contribution. Can you tell me who brought it in?"

"Brought it in?" She thought on it for a moment. "It just came in the mail."

"Of course it did." He wasn't surprised. "Well, when it came in the mail, did anything come with it?"

"Just the disc you asked us about." She returned to her desk and pulled an envelope out of the top drawer. "I gave it to several of the folks who volunteer here but none of them could identify it." She seemed disappointed for him. "But they're all certain it's not one of Mr. Dixon's works."

"May I?" He held out his hand.

She gave him the envelope with the disc. "I'm sorry to tell you that they think you may have been…" She clearly didn't want to say it out loud. "Well, the victim of a fraud. Or of a joke," she added quickly, eager to put a sunny spin on it.

"Oh, I'm the victim of a joke, all right." If he was certain of nothing else, he was certain of that.

CHAPTER THIRTY-FOUR

As soon as they climbed into Rabidoso's stolen brothel on wheels, Moog checked over the package they'd received and asked, "Now what?"

"Now we listen." Daniel pointed to the in-dash stereo that was pumping out someone rapping over a Tejano tune with a throbbing bass line at a window-rattling volume.

Moog silenced it and slid in the new disc.

"Hey, man!" Rabidoso objected. "I was listening to—"

"Shut up," the big man said without taking his eyes from the complicated stereo unit he was trying to operate. "We gotta listen to this."

"Don't tell me to shut up."

"It's less painful if I *tell* you." Moog pressed play. "We gotta listen to this."

Rabidoso grumbled something under his breath, but it was drowned out by a swelling blast of solid brass. Behind the horns, there was an electric bass line that was as melodic as it was rhythmic. Right alongside it, a pair of funked-out guitars shared a part that was as rhythmic as it was melodic. Backing it all up was a layered percussion line that Daniel's ears heard as multiple tracks that had been overdubbed but might have been two actual drums, with a tambourine hitting all the back beats.

"You turned my joint off for this shit?" Rabidoso griped.

Moog meant to pause the track but the button he pushed ejected the disc, which only heightened his growing frustration. "I've been riding with your psychotic ass for the last six days." He spoke in measured tones, as if his growing anger was something even he was barely strong enough to control. "We need to listen to this and figure out where we find the money. And right now the shit you say is getting in the way of that."

The little man began to answer, but Moog held up his hand to stop him. "I don't want to hear it. I don't want to hear anything except this damn song. And if I hear anything else, I'm going to silence it."

"But—"

"Silence. It."

"Fuck you," Rabidoso spat. He hopped out of the truck's cab, slammed the door, and walked angrily down the sidewalk headed south.

And then it was silent. Moog pushed the disc back into the stereo and the same funky bass and driving rhythm resumed. The same vocalist, his voice smoother and higher, started to sing.

> *Well, now it seems to you that you lost everything*
> *Sometimes I feel like I lost it all too*
> *But, baby, what we got ain't nothing*
> *What we got is nothing to lose*
> *We got nothing to be scared of*

And there's nothing to regret
Ain't nothing holding us back
There's nothing that we can't get
No, there's nothing that we can't get
Nothing that we can't get

Moog couldn't help tapping along on the dashboard, his head bobbing rhythmically back and forth.

Roll around this town, looks like a bomb's been dropped
But those who stayed, we ain't going away and we can't be
*   stopped*
Because the Comeback City is still our home and it will always be
And we'll be back, baby, we'll be back, baby, you and me

'Cause there's nothing to be scared of
And there's nothing to regret
Ain't nothing holding us back
There's nothing that we can't get
No, there's nothing that we can't get
Nothing that we can't get

Lincoln Mammett was a good man, he could slap that bass line
*   down*
He hung with the Funk Brothers, he's still knockin' 'round this town
Now Danny he's so much like you, he's a man that you should meet
You'll find him out there every night, 'cause he's living on the street

But he's got nothing to be scared of
And, Danny, there's nothing to regret

Ain't nothing holding either of you back
There's nothing that you can't get
No, there's nothing that you can't get
Nothing that you can't get

The track drew to a close with a flourish of horns and bass, guitars and drums, and then—BOOM—came to a sudden stop.

"Detroit."

"What's that?" Moog wondered aloud.

"Detroit," Daniel repeated, although he wasn't sure why he had to. "Our next stop is Detroit."

"How you figure that?"

"The song had a Motown feel to it, with all the brass and the tambourine keeping time like a drum," he answered, as the first of a list of clues he was prepared to rattle off. "Detroit's always been known as the Comeback City, but if there's ever been a city that looks like a bomb's been dropped on it—"

"All right," the big man cut him off so he could consider the argument. "Suppose we go to Detroit...then what?"

"I don't know." Daniel shrugged. "I suppose we go looking for that man."

"What man?"

"Lincoln Mammett."

"The name mean anything to you?" Moog wondered.

Daniel shook his head. "The Funk Brothers were Motown's house band. Like Booker T. and the MGs down at Stax." He took a deep breath while he tried to put clues together, but there was nothing else. "I guess we'll just have to go looking for him."

The big man smiled. "My gramma used to play all that Motown every Sunday when I was growing up. Supremes. Smokey. Marvin

Gaye." He took a moment to enjoy the memory and then got right back to business. "Man, I loved that shit."

The memory was interrupted by a tapping at the rear passenger window, right by Daniel's head. He turned reflexively, expecting to find a disgruntled Rabidoso standing there, but found instead a stranger looking into the cabin longingly. "You got a dollar or two, mister?"

Daniel was surprised by his appearance at the side of their stolen truck and could only respond with a bewildered, "What?"

"A dollar or two?" The man was tall and lean, with an air and wardrobe that suggested he was a citizen of the streets. "Ain't gonna lie to you. It ain't for food."

"I understand." Daniel pulled a handful of change out of his pocket and lowered the electric window so he could hand the offering out. "I do."

The stranger snatched the coins out of Daniel's hand. "That's mighty kind of you, mister." He couldn't help but turn the contribution over and smile broadly at Daniel's grim face. "But if'in I was you, I'd keep my head down, *mi key.*"

"What did you—" Daniel turned back to the window, but caught only a glimpse of the stranger running back up South Michigan Avenue. He might have thought it was an odd encounter, maybe even have called after the gentleman if his attention hadn't been immediately diverted by the sight of another man advancing on the truck.

"Get down!" Daniel screamed as he threw himself to the floorboards.

A split instant later there was a thunderous blast outside and the rear window—with its decal murals of two skeletons gunfighting under the name Ramirez—shattered into black-tinted shards as eight three-quarter-ounce lead pellets tore through the cabin of the truck and embedded themselves in the dash.

Moog threw open the front passenger door and leaned out with his .50-caliber in his hand. There were three quick concussive blasts. Then the big man leaned back into the truck and slammed the door behind him. Though Daniel couldn't see a thing from his hiding place on the backseat carpet, he figured the big man must have gotten his man.

"Where the fuck is he?" Moog screamed at the empty driver's seat.

Figuring the coast had been cleared, Daniel's head popped up like a meerkat surveying the savannah, only to catch with his peripheral vision the image of a black Escalade stopping traffic on South Michigan Avenue as it pulled up right beside them. "Moog!"

The passenger-side windows on the Cadillac came down. A second later the driver's side windows of the purple pimpmobile shattered in a hail of gunfire. Daniel tried to flatten himself even farther into the floor as the attack showered him in a blizzard of tinted glass.

"Fuck!" Moog screamed, proving it was possible to hide a man of his size in the front passenger footwell. "I'm not waiting for that cocksucker any longer." Without raising his head any farther than he had to, he fired off two shots from his hand cannon and then reached over with his left hand to turn the keys dangling from the ignition. The engine came to life. He reached up for the gear shift and pressed on the brake and then the accelerator with the long barrel of his pistol.

The truck lurched backward and then rocked violently as it smashed into the Chevy minivan parked behind it. The truck was still rocking from the collision when Moog shifted again and this time the pimpmobile rocketed forward into the Celica parked there. "Fuck!" Moog screamed at the second collision. A second volley of gunfire poured in from the Escalade.

Still pinned to the floor, Daniel guessed the problem. "You have to turn the wheel!"

"You turn the motherfucking wheel!" Moog yelled, firing off two more rounds into the Escalade. He waited for Daniel, who'd taken the comment more as an angry response than an instruction. "Get your fucking ass up here and steer, mother-fucker!" With that, the big man raised up and planted his size 14 on the accelerator while he emptied what was left in the clip into the Escalade.

Daniel sprung up under the cover fire and grabbed the wheel, turning it as hard as he could to the left. The truck groaned as it struggled to push the Celica out of its way and then roared as it finally freed itself and shot out onto South Michigan Avenue, taking off the front panel of the Escalade as it did.

Moog ejected the spent clip from the Desert Eagle, slapped in a new one, and immediately began to fire through the shattered rear window at the Escalade that was now in pursuit. Daniel leaned forward across the center console, trying his best to navigate through southbound traffic that was speeding to escape the shootout.

"What the fuck, man!"

Daniel looked over through what had once been the driver's window and saw Rabidoso running at top speed beside the fleeing truck. "Stop the car!" he yelled to Moog.

"What?" the big man asked over the deafening boom of his own pistol.

"Stop the car!"

Moog looked over and moved his foot from the accelerator to the brake. The truck screeched to a stop. The Escalade collided into the rear end. The jolt sent Daniel sailing up into the driver's seat but couldn't dislodge Moog, who suddenly had a close and steady target. Six shots fired in rapid succession and Daniel could tell from the cold, satisfied look in the big man's eyes that he'd taken care of the problem once and for all.

Daniel crawled into the backseat as Rabidoso pulled open what was left of the driver's door and climbed back in behind the wheel. "What the fuck are you two doing?"

The big man glared. "One more won't make any difference to me right now, motherfucker." For once, the psychotic Mexican was silent. "Now get us the fuck out of here. Now!"

No one was surprised the Escalade did not resume its pursuit. Smoke poured out of its engine like blood flowed from its passengers.

"Man," Rabidoso interjected. "What do you think that was about?"

"I don't know," Moog said sarcastically. "Maybe we shoulda asked Senior Ramirez why he was so upset about you jacking his fucking truck."

"I don't know," Daniel said, finding a seat on the back bench. "I don't think that was Mr. Ramirez. The guy on the sidewalk was wearing a biker jacket." Sirens grew louder in the distance. "Like the guys in New Orleans. Remember?"

"What are you saying?" Moog wondered, although he was pretty certain he already knew what Daniel was trying to get at. And he didn't want to hear it.

"I think your boss has put a bounty out on us," Daniel answered. "All of us."

"Don't be stupid," the big man answered defensively, though not with his characteristic confidence. "Mr. P. knows I got this shit locked down."

His partner didn't say anything.

"Right?"

His partner didn't say anything at all.

CHAPTER THIRTY-FIVE

They ditched the critically wounded pimpmobile at the valet stand at McCormick Place and tried their best to blend into the crowd of actuaries holding their annual conference there. They cruised through the gathering like sharks in a kiddie pool and then made straight for the parking lot behind the convention center.

Moog chose the car this time: a beige Lexus. Without breaking a sweat, Rabidoso was inside and the car was started. But Moog held the driver's door open and stared silently at the little assassin until he slunk out from behind the wheel and retook the shotgun seat to which he'd been permanently demoted.

Knowing they couldn't afford even the simplest run-in with the police, the big man drove careful and slowly. With traffic out of Chicago at rush hour (one of five rush hours, anyway), a cruising speed set at the posted limit, and a stop for something to eat at the Bob Evans at Exit 43A off 94, they didn't make Detroit until well after dark.

"We need a place for the night," Rabidoso grumbled.

"No time," Moog advised without bothering to take his eyes from the road.

"No time?"

"Tick. Tock." He pointed at the watch strapped to his tree branch of a wrist. "We gotta find that Lincoln Mammett guy. And we gotta find him soon." Without another word he kept driving through Detroit's largely deserted streets.

They drove past the railway station that had long since been abandoned to the ghosts of a million joyous reunions and just as many heart-wrenching farewells. In silence they rolled down streets lined with shelled-out skyscrapers that made it seem history must have forgotten to add a war to its endless roster, and past tracts and tracts that had once been someone's yard but were now just more patches in an ever-expanding quilt of wilderness.

And every time they happened to spot a soul making his way along the lifeless streets, the zombified landscape, Moog would pull the car along upside and tell them, "I'm looking for a Lincoln Mammett."

Some thought the big man was obviously a cop. Others clearly suspected he was something worse. Most gave him a silent shake of the head or, if they could muster it, a simple no. There were a couple who cursed at him and more than a few who asked for money in return for information they couldn't even pretend to have.

Moog was just about to concede and call off the search when he spotted a man stumbling toward the ruins of the United Artists Theatre Building on Bagley Street. He pulled up to the curb and called out, "You know a Lincoln Mammett?"

"I know him," the man in the blue parka answered. "What you want with him?"

"You let us worry about that." His deep voice was colder than the night.

The man considered his situation and options and must have concluded he didn't have much left to lose. "I'm Lincoln Mammett."

The man was six foot, although it was probably a safe guess that he'd been taller before his body had been broken by a life on the streets. He had a blue parka, old and tattered, with the right sleeve pinned up at the elbow.

"I'm not letting that old goat in the car," Rabidoso complained. "We'll have the fucking smell with us till we get back to Vegas."

"You won't have to," Daniel said calmly as he closed the door behind him.

"Hey," Moog called out after him. "Get back in this car." It wasn't clear whether he was being protective or if he just didn't want to lose Daniel again.

Whatever the case, Daniel ignored him and offered his hand to the man. "I'm Daniel Erickson."

The man took it with his left hand. "Lincoln Mammett. You have to excuse the hand," he looked down at their awkward attempt at a shake. "I only got the one."

"I'm sorry."

"Don't be," Mammett said, his breath heavy with booze. "My own goddamn fault." Without explaining anything more, he turned and started walking slowly down the street.

Daniel followed. "You don't seem surprised we're looking for you."

"They said you'd find me." He looked around at the devastation that surrounded him. "I told 'em it was damn near impossible to find a single man in this ocean of decay, but they said you would."

"Who?"

"Don't know."

"Did they give you a name?"

"Nope."

Daniel was desperate to narrow the list of suspects. "Do you remember what they looked like?"

Lincoln considered the question. "White guys," Lincoln said with a shrug. "Skinny white guys with long hair."

That didn't narrow Daniel's list that much.

"I remember they was musicians, 'cause we talked about music for a long time."

"What did they say?"

"They said you was a musician too. Guitar player," he said brightly.

"I used to be." Daniel found it hard to explain. "I was in the music business."

"I played once or twice with the Funk Brothers," Lincoln said, still proud of that.

"I heard."

"You know, they recorded more number ones than Elvis and the Beatles and the Rolling Stones. All of them put together. They recorded more number ones than anyone." What he'd begun as a boast left him feeling sad.

"The guys who told you I'd be coming—"

"It wasn't always like this," he offered apologetically. "The city." He shook his head. "Or me." He took a step and then another. Daniel followed.

"There was a time when Detroit was as fine a city as you find west of New York. Folks from Chicago will tell you different, but what the hell do they know. Chicago was bigger, but Detroit was always finer."

Daniel nodded that he understood the distinction.

"That was the thing about Motown. Mr. Gordy always told everyone, you're what the whites are going to see. And when they look at you I want them to see *royalty*." His eyes sparkled with the recollection. "And that's what we was." He straightened his bent back and puffed out his chest. "Royalty."

Daniel got a sense of what that had once meant to the man. And smiled.

"But then Mr. Gordy upped and moved everything out to Los Angeles."

"And you stayed here?"

"Shit, no. I ain't stupid." He laughed a hoarse, hacking laugh. "I packed my bags and got out of Detroit—are you kidding me?" He had another laugh. "But Los Angeles—that was something else."

Daniel couldn't tell whether it was an expression of melancholy or wonderment. Either way, Daniel understood.

"Man, the women…" Lincoln let his voice trail away before correcting himself. "The woman."

Daniel nodded again.

"Her name was Lola." Mammett chuckled to himself. "You woulda thought I'da known better than to mess around with a woman named Lola."

Daniel understood that part too. "You lose your head when you're in her arms, don't you?"

"Ain't that the damn truth." He coughed again. "Anyway, we was happy—more or less—for a couple years at least. And then—" He shook off the memory. "People always go on about musicians living that life: partying and drinking and chasing all the skirts. What everyone always forgets is that while you out at your gig doing your thing, your old lady is back home all alone." He took a couple of steps in silence. "Or she's not."

Daniel could nod to that one too.

"I took it bad. Thought I'd show her how much I loved her, thought if I convinced her I'd die without her..." He walked some more. "I took an overdose. Heroin. Only I didn't die. Got an infection. They took my arm. I came back to Detroit and we've been falling apart together ever since."

It wasn't that Daniel was unsympathetic to a story that reminded him of his own, but he had to find the money. And he was running out of time. "The men who talked to you about me—"

"They gave me this." Lincoln pulled an envelope out of his coat and offered it to Daniel before pulling it back. "They said you'd pay me for it."

Daniel shook his head with regret. "I'm afraid I don't have anything right now."

Mammett thought for a minute. "Here, you take this anyway." He put the envelope in Daniel's hands. "Whatever it is, you must need it bad or you wouldn't be out here with me."

Daniel took the envelope and then reconsidered what he'd just said about not having anything. Without thinking about it further, he reached for the watch on his wrist. A Panerai. Limited edition. One of a hundred. He unfastened the clasp and slipped it into the old man's hand. "Here, take this."

"Oh, no. I can't take something like this."

Daniel looked at the timepiece, remembering the day Connie had given it to him. "One thing I've learned—"

"What's that?"

"Life will shit on you for years at a time."

"Ain't that the truth."

"So, when your luck changes, you don't fight it."

"Don't fight it?"

Daniel pressed the watch into the man's hand. "You just roll with it."

The man smiled. "Roll with it."

Daniel held up the envelope. "Thank you."

Lincoln held up the watch. "Thanks are mine."

"You got it?" Moog called from the car.

Daniel showed him that he did.

"Then come on. Let's go!"

"Now that's worth some money," Daniel advised Lincoln as he started toward the car. "You make sure you get a couple of dollars for that, don't let them screw you too bad when you pawn it." He started to climb into the backseat.

"Don't worry about me," Lincoln assured him. "I know what it's worth, *mi key.*"

"What did you say?" Daniel asked as he spun back toward the sidewalk.

Lincoln Mammett was gone.

CHAPTER THIRTY-SIX

Daniel stared out into the darkness, taking special notice of each house they passed. None of them appeared to be more than a single point of light in the distance. And yet he knew there was a family inside each one. Mothers and fathers. Daughters and sons. Probably sleeping, he thought, comfortable and snug in their beds in their little houses at the edge of the highway. He envied them. All of them.

"You're sure about this?" Moog wanted to know.

"Yes," Daniel answered without taking his eyes from the parade of houses he was watching. "If you doubt me, just play it again."

Doubt wasn't the right word, but Moog still wanted to be certain. "I've listened to that song two dozen times and I still don't hear where you get Cleveland out of it."

He pushed play on the CD player that had been silent for twenty miles or more.

The same counting of time as a drummer clicked his sticks. "One-two-one-two-three-four."

And then right on the beat there was an explosion of drums and bass and guitars that shook Rabidoso from his sound sleep.

"What the—" He rubbed his eyes. "This shit again?"

Moog just kept on driving. "Yes."

As Rabidoso snuggled himself back into the passenger seat, the music chugged on like the little engine that knew it could. And then the vocalist joined in.

This life is rough, it'll knock you down
Mess you up, spin your head around
But when times get tough, you're pinned to the ground
You just suck it up, it's time to throw down

Rock. Rock. Rock.
When you fear you can't go on
Rock. Rock. Rock.
When you think you lost the fight
Rock. Rock. Rock.
When they tell you that you're wrong
Rock. Rock. Rock.
Till you get it right

"It's the first pure rock-and-roll song I've heard in all of this," Daniel explained. "All of the others have just been leading up to this. From the Delta to New Orleans and Memphis to Chicago and Detroit. They were blues. Rhythm and blues. Nashville was country. But they were all just the pieces that built the rock-and-roll machine."

"But Cleveland?"

"Wasn't always a punch line," Daniel answered. "It was a city ahead of its time."

Now when the Moondog threw his Coronation Ball
There were twenty thousand kids came to answer the call

Blacks and whites together, for the love of it all
Everybody singing, "Jim Crow tear down your wall"

Rock. Rock. Rock.
When you fear you can't go on
Rock. Rock. Rock.
When you think you lost the fight
Rock. Rock. Rock.
When they tell you that you're wrong
Rock. Rock. Rock.
Till you get it right

"The Moondog in the song was the nickname of a DJ named Alan Freed."

"Never heard of him."

"I guess he's faded with time. But he's *the* Father of Rock and Roll. In fact, he's the first one who called it that. He was the first man in the country to play black music for a white audience, white music for a black audience. He just played music, you know? He was the first one to see through the ugliness. Completely color blind." Daniel thought for a minute. "I can't imagine what that must have taken back in the 1950s."

Moog just nodded from the front seat.

"And he organized the Moondog Coronation Ball in 1952. It was the first rock concert ever. Ten years before the freedom marches or the March on Washington, he brought twenty thousand kids, black and white, to see a rock show with a completely integrated lineup. And it was held in—"

Moog knew the answer to that one. "Cleveland."

"Cleveland."

Now rock and roll's a river fed by many other streams
There's rhythm and there's blues, of course, and stuff that's in
    between
There's boogie-woogie, jazz, and sweet gospel soul
That's the special stuff that gives the rock its jelly roll
There's cowboy swing and other things like country jamboree
Bluegrass, folk, all play their part in driving that Big Beat

Rock. Rock. Rock.
When you fear you can't go on
Rock. Rock. Rock.
When you think you lost the fight
Rock. Rock. Rock.
When they tell you that you're wrong
Rock. Rock. Rock.
Till you get it right

Now, Danny, you've had hard times, but you're not alone
And dying, it won't get you where you need to be goin'
Just think about all the things that you've been shown
Yeah, you're oh so, close now, you're almost home

Rock. Rock. Rock.
When you fear you can't go on
Rock. Rock. Rock.
When you think you lost the fight
Rock. Rock. Rock.
When they tell you that you're wrong
Rock. Rock. Rock.
Till you get it right

The song came to a cacophonous sustain and then ended with a flourish of guitars and drums that burst with one final cymbal crash.

"All right then," Moog finally agreed. "Let's go to Cleveland."

CHAPTER THIRTY-SEVEN

Along the western shoreline of Lake Erie, a seven-story tower seems to rise up out of those questionable waters. In front of this building stands an enormous pyramid constructed of glass and steel. It's a visually startling sight and one that can't help but call to mind a similar structure that sits in front of the Louvre in Paris. And for good reason, as both edifices are the work of architect I.M. Pei.

It is not a natural combination, the master of modern architecture, I.M. Pei, and the Rust Belt's capital city, Cleveland. In fact, when Pei first agreed to take on the project on the banks of Lake Erie, there were many within the architectural community who were aghast that the grand master had agreed to lend his talents to a building honoring what they considered to be a culturally insignificant art form. That building was the Rock and Roll Hall of Fame.

As the three men sat in silence in their stolen car, Daniel stared out the window at the modern edifice wondering how Charlie Patton playing his five-string guitar for a young Son House on the porch of a company house at Dockery Plantation could have set off a spark so combustible that it could have led to something so spectacular. Pei designed a lot of buildings over the course of his career, but *this* was his only cathedral.

What a long, strange trip, indeed.

"What time they open?" Moog asked.

"Ten." It wasn't the first time Daniel had answered that question.

"What time is it now?"

Instinctively, Daniel looked for his watch before realizing it wasn't there anymore. A momentary pang of regret washed over him. He pointed instead to the digital clock on the dash right in front of the big man. "Nine fifty."

"You think it's going to be in there?" It wasn't the first time that question had been asked either.

It was like being on vacation with an oversized child. "Yeah."

"Where?"

"I don't know." Even as he said it, Daniel knew it wasn't a confidence-inspiring answer. Still, it was the truth. "They're always there. You know, something—"

"Will turn up." Moog had heard that before too. "Well, I hope something turns up to lead us to that money soon. Mr. P. ain't gonna sit still for us taking some field trip."

And what could Daniel say? He knew his time was running out. A day was coming—maybe even this day—when Moog and Rabidoso's own survival would necessitate ending the wild goose chase and returning him to Vegas, with or without the money.

"We're getting to the end of the trail." Daniel wasn't nearly as optimistic as he sounded, but he thought it might buy him some more time. "We have to be."

"What do you mean?" Moog wasn't necessary interested, but there was a still a minute or two to kill before they could get inside.

"It's clear we're tracing the evolution of rock and roll, right?"

When he was a kid, Moog always hated those days when there was nothing better to do than go to school and the teachers would ask him questions they knew he didn't know the answer to just to make him feel dumber than he already did. "OK?"

"Well, we've come all the way from the Delta, where the blues began, to here, Cleveland, birthplace of rock and roll. It just doesn't go all that much farther now."

"What do you mean?"

"Cleveland was the epicenter of an explosion that sent rock and roll splintering on a thousand different geographical directions—including other continents—where it developed completely different regional styles and sounds." Daniel worried what would happen if the next clue sent them off in some unexpected direction, like England.

"You know what I wanna know, Mr. Professor?" Rabidoso moved in his seat like a snake with the taste of prey in the air. He curled around the side of the passenger seat until he was looking straight at Daniel. "I been thinking and thinking on something I can't figure out."

Daniel said nothing.

"Back in Chicago. Why were all those police after you?" His eyes narrowed when he grinned.

"What?"

"Five-oh, *esse*. What they want with a straight shooter like you?"

"I don't know."

Rabidoso expressed his doubt—and the fact that he knew it was a lie—by broadening his reptilian grin. "Don'tchu?"

The car was colder than the meat-packing plants down on West Sixty-Eighth Street, but Daniel was beginning to sweat. "You tell me. You were there waiting for me. You must know something I don't."

"Oh, I know a lot you don't." The grin oozed into a sneer.

"What the hell does that even mean?" Daniel bluffed, though he was terrified he knew exactly where his tiny tormentor was headed.

"Ever since we plucked you outta the streets, I've been waiting for you."

Daniel pretended he didn't understand.

"I figured even a piece of *mierda* like you would have to do something to get revenge on the man who—"

"I don't know what you're talking about," Daniel lied just to keep him from going further.

"Don't you?"

He needed Rabidoso to continue believing he'd killed Zack. "No." The denial came out louder than he intended, and the extra volume didn't make it any more convincing.

"Really?"

Daniel leaned back in his seat and looked out the window, pretending not to be interested in continuing the inquiry. What he really felt, however, was afraid.

Ever since Moog and Rabidoso had recaptured him, Daniel had struggled with how he should react to the man who thought he'd killed his son. If he tried to feign a father's natural desire for retribution and failed to be convincing, he might betray the lie. If he was too convincing, the situation might escalate to violence.

A dead Rabidoso did nothing to help the situation. And a dead Daniel was even worse.

The risk with doing nothing, however, was that Rabidoso would begin to suspect he'd made a mistake back in California, that he'd somehow claimed the wrong victim. And if that suspicion began to fester in his psychotic little brain, it might soon lead to the conclusion that Daniel's only son was still out there. Alive. And available to be tortured to death all over again.

"Let's go." Moog opened his door.

Daniel climbed out, relieved to have escaped Rabidoso's tightening coils.

"We're not done with this," the little man called, then followed after them.

Moog pulled up the collar on his suit coat. "For an antisocial psychotic, he is one chatty little motherfucker."

"Yeah." Daniel was surprised by, but grateful for, the comment. He thought it might be the germ of a confidence that could be cultivated into something useful when the time came. "Yap, yap."

Behind them the *click-clack* of size 7 cowboy boots running across the slush-covered pavement to catch up with them echoed out across the lake.

Daniel knew that any appearance in public was risky. A risk that was growing exponentially with every hit on Yahoo! or loop of headline news. Whatever the news services might have dug up, he hoped they weren't using the ridiculous headshot he'd been cajoled into taking to promote *Rock and Roll Relapse*.

Still, whatever picture they were using, it was a certainty that at least some of the rock-and-roll faithful filling the museum had seen it. Daniel kept his eyes down as he moved through the front doors, trying hard to be as inconspicuous as anyone can be when they're accompanied by a giant and an evil elf.

"Excuse me," Daniel said without looking directly at the young woman behind the information kiosk.

She didn't look up at him either. "May I help you?" Her tone made clear she'd rather he just went away.

"Could you tell me if anything was left for me here?"

"Left for you?" She raised her head to catch a look at the crazy question-asker.

"Maybe a package? An envelope?"

"Who would've left you something here?" Every word dripped with contempt. "Elvis? Jimi Hendrix? Did Kurt Cobain leave something—"

"Do you have a package for this asshole or not?" Rabidoso interrupted. The brutal fantasy he was having about her and a length of nylon rope burned bright in his eyes. "His name's Erickson. Daniel Erickson."

She moved back in her seat and her right hand reached not so subtly for the alarm button beneath her desk.

"It's all right," Moog assured her as he ushered the other two away from her desk and into the museum. "They didn't mean nuthin' by it." The woman pulled back her hand.

"What?" Rabidoso wanted to know. "I thought we came in here to get one of those CDs?"

"Just keep walking." Moog turned back and smiled at the still-rattled receptionist as he pushed his two companions into the crowd. "Now what?"

Daniel had no idea. "I guess we just look around."

"Look around?" Rabidoso challenged. It didn't seem like much of a plan. "There's seven floors!"

Looking up at the atrium rising high above him, Daniel realized searching the entire collection would be impossible. He was just about to make that admission when the answer came to him. "Alan Freed."

"Who?"

"Alan Freed," Daniel repeated. "The DJ I told you about."

"Where do we find him?" Rabidoso asked, apparently eager to hurt someone before the morning was through.

"He's already dead," Daniel said dryly as he looked around. "The song kept referring to Alan Freed. That's gotta be the connection." He wasn't as sure as he sounded, but he knew if they left empty-handed the next stop would be Vegas.

Together the three toured the *Architects of Rock and Roll* exhibit. They listened to excerpts from rock-and-roll shows Freed had produced. They looked at movie stills from *Rock Around the Clock* and *Don't Knock the Rock* and flipped through an endless assortment of record albums Freed had produced or endorsed. They watched clips from his TV appearances and even toured a mock-up of his old radio studio. But nowhere was there any sign that something had been left behind for Daniel.

All three had silently concluded that their treasure hunt was a wild goose chase when then they came upon what is unquestionably the oddest piece in the hall's immense collection: Alan Freed. Right there, behind a Plexiglas window set into the wall, was a bronze urn that held the ashes of the Father of Rock and Roll.

"Yeah," Rabidoso quipped, "I don't think the dead guy in the fancy bong has your little CD or whatever."

Daniel smiled. "Don't be so sure about that."

"What do you mean?" Moog was interested, even if his partner wasn't.

"Look back there," Daniel said, pointing out a thin strip of metal beneath the urn's base. "Is that—"

Moog nodded. "I think that's a CD back there."

"Where is it?" Rabidoso asked, squirming like a kid trying to get a look at whatever everybody else was looking at. "I see it," he announced with what seemed like genuine enthusiasm.

And then, without another word, the little man gave the Plexiglass a swift shot from his elbow. The display case shattered on impact as alarm bells began to sound and emergency lights started flashing.

The same camera-toting, concert-shirt-wearing crowd that had been wandering through the exhibits at a snail's pace suddenly began to scream and run like they were Who fans in Cincinnati—and the band was beginning to play.

In the midst of the chaos, Rabidoso reached into the exhibit, pulled out the urn, and casually let it drop as he picked up the disc behind it.

Daniel dove to the floor, catching the urn before it hit. When he looked up, Rabidoso was standing over him, triumphantly holding up the CD. "Got it."

"I got it." Moog snatched the disc and put it in his coat pocket.

"Hey!" Rabidoso objected.

"We gotta get out of this place," Daniel called out before the mismatched partners could break into yet another sibling squabble.

The three turned for the exit but only got a step or two before a security guard came charging in, his right hand readying the pistol holstered at his hip. "Stop right where—"

Before he could draw his weapon or finish his command, Moog's oversized fist silenced him. The guard dropped to the ground with a sickening *thud* and lay motionless as the three moved quickly past him. They ran down the hall toward the stairs, trying to blend in with the rest of the tourists frantically rushing toward the exits.

At the head of the stairs, Moog noticed that the flow of fleeing tourists pouring downward was being interrupted at the bottom by five guys who looked like they'd just escaped from the Altamont exhibit. With their biker colors in full display, the gang pushed their way through the crowd as they made their ascent.

The big man put a hand out to stop Daniel and pointed the group out. He thought he recognized two or three of them from New Orleans, but the leader of their pack was new. A guy with a tattoo across his face, a brute who was even bigger than Moog.

"Oh, shit!" It wasn't that Moog was scared—he hadn't been scared of another man since he was eleven years old—but his grandmother hadn't raised no fool. He turned and started looking for another exit. "Come on, let's go this way."

When he noticed a pair of security guards running toward them, he called out, "There's five bikers! They all have guns! They're screaming crazy shit like they're going to kill all the cops!"

The security guards stopped in their tracks. The one who looked like Paul Blart's fatter, older brother yelled at the crowd, "Everybody remain calm! Remain calm!"

But the one who seemed like he could have played point guard for the Cavs stopped them in their tracks with an oversized palm in the center of Moog's chest. "Stop your running," he told them. "There's an exit right over there." He pointed them away from the crowd toward a door at the other end of the hall marked EMPLOYEES ONLY. Moog and Rabidoso did as they were told, but Daniel stood for a moment, struck by something undefined in the man. The guard just smiled. And laughed. "You best get your asses on the other side of it, *mi key.*"

"But—"

"Go! Now!" the guard shouted before diverting more of the crowd into the path of the bikers. Daniel understood—and turned and ran after his companions toward the door.

Rabidoso was still laughing when he slid into the Lexus's passenger seat. "Can you believe that shit?"

Moog wasn't amused. He forced himself behind the wheel and slammed the driver's door closed. "Goddamn it! Do you realize what you just did?"

"Yeah. I got what we were after," the pint-size killer bragged. "And I did it in about two and a half hours less than it would've taken the two of you."

Sirens wailed in the near distance, louder and louder, their numbers increasing.

"This place is going to be swarming with cops in a minute. They're gonna be looking at videotape in an hour. And they're fucking going to see us!" Moog shook his head. "If this goes bad because of you, I swear—"

"You'll what?" Rabidoso's grin dared him to finish.

Moog put the car in reverse instead. "We're never working together again." He pulled out of their parking spot. " 'Cause one of us is never *working* after this."

"Good."

"Good."

The Lexus pulled out of the lot just before the Cleveland police arrived to cordon it off. As squad car after squad car sped past them, Moog drove at a very reasonable speed out of the city.

"Are we not talking about the biker gang?" Daniel wanted to know. "Or are we going to pretend it's just a coincidence they keep showing up trying to kill us."

"Did you see that big motherfucker?" Rabidoso laughed. "I wouldn't have believed it, man," he said to Moog, "but he scared the shit out of you. You were like a little fucking girl when you saw that horse."

Moog told his partner to fuck off, but he didn't call him a liar. Then he looked back at Daniel. "Ain't nothing to talk about. I got a job to do and I'm gonna do it."

"Are you kidding me?" Daniel was starting to worry that even if he stayed with Moog and Rabidoso he might not make it back to Vegas alive. "Your boss has pulled the plug on both of you."

Moog didn't want to hear it. "I don't know what you did to those guys. Maybe they're still pissed about how it went down in New Orleans. I don't know. But Mr. Preezrakevich ain't gonna do me like that."

His partner didn't say anything at all.

CHAPTER THIRTY-EIGHT

When Cleveland's skyline was shrinking in the rearview and Moog was reasonably certain they'd left the police back at the Rock and Roll Hall of Fame, he slid the disc into the player. "All right, Music Man, do your thing."

Daniel leaned forward on the seat and readied himself.

The track started with a funkified bass line that whoever was laying it down would have termed "sexalicious" or "orgasmatastic." It percolated and throbbed on its own before being joined by a drumbeat that sounded like a factory working overtime. They completed the sound with two wha-wha guitars that rolled and tumbled to the rhythm like two lovers trapped in sweat-soaked sheets.

When the vocals joined in, it wasn't the singer Daniel had come to know (and grudgingly appreciate) from the previous tracks, or at least it wasn't just him. This time the vocals came as a harmony of two or three voices. Daniel thought it might just be an overdub effect, but it was probably an extra vocalist who'd been added to the project.

Cash money
Some people will sell their souls for it
Some folks will give up their dreams
Some people will trade you their flesh
But it's never what it seems

Cash money
It's all some people want

"It's all I want," Rabidoso interrupted.
Moog flashed him a look. "Will you shut up."

Cash money
It's all they think they need
Cash money
In my pocket
Cash money
But it don't own me

Some people they don't care who they hurt
Some people they will steal just what they can
Some people they will take another's life
But it don't make them a man

"Makes *me* a man," Rabidoso joked again. "Who comes up
with this shit?"
"If you don't shut up, I'm going to push you out of this car,"
Moog threatened. "And we're going eighty."

Cash money
It's all some people want

Cash money
It's all they think they need
Cash money
In my pocket
Cash money
But it don't own me

'Cause you can't buy your way to heaven
And you can't bribe the hands of fate
True love, it's not for sale
And you can't buy more time when it's too late

Cash money
It's all some people want
Cash money
It's all they think they need
Cash money
In my pocket
Cash money
But it don't own me

Danny, spent your whole life trying to earn a buck

Daniel couldn't help but bristle whenever the track began to address him personally.

How'd that end up for you
With a woman that didn't give you love
Made you do those things you do

But now you get yourself a second chance
That trip of yours is at its end
You got just few more stops
And then it's all yours again

Cash money
It's all some people want
Cash money
It's all they think they need
Cash money
In my pocket
Cash money
But it don't own me

The funk bubbled and brewed on and on and then came to a sudden end as everything broke down in a crashing cacophony. And then silence.

The answer was clear to Daniel. "Philadelphia."

Moog didn't need to work the tracks out any longer. Daniel had proven himself and that was good enough for the big man. He nodded, pleased that something was working out. "We're on our way."

"How you get Philadelphia out of that shit?" Rabidoso asked, his question suggesting there was no good answer.

"It's Philadelphia soul," Daniel explained.

Rabidoso changed his mind. "I don't even want to know."

"Now that's some good shit, right there," Moog offered enthusiastically. "The O'Jays. The Spinners."

"The Three Degrees." Daniel was quick to contribute. "Harold Melvin and the Blue Notes."

Moog nodded his big head. "Yeah, that's some good shit right there."

"Chubby Checker and 'The Twist' came out of Philly," Daniel added just for the sake of thoroughness.

"I did not know that," the big man admitted.

"What are you, going to school now?" Rabidoso challenged.

"I'm not getting into this with you right now." That was all Moog had to say on the subject. "And you can always learn something new. You oughta try it sometime. Ain't nothing to be proud of, going through life ignorant."

It's a little over four hundred miles between Cleveland and Philadelphia and Moog and Daniel spent most of the trip calling out and trying their best to sing along to the songs they'd each grown up with.

Somewhere along the way, Rabidoso turned back to Daniel and motioned at Moog. "He's not your friend, you know. He's not going to save you."

"Man, what are you talking about?" Moog protested.

"I'm just setting him straight. You're singing songs together like this is *American* fucking *Idol*, but we both know when this is all over you're going to kill him. Just like I'm gonna." He looked over the seat, focusing his reptilian eyes on Daniel. "Only you'll do it quicker. A lot quicker."

"Yeah, well, don't you go drawing any conclusions about just who I'm going to be killing at the end of all this." Moog's stern look underscored his point. "I might just surprise you."

"I might surprise you too." Daniel's voice came as a surprise to the killers, who looked back at him, unnerved.

CHAPTER THIRTY-NINE

Every city in the world has a nickname or two, but there is no greater municipal misnomer than Philadelphia being called the City of Brotherly Love. At last count there were a little over a million and a half Philadelphians—and all but a handful are looking for a fight.

Moog pulled the car to the curb and surveyed the block. "You're sure this is where we wanna be?"

"Two-twelve North Twelfth Street." Daniel confirmed. "This is Sigma Sound. If the song was considered Philly soul, then it's a good bet it was recorded right here."

"That's good enough for me." The big man slid out from behind the wheel of the Lexus and closed the door.

Rabidoso climbed out of the car but was less impressed with the plan. "I say it's enough of this bullshit. He's just running us around. Let's stuff him in the trunk, take him back to Mr. P., and see what we can get out of him."

Before the big man could respond, a voice called out, "Cowboys suck!"

Rabidoso, proudly wearing his Dallas jersey, wheeled around to find a group of four men on the opposite side of the street. "You suck!" he called back, following it up with "*Chinga a tu madre!*" Satisfied he'd settled the matter, he turned back to Moog. "We need to stop all this musical shit and—"

Hardness is a measure of the degree to which an object resists changing its shape when it is put under some pressure or force. The ice ball that whizzed across Twelfth Street had been compacted to a degree of hardness that could've been tested by a Schmidt hammer. When it struck Rabidoso—just above his right ear—the impact was enough to drop him to the ground like he'd been shot.

A burst of uproarious laughter went up across the street as all four Cowboy-haters doubled over in high-pitched hysterics. "Suck on that!" one of them yelled and then rejoined the other three in more laughing. And a cheer. "E-A-G-L-E-S! Eagles!"

Rabidoso was quick to get back to his feet as a matter of pride, but it was clear he was still a little stunned. He touched his right ear and calmly noted the thin trail of blood trickling from it.

"Don't do this," Moog warned, but even the big man knew this was not the time to engage the psychotic hit man.

Rabidoso rubbed his blood between his fingers, as if the feel of it was arousing to him. "*La concha tu madre!*" he screamed, as his tiny cowboy boots marched purposefully across North Twelfth Street.

"Don't do this," the big man called after him, but he didn't make any attempt to interfere. "Just let it be." Rabidoso didn't stop and Moog hadn't expected him to.

As the pint-size assassin approached the four Eagles fans, their laughter died to a Greek chorus of "Ooooooohs" and "Look at this! Look at this!"

The biggest of the four stood up straight and puffed out his chest. He made his challenge sound like a single word, "Whatthefuckyouwant?"

Rabidoso didn't utter a word, but the answer was simple enough. He reached into the waistband of his jeans.

Maybe the four men across the street had assumed their target was too small to stand up to their bullying. Maybe they'd miscalculated that any fighting would be limited to punches—and kicks, once the little guy was down on the ground. (It was Philly, after all.) But apparently none of them figured it might turn into a gunfight, because they all seemed genuinely surprised when he pulled out his 9mm and started firing.

Crack. Crack. Crack.

It all happened so fast that by the time Daniel, still standing by the Lexus, realized why the men were falling down, there were already three bodies on the ground.

Moog started across the street and then thought better of getting directly involved in a multiple homicide. He turned back toward the car, shouting to Daniel, "Get in the car! We gotta get out of here!"

The fourth man—the only one still standing—looked into Rabidoso's eyes but only saw the devil looking back. He turned and ran as fast as he could, leaving his fallen friends behind.

Rabidoso chased after him, stopping every four or five strides to fire another shot.

Crack. Crack. Crack. Crack.

The first two went far and wide, but the third and fourth hit their target and brought the man down like a whitetail on the Monday after Thanksgiving. He crumpled to the slush-covered street, twitched once or twice, and then went still.

Rabidoso stopped running and walked calmly to where the man had fallen. He stood over him for a minute, savoring the terror contained in the man's tearful whimper, "Jesus Christ, man. Please! I got a wife and kids, man! Please don't do this!"

Rabidoso crouched beside the man and looked him over. "You're worried about leaving them behind? Your wife and your kids?"

Blood and mucus streamed from the man's nose and mouth as he gagged out a weak, "Yes."

"I tell you what—" Rabidoso reached for the man's wallet and met no resistance pulling it free. "I'll tell you what, Anthony Esposo, 1411 Carning Street. I'm not a complete monster. I understand you're worried how your wife and kids are gonna take care of themselves if I kill you here and now."

"Thank you," the man offered for what he mistook as mercy.

"So, you die easy now, 'cause when I'm done here I'm going straight to your fucking house to kill that cunt and your little fuckers!" The man started to squeal. Rabidoso put a single round in his head. *Crack!*

Back on the sidewalk, one of the bullies was crying and screaming in pain. "Jesus Christ! Jesus Christ!"

Moog knew there was more killing yet to come. He started up the car and yelled with urgency to Daniel, "Get in the goddamn car!"

Daniel stood dumbstruck by what he was witnessing. Moog's voice jarred him from his stupor and he ran back to the Lexus, pulled open the door, but then froze again.

"Get in the goddamn car," Moog ordered. "We gotta get—"

Whatever hope they'd had when they come to Philly, it was all gone now. *Hope* was the fifth victim of Rabidoso's rampage. After a multiple homicide, there was no way they could roam the city looking for musical clues to the secret location of his money. There was only one possible destination now: Vegas.

If he even made it to Vegas. Daniel had just witnessed four murders. Was Rabidoso going to let him live?

No, if there was any chance of saving himself or his son he had to go. Now.

Behind him, Daniel heard Moog screaming, "Erickson! Get back here!" Then several more cracks as Rabidoso finished what he'd started. There was a brief moment of silence, suddenly shattered by the mournful wails of approaching police sirens in the distance.

Daniel didn't pay attention to any of it. He just ran.

He ran, but he knew he couldn't run fast enough or far enough. There would be people looking for him now. Lots of people. All sorts of people. He had to find a place to hide. And a way out of the city. His mind raced, searching his surroundings. The seafood delivery truck he noticed parked at the back end of the alley off Race Street seemed to offer both.

After his last ride in a truck, Daniel didn't bother to ask the driver for permission to come aboard. Instead, he slid open the back door and climbed up into the empty cargo hold, taking a seat with his back against the far wall. Uneasily, he waited for the driver to complete his delivery and then get him somewhere far, far away.

Alone in the dark, his thoughts drifted from his time with Connie to when their lives had begun to unravel, from a time when they were too much in love (or too young) to think that the world could ever touch them, to their end when they limped off to their respective corners after the world had torn them apart.

He wondered where his son was. And why he hadn't heard from him. He worried Zack had been one of those millions who must have clicked on a story about a maniac on a cross-country crime spree.

He worried there were others out there, others like Rabidoso, who were searching for him, who would find him—or Zack.

And what could he do about it now? Whatever was hidden and waiting for him in Philadelphia was out of his reach forever. The answer to the riddle would remain a mystery. There was nothing he could do. Nothing.

CHAPTER FORTY

The squeal of brakes and the sudden shifting of his body shook Daniel from his unintended sleep. He sat there, momentarily disoriented in the dark, and listened, not quite sure just what he was listening for. He heard the driver's door open and close. And then nothing at all.

When it finally seemed to him that the uninterrupted silence meant it was safe, he got to his feet and walked to the end of the cargo hold, listened for a moment, and then lifted the gate as quietly as he could. There were a dozen other trucks parked in rows, but nobody in sight.

Daniel climbed out of the truck and pulled the door closed behind him. He turned and began to take quiet, careful steps across the abandoned truck yard. Step. Step. Step.

There was a chain-link fence around the perimeter of the lot and he moved toward it as quietly as he could, wincing at the loud crunch each step made against the frozen snow beneath his feet. Step. Crunch. Another step and another crunch. A step and then a crunch. And then another crunch—an *extra* crunch.

He froze in place. There was someone else with him in the truck yard. Daniel looked around the fenced yard but couldn't see anything but trucks and darkness.

He took a step. Crunch. Crunch. Crunch. Two extra crunches.

Daniel turned toward the sounds, but he only managed to see the dog out of the corner of his eye. An instant later a German shepherd the size of a circus pony was just an arm's length away.

He sprinted for the fence with the dog right behind him. In a single move, Daniel jumped up toward the fence, caught two handfuls of links, and forced himself up and over. It was a display of athletic prowess he never would've guessed he had.

The landing, however, was trickier. Propelling himself over the fence, he twisted in midair and proved Newton's theory of gravity by dropping like a stone and landing on the flat of his back.

Six inches behind him, the dog hit the fence like a bullet train meeting the sound barrier. The collision rattled the chains and made them sing as the shepherd barked wildly, its teeth bared, furious that its prey was so close yet so out of reach.

Daniel got to his feet and began to run. He wasn't sure, but he thought he heard laughter in the distance behind him. He was certain it must've been his imagination, but he thought he heard someone call out, "Run, *mi key*, run!" He didn't look back, he just kept running.

Just two blocks later, Daniel had completely run out of running room. Ahead of him, the Atlantic rolled into the sand. Daniel stood and looked at the rolling surf as incredulously as if it contained a half-submerged Statue of Liberty. It seemed impossible to him, but the frothing surf was undeniable proof that he had stowed away to a shore town in New Jersey.

There was no point in heading out onto the sand and so he wandered down the street that lined the beach. Looking for some refuge from the night, he found there was still one place open despite the late hour. He opened the door and stepped inside.

"We're closed," the woman behind the bar yelled without paying him any particular attention.

He looked around the barroom and noticed all of the chairs had been turned up for the night. "I'm sorry. I just—"

She raised her eyes from the bar she was wiping down and ran them up and down him, from head to toes and back again. "You look like a man who could use a drink."

"I could," he agreed, although he hadn't thought of it until she extended the invitation.

She nodded at a spot at the bar in front of her. "One drink to get you back on your feet and then you can use them to take yourself out of here."

"Thanks." He moved to the seat she'd offered.

"What'll it be?"

He knew what his dire circumstances required: "Whisky."

She poured a double and set in down in front of him. "There you go."

"Thanks." He took a drink, unprepared for the burning sensation down his throat and into his empty stomach.

"Easy, Tiger."

"I'm Daniel," he said, before it occurred to him that he probably shouldn't.

"Vicki."

She was more attractive than Daniel would've expected to find behind the bar at some seaside joint in the off-season. He guessed she'd spent happier days (and nights) behind a bar when she was younger and then retreated back there when her life didn't play out as she planned in those halcyon days. Still, whatever collection of life's disappointments had returned her behind the bar, they'd done little to dim her bright smile or to dampen the sparkle in her eye.

"I'm all right," Daniel assured her.

"I'm sure you will be."

The conversation was joined—or interrupted, as Daniel saw it—by another man he hadn't realized was in the otherwise empty barroom. Uninvited, the guy took the stool next to Daniel's and put a hard-shell electric guitar case between them.

"How'd you like the show?" he asked the bartender, who paid him even less attention than she'd paid Daniel's entrance. Her pointed silence did not dissuade him. "Yeah, the band was really tight tonight."

She either disagreed or didn't care. "What'll you have?"

For the first time, the man admitted taking notice of Daniel. "I'll have what he's having."

She shook her head. "You'll get a beer."

The guy seemed disappointed when she put the amber bottle in front of him, but he took a big swig from it anyway. "I'm wearing her down," he whispered to Daniel, loudly enough that she could hear.

"The only thing you're wearing down is your welcome. Now drink up and get out." She picked up a tray of clean glasses from beneath the bar and carried them out through a pair of swinging doors.

He watched her go. "I'm pretty sure she's a dyke. But just 'cause the door's closed doesn't mean there's no use in knocking, right?"

The man turned to Daniel and offered him his hand. "George Beamer. George Beamer and the High Beams." He used the top of his bottle to point at an E-Z Print banner that hung over a small stage area in the far back. "That's me."

"Dan—" The whole fugitive thing was hard for him to get. "Eric Danielson."

"Well, nice to meet you, Dan Eric Danielson. What is that, Norwegian?" He snorted a laugh. "I'm only joking."

He caught Daniel looking down at his case. "She's a '52 Telecaster. Just like *his*." He smiled as if he'd just said something important about himself and took a drink. "And, yes, before you ask, I've played with *him*. Played with the Boss many times." He took another drink. "Couple a times. But that's what everybody asks, 'You ever played with *him*?'"

Daniel had more important things on his mind than playing a rock-and-roll version of Six Degrees of Separation. "Uh-huh."

If thirty years of playing fifty-seat bars up and down the Atlantic shoreline had taught George Beamer anything, it was not to be discouraged just because people aren't listening.

"I tell you what gives me the biggest kick about *him*," he continued unasked. "*He's* always here. Well, not *here*," he said, gesturing to that particular barroom, "but *he's* constantly drifting in and out of all these little places, walking up and down the Boardwalk at all hours. *He's* like a rock-and-roll ghost."

Daniel wasn't sure what to say. "OK."

"I mean, people always say to me, 'Isn't it hard, you know, you been playing as long as *he* has, you rock just as hard as *he* does.'"

Daniel had never seen a High Beams show, but he found it difficult to believe.

"They say, 'You work as hard as *he* does, but *he's* where he is and you're where you are.'" He took a breather and a swig of beer. "But I tell them they're missing the point, 'cause *he's* where I am. You know?" He laughed harder than he had to and gestured around the barroom again. "*He's* right here. I mean, *he's* got the mansion on the hill, but I got the keys to the kingdom."

He looked at Daniel as if he expected some comment from him. He got none.

"I've played some large venues in my day," George said, lightly tapping the guitar case. "I opened up for Southside on this benefit gig out at Jones Beach. Must've been twenty thousand people there. Not when we were playing, but, you know, there were a lot of people there. And, you know what?"

Daniel didn't say anything.

"It was just the worst. Couldn't see anybody. Couldn't connect with anybody. But a place like this," he turned to look around the cramped confines of a room that couldn't hold more than a hundred fifty people without giving the local fire marshal angina. "You get up on stage in a place like this and you can look into everyone's eyes. You can feel them. In a place like this you can create real magic." He took a sip of beer, disappointed that it was his last.

"Today music," Daniel said under his breath.

George didn't understand. "What?"

"I met a man who told me that what made the old blues players so great was they were never playing for tomorrow. Everything was about playing for today. It's not about the money or the venue. It's just about the music. Playing for today. Today music. 'He plays Today music.' That's got nothing to do with paid attendance or revenue receipts."

Somehow Daniel's words had insulted him. "Yeah. I don't know anything about that. Truth of the matter is that that show in Jones Beach was a rush. Like riding a fucking dragon. And whoever thinks money doesn't matter doesn't have a mortgage to make and an old lady buggin' him for a new used car." He looked around the dingy bar. "I can't for the life of me understand why *he* keeps coming back. I get out of here, I ain't ever coming back. That's for fucking sure."

"Well, now that you're all talked out," Vicki informed him as she reappeared from behind the swinging double doors. "You should get going. I've gotta lock up."

"Sure enough." George took another hit on the bottle, somehow surprised to find it was still empty. "All right, Eric van Toaster Slam. Let's say you and I—"

"He's staying."

It was hard to say whether Daniel or George was more surprised by what she'd said, but George was the one who said, "What?"

"He's my ride home," Vicki told him, her tone making it clear she resented the explanation she'd given him and had no intention of expounding on it.

"I'll be more than happy to—" George was quick to offer.

She was quicker still to cut him off. "I didn't ask you." She made a motion with her hand like he was so much dust on the bar that she was brushing away.

He reached down to pick up his case and as he did, Daniel—as surprised as anyone by the turn of events—offered him his hand. "It was nice to meet you."

Beamer grabbed the case handle instead. "Piss off." And with his replica Telecaster dangling from his hand, George Beamer stomped off into the night.

Vicki shook her head when he was gone. "He's such a bore. Did he give you his whole 'I'm Better Off Not Being Successful' spiel?"

"Yeah."

She laughed to herself. "What a load of shit."

Daniel looked back over his shoulder toward the door George had just let slam behind him. "He seems convinced."

"Well, he's had thirty years to work on it."

She pointed at Daniel's glass, which was still half full. "You finished?"

He steeled himself, threw back the rest, and placed the glass back on the bar, proud of himself that he didn't let a single cough, gasp, or choke escape. "Yes."

She took the glass, wiped it with the towel she'd been cleaning the bar with, and then placed it back on the shelf.

"What?" she asked when she noticed the look he'd given her less-than-hygienic actions. "It's not like *you're* going to be back in here tomorrow to drink out of it."

It was true, but somehow the way she said it made it sound like an unnecessarily harsh accusation.

"You got a smoke?" she asked.

"No. I don't smoke."

"I don't either," she announced proudly. "I just quit."

"How long?"

"No, that's it. I just quit. Right now," she smiled. "If you'd had a cigarette I'd still be smoking."

"Well, it's probably for the best."

"Think so? It hasn't even been a minute and I'm already having my doubts." She drummed her fingers on the bar. "I just wish I had one last one."

Her request triggered a memory about something Moog had told him about cigarettes buying things that cash couldn't. "Wait a minute, I do have a pack."

"Never mind." She shook it off, but regarded him suspiciously. "You don't know your own name. Don't know whether you smoke or not."

There wasn't much he could offer in his defense. "It's a long story."

"Tiger, you look like a guy who's got a lot of long stories."

He thought on it. "Really, just the one. But it's a killer."

"I'll bet it is."

CHAPTER FORTY-ONE

The man stared out of the photo with lost, empty eyes that were ringed by dark circles. His face was expressionless, not so much accepting of what had happened to him as resigned to it. Nothing about the man seemed particularly threatening; he was more melancholy than maniacal.

"Who the hell is this? And why am I looking at his picture at two in the goddamn morning?" Regional Director Casey asked. "Can you tell me that, Agent Feller?"

"That's Daniel Erickson, sir. The picture is a mug shot taken in conjunction with an involuntary commitment in California two years ago."

"You're running out of time to get to the *why* am I here looking at this, Agent Feller." The older man in the bigger chair threw the photo on top of the rest of the dossier Feller had handed him. "Get to the goddamn *why*."

Feller didn't flinch an inch. "Because he's left crime scenes clear across the country in the last week."

The head of the FBI's Philadelphia office picked up the photo with renewed interest. But still the same doubt. "This guy?"

"It started with a shooting on the Pacific Coast Highway out-side a home he was renting in Malibu."

The file Feller had prepared contained several photos of the cars that had collided with one another after Daniel had stepped out into the northbound lanes. The gruff old man was unimpressed. "A goddamn pileup is no crime, Agent Feller."

"We believe he was fleeing this domicile after murdering a Maria Gonzalez, whom he employed as a domestic." Feller indicated a series of pictures of a female corpse, topless and reclined in a pool of its own blood.

The gruesome scene piqued the regional director's interest. "Good God!"

"From that crime scene we believe Mr. Erickson stole a vehicle—a late-model Lotus Elise—and drove to the house of his ex-wife, where he subsequently murdered her live-in, a Randall James Baldwick." The accompanying photographs showed a group of crime-scene technicians pulling up a freshly scrubbed carpet to reveal large, dark blood stains. "We haven't found a body yet, but he's currently missing and evidence at the scene strongly suggests there was a murder here. There's more blood under those carpets than in a slaughterhouse slough trough."

"The woman file a missing persons report?" Casey wondered aloud, sifting through the photos.

"Sir?"

"On the missing boyfriend. Did this ex-wife file—"

Feller understood. "Oh, yes, sir."

"Good."

"Again he stole a vehicle and it seems he drove east. Presumably fleeing his crimes. Eventually, he wound up at a service station in New Mexico." The photo showed a surveillance camera image of Daniel at the pumps, suspiciously looking around as he fueled the Kia. "The surveillance tapes were stolen for the night of the crime, but we believe that he went back to the same station the following night and murdered the cashier, Nancy Ravensong." There was a picture of that corpse too: a young woman with her throat cut open. Casey silently shook his head.

"Next—"

"Jesus, there's more?"

"Yes, sir. We next caught sight of him in New Orleans. He's at the center of a riot at Mardi Gras." There were more grainy pictures from a security camera that showed a man who looked like Daniel—or two and a half million other men—getting into an altercation that quickly developed into a riot. If Casey flipped through the collection, the images seemed to come to life.

"He next serviced in Memphis. Where we apprehended the car he'd stolen. The suspect, however, eluded capture."

"How was that, Feller?" The edge in Casey's voice was no accident.

"All I can say, sir, is that the local law enforcement agencies down there leave something to be desired, sir."

The old man considered it. "Memphis, hmm?" Then he snorted his understanding and agreement.

"Now the next we heard of him, he was in Chicago."

"He's on a goddamn rock tour," Casey observed.

"Exactly, sir." Feller cleared his throat. "In Chicago, the suspect again evaded apprehension and, in so doing, endangered the lives of numerous law enforcement officers."

"Right." The incident rang a bell with the old man. "Regional Director Buckley told me about what happened there." He shook his head. "He's still trying to sort out all the goddamn paperwork on that one."

Feller uncomfortably shifted in his seat and tried to move on. "Later that morning, Erickson was involved in a shoot-out on Michigan Avenue. Six dead. This is surveillance footage we have of him making his escape through the McCormick Place." There was a pixilated black-and-white image of Daniel running through a lobby and dashing up an escalator.

"Who's that with him?" Casey asked, pointing out the two men running right behind him.

"Here's where it starts to get a little weird, sir."

"Jesus Christ," Casey exclaimed. "It wasn't weird before?"

"Well, the larger man, the African American, is Vernon 'Moog' Turner." Feller put a mug shot of Moog in front of Casey. It was a youthful shadow of the man he'd become, but the tombstone eyes were still set in his face. "He's an enforcer. A hired killer. Started in Kansas City. Branched out. We believe he was a contract killer under the tutelage of Harrison 'Bumper' Marcus until he, in turn, killed Mr. Marcus. We last heard of him as the main muscle for Filat Preezrakevich, former Russian Mafia."

"Russian Mafia? I don't get it. What's a psycho killer like Erickson doing in the company of muscle for a Russian mobster?"

"As I said, sir—weird. And it gets weirder. The smaller man, the Mexican there, is Señor Jesus Arturo Castillo del Savacar. He was an *asesino* from Cártel del Golfo."

Casey scratched his bald head. "So, what are a psycho killer, Russian mafia muscle, and a Mexican cartel killer doing on the lam together?"

"Raising hell, sir. They were at the Rock and Roll Hall of Fame. Where another riot broke out. And then tonight they surfaced in Philadelphia. Four men were shot to death."

"Jesus Christ." The regional director shook his head with one final display of disgust. "What does it all mean, Feller?"

"I'm not sure. We know the Russians and the Mexicans have been working together to expand the cartels. This may be proof positive of that cooperation."

"And the psycho killer?"

"Apparently he served to launder money for Preezrakevich on some crazy, harebrained television swindle. My guess right now is that the Russians are financing Mexican cartel expansion into the US and Erickson is a part of moving the money. My guess is that he got greedy and jumped the track. The other two have been ordered to bring him back."

"Bring him back? Back where?"

"That's just the thing, sir. I know where Erickson's going. I'm certain of it."

Casey thought about it for moment. "Then go get him."

Agent Feller thought a smile would be perceived as unprofessional or—worse yet—unmanly, so he suppressed his. "Yes, sir."

"You've done some real fine work here, Feller."

"Thank you, sir." A real career maker.

"But don't fuck up like you did in Chicago. You won't survive another fuckup like that." It wasn't a threat, just a statement of fact.

"Yes, sir." Or breaker.

CHAPTER FORTY-TWO

Vicki Bean wasn't the first woman Daniel had slept with since his wife left him for another man.

To be sure, in the weeks and months that followed Connie leaving him, the only thing Daniel's quest for vengeance (and reaffirmation) lacked was a funkadelic '70s bass line for a soundtrack. There were all sorts of women, all sorts of arrangements, and all sorts of situations. None of them ever made him forget Connie for more than an hour at a time. And maybe because of that, none of it had ever made Daniel feel the slightest bit guilty.

This night was different. He hovered between waking thoughts and sleep's deep dreams, momentarily bothered by some gnawing feeling of betrayal—his. It wasn't that he felt guilty about having had sex with Vicki Bean, it was that they were sleeping together. Really sleeping.

He felt culpable for the way her body seemed to melt into his or how she pulled his arms around her to hold her closer as she dreamed. He felt guilty for feeling all the things he hadn't felt since Connie: Satisfied. Happy. At peace.

He felt guilty—and grateful—all at once.

This night was wonderfully different. And he did not want to waste it fretting that it would end soon. Or wondering how it was that he could have found something he'd lost in himself in a stranger. It was what it was and all he wanted to do was to live that moment. There, beneath her crinkly down comforter, with Vicki Bean in his arms, Daniel was playing Today music.

It could have been hours or maybe just minutes, but Daniel woke, relieved to find she was still in his arms.

"Everything all right?" she asked when she felt him stir, her voice soft and sleepy.

He pulled her closer. "I'm great. How about you?"

She turned in his arms to face him. "All things considered, I'm doing much better than I expected."

"That's encouraging."

"What do you want me to say?" She propped herself on her arm. "You come staggering into the bar after-hours looking like you just fell off a fish truck, with a fake name and a long story— that you're still keeping a secret."

He was embarrassed she'd caught him in the lie he hadn't told her. "I thought women loved a mysterious man."

"Obviously we do." She moved against him. "I saw you and said to myself, 'There's a guy with real problems.'"

"Now you're just trying to flatter me." She laughed but didn't saying anything more. When he couldn't bear her silence anymore, he asked, "Why me, then?"

She didn't answer at first, but when she was ready she said, "I finally admitted to myself that my chooser's broken."

"Your what?"

"My chooser." He liked the way she smiled when she was trying not to let on she was embarrassed. "You know, whatever it is that makes you choose one person over another. One opportunity over another."

"Oh, that."

"Yeah. So when you shambled into the bar looking like you'd just gone twelve rounds with the world, I said to myself, 'Now here is a guy who's an absolute mess.'"

"Thank you very much."

"Seriously," she giggled. "Here's a guy who's nothing but trouble." She wondered if that was putting it too strongly and then decided it wasn't. "I mean really just a complete train wreck."

"I understand."

"No," she laughed, suggesting it wasn't nearly as horrible as she made it all sound. "You walked in and my chooser was screaming this is the absolutely worst guy you could ever be with. Ever. And I have been with some guys like you can't believe."

He smiled uncomfortably. "You're making me feel so much better."

"Good." She kissed him. "See...my plan is working."

He thought he might actually have understood. "Choose against the chooser?"

"Choose against the chooser," she confirmed.

"Suppose for once in your life your chooser was dead on the money?" he wanted to know.

"What do you mean?" She sounded somewhere between cautious and curious.

"I am trouble," he admitted. "Well, *I'm* not trouble, but I'm in trouble. Some pretty serious trouble."

"Zack?" she asked.

The question alarmed him. "How did you—"

"You kept calling the name out in your sleep."

The look in his eyes answered before his words could. "He's my son. And I'm in a situation—" How to explain it? "There are some very bad people who may go looking for my son if I don't—"

"What?"

He wasn't sure. "There's some money that's been stolen from me."

She wasn't surprised. "You looked like trouble—but *moneyed* trouble."

"It's just that the men who stole the money, they've been leading me on this wild goose chase, setting up these musical clues."

"Musical clues?"

"I know it sounds strange." He was in the middle of it all and it *still* seemed strange to him. "See, I was in the music business for—"

She sat up, now clearly alarmed. "No wonder my chooser hated you."

"Hated?" The word seemed kind of harsh.

"I can totally see you as some label suit." She laughed to herself. Or maybe she was laughing at herself. "I'm tending bar as a kinda rehab after wasting the last fifteen years."

He furrowed his brow. "You were in music?"

She seemed hurt that he couldn't picture her that way. "Don't look so surprised."

"No, it's just you don't look like—"

"I wasn't a suit," she said, as if the suggestion was insulting. "You ever hear of the band The Bitch You Miss?"

He wanted to have heard of them, but had to admit, "No."

She wasn't disappointed—or surprised. "We had our fans," she told him, suggesting the band hadn't missed his support. She reached to her nightstand, pulled out a relapse cigarette, lit it, and took a drag. "We never cracked that big commercial market, but it's not like punk has a big commercial market to crack."

"What?" Daniel looked like he'd been struck with a jolt of 220 volts.

"What do you mean *what*?" She took another puff. "You're not one of those dinosaurs who thinks the only opportunity for a woman in rock is on her knees in front of some douche bag with a mullet?"

"No," he assured her, though he was paying more attention to the thoughts in his head than he was to anything she was saying.

"That's the only reason I treat George Beamer the way I do. He walks around like he's rock and roll's saving grace and I should be lucky to catch a bone from him." She took a puff and watched it drift to the ceiling. "The truth of it is that I could play him off-stage any night of the week."

"Punk," he repeated.

"Yes. Punk." She ran her fingers through her long red hair. "I'm a punk rocker," she said, making it clear that was something he was going to have to deal with.

"No, not like that," he dismissed her concerns, while still trying to fit his thoughts into place. "Punk. That's the last clue."

"What are you talking about?"

He sat up and explained, "All the clues led me from city to city tracing the evolution of rock and roll."

"OK." She didn't understand what he was saying or the enthusiasm with which he was saying it, but she was willing to listen.

He collected his thoughts. "But I was explaining to Moog—"

"Who's Moog?"

"One of the bad guys."

"Of course."

"I was explaining that once that mixture of blues and rhythm and country, once it all hit Cleveland, rock and roll just sort of exploded. It went everywhere and when it did it just fragmented. It went a thousand different places and there wasn't really another major movement until—"

She was willing to take a guess. "Punk?"

"Until the punks hit New York, yeah. The Ramones. The Dolls. Hell, the Pistols fell apart there." He felt euphoric. "I don't need the last clue, because I know where the music goes."

She thought he was cute when he got all excited, even if his enthusiasm was a little scary. "Well, that's good I guess. Right?"

"It's awesome." It meant he still had a chance.

"Well, all right."

"Listen." He grabbed her gently by the shoulders and looked deeply into her mischievous eyes. "I know I don't have any right to ask anything of you."

"No, you don't."

"But I'm going to anyway."

"I figured." She braced herself with a puff of her cigarette. "Go ahead."

"The first thing, maybe the most important thing, is that I need you to believe me."

She was worried. It had just been one night; usually she had to invest in a week or two before men started telling her they needed her to believe them. "About what?"

"About everything." He took a moment. "There's going to be some things that you're going to hear about me—"

"What kind of things?" She'd already given up on her decision to quit smoking and she was having serious reservations about the whole "choose against the chooser" thing too.

There was no way around it. "Bad things," he admitted. He thought he saw her make that "Here-we-go-again" face. "No. None of it's true," he assured her. "You have to believe me."

"Well, my chooser is saying you're completely crazy and I'd have to be crazier to trust you, so let's just say for the time being that I do. What else do you need from me?"

"I need you not to say anything about me. Not to anyone."

She mulled it over. "All right. Anything else?"

"I need you to let me steal your car."

This request alarmed her. "What?"

"I need to get into Manhattan."

A simple enough request to fulfill. "Well, I'll take you," she said.

"No. I told you, there are some very bad people after me—"

She thought she'd caught him. "I thought you said they were after your son?"

"They're after us both, OK? That's why I can't have you anywhere near me. It's just too dangerous."

She thought it over for a second. Took a deep breath and decided to disregard everything her chooser—and common sense—was telling her to do. "Well, then just take it. Go into the city and do what you have to do and then—"

"I can't take that chance. If I get caught and they trace the car back to you—"

"I'd be in danger?"

"No." He wasn't as confident as his denial sounded. "But I don't want to take that chance. Just give me an hour and then call the police and report it as stolen. Then, whatever happens, no one will ever be able to trace me back to you."

"Gee," she scoffed. "Fuck me. Leave me. Steal my car. What girl could resist?"

"It's not like that." His voice conveyed the depths of his desperation for her to have a little faith in him. Of all the men she'd had in her life, she wasn't sure if any of them had ever *needed* her to have faith in them. None of them until now. "I know."

CHAPTER FORTY-THREE

It was either very fitting or very ironic that the revolutionary response to rock and roll's bloated excess began in a small club in New York's Bowery section called Country Bluegrass Blues and Other Music for Uplifting Gormandizers. CBGB & OMFUG, to its friends.

Like so much of America's musical heritage, however, the original CBGB has disappeared. The space at 315 Bowery at Bleecker Street—once the staging ground for punk's counter-assault on rock's establishment—had been turned into a boutique for a high-end men's fashion designer.

Daniel parked Vicki's Monte Carlo, which he figured she'd be reporting as stolen just about then, and went inside.

"May I help you?" a young man in gray slacks and a brown turtleneck asked.

"I was wondering if anybody left anything for me here." Daniel had become comfortable asking the question.

"I'm afraid I don't know what you mean."

Daniel ignored the unpleasant tone. "A package? Maybe a manila envelope? For Daniel Erickson?"

"I'm afraid we sell men's clothes," the clerk snapped snarkily. "We're not actually a *drop*." He put the word with air quotes. "But there's an alley out back, you might want to check there."

Daniel left the shop, disappointed but undeterred.

Although CBGB was certainly *the* seminal punk club, there were other venues that played significant roles in punk's development. He could head over to Max's Kansas City—although that too, had disappeared only to be replaced by a Korean deli. And there was the Mudd Club in Tribeca—now a bagel place.

Daniel stood on the sidewalk, not sure where to go next. Should he continue his search for the money or concede that it had eluded him? Should he go straight to Vegas and accept whatever punishment the mad Russian might mete out? Would it be so bad if he just went back to Vicki and tried to run?

And then, with all of these questions swirling around his brain, he found that the answer was right in front of him. There on a light post outside of the ghost of CBGB's was a flyer for a band that had recently played a show in New York.

They were called Dockery Plantation, an homage to the place where Charlie Patton had started it all. But unlike their flyer in Nashville, this one had a picture of all six members of the band. Five of them he'd never seen before, but he recognized the one holding the Gibson ES-335. And there was one more show on their tour.

CHAPTER FORTY-FOUR

There are almost three thousand miles between Manhattan and Seattle. An average driver in a reasonable automobile can make the trip in just over forty hours. A desperate man in a battered, old Monte Carlo can do it even quicker.

Over the years Daniel had amassed a collection of twelve charge cards. No longer worried now about maintaining his credit score, he financed the trip to Seattle by selling them off one by one to whatever shady truck-stop characters had ready cash. The genius of his plan was that not only did it provide the necessary gas money, but those who bought the cards went on outlandish spending sprees that created an impenetrable cover. Whoever might have been monitoring his transaction activity in hopes of locating him would have had to follow up on an electronics shop-a-palooza in Columbus, a new wardrobe of women's wear in St. Paul, and even a junket to Vegas.

The Central Tavern is a Seattle institution. Not only because it's the city's oldest drinking establishment, but because it served as the first venue for a local band that took the small stage under the name Nirvana.

When Daniel finally pulled up in front of the place, the band on the marquis was called Dockery Plantation.

He walked into the place and knew at once he'd finally solved his mystery.

There were six guys in the band: a drummer, a bassist, a keyboard player, two guitarists, and a singer. On stage they shared the kind of easy camaraderie that's sometimes formed when a band goes out on the road.

"Thank you for coming out tonight," the vocalist called out to the crowd in an all-too-familiar voice. There were maybe fifty people still left in the place, which, considering it was a Monday in February, seemed to Daniel like a fairly strong showing.

"Before we go tonight, I'd like to introduce you to the members of the band. On drums, Ryan Helms." There was a smattering of applause and a few whistles. "London Haynes on the bass." The crowd responded with more of the same. "We got Kevin Connor on keyboards. On guitars, our twin diesel engine: Jake Robertson. And Zack Erickson."

As soon as the name was announced, Daniel clapped so hard and whistled so loudly that it took a moment or two before the vocalist could complete the band's introduction with, "And I'm Joe Vigilatura. We're the Dockery Plantation and tonight were going to leave you with this. This is 'The End of the Road.'"

The other guitarist began to strum that same, simple chord progression on a twelve-string acoustic as Zack wove in a soft, haunting melody on Daniel's ES-335. Then the singer joined in.

Put the past behind you
Set your burden down
There's nothing to remind you
It's all over now

Take your first steps forward
You've paid all the debts you owed
It's your life to run
Run it to the end of the road

With a sudden punch, the drums and bass and keyboards joined in for the chorus.

To the end of the road, till you're late for the sky
Run as fast as you can, till you take off and fly
And if you soar with the angels, or crash to the ground
You can count on me to always be around
I'll get you back on your feet, and carry the load
I'll be by your side, to the end of the road

When the show was over, the rest of Dockery Plantation went to the bar for a round of beers on the house. All but one. Zack Erickson knew he had unfinished business to take care of.

Daniel was seated at a table in the far corner of the Tavern and Zack moved slowly toward him, unsure what the reception would be like. He made a point of keeping his back straight, trying to conceal from his bandmates (and his father) that the twenty steps from the stage to the table had transferred him from bold rock guitarist to penitent boy. "Dad."

Relief. Fury. Joy. Frustration. Feelings that didn't have names and others that Daniel had never experienced before. He rose from his seat silently, struggling to maintain the emotional New Orleans levee that threatened to break at any moment.

They stood face-to-face, neither one sure what to say to the other, what to do.

And then Daniel wrapped his arms around his son, not so much hugging him as taking hold of him and hanging on like his son was the only fixed, deeply rooted piece in his life that could keep his head above the rushing flood waters as those levee walls betrayed him and gave way.

"It's all right, Dad." Zack patted Daniel's back like *he* was the parent, but nervously looked around the thinning crowd to see if his bandmates or anyone else at the bar had noticed what was happening between them. "It's all right."

Daniel pulled himself away. "No." He ran his sleeve across his eyes, too exhausted and emotionally spent to be embarrassed by his tears. "No, Zack, it's not."

Afraid his legs might simply give way, Daniel took his seat. He started to say something, then stopped, tried to start again, and found he had no means to express all of the thoughts and emotions that were running around his overloaded brain demanding expression.

Anger was the most persistent. He wanted to yell, wanted to rage at the immature and ill-conceived antics that had dragged him, kicking and screaming, through hell.

There was profound sadness too. Whatever his son's motivations, it pained him that the bond between them was not strong enough or had been so deteriorated over the past few years.

He was awash with pride for his boy for having conceived of and executed such a sophisticated plot, one that demonstrated such admirable musical tastes. There was something melancholic in the realization that his boy was no longer a boy. And there was joyous relief that his son was alive and sitting there in front of him.

So much that needed to be said, but all that came out was: "What the fuck?"

Though he'd clearly become a man, Zack took the same boyish breath he used to draw before explaining the unforeseeable series of events that had resulted in a shattered flat-screen or the family dog sporting a Mohawk.

He had explanations ready, of course. Since he'd first conceived his plan, he'd worked on explanations. At every step of the journey, he'd honed his story so he could meet his father's inevitable questions with answers that were razor-sharp and succinct.

At the last minute, however, he decided to just tell the truth. "I was afraid."

"Afraid?" Daniel had anticipated an amusing variety of alibis, but fear had not been among them. "Afraid of what?"

Zack took another breath, but not his juvenile, carnival-barker-playing-three-card-monte preparatory breath. This was a desperate attempt to keep his own emotions from overflowing their banks. When he could, he answered, "Of losing you."

The words hit Daniel with a physical force more terrible than anything Moog could have ever dished out, and he brought his hand to his mouth to keep from losing his breath. "Zack."

"When you tried to kill yourself—" He wished he hadn't begun, but it was out now and Zack could not stop. "When you did *that*. Something inside me died."

Daniel wanted to offer explanations of his own but said nothing, knowing his son wasn't finished with him yet.

"And even after you came home, even after they said you were all right. You just weren't—" Zack paused, searching for the words to say, "You just weren't *you*."

"And you thought by robbing me—"

"I didn't rob you," Zack snapped. "The fucking money is still here." He did a quick accounting in his head. There had been expenses. "Most of it."

Daniel shook his head, overwhelmed by the weight of everything that had happened—and was still left to happen. "What were you thinking, Zack?"

"I was thinking that the only thing you ever loved—" Zack hadn't wanted to bring her up, but there she was. "Besides Mom—"

"I love you." Daniel had never really understood the depth of those words until saying them to his son like that.

"Besides me and Mom." Zack was willing to spot him. "The only other thing you loved was music. But somewhere, somehow you lost that."

Daniel winced. "There was a lot going on for me."

His son had heard it before and ignored it this time too.

"The night they took you away," Zack continued, "I stayed at the house alone. I don't know, I just wanted you near. And I found all these old albums, these old records you'd had when you were my age. I realized these were what had inspired you to pick up a guitar. You know, to create something. They were what had made you feel alive. And I just thought that if I made you rediscover the music, if I could give that back to you…then maybe you could be alive. Again."

Daniel knew exactly which box of records Zack was talking about, but the dark irony was that he'd never listened to one of them. The old man from whom Daniel had bought his ES-335 from back when he still thought he might have a shot at the rock-and-roll dream had given him the records. The old man had told him he was wasting his time and his money on such a guitar until he learned the music behind it. Three weeks later "Driving You

Out of My Mind" hit. The guitar went up on the wall as a decoration and the box of records went in storage.

Daniel was moved that his son had thought of the scheme. And crushed his son felt he'd had to.

Zack struggled to continue. "And maybe I could be alive again too."

"Oh, Zack." Daniel closed his eyes and shook his head at the tragic irony. How could he tell his son that this well-intentioned (though misguided) attempt to save his life was the reason he was going to lose it. "You have no idea."

"And you did, didn't you?" Zack interrupted enthusiastically, sensing they might just be turning a corner. "You found something out there on the road."

Daniel knew the reason for his son's optimism. "You haven't seen the news recently, have you?"

"No. We've just been on tour the last couple days." He started to explain then realized he didn't have to. "Well, you've been right behind us so you know—"

"Yeah. I know."

"But you feel better now, don't you?"

Daniel considered the question, making sure to keep his hand with its missing finger hidden in his coat pocket. "There were complications."

And then in a moment of what Jung—or Sting—would call synchronicity, the barroom door opened wide and Daniel's two complications stepped inside.

"Oh, Jesus no," Daniel cried beneath his breath as he slouched in his seat to avoid being seen.

"Dad, what's wrong?"

"Where is the money?"

"I've got it, Dad." His tone suggested there was no "big deal" to any of this.

"Where?" Daniel shouted in a whisper.

"Those two Marshall amps don't actually work," Zack said, pointing to two unused guitar amps. "What I didn't spend setting all of this up is stashed inside."

"Listen to me." Daniel's voice was low and to-the-point, like they were in a huddle and he was drawing up the last-minute game winner for a Thanksgiving Day touch football game. "I want you to take one of those amps and I want you to get as far away from here as you can. Drop the Erickson. Pick up something like Flea or Bono or something."

"Dad, what are you—"

"For once in your life, just listen to me." He nervously checked the two at the door. They hadn't noticed him yet, but time was running out. "I'm going to take one of the amps—"

"I don't want the money, Dad." It was important to Zack that his father understood. "The money's not what this was about."

"It was always going to be yours, that was what I was saving the money for. But I need some of it now."

"Sure."

"Now take that amp and pack up your band and go." He tried to gauge his voice to convey urgency without conveying the panic he felt rising within. "Right now. Get out of Dodge."

"Dad?"

"I need you to do this for me, Zack." He looked over and saw Moog and Rabidoso talking to the girl behind the bar. "Go. Now."

Zack got to his feet, nodding his consent but still not understanding.

Daniel looked up at his son. "I'm proud of you. And I love you."

"I love you too."

The young man turned and started away. It was only then that it dawned on Daniel that he was saying good-bye to his son. Forever.

"And, Zack."

His son turned.

"I fucked up my whole life." Zack started to say something in his father's defense, but Daniel stopped him. "I've never done anything that really matters." He needed his son to know. "Nothing but you. People have built pyramids. And painted masterpieces. They recorded *Exile on Main Street*. So many people have done so many amazing things. But I look at you, at the man you've become, and I realize I had a small part in something so much greater than any of that." There was more he wanted to say, but no more words. Or time. "Thanks."

Zack smiled, "Sure thing."

He'd run out of time, but Daniel realized there was just one more thing he needed to say. "And, Zack."

"Yeah?"

"You know how I told you that music wasn't any kind of life, that rock was dead?" His son nodded. "Maybe I just didn't know where to take the pulse." Zack smiled. Daniel smiled too. "You keep rockin' it as hard as you can. And don't you ever let them make you stop."

"Count on it." With that his son turned and joined his bandmates at the bar.

Daniel watched him go.

And now he was ready. Daniel got up, walked over to the band's equipment, and casually picked up one of the amps Zack had indicated was stuffed full of cash.

He turned to go but found the way blocked by a side-by-side refrigerator in an overcoat. "Hello, Daniel."

343

"Moog." He wasn't surprised they'd managed to follow him there, but he had to know. "How'd you find me?"

Moog understood and was happy to oblige. "The pack of cigarettes I put in your pocket when I gave you that coat—"

"Yeah?"

"Personal tracker," the big man answered matter-of-factly. "I tracked you all the way here."

Daniel grinned and shook his head. How many times had he thought to throw those things out? "When they warn cigarettes'll kill you, you never think of it like that."

"You shouldn't have run, Daniel." Moog's voice was low and quiet.

"Yeah, you shouldn't have run, you little shit," Rabidoso chimed in.

"No," Daniel insisted. "It was the right thing to do." He held up the amp. "You didn't want to go back to Vegas empty-handed, did you?"

"That don't matter now," Rabidoso hissed.

"Really?" Daniel taunted. "Because I got your money."

"Where?" Moog wanted to know.

"Right here." Daniel held the amp up as high as he could.

Rabidoso looked over at the band gathered at the bar and started toward them.

"Hey," Daniel called out to stop him. "It was just a practical joke played on me by a band I used to manage."

"That so?" Rabidoso turned, more interested now in getting the lie out of him.

Moog looked over at the band skeptically.

Rabidoso's gaze was more predatory. "I think we should kill them all just for the trouble they caused us."

"No." Daniel snapped it like an order, then realized his mistake and looked to Moog. "I think about the only thing you guys could do to bring more attention to Filat is shoot up a bar in Seattle and kill some innocent kids. That'd really help you guys out." He could tell Moog saw the sense in what he was saying. "Besides, I have the money. And you have me. What do you need with any of them?"

Moog's verdict was quick. "He's right." And beyond appeal.

"What do you mean he's right? You're telling me those kids ran us all around this goddamn country, cost us ten days, and we're just going to let them—"

"I'm telling you we got what we came for. Now let's go." Moog pointed toward the exit sign at the back of the building and herded both men toward it.

"Don't you push me, man," Rabidoso started.

"Push you?" Moog stopped. "I'll put your ass right through that goddamn door if you don't open it and get to steppin'."

Wanting the pair out of the bar as quickly as possible, Daniel walked quickly to the door, opened it himself, and took a step out into the alley behind the tavern. "Guys, let's just get going."

Moog prodded the little man through the door and then followed. Holding the door open, Daniel turned over his shoulder and took one last look at his son. Then he let the door slam shut. Everything would be all right now—everything that mattered.

"Man, I'm telling you, this is bullshit," Rabidoso continued out in the alley.

Moog wasn't having any of it. "Will you just shut up on that now!"

"There's no practical joke here." Rabidoso walked up to Daniel. "You know what I think? I think I killed the wrong *puta* back in California. I think that's why you never tried to avenge your own son. I think somehow you called your son from Vegas and told him to get your money out of the house."

Daniel was worried. Not only had Moog not told Rabidoso to shut up, but he seemed genuinely interested in what the petite psycho was saying.

"I think you just ran us around and around until you thought you could get free," Rabidoso continued. "Then you came here to pick up some money so you could go deep underground. I think your son's still in that bar. And I think that Mr. P. would love to see the look on your face when I throw the little fuck over his balcony railing. I think *that's* an offering that would make all of this up to Mr. P."

Moog thought about it. And then rejected it. "None of that's got nothing to do with the job we were hired to do."

"I'm not asking your permission, Gigantor." Rabidoso's 9mm was already in his hand. "I'm going in there and getting that little *puta* and I'm giving him to Mr. P. as gift. And if he doesn't want him, then I'm offering him to *Santa Muerte*." Rabidoso turned to go back in through the exit door.

Daniel brought the cash-filled amp down on Rabidoso's head with such force that the little man crumbled to the pavement.

He raised the amp high above his head, prepared to deliver the *coup de grace*, but a sharp click drew Daniel's attention. He turned to find Moog had drawn his Desert Eagle and had it pointed straight at him. "I hate the little fucker too, but that was a seriously bad mistake."

Before he could explain, Daniel felt the cold chromed steel of Rabidoso's pistol against the back of his neck. "I'm going to kill you so hard—"

The sights of Moog's pistol shifted from Daniel to Rabidoso. "Don't!"

The Mexican looked over and saw the intent in the big man's eyes. There was, he knew, nothing to be gained in calling him on it now. He returned his pistol to its place in his jeans' waistband and raised his empty hands for his partner to see. "Satisfied."

"I ain't been satisfied since we started this mess."

Rabidoso just laughed. And then punched Daniel right in the throat.

The amp fell to the pavement as Daniel's hands instinctively came up to clutch his throat. A second later Rabidoso's cue ball of a fist struck him hard in the nose. Blood erupted like a broken water main. And then in the right eye. The nose again.

Daniel staggered backward. He wobbled on his feet.

A moment of silence. And then blackness.

An instant later, Daniel was looking up at the sky. Rabidoso was straddling his chest and punches were falling like rain in the Pacific Northwest.

"Stop it!" Moog ordered.

Rabidoso ignored him.

A size 14 Ferragamo kicked Rabidoso to the ground. The Desert Eagle convinced him not to push the matter. "Now get him up and let's go."

"Fuck you!" Rabidoso got to his feet, but he wasn't compliant. Not anymore. "You think you're running this show? You ain't been running shit! Not since we left! You think you the only motherfucker with a cell phone?" He pulled his phone out of his pants. "Fucking Motorola Android, *esse*. Top of the line. You not the only one talking to Mr. P. Why you think he sent me along anyway, you stupid ape?" He put his phone away. "How you think those fucking bikers keep finding us, you dumb motherfucker?

I'm the fucking *capitan* calling the shots. You think you got a future, asshole?"

Under other circumstances, Moog would have finished their discussion with his fists, but something about the question—an uncertainty that had dogged him since they'd started their trip—left him speechless and flat-footed.

"You're the past, *esse*. I'm the motherfucking future. And you ain't in my plans. And you ain't in Mr. P.'s plans. Now, I'm going in there and I'm getting this cocksucker's fucking son. And if you want to stop me, you take your shot now. But if I get back to Vegas and tell Mr. P. what he could have had, what you kept from him, it's only going to make your retirement party that much more painful. Trust me," he glared back at the big man. "I know. *I'm* the fucking retirement committee!"

Daniel used the time they'd spent arguing to struggle to his feet. "No!" He'd come too far, gone through too much to let anything happen to Zack now. He stumbled forward like a George Romero zombie. "I won't let you hurt my—" He made a desperate rush at the Mexican, grabbed him around the waist, and dragged him back to the ground.

There was nothing skilled or noble in the way Daniel fought. It probably wasn't even fighting as much as it was a flurry of mammalian fury, a parent protecting its child. He pressed his thumbs as hard as he could into Rabidoso's eye sockets and then swung his fists wildly. He grabbed handfuls of hair and bit down hard on the little man's ear, all the while growling and snarling like an animal.

Pound-for-pound Rabidoso was as tough as they came, but even he could endure such an attack for only so long. He struggled to push himself away and got to his feet, staggering around unsteadily as his brain worked feverishly to process the pain that had been inflicted on him. When he'd gained sufficient sense of it, Rabidoso rushed at Daniel, who was just getting to his feet. He tackled him hard and drove him into the green Dumpster at the end of the alley.

The two men hit the Dumpster with such force that they drove the heavy metal receptacle back a full foot. The crash of their impact echoed in the night as they bounced off it and fell to the pavement. They rolled and tumbled back and forth, but it was Rabidoso who ultimately got the best of the struggle and pinned Daniel beneath him.

Bloodied and beaten and with all his psychoses fully engaged, Rabidoso was no longer thinking about satisfying his employer or career advancement—or anything else. When he pulled the blade from his pants pocket, the only thought in his twisted head was cutting Daniel's heart from his chest. He raised the knife high above his head.

There was no telling where the dog might have come from. The most logical explanation would have been that the pup was a stray that had made a home behind the Dumpster and was responding instinctively to a perceived threat to its territory. It could have been that it was a runaway from the neighborhood that occasionally supplemented its kibble rations with a trip to the Dumpster. Or maybe it was simply that from time to time, things happen that are beyond explanation or understanding, things like love and music—and even the occasional charging dog.

The dog was tan and white, seventy pounds or more, and even more vicious than Rabidoso. It went straight for the arm that was poised to bring the knife down into Daniel's chest and sank its teeth into the flesh until tooth hit bone. As the dog's jaws tightened, it rolled its head violently back and forth, sinking them in farther and tearing the wound wider and wider.

Rabidoso screamed and cursed as he tried in vain to shake his arm free of the mutt's snarling maw. Gritting his teeth, he transferred the knife to his left hand and then slashed at the dog, opening a wound along its left side. The dog squealed in pain, released the arm, and then ran scampering off behind the Dumpster.

"What did I tell you!" The words came out of Moog's mouth, but the voice was deeper, colder, and crueler than his own. "What did I *fuckin'* tell you!"

Rabidoso was focused on inspecting the deep wound in his arm and so was surprised to find the big man advancing on him. "What?"

"I told you if I ever saw you touch another dog again—" The big man's eyes flared with rage.

Uninterested in continuing their rivalry any further, Rabidoso turned his attention back to the wound, which he was certain would require stitches. And a shot.

"I warned you," the big man growled.

He looked up, distracted and annoyed. "What are you talking about?"

Moog's right hand wrapped itself into the front of Rabidoso's jersey and lifted him off the ground and above his head like he was just a *toy* psycho killer. "You love her so much? Meet your motherfucking *Muerte!*"

Maybe Rabidoso's boasts that he'd never known fear in his life were true, but he more than made up for it in that moment. Frantically, he reached back for his pistol, but just as he found its grip the big man brought him down, crashing him into the steel Dumpster with a force that dented the Dumpster and shattered bones. The pistol tumbled from the Mexican's limp hand.

Again and again, Moog repeated that simple motion, lifting Rabidoso up into the air and then bringing him down on the

Dumpster. Over and over, he smashed him until the Mexican's body was completely limp. Moog held the broken body over his head and then let it fall to the ground.

A second later the big man staggered back, unsure what had happened or what he'd done. He looked down the alley. Rabidoso lay motionless in a deepening pool of his own blood. He looked up the alley. Daniel was gone. The money was gone too.

In the distance, Moog could hear sirens. He couldn't be sure who'd witnessed what he'd done there, but he was certain the cops were coming for him now. He looked down at his feet; they were splattered with blood. His suit pants too.

The sirens drew closer.

He wondered if he should even bother to run. Would his escape be worth the effort? Escape to what? His fate was set. But he couldn't help wishing that for just once in his life…he could beat his fate.

Tires squealed at the end of the alley. He looked up at the car. It was a maroon Monte Carlo. Daniel was behind the wheel.

"Get in the goddamn car!"

CHAPTER FORTY-FIVE

Daniel had driven almost to Yakima by the time Moog was ready to speak. And even then it was only a hushed, "Why?"

"That's a big question," Daniel quipped. "Why what?"

"Why would you come back for me? You were out. You had the money. Why not just keep running? Why'd you come back to pull me outta there?" The big man's voice was hushed and troubled. "I'm thirty-two goddamn years old and nobody ever helped me outta nuthin'." He'd intended those words to resonate with pride, but after hearing his declaration out loud he wasn't sure what there was to be proud of.

They rode for a while in silence, though it was clear something was still troubling Moog. After a dozen miles had gone past, he turned to Daniel and admitted, "You savin' me makes me feel funny. Like I owe you, but it's like you sold me something I didn't wanna buy."

"Forget it." Daniel didn't bother to take his eyes from the highway. "That one's on the house. You don't owe me anything."

"'Cause this don't change nothing," Moog announced, more vehemently than he knew he needed to. "We can share some miles, but you ain't my friend. You just a paycheck. That's all, all you ever gonna be."

"Got it." Daniel ran a hand through his thinning hair. "I just thought—"

"Well, don't," Moog snapped. "You think too goddamn much!" He crossed his arms across his massive chest. "Just don't you do it again. I look like I'm goin' down, you just let me sink."

Daniel was too tired to say anything more than "All right."

It wasn't enough to satisfy whatever was eating at the big man. "If you ain't nothin' to me, then how can I be anything to you? How can I be anything but the badass motherfucker who's gonna turn you over to that crazy Russian cocksucker?" He asked the question like he knew it didn't make sense. " 'Cause that's what I'm gonna do."

"Maybe my chooser's broken?" Daniel offered. The thought of her brought a smile to his face.

"What the fuck is that supposed to mean?"

Daniel had no intention of sharing. "What do you want me to say? I guess I thought that buried underneath all your homicidal intent there's a good man, too good to just leave with the trash in the back of an alley." He sighed, weighing whether to continue. "And I still think you're too good to—" And then he stopped.

"Too good to what?"

Daniel shook his head. "I don't know, I just don't understand what someone like you is doing as a muscled manservant to that Soviet psycho."

"You just check yourself one damn minute." The big man held up an open hand like he was an oversized crossing guard stopping a car in a crosswalk. "I ain't nobody's servant. I'm an independent contractor."

"All right. You're an independent whatever-you-say-you-are."

"I'm an independent contractor, motherfucker," Moog repeated, in case there was any confusion. "That's what I am. It ain't much but—"

"Then why be it?"

"'Scuse me?"

To Daniel the question was simple. "If what you are 'ain't much,' then why not be something different? You know, something more."

To Moog the question was a complicated one, but the answer was simple. "I was born on the bad side of Kansas City. Whatchu think I was going to turn out to be? A fucking doctor or lawyer?"

Daniel just smiled. "I've just spent the last two weeks following the path of dozens of guys who were born into situations that were a fucksight tougher than yours. And you know what they did?" He didn't bother to wait for an answer. "They changed the fucking world!"

"First off," Moog was getting wildly angry now. "It hasn't been no two weeks yet."

"All right," Daniel easily conceded. "It hasn't been two weeks, what else did I say that was wrong?"

Moog was furious, but he wasn't sure at whom. After a silent mile or two, he muttered something like, "Make more money than any of those old guys ever did." Daniel didn't respond and that only made the big man grumble more. "Independent contractor, goddamn it."

They didn't talk for a long while. Daniel just drove and Moog just fumed.

When the silence finally began to bother him more than what Daniel had said, the big man asked, "You know he's just gonna kill you, right?"

"I think we're both pretty sure of that." His calmness surprised even Daniel.

"Then why you doing it? 'Cause he ain't gonna kill you easy." Moog felt bad saying it out loud to someone who'd probably just saved him a life stretch in the Washington State Pen, but it was a truth. "Hell, if you want to die so badly," he said, "get yourself a room and a girl, a bottle, and some pills. Go out real easy."

"It's not as easy as you'd think," Daniel said with a degree of authority that surprised his traveling companion.

"Whatchu mean?"

They had nothing but time and miles in front of them. "You ever been in love?"

"Proper love?"

"Any kind of love."

"No. Probably not."

"You're a lucky man," Daniel assured him. "I was in love once."

Moog had been to Connie's house and already knew the story's ending. "Went bad, huh?"

"When my son, Zack, graduated high school," Daniel explained, "my wife and I threw him a big party at our house. All our friends and family. His friends. His girlfriend. Her family." Daniel's voice trailed off.

"And?"

Bad thoughts can be hard to escape and Daniel had a lot to get lost in. "What?"

"You were saying something about a graduation party," the big man prompted.

"Right. Well, Zack's girlfriend brought her parents and little sister. She brought her older brother too. And to give you some idea of this guy, he'd just dropped out of community college to pursue a career as an actor because he'd landed a walk-on in *Mega-Python versus Gatoroid II: The Rematch*."

"I saw that movie," Moog chimed in before realizing that wasn't really the point.

Daniel chuckled anyway. "Well, halfway through the party everyone's out on the main deck and there's a large crash. Of course, everyone turns and there's my wife and this kid. They'd been upstairs in our bedroom and—whatever contortions they'd gotten tangled in—they managed to crash through the sliding glass door and land right on the balcony."

After all the years passed, Daniel only wished he could find it as funny as Moog did. "I'm sorry," the big man whined after he finally stopped laughing. "For reals?"

"For reals."

Moog wiped away a tear and shook his head. "Well, a woman's like a dresser."

"How's that?"

"Always someone running through her drawers."

Daniel laughed.

"And the dude?"

Daniel gritted his teeth. "Randy."

The pieces fit. "That the boy that Rabidoso did back at your old lady's place?"

Daniel nodded.

"*Maaaaaaan*," Moog stretched the word out to express his amazement. "If it makes you feel any better, that crazy little Mexican hurt the boy all kinds of ways before he finally put him down and out."

"It really doesn't." Daniel felt he had to be honest. "Not *a lot* anyway."

"I knew that wasn't your son." Moog wanted Daniel to know.

"I thought you did. But I couldn't figure out why you didn't tell Rabidoso."

"That psycho was sick. Turning someone like that loose on someone's kid, man, that ain't right. Ain't professional."

Daniel was curious. "How'd you know it wasn't Zack?"

"When we first broke into your ex's, I was lookin' around upstairs. Saw your boy's bedroom. Lots of pictures of him in there. Saw your ex's bedroom too. Lots of pictures of her with the guy Rabidoso worked on, so I just figured he wasn't the son."

Daniel nodded. "Can't argue with that logic."

"Freaky pictures."

"I get it."

"I mean some freaky, nasty pictures." Moog shook his head. "I mean the things were just unnatural...I mean—"

"I get it," Daniel snapped.

Moog smiled sheepishly and tried to steer the conversation back. "So what happened with you after all that?"

"After my wife fell out of the window screwing my son's girlfriend's brother?"

"Right."

"Well, she went off with him. Sued me for divorce and took half of everything."

"Except your cash," Moog pointed out, ever the glass-half-full kinda guy.

"No, she took most of that too." Daniel was growing tired and the story wasn't helping. "I fell into a depression. Tried to deal with it with the bottle. Tried to deal with it with pills. Tried to deal with it with the bottle *and* pills. After a while, I couldn't work. Couldn't be a father. Couldn't be anything. And so one night I decided I didn't *want* to be anything."

"Dark times, huh?" Moog had seen his share.

"People think hell is all about the evil, but that's not how the story goes. Devil doesn't start out hating God. He loves Him more than anything. But it's not enough. God loves someone else. That's what hell is. It's not sulfur and flame, it's being discarded. It's being told that your love—everything you got, everything you are—just doesn't matter. You're inconsequential. That's what hell is."

Moog knew there were all sorts of hells, but he didn't bother to interrupt.

"So one night I took a handful of pills. Antidepressants. Anti-anxiety. Pain relievers. Sleeping pills. Everything that had been prescribed to me over the course of my descent. Took it all and washed it down with whisky."

"What happened?"

"Turns out hell's not that easy to escape. My son stopped by my place unexpectedly. Found me there in a pool of pharmaceutical-grade, Technicolor vomit and called the ambulance. I spent thirty days in a psych ward." He shook his head wistfully. "If you think success can build you up quickly, you ought to see how quickly the sickly stench of failure will bring you right back down again. The whole thing wiped me out."

"And that where Mr. P. come in?"

Daniel nodded. "I got an idea for a reality show. I used to handle a band called Mission." He turned expectantly.

Moog nodded halfheartedly. He'd heard the name but not the music.

"Well," Daniel said with a shrug. "They were fairly big about ten years ago. And then they imploded. Booze. And coke. And pills. But I got an idea that I could resurrect them and follow them on tour—not headlining or anything—but, you know, hit the state fairs and just show how they handled their sobriety out on the road."

"I'd watch it." Moog didn't own a TV, but it seemed like the right thing to say.

"I think a lot of people would have, but your boss didn't like the rough cut I sent him. He said it needed more spice."

"Spice?"

"The very next stop on the tour, he sent over some girls with a free supply of 'spice.'" There was more to the story, but his guilt made him hesitate telling it. "I could've stopped it, but I was afraid to lose Filat's financing. So I let it happen. And the next thing I knew everyone in the band was using worse than ever." He sighed sadly. "There's nothing more pathetic than some comatose, potbellied, middle-aged rocker shitting his leather pants. No one wants to see that." He reconsidered what he'd said. "Not more than once anyway."

Daniel thought to himself and chuckled. "The funny thing is that I was going to use my own money to finance the pilot, but then I met your boss and thought he was just a little shmuck. I thought I could use his money for the show and not have to touch my safety net. But now, I'm not only going to lose all my money anyway, but I'm going to lose my life too." He stopped to consider the true absurdity of it.

"That's why I'm certain there's a god out there," Daniel continued.

"How's that?"

"Because life is so damn funny and humor doesn't just happen, humor's hard. I just can't believe that all of this could happen just by chance. I mean, my son set up that little musical goose chase as a way to make me want to live again. And it worked. But because of it, I'm going to die. That kind of irony is just too perfect to be happenchance. It takes real effort."

Moog was quiet for a moment. It wasn't something he normally liked to talk about. "I hope He keeps his sense of humor
for me."

"You believe in God?"

"My gramma said so, but I don't know. After all the things I
done, I kinda hope there ain't nothing there."

"Well, I'll know soon enough." Daniel's voice was quietly
resigned.

"I still don't understand why you're going."

"You have anything you'd die for?"

"Lots I'd kill for," the big man hedged.

"That's not the same thing."

Moog knew it wasn't.

"Well, I'd die for my son. And that's what I'm going to do.
I'm going to face up to that crazy Russian and settle this account
without involving my boy."

"Is that why you saved me back there?" Moog was uncom-
fortable with the thought. "'Cause I don't know if I'm going to be
all that much help when we get there."

"You think he's going to kill you too?"

"Mr. P.?"

Daniel nodded.

"Things got pretty messed up out here."

"They sure did."

Ever the professional, Moog was willing to take responsibility
for everything that had happened on his shift. "And it was all on
me."

Daniel knew there was something else. "He won't like what
happened to Rabidoso, will he?"

"Well, I ain't gonna tell him. And you ain't gonna tell him." The big man turned suddenly, like he needed to be reassured about that.

"No, I'm not going to tell him."

Moog made a gesture with his oversized hand like he was dismissing all of those concerns. "I don't know. Someone's gonna kill me sometime. I guess it could just as easily be Mr. P. tonight. Shit, you know him; not even *he* will know what he's gonna do until he does it."

They drove in silence for a mile or two.

"If it helps," Daniel started, "all the reasons I gave you are true."

"About why you came back for me?" Moog clarified.

Daniel nodded. "I thought about not coming back for you, about just running."

"It's what I would've done."

"In the end I figured you were just too good a man to leave in an alley like that."

They drove on for another couple of silent miles. Moog was the first to break the silence. "It's not completely lost on me, you know?"

"What's that?"

"Why you did what you did. Why you're going back now."

"How's that?"

"I got a kid of my own." There was a note of solemnity in his voice.

"Really?" The question reflected Daniel's surprise, but also a degree of happiness. "Where is—"

"She's with her momma," Moog explained. "I don't really see her all that much. She's better off without me." That truth hurt him. "I send her money," he was quick to point out. "Take good care of her and her momma."

That didn't surprise Daniel.

"I just ain't fit to be no father."

Daniel nodded. "None of us are."

Moog nodded back. "In my whole life, it's the only thing I feel guilty about."

Daniel stared out at the endless highway. "I guess you do understand."

CHAPTER FORTY-SIX

Oregon. The Beaver State. The name brings to mind rugged, rocky Pacific coasts and dense evergreen forests.

Like so much in life, however, the reality of it all is very, very different. US 84 cuts down deep through an Oregon that is an endless wasteland, a barren landscape that resembles nothing so much as the dark side of the moon.

Mile after mile passed with the Monte Carlo's speedometer quivering up near ninety, but without any features to mark their bearings, it seemed they were standing still, as if they could've opened their doors and stepped out into the gray nothingness.

Daniel's eyes grew heavy, and then heavier. He tried to shake away the fatigue. He slapped his face and bit the inside of his cheek. He rolled down the window and then rolled it back up again. Nothing he tried did anything to free him from the sleepiness that threatened to pull him down in a warm, comfortable stranglehold.

The tires screamed and the steering wheel shook when he drifted over the shoulder and onto the rumble strips. Startled,

Daniel pulled the sedan back onto the highway and nervously looked over at Moog. The incident hadn't woken him.

Concentrating on his fight to stay awake and on the road, Daniel hadn't noticed the bikers at first. By the time he did, they were right on his bumper, riding as a pack of four, with two pairs riding two abreast. Their throaty pipes rattled the windows with a predatory roar.

He sped up a little. And then sped up a little more. He pressed the accelerator until the Monte Carlo began to shake and shimmy. The bikes stayed right behind him. He remembered what had happened in New Orleans. And Chicago. And Cleveland. Stealing a check in the rearview mirror, it occurred to him that they were in very big trouble.

"Wake up," Daniel called across the armrest.

Moog stirred in his seat, but only slightly. He said something that sounded like "Hrmmmph" and then fell back into the depths of sleep.

"Wake up!" Nothing.

Daniel reached across and poked the big man, who shot up out of his slumber with a reflexive reach for the pistol holstered beneath his left arm. "What th—"

He looked out the window and then over at Daniel. "What the hell is wrong with you? You don't go just poking a man when he's asleep." He made a point of pulling his hand away from his Desert Eagle's grip. "Not a man like me." He made some disgruntled smacking noises like a bear woken too early from his hibernation.

Daniel ignored the tantrum. "I think we've got company."

"Company?"

Daniel motioned with his thumb and Moog followed the gesture to the back window. "What?"

"The bikers," Daniel answered incredulously.

"Bikers?"

When he turned back to the window one of them had pulled up alongside them and was taking aim with a cannon almost as big as Moog's.

A second later the Monte Carlo's chassis dipped down to the pavement as Daniel stood on the brakes. The thread-worn tires squealed in protest and left rubber they couldn't afford to lose on the pavement as the car fishtailed to a stop.

The shot from the biker's oversized hand cannon sounded like a clap of thunder, but the shot missed the mark.

The bikes growled loudly as they split in pairs, swerving to either side in a desperate attempt to avoid the sedan. Only three of them made it clear. The fourth clipped the Monte Carlo's right rear quarter panel and dropped the bike straight down to the road. Sparks shot up from the wreckage like it was a dancing dragon in a Chinatown parade on New Year's night.

The biker bounced off the pavement, went high in the air like he was made of rubber, twisted in midair, came down, and bounced again. He slid three hundred yards down the highway as Exhibit A in the ongoing debate over the importance of helmets. And proper riding clothes. And safe riding habits.

"Jesus Christ!" Moog screamed as he instinctively grabbed the dash.

Ahead of them on the barren highway, the three bikers had turned and come to a stop, lined three abreast across the highway.

Daniel turned to Moog. "What do I do?"

Moog's answer was simple. "Get rid of them."

"How?"

The big man just shook his head. "Don't you ever get tired?"

"Tired?" Daniel didn't understand the big man's point or what it had to do with the three bikers who sat five hundred yards down the road menacingly revving their bikes, making them roar like wild beasts begging to be freed to attack.

"Of always asking for things. Asking for help. Asking for permission. Asking for forgiveness." Moog made no effort to disguise his disdain as he pointed across the dash to the riders who were waiting for them. "Those guys want to kill your ass."

Daniel looked nervously toward them and then back to Moog.

"Before you go and throw your life away, just once…when they try to push you 'round, stand up and be a Push Back Man."

From the car's stereo Elmore James made his guitar pay the price. And suddenly Daniel understood. He thought about the life he'd led. And the one he wished he had. He thought about everything Atibon had told him about Today music. Suddenly he knew why he'd come to the crossroads and he could admit what he'd wanted all along.

The Monte Carlo squealed again as he dropped her into drive and brought the accelerator down as hard as she'd tolerate.

The bikers answered the call and rolled back hard on their throttles, erupting from the point like three leather-clad missiles.

Moog pulled his Desert Eagle and turned to Daniel. "Now, what's the plan?"

"Plan?" He stared down the highway. "Something will turn up."

The big man smiled as the distance to the bikers closed quickly.

Shots from the bikers popped holes in the windshield, which each instantly connected itself to the others with an intricate spread of spider webs in the glass.

Return fire from Moog's Desert Eagle popped holes in one of the bikers. He was dead before he hit the pavement with a sickening thud. Blood and sparks sprayed across the pavement.

The two other bikers kept coming. Closer and closer.

More shots hit the Monte Carlo.

More shots whizzed past the bikers.

And then, just as the two converging forces were about to collide, Daniel pulled the steering hard to the left and stomped on the brake. The car began to spin wildly around and around.

The bikers had been preparing to dodge the oncoming car, swerving to either side to avoid the five-foot span of the sedan's hood. They hadn't counted on the Monte Carlo spinning down the highway like a two-ton, Detroit-made, rotating blade of a meat grinder. There was no escape.

One rider hit the hood, slid across it from left to right, and then disappeared somewhere beneath the skidding wheels, smeared across the asphalt like a dollop of strawberry jam across a hot piece of toast.

The last rider hit the Monte Carlo's trunk, took a tumble over it, then ricocheted off it, up into the air. He landed on the shoulder of the road and rolled down the pavement.

"Now," Moog asked, "was that so hard?"

Daniel slowed then pulled to the side of the road and stepped out of the car. He left the engine running and the door wide open.

The horizon he looked out on was strewn with wreckage. Man and machine. All of it linked by lines of crimson blood, burnt rubber, and spilled oil like some gruesome connect-the-dots picture. Daniel took it all in with a cold eye and then began to walk toward the scene, his legs surprisingly steady and strong.

Daniel looked down on what had once been a man but was now reduced to a mass of wheezing and convulsing parts, not coldly, but with a certain detachment. The rider's twitching hand suddenly reached up and grabbed hold of Daniel's pant leg. "You didn't come to the crossroads to die," the shattered man gasped.

"What you come there for, *mi key*." The grip on his leg tightened with one final spasm and then fell lifeless.

Moog came up behind him and then stood next to him. "You all right?"

"You don't have to go back," Daniel told him without taking his eyes off the still-smoking wreckage. "I can do this myself."

Moog looked past the carnage, out toward the endless horizon. "I got a job to do. And I'm going to see that through."

Daniel just nodded.

"You know, you could too," Moog offered. "You could head someplace," the big man told him. "You could run now and I wouldn't come after."

Daniel looked down at his feet. The bloody mass wasn't wheezing or twitching anymore. "You're not the only one with something to finish."

Moog turned back toward the Monte Carlo, waiting for them there with its doors open wide at the berm of the road. "Then let's go."

Daniel leaned down and pulled a .45 free from the corpse's waistband. It felt good in his hand. Like it belonged there. "Yeah. Let's finish this."

CHAPTER FORTY-SEVEN

It wasn't quite midnight when they finally pulled the Monte Carlo up to the valet's stand at the Hotel du Monde—twelve hundred miles and a handful of street-legal speed from Seattle.

Through the shot-out windshield, Daniel saw the kid in the maroon valet jacket jump back as the bullet-riddled sedan rolled to a stop and then shuttered like it was going through death throes. When he was reasonably sure the heap wasn't about to burst into flames, the kid came around and pulled on the dented driver's door. It took three hard tugs before it finally came open with the shrill sound of metal on metal, like opening a steel coffin.

Daniel got out and handed him the keys. "Don't scratch it."

"No, sir," the kid said earnestly.

Daniel reached into the backseat and pulled out the cash-stuffed amp with his right hand.

"You want me take that?" Moog offered.

"I'd like to go up there carrying it myself."

The big man nodded. "I get it."

Daniel shifted the amp to his left hand and then reached behind him with his right to make certain his pistol was ready.

Together they walked to the far end of the hotel's casino lobby, to the bank of elevators that serviced the penthouse. Moog pushed the up button and then turned to his traveling companion. "However this ends for you—" He wasn't particularly good with saying things unrelated to his professional duties. He felt awkward, aware of his lack of eloquence. "I hope it goes how you want it to go."

Daniel said, "Thanks." And meant it.

The elevator doors opened, but Daniel put his hand out to stop Moog from getting on. "Before we go up there, there's something I need to tell you."

Moog watched the doors slide closed again. "What?"

"When this all started and you took me to Malibu—"

"Yeah?"

"I thought the money would be there. I did."

"All right." It didn't matter anymore.

"But I knew the gun was in there too." The relief Daniel found in the troubling revelation made it sound glib in a way he hadn't intended.

Moog wasn't entirely sure how to take it. Or if there was more. "OK."

"If the money had been there, my plan was to shoot both of you." Daniel hung his head. "I've felt bad about that for a while now. I just wanted you to know that."

"All right."

"And I want you to know, with everything that's happened—" Daniel pushed the up button, ready to go now. "I'm glad I didn't."

The doors opened and both men stepped into the car. They rode up in silence until the "P" on the light pad lit up and an electronic female voice announced, "Penthouse." The doors opened. Moog stepped out.

And someone punched Daniel right in the face.

It took a minute for the lights to come back on in his head. By that time there was a heavily muscled man with a dragon tattoo wrapped around his neck standing over him, with his left hand clenching Daniel's shirt front and his right balled up in a fist. "This is for New Orleans." The punch fell so hard it seemed to shake the entire elevator car.

"This is for Shakey up in Chicago," the man growled as his biker boot kicked Daniel in the ribs. Another kick.

Daniel tried to crawl away, but there was no place to go.

"And this is for today," the bulked-up biker continued. "This is for Black Greg." A kick. "And Lobo." A kick. "Turtle." A kick. "And Kingpin." A kick.

"Dragon, that's enough," the potbellied biker Daniel remembered from New Orleans yelled as he grabbed his brother-in-arms by the arm. "The Russian didn't want him touched!"

"Fuck the Russian!" Dragon shouted as he let another kick fly. Another kick, and then he suddenly realized the risk in defying Filat. "This ain't over!" he promised.

Daniel coughed and the clump of blood and mucus it produced made him gag. "No." He spat and then looked Dragon in the eye. "This is a long way from over."

Potbelly pulled Daniel from the elevator car and patted him down, immediately discovering the pistol concealed at the small of his back and pulling it free. He tucked the confiscated gun into his own waistband and then pushed Daniel into the suite's main living area.

Filat Preezrakevich was waiting there, sprawled out on an enormous couch that he shared with half a dozen young women in various stages of undress. A dozen more girls circulated in the bar area behind him like exotic zoo animals in lingerie.

"Ahhhh!" the mad Russian called out. "Look who's returned from his cross-country vaca—" He stopped midmock when he noticed Daniel's condition. "What is this? Did I ask any of you beat him? No. I deed not!"

"No." Potbelly looked like he'd been caught peeing in the hotel pool with the telltale blue ring of Wee-Wee-See spreading out across the water all around him. It was time to shift the blame. "It was Dragon. I never touched the guy."

Filat rolled his eyes the way he used to do with his kids (before he'd had to kill them) and called for his disobedient biker. "Dragon! Get in here!"

A couple of seconds later, the muscle-bound biker walked into the living area, still trying to wipe Daniel's blood from the assortment of inked demons, monsters, and naked women that wrapped around his massive forearms. "What?"

"What is this?"

Dragon looked disinterestedly at the man he'd just beaten. "What?"

"He is broke-een already!" the little man complained. "Did I not say no one touches him?"

"I had a score to settle with him." Dragon shrugged it all off.

"No. No! NO!" The Russian jumped to his feet. "If I ask you to my table, do you eat before me? If I ask you to par-tee, do you drink before me? Fuck my girls before me?" He gestured at the strippers, who'd all stopped their gyrations and were staring at their patron like so many heavily medicated fawns caught in high beams.

Dragon still wasn't seeing the problem with the warm-up ass-kicking he'd delivered. "What do you want me to do? *Un*-punch him?" He might not have meant it to come out of his mouth as flippantly as it did, but the offhand comment made everyone in the room suck in their collective breath.

"Un-punch him?" Filat asked the question almost gently. "You talk to me like this?" He took a step or two toward the biker, picking up a bottle of Jack Daniels from the coffee table as he went. "That funny. Un-punch him?"

Dragon took it as a good sign, a conciliatory draw on a shared bottle of Jack. "What? I can't do nothin' about it now." And as far as he was concerned that was all there was to it.

He was wrong. Filat smiled and then a second later he swung the whisky bottle with incredible speed up toward Dragon's head. It shattered against his left temple. Some of the strippers squealed at the collision of flesh and glass. Some of the bikers winced, but everyone in the room knew better than to interfere.

Dragon collapsed to the floor in a shower of Jack and glass shards. A second later there was a psychotic Russian on him too.

The Raging Runt of Rublyovka slashed wildly at the unconscious biker's face. The wounds were so deep that the body jumped and convulsed as each was opened, but the pain was never enough to stir him back to consciousness. Again and again, Filat cut at the face until the only thing vaguely human about it was the gaping mouth where bubbles formed in the pooling blood as Dragon struggled to breathe.

Filat stuck the razor-sharp end of the bottle neck into Dragon's mouth and began moving it about like it was a plumbing tool and he was laboring to get something out of a clogged sink. As he worked, he screamed, "Nobody talk to Filat like that! Nobody! Nobody!"

When he was finished or exhausted or simply figured his insubordinate biker minion had had enough, he rose to his feet, leaving the broken bottle protruding out of Dragon's mouth. It was clear the adrenaline rush (and crystal high) had left his legs a little shaky and Filat took a deep breath and a moment to collect himself. He shook out his robe, as if that did anything for the blood patterns that were splattered all over it. "Now. Where were we?" He returned to his spot on the couch.

None of the girls wanted to sit next to the blood-drenched psychotic, but he patted the seat next to him insistently and a blue-haired girl who looked like she might still remember faintly what it was like to be happy took the seat, figuring it was better than taking a chance on pissing him off. He put an arm around her and she tried not recoil at his blood-covered touch.

"Right," Filat said flatly and then turned his still-crazy-wide eyes on Daniel. "That was regrettable. It's been so long, I wanted to be the one to welcome you personally." He fingered one of the necklaces around his neck, a gold chain that featured a severed finger dangling from it. "I had a whole thing where I tell you I keep promise and keep finger until you return." He looked disdainfully at the corpse on the floor. "But Dragon ruined all that." Daniel didn't say anything and that seemed to please the Russian. "We were talking about vacations, *da*?"

"Mine was sort of a working vacation," Daniel conceded.

"Moog—" The Russian turned like he was a trial lawyer and this was the time to call the surprise witness. "You enjoy *your* vacation?"

The big man didn't seem to be actively restrained, but he was surrounded by four bikers, all of whom had their attention and their best "I'm a badass" looks focused on him. Daniel remembered them all from New Orleans: Zit-face, Shorty, Toothless. And Ape-Face.

"There wasn't no vacation 'bout it, Mr. P." Moog sounded respectful but unshakable. "It was all business."

"Good. Good. That's what I like to hear: all bees-ness." Filat laughed and everybody in the room was too scared not to laugh along—everybody but Moog and Daniel.

"Speaking of the bees-ness, Moog." Filat sat up and adjusted himself on the couch, like he was getting ready to say something important. "Where is Rabidoso?"

Moog had expected the question and answered it as simply as he'd planned. "I don't know."

"Don't know?" The Russian's brow furled. "I send with you. Ask you show him ropes. Why you no know, Moog?"

"He was kinda crazy, Mr. P."

"He was fuck-eeng cra-zee, Moog!" The Russian laughed and everyone who was afraid of sucking on a broken Jack bottle chortled right along. "That why I hire him. What I want to know is where he is now?"

"I don't know." And that was the truth. "He's just gone."

"You try to be the funny?" He asked the question looking pointedly at Dragon's still-warm corpse. "You see what happen with the funny."

Moog squirmed, not afraid but knowing he'd have to offer some explanation. "He was shooting everything that moved."

The Russian smiled proudly. "That sounds like Rabidoso."

"We had our differences and he took off." It wasn't the whole truth, but he thought it was close enough to work.

"Took off?" Preezrakevich scoffed.

"Yes, sir."

The Russian seemed to weigh the plausibility of the explanation Moog offered and surprised everyone in the room by accepting it. "Well, maybe we see him soon."

"Yes, sir," Moog answered, confident that no one was likely to see his pint-size antagonist until King County's trash pick-up day.

"Enough of this," the mad Russian declared with a grand gesture. "It's party in here with all these pretty girls." All the women had stopped dancing and gyrating, paralyzed like statutes by the rising tension in the room. "We men go out on balcony. Finish business out there."

"Sure thing, Mr. P." Moog wasn't intimidated by the offer.

Waiting for them out on the balcony was the Viking biker Moog had first seen charging up the stairs of the Rock and Roll Hall of Fame. He was a good head or two taller than Moog and at least a hundred pounds heavier. Almost every inch of flesh not hidden by his club colors and jeans was covered in tattoos, including a Nordic pattern that ran from one scarred cheek across his often-broken nose to his other scarred cheek. He stared straight at Moog like a linebacker picking up his assignment.

It was impossible not to take immediate notice of the Viking giant, like Bigfoot just hanging out on the balcony, but Moog pretended not pay him any particular attention. Instead, he pushed open the sliding glass door and calmly stepped through. His escorts followed closely behind but stopped as soon as they got outside, as if their orders were to guard the door, not the big man. Moog walked to the far end of the deck and stood alone, careful not to let on he was watching the Viking out of the corner of his eye.

Ponytail dragged Daniel out onto the balcony and pushed him toward the railing over which there was every chance he'd be sailing soon. The night air was bracing and the winter wind blew away the thick layer of daze that had clouded Daniel's thoughts since his stomping in the elevator. He looked out at the lights of the city below and the stars up above, marveling at their brilliance and wondering which were brighter. They seemed so much more beautiful since the last time he saw them.

Filat Preezrakevich was the last to come out, making a dramatic entrance by stepping through a curtain of biker outlaws. "So, I ask for money back in twenty-four hours. You come, what? Twelve days?" He was clearly biting back on his anger.

"Eleven days," Moog corrected after checking his watch. "It's not midnight yet."

"Eleven days?" The Russian laughed, but the four behind him only tittered nervously. He drew his blood-soaked bathrobe around him. "Not argue about little things."

"Yes, sir."

"I ask for my money. But what is this?" The Russian pointed to the amp one of the bikers had brought out with them.

"It's a Marshall Class Five tube amp," Daniel was quick to identify.

"And you bring this why?"

"Because the cash is in it," Daniel answered. And then added with a smile, "And 'cause you can't rock a satchel."

"The whole million?" the Russian wanted to know.

"About half." Daniel shrugged, surprisingly calm about it all. "Give or take."

"Doesn't matter," Filat said dismissively, not willing to concede he'd been disrespected. "You owe me far more now."

"Is that right?"

"Interest of fifty percent for," Filat turned to Moog, "eleven days, right?"

The big man nodded, although it was clear he didn't want to.

"Expenses. Not cheap tracking you down. My men don't work free. Do they, Moog?"

The big man reluctantly shook his head again. "No, sir."

"And penalties! For thinking you can make fool of me! Of me!" His voice was so filled with furious psychoses that Moog and Daniel were the only ones on the balcony who didn't flinch. He looked up at the night sky as if there were a calculator up among the stars. "Twenty-five million will cover it. If you don't have that, my friend, then we have very serious prob-leem."

Daniel looked over at the amp and then back to Filat. "I started out thinking I could come here and beg you."

"Oh, you will beg me." The Russian seemed certain of it.

"No, I don't think I'm going to." It was one of those rare moments when a person naturally realizes the importance of words, and Daniel paused to collect exactly what he wanted to say. "As I was running around chasing down this money—Memphis, New Orleans, Chicago, Ruleville." He laughed at a dozen memories all at once. "It's a long story. But I found," he corrected himself, "I rediscovered something."

"And what is that?" Mr. P. asked sarcastically.

It was a simple lesson, really. "The goddamn necessity of living your whole life like you were playing Today music."

The Russian looked at Moog, equal parts confused and outraged. "What is he talking about?"

Moog stammered, but Daniel could speak for himself. "I'm telling you I set out to beg you, but along the way I realized I never got a goddamn thing by begging for it. And I'm never going to beg for anything ever again in my life."

"Lucky for you that won't be much longer," Preezrakevich snarled.

"Maybe." Daniel seemed, not indifferent, but situationally confident. "But I got the feeling that something's going to turn up. So, before things get all shooty and stabby out here, I'm going tell you something I've wanted to tell you for the longest time."

"And what is that?"

"Go. Fuck. Yourself!" Daniel shot the words out like bullets.

It had been so long since someone had said something like that to the mad Russian that he stood silently for a moment or two, wondering whether it was even humanly possible. "What?"

It was more than possible. "Go. Fuck. Yourself," Daniel repeated, relishing each syllable like a fine cigar or an aged Scotch. He was living. Even if there were only moments left, he was playing Today music.

"You think you have *ya-eechko* say that to me?" The Russian would have had to calm down just to be furious. "We see what music you make on way down to street!"

"It won't matter," Daniel said confidently. "No matter what you do to me now, I'll always be in your head as the one man who stood up to you and called you out as the malignant little cocksucker you are. You'll always remember me looking you in the eyes and telling you to fuck yourself. And no matter what you do or buy, no matter who you kill or fuck, no matter what you do, that'll always make you feel just as small as the twisted, pathetic piece of shit you are."

"I want him dead! Now!" Preezrakevich turned to Moog. "Throw him over railing, I want to see him pop like meat pie when he hits street."

Nobody moved. Not Daniel. Not the bikers. And not Moog.

"I said, throw this fuck over railing!" Preezrakevich screamed, but the extra volume didn't move Moog either.

He decided to take a different approach. "You already piss me off, Moog. Throw him over." He stared at the big man, who didn't do anything but stare right back. "Or you can take his fucking place!"

"No."

It had been awhile since anyone had said that to the Russian too. "Maybe you not hear me—"

"I heard you fine. You're all screaming and shit, but I'm not going to throw him over any damn railing for you." Moog shook his head, disappointed with himself. "I'm my own man."

"You're nobody's man!" the Russian screamed. "You my boy!"

Moog's eyes got crazy wide, dilated by the rage inside. "What did you just say?"

Daniel leaned back to tell Ponytail, "I told you things were about to get all stabby and shooty out here."

Moog started toward the man he'd called "Boss" for most of his adult life. "Don't you ever—"

Of all of the club members who'd been hired on as security, Ape-Face was the one who thought he'd be the boss's new hero. As he moved to intercept Moog there was a sharp click, and a thin blade appeared in the biker's right hand.

It was like hunting a grizzly with a butter knife. Moog looked past Ape-Face like he wasn't even there, already calculating in his head how he was going to kill the others. When the biker brought up the blade, the big man caught his arm, twisted it back on itself till it made a terrible snapping sound, and then forced the limp limb back, driving the knife into Ape-Face's belly. Before the simian-looking tough guy could even cry out, Moog struck him with the palm of his oversized hand, shattering the nasal bones and driving them up into his brain. The man whose mother had named him Kevin dropped to the deck like a two-hundred-pound sack of ground meat, nobody's boy any longer.

Zit-Face and Shorty stepped in front of Filat, inexplicably eager for their turns at Moog.

Meanwhile, Toothless reached behind his back and pulled a blued .38 out of his tattered jeans. He drew down on Moog, but before he could pull the trigger, Daniel ran for him, tackling him and knocking the revolver from his hand.

Preezrakevich's new security crew had searched Moog when he came in and taken his Desert Eagle from him. For some reason, however, the jeans-and-T-shirt-wearing bikers had never thought to check the necktie that Moog was never without. It was a fatal oversight. Concealed in the dapper neckwear was a single throwing blade. It whistled through the air and then buried itself in Shorty's left eye.

At the same time, Ponytail and Potbelly descended on Daniel, who was already getting more of a fight than he could handle from Toothless. Together, they pulled him off their comrade and held his arms back as Toothless got up to his feet.

Zit-Face had a gun too, but he was late in pulling it. The Colt wasn't even cocked when it dropped to the ground as Moog twisted his head violently to the right until vertebrae snapped.

As the big man bent down to pick up the weapon, Shorty—still screaming with a knife in his eye—jumped on Moog's back, perhaps thinking he was going to rodeo the big man to death. Moog flipped him over his shoulder like he was a doll and then reached down and grabbed the man by his ankles.

"I'm going to cut you balls to chin," Toothless bragged to Daniel as he produced a blade. But before he could use it, he was struck from behind by Shorty, who was being wielded by Moog like a human Louisville Slugger. The collision sent Toothless sprawling across the deck.

Moog swung Shorty again and hit Potbelly with a force that sent him staggering back to the balcony railing.

Moog lifted Shorty a third time, over his head, and then brought him straight down into the concrete deck. His head slammed into the surface and produced the same sound and effect as a Halloween pumpkin being tossed off a highway over-pass by a costumed prankster.

Ponytail was debating whether he was going to be the next to move on Moog or whether he might just exercise some sound judgment and make for the door when Daniel came up behind him and grabbed him. He couldn't do much more than clench Ponytail, but it prevented the biker from raising his hands to defend against the knife-edge chop Moog delivered to his throat. There was a savage popping sound and then it was Ponytail, his breath leaking out of his shattered throat, who was hanging onto Daniel. He tried to say something, but his last words came out as an unintelligible hiss. Daniel let him fall and Potbelly realized it was his turn to spin Moog's Wheel of Pain.

It turned out that the rotund little man was the smartest of his brothers. He decided to make a run for it, pushing Daniel to the ground as he rushed toward the door. If he'd carried a little less weight and moved a step or two faster, he might have made it.

The shot hit Potbelly in the crown of the skull. He dropped straight to his knees, let out a little squeal like a spiked boar, and fell dead on his side.

"This is my fault," Preezrakevich said with a heavy sigh, the still-smoking pistol dangling casually from his hand. "Do you see? To replace you, Moog, I go hire army." He looked around to take stock of his corpse-strewn balcony. "Always go with quality." He nodded, like he was making that point to himself. "Always the quality. Of course, there is still Rollo here," he gestured at the Viking who was now standing behind him like an oak tree with its branches folded across an impossibly broad trunk. Filat barely came up to his prized bull's belt buckle and together they looked like they were participating in some twisted Take Your Evil Son to Evil Work Day event. "I think you two will work good together."

"We're not done, you and me," Moog yelled. "Not by a long shot."

Preezrakevich turned back to him. "*Da*, we are. You fuck up. I forgive. That's all done now." He looked over at Daniel, who was still on the ground. "Now take care of him. And make it *huuuuurt*." He purred the word like the thought of it excited him.

"You forgive me?" Moog growled. "I give you eight motherfucking years. And then you send these backwoods, redneck motherfuckers after me, and *you* forgive *me*?"

"Moog. You talk crazy now. It's not personal. Just bees-ness."

"Not personal? Taking my goddamn life is not personal? How much more personal can it get than taking a man's—" His own words stuck in his throat, choked him, and brought him to a stop. How *could* it get more personal? He thought back to the lives he'd taken in the Russian's employ. His voice was soft and tired. "I'm done. I done everything you paid me to do, but I ain't workin' on your farm no more."

"Done?" The thought of it made the little Russian chuckle like a murderous elf. "You think you just retire from me? From Filat Preezrakevich?" The thought enraged him. "You not done, until I tell you. Do you understand me," his eyes flared, "boy!"

"Now that's the second time you called me that. I let the first one slide because, goddamn it, I deserved it—bein' your bitch and all. That second one there is a professional courtesy. But you call me 'boy' again and it's gonna be your motherfucking ass that's going airborne over that railing."

"Are you threat-een-ing me, Moog?" the Russian asked. "Do you think you frighten me?"

There was one thing Moog was absolutely sure of. "I terrify you."

"No, Moog." The little man slid on his best poker face. "You make me wonder how I ever put faith in you." He stared into the big man's eyes. "Boy!"

The Russian turned to look way up at the giant with the Nordic tattoo across the bridge of his nose. "Show me what you can do."

Moog and the Viking rushed at one another and the two men collided like a thunder clap, but it was Rollo who drove Moog backward.

Moog couldn't remember the last time he wasn't the biggest man in the fight and so it took him by surprise to find himself falling backward through the air. His size and strength had allowed him to move through life fearlessly, certain that his force was more than enough to enforce his will, and so he was caught momentarily off guard to be the one on his back with someone else straddling his chest.

Rollo's fist landed on the left side of Moog's face like a wrecking ball. It was not the only punch Moog had ever taken, but he'd never taken one like it before. The whole world seemed to skip a frame, as if life were a badly scratched DVD.

The second punch was even harder and opened Moog's nose like a Mount St. Helens of blood. It was just a busted nose, but for the very first time in his life, the blood filling his mouth and running into his eyes left him to ponder something he'd never even considered before: he might lose this fight.

It was more than that. He might die. Actually die.

It made him angry. And maybe even scared.

Before a third punch could fall, Daniel rushed across the balcony and threw himself on Rollo's back, knowing all he could hope to offer Moog was a momentary distraction.

The Viking flung Daniel across the balcony deck like a petulant child throwing a stuffed bear. But in the split second that the giant's attention was diverted, Moog reached up and grabbed Rollo's head, a hand on either side. And instant later, Rollo howled in agony as two black thumbs burrowed into his eye sockets.

Tears of dark red blood streamed down the Viking's face as he cleared Moog's hands away from his face and focused his fury into a third punch. Moog survived it but knew he wouldn't remain conscious if there was a fourth. And if he got knocked out, Moog was certain he would die.

The Viking raised his hand, but there was no fourth punch coming. This time his right hand was filled with the handle of an Arkansas pig-sticker, a jagged-blade knife about a foot and a half long he'd had sheathed beneath his leather jacket.

Moog wondered if this was what all those others had felt when *he'd* been the one delivering the beating, when he'd been the one taking *their* lives. Had the pain been as intense for them? Had they'd been as frightened of losing themselves in the spiraling abyss of shock? Had they'd been as terrified of the inevitable end, the dark finality that was waiting to close them out?

And if they had, Moog wondered, why the hell hadn't they fought harder?

As the blade descended, Moog reached up with his left hand and seized Rollo's wrist, struggling to keep the blade from plunging into his racing heart. With the knife's steel tip just inches from his chest, Moog reached up with his right hand and cupped it around the back of the Viking's head.

In what seemed like a scene from *Backwoods Man Love*, Moog pulled the Viking's face down to his open mouth, but it was no kiss of passion. Rollo roared in pain for what seemed like a full minute. When he finally managed to free himself from Moog's toothy grip, the Nordic tattoo across the bridge of his nose was completely gone. Moog rolled to his side, gagged, and spit it out.

Instinctively, Rollo's left hand searched his face in vain for the nose that had been there only a second ago. In its place was a deep hole and a geyser of blood.

By the time the Viking could refocus his thoughts and seek a target for his rage, Moog had already gotten back to his feet with a catlike nimbleness anyone would have thought beyond a man of his size. Rollo's bloodied eyes burned with a lust for revenge, but it was already too late for him.

Moog seized the Viking's knife hand and twisted it back until it snapped; the size of the limb only amplified the disturbing *crack* of a human bone breaking, as the Rollo-size knife dropped to the ground. Moog pushed forward on the broken arm he still held and drove his victim to the ground. Then with his left hand, he picked up the fallen blade.

Moog let go of the Viking's useless arm, grabbed a handful of the man's long, blond hair, and pulled back until the soft, tattoo-covered flesh of his throat was exposed. He pressed the sharpened steel of the blade against his throat. It was now just a matter of simple anatomy. Or basic butchery.

But because their struggle had become intimate and personal, because Moog had surrendered his prized professionalism, he didn't slit the man's throat as he normally would have. Instead, he leaned forward and spoke into the giant's ear. "I was the baddest motherfucker before you came on the scene, and I'm still going to be the baddest motherfucker long after you're dead."

The brief monologue took about four seconds to deliver. Not long, but it was all the time the Viking needed to reach for the small .22 he kept in his back pocket for just such unforeseen emergencies. Moog—concentrating more on settling the score than taking care of business—never noticed.

BANG! The concussion of the shot echoed in the valley of the Strip so that it sounded like there were dozens of shots, one right after the other.

The Viking dropped his .22. It made a small, tinny sound as it hit the deck. Then he lurched forward and fell from Moog's grasp to the balcony. There was a bright red bullet hole in the left side of his head and an exit wound, bigger and redder, in the right.

Moog looked across the deck and was startled to see Daniel standing there, Ponytail's pistol still smoking in his hand. "He was going for a gun," Daniel said, pointing out the fallen weapon.

"Didn't I just tell you I didn't want you doing nothing for me?" Moog exploded. "Didn't we *just* have that exact conversation?"

"He was going to shoot you."

"I had that shit handled," the big man insisted.

Daniel didn't want to fight about it, but still. "He was going to shoot you."

"This ain't through," Moog said, pointing a warning figure toward Daniel. But he had other business that needed settling first.

His face was already swelling and the beating he'd gotten had left his senses whirling around his head like a child's gyroscope. Splattered with blood—some of it his own—Moog lumbered toward the Russian.

"You always best," Filat said, his voice tinged with nostalgia. "But even you not better than bullet." He raised the pistol he'd used to stop Potbelly's desertion and aimed it at Moog's chest.

"Neither are you." Daniel stood off to the side with Ponytail's pistol still in his hand and the Russian's head in his sights.

"So," Filat said with a toothy grin, trying not to let on that he hadn't anticipated these turns of events. "We have the Mexican stand-you-off?"

"We don't have any fucking stand-off, 'cause I'm not with him," Moog said angrily, pointing back at Daniel.

"But I'm still going to shoot you if you shoot Moog," Daniel warned the Russian.

"And I will shoot Moog if you don't put gun down." Filat raised his pistol higher, trying to illustrate just how serious he was.

"I'm not going to put my gun down." The suggestions didn't even make sense to Daniel. "I mean, he's still the guy you sent to kill me."

"Thank you," Moog acknowledged as if he'd just made some long-denied point.

Daniel continued, "The guy who's been hunting me for two weeks."

"Eleven days," Moog cut in again.

"But I am going to shoot you afterward. So, I think that calls your bluff." Daniel flashed a satisfied smile. "Doesn't seem like you've got much of a hand there."

The Russian, however, had a grin of his own. "You forget one thing."

"What's that?"

"I always have card up sleeve," he said slyly.

"I don't see any card." Daniel took a deep breath and tried to ready himself to take his shot.

"No, of course not," the Russian laughed. "He's over there."

"*Hola, pendejos!*" The voice was little more than a crackling whisper but instantly recognizable just the same. Everyone left alive on the balcony turned as Rabidoso stepped out of the shadows. He had a cervical collar around his broken neck and a pistol in his hand. "Did you really think *Santa Muerte* would let me die?" If his throat hadn't been crushed the words would've come out as a triumphant, thunderous shout. Instead, they were merely a barely intelligible croaking. "Did you think she would let someone like *you* claim my soul?"

"Didn't figure you had a soul to claim," Moog said, wiping blood from his face.

"Of course, the blessed lady requires a soul for a soul," Rabidoso hissed. "I thought I'd give her this one." Without diverting his attention he reached back into the dark shadows and pulled out a living but beaten body.

"Zack!" Daniel's heart fell.

And Moog saw Daniel's pistol dip too. "Keep your goddamn shot!" he yelled loudly enough to recapture his attention. "It's the only chance any of us got!"

"You have no chance," Filat chimed in. "What's this sound I hear now?" He cupped his free hand to his ear for effect. "I think I hear fat lady. Singing!"

Daniel was too overwhelmed to respond.

"I knew it would come to this," Rabidoso rasped. "I never enjoyed killing anything as much as I'm going to enjoy killing you two." He put the muzzle of his pistol to Zack's temple. "Put down the gun."

On his knees, with a gun to his head, Zack's eyes filled with tears as he looked for his salvation. "Dad!"

"Don't do it," Moog yelled at Daniel. "Focus on your target."

"Dad?"

"Drop the gun!" Rabidoso's hoarse whisper was louder and angrier. He pressed the gun harder until its target winced.

"Dad, please!"

Daniel looked at his boy on his knees and then back to the pistol in his hand.

"Drop the fucking gun!"

"Dad! Please!"

Rabidoso thumbed back the hammer. "Your last chance, *papi*."

"Dad!"

"Focus on the fucking target!"

"Drop it!"

"Dad!"

The screaming became an assault on his senses, a cacophonous chorus of voices, all demanding his attention and compliance. And yet the only thing Daniel heard clearly was Mr. Atibon's voice in his head. "No man got possession over Judgment Day. You can try hidin' from Death, but the only thing you'll miss out on is Life."

Daniel let Filat out of his pistol's sight and aimed at Rabidoso's chest.

"That's how it is, *puta*?" Rabidoso reacted to the challenge. "You think you got the *cojones*?" In his bravado, he took the gun from Zack's head and threw his arms in the air, daring Daniel to take the shot. When he saw that Daniel was ready to do just that, he ducked back behind his hostage.

"Zack," Daniel called out to his son. "I need you to do something for me now. I need you to trust me."

There wasn't a lot of confidence in the young man's desperate eyes. "Please, Dad. Just do what he says. He's going to kill me."

"That's right. I'm going to kill him," Rabidoso confirmed.

Daniel ignored them both. "Zack. Listen to me. I need you to get to your feet."

"Dad," the boy pleaded. "I can't."

"That's right," Rabidoso told him. "Don't you move."

"I know you feel that way," Daniel continued patiently. "But you can't do anything when you're down on your knees."

"He can't do anything anyways," Rabidoso called back.

Daniel wasn't listening. "This trip you sent me on, Zack, it taught me that no matter what, you've got to get up on your feet."

"What are you doing, man?" Rabidoso asked. "I already killed your son once, you think I won't—"

"Don't listen to him, Zack. Get up off your knees." Daniel's voice was stronger than his son had ever heard it before. "Get to your feet."

And to his own surprise, Zack found himself rising to his full height. He towered over Rabidoso, who wasn't sure what was happening. "You think I won't—"

"Now just put him out of your way." Daniel explained, as if dealing with an armed killer was just that easy.

"Are you crazy, man?" Rabidoso put his gun back to Zack's head. "I will kill him right here, right now!"

"Put this fear out of your life," Daniel instructed. "Push it out of your way and there won't be anything you can't do. You'll own your life."

"Don't do it, man," Rabidoso warned.

"Dad!"

"Zack!"

In an instant, Zack turned and pushed Rabidoso back. If the assassin hadn't been broken and bruised and bandaged, he certainly would have killed Daniel's son; maybe he would have killed Daniel too.

But "ifs" and "maybes" don't matter to desperate dads. Or the laws of physics.

Rabidoso staggered back a step or two and then looked down at the wound in the center of his chest. "*San Amado. Como podría usted me va a entregar?*" His voice was small, like the child he'd never been. No one was quite sure what he'd asked, but a second shot answered the question just the same. And then just like an old man had once promised him, Rabidoso's head went BOOM!

A second later Daniel's pistol was trained on the Russian again, and this time the threat was much more menacing.

A gloating grin spread across Moog's face as he slowly approached Filat. "Looks like my ace in the hole just trumped the fuck out of the card up your sleeve."

His pistol hit the ground and his hands floated harmlessly above his head. "W-w-w-wait minute, Moog," Filat stammered.

The big man was not in a waiting mood. "You want to see someone go over this railing so badly, check it out your own damn self." He swept the tiny Russian up into his arms and carried him over toward the railing.

"Moog," he squealed as he squirmed. "I have money. Here. In suite. All yours."

The big man hoisted his former employer up over his head like he was doing a squat and clear. "I'm not interested in your money anymore."

"Moog," he begged. "Be reasonable. Be businessman."

"I'm done doing your business," he declared. "I ain't nobody's *boy* no more."

Three and a half seconds later a dull thud echoed above the traffic noises of the Vegas Strip. Down below they could hear screeching tires and a woman screaming, but neither Daniel nor Moog bothered to look over the railing.

Instead, Daniel went to his son, hugging him and then checking him up and down. He was bruised, but nothing that wouldn't heal with time. "Are you all right?"

"I think so." Zack felt exhausted and elated at the same time. "What the hell happened here?"

"It doesn't matter," Daniel tried to reassure him. "It's over now."

"Is that what you think?" Both Daniel and Zack turned to the booming voice behind them. A pistol dangled from Moog's hand. "There's close to a million dollars in that amp. Another five in the suite. And you two are my one-way ticket to a lifetime stay at High Desert State Penitentiary. You think you're just going to walk out of here?"

"Moog?" Daniel considered the pistol in his own hand and the man he was hoping he wouldn't have to shoot. "What are you doing?"

The big man's face was swollen and bruised, but not so disfigured that Daniel couldn't read the grim determination in it. And then suddenly it all cracked into a wide smile. "Nah, I'm just fucking with you."

It made Daniel feel better, but not much. "What—"

"I never owed nobody nothing in my whole goddamn life, but I guess I owe you—whether I want to or not." A big, bloody grin revealed some lost teeth. "As far as I'm concerned my contract to burn your ass was terminated when that fucker found out he couldn't call me boy—or fly. So we're all good." He looked around at the bodies scattered across the balcony deck. "But seriously, we all need to get our asses out of here quick before the po-po show up."

"And the money?" Daniel wondered.

Moog shook his head. "I'm a lot of things, but I ain't no thief. Money's yours."

Daniel went over to the amp, picked it up, and handed it to Zack. "Here. This is yours."

His son looked at it tentatively before taking it. "I don't—"

"I'm going to have to go underground for a while." He looked over his shoulder at Moog for confirmation.

The big man surveyed the damage they'd caused and made a quick calculation in his head. "Oh, you're in some subterranean shit here."

"Take it," Daniel insisted. "No one knows about you." He looked past his son to Rabidoso's lifeless body. "You'll be fine."

That wasn't enough for Zack. "And you?"

"I'll be fine too. But I need to know that you're safe, so you have to go now." He pointed at the amp. "That's enough money to float all your rock-and-roll dreams."

"All right."

"And go check in with your mom," Daniel told him. "She's going to need someone to take care of her for a while."

"I will." He wanted to say something more, but all that came to him was, "Thanks."

Daniel shook it off. "The money was always for you."

"Not the money," Zack said, "For everything else."

Daniel hugged his son as tightly as he thought the boy would tolerate, held on to him as if he was letting him go forever. And then he did. "Hurry up," he said, leading him through the now-abandoned suite and putting him on the elevator. "You take care of yourself."

"I will." The elevator doors opened and Zack stepped on.

"And don't ever give up on those dreams." Daniel felt overwhelmed with emotion. "Promise me that."

"Promise."

"And when you play—" Zack waited. "You play just for today."

"Promise."

Daniel leaned forward and kissed his boy one last time. Then the elevator doors closed and he was gone.

"What you planning to do now?" Moog wondered aloud.

"I'll tell you in a minute." Daniel went to work and in a minute and a half he'd found the Russian's stash of cash and packed it away in a leather duffel.

"How about we split this," Daniel offered, opening the bag and showing him the cash he was taking.

"Told you," Moog said resolutely. "I ain't no thief."

"It's hard to live on nothing but principles," Daniel warned. "And I'm guessing your employment prospects are dim considering you just tossed your last boss sixty stories to the pavement."

"I'll be all right," the big man assured him.

"But I might not be, right? I'm guessing I pissed off some people tonight."

Moog nodded his head. "Oh, there's folks going to be plenty pissed about what we just done." He pointed at the bag Daniel was carrying. "And that's five million more reason some folks are going to want to take you out."

Daniel had a thought. "Well, since you're out of work. And I need protection. And since I've recently come into a sum of money—"

It didn't take Moog long to consider. "I ain't calling you Boss."

"I wouldn't ask you to."

"Well, all right."

"All right."

And like that a deal was struck.

They walked together to the elevator and rode down in silence.

CHAPTER FORTY-EIGHT

Ten minutes later, a task force of FBI agents entered the Hotel du Monde's penthouse suite in a classic single-file "snake" formation. Every one of them had spent enough time in the bureau to see death's handiwork up close before. It was just none of them had ever seen so much of it in one place before.

The agent at point stopped as soon as he saw the scene. "Holy fuck!" The 9mm he held at the ready dipped slightly for a second as his mind struggled to make sense of the endless buffet of carnage stretched out before him. "Everybody's dead!"

Special Agent Feller pushed past him, wanting to get his own eyes on the situation. "Goddamn it!" The other agents saw corpses on the ground, but Feller saw his one chance to redeem himself after Chicago lying as a casualty among them. "Goddamn it!"

For a split second, he panicked, lost sight of his need to take control of the situation. For a brief moment, his professional life flashed before his eyes. It was a *very* brief moment.

"Agent Feller?" one of them asked, his tone of voice making clear it wasn't the first time he'd put the request for instructions to their team leader.

"What? Right." Whether it was procedure or not, there was only one thing he wanted. "I want IDs on all of these bodies. Do we have Erickson here?"

"Negative!" one of the agents called out as he looked down on Potbelly's remains.

Another agent checked Ponytail's. "Negative!"

And the practically headless corpse of Rabidoso. "Negative!"

With each response Special Agent Feller's hopes took on just a little more water. "Where the hell is Erickson?"

The agent who'd led the "snake" into the suite was the first one to answer. "He's not here." He looked from corpse to corpse. "Turner or Preezrakevich either."

It just kept getting worse. "Well, where the hell are they?"

No one wanted to wade into that one.

It couldn't end like this. He wouldn't let it. He'd go back to the deputy director and make a case that what had happened in the penthouse suite was just another example of why it was so important to apprehend Daniel Erickson—and that he was still the best-suited agent in the bureau to get that done. He could turn it into a positive. All of this could be a positive.

The point guy interrupted his inner pep talk. "What the hell happened here?"

Feller wondered how there could be any confusion about that. "Offhand, Agent Hosney, I'd say he killed everyone."

"But I thought you said he was just some music weasel."

"Well, it's obvious that he's changed, hasn't he?"

CHAPTER
FORTY-NINE

The casino's driveway was ringed with the complete spectrum of emergency vehicles: patrol cars, fire trucks, and an ambulance. There was an emergency crew tending to a situation that a ring of police officers were trying hard to keep the gathered crowd from seeing. There were still more officers beginning to canvas the people on the ground, asking each of them if they'd seen anything. All of them were too interested in the twisted corpse on the main drive to take any note of the battered pair walking toward the valet stand. Daniel and Moog walked past the whole scene, disinterested.

The Monte Carlo shimmied and knocked to a stop at the valet kiosk and the same kid in the maroon jacket popped out from behind the wheel. He handed Daniel the keys. "Not a scratch."

Daniel put the bag in the back, took a C-note off the top of a stack, and handed it to the kid. "Thanks."

The kid looked down at the Franklin and smiled. "Well, you look like you have a grand, long story to tell."

Daniel looked up. "What did you say?"

"Exactly what I meant to say. I always do." The kid held the dented door open and waited as Daniel eyed him suspiciously for a moment. The kid slammed the door and muttered, "You better get going, *mi key*." The voice was raspy and rough.

Daniel wasn't surprised any longer, he just smiled. "Thanks." He looked hard into the kid's eyes and saw exactly what he'd wanted to see. "For everything." Then he reached out through the window and pressed a wad of hundreds into the kid's hand.

"I take your cash money. And I give you this." He put something into Daniel's hand. Daniel opened it and it was the bones of his finger suspended from a gold chain. "I figured you'd want it back."

"Thanks?"

The kid grinned wider. And ran back to his stand. He watched the battered Monte Carlo pull away. "You on your way. But I ain't through with you yet, *mi key*."

"Where we headed?" Moog asked as Daniel eased the battered Monte Carlo out into the traffic cruising up the Strip.

"I was thinking maybe the islands, lay low like a lizard."

Moog thought about some time with nothing but the surf to interrupt the quiet. "Sounds good."

Daniel had just one proviso. "I just have to make a quick pit stop in Jersey."

"We're going to the Caribbean via Jersey?"

"It shouldn't take long. I made a promise."

Moog was in no hurry. "Man's gotta keep his promises."

They drove silently until the very last sign on the Strip offered them a neon farewell: "Drive Carefully. Come Back Soon." Daniel headed off into the pitch-black desert with no intention of ever coming back again.

He switched on the stereo and a blues vamp began with a single electric guitar. Daniel was expecting Dockery Plantation's vocalist, but this singer had a rougher and raspier voice.

Hard promises that you made in the night
The bargain you struck for the fire to fight

"I thought we was all done with this?" Moog asked, obviously alarmed.

"I never heard this one before," Daniel insisted.

"And you ain't gonna hear it now." He pressed a button and pulled out the disc he'd ejected. Without giving Daniel a chance to object, he flipped the disc out into the cold, black night. "That's that. Let's get us some Jeezy up in here. Somethin' to travel by."

Daniel didn't object and Moog switched on the radio. The same blues guitar vamp came on. The same lyrics.

Hard promises that you made in the night
The bargain you struck for the fire to fight

"What the—" Moog tuned through the dial but every time the hiss of static subsided, the same blues vamp would begin.

Hard promises that you made in the night
The bargain you struck for the fire to fight
Blood has been spilled, lives have been lost
There's no walking away without paying the cost

And there's a heavy
There's a heavy
A heavy price to pay

"Just turn it off." Daniel reached over and did it himself. It was silent in the car until damn near Cedar City, but he couldn't get the tune out of his head.

Hard promises that you made in the night
The bargain you struck for the fire to fight
Blood has been spilled, lives have been lost
There's no walking away without paying the cost

And there's a heavy
There's a heavy
A heavy price to pay

ABOUT THE AUTHOR

Photograph by Eyre Price, 2011

Eyre Price has traveled the Blues Highway, from Bob Dylan's boyhood Minnesota home all the way to Professor Longhair's shrine in New Orleans. With his son by his side, he's made pilgrimages to Graceland, Sun Studios, Stax, and Chess Records. He's stood at the crossroads where legend says Robert Johnson sold his soul, and he's walked the alley between the Ryman and Hank Williams's favorite honky tonk. The result is *Blues Highway Blues*, a novel reflecting his passion for American music, from the Delta's blues to Seattle's grunge. Eyre and his wife, Jaime, live in central Illinois (for now), where they are raising their son to have a wandering heart and a musical ear.